KT-559-186

Praise for P L Kane

'Stunning suspense . . . You'll be turning those
ages faster than you can say, "Didn't see that coming."
Fabulous book. 5* from me.'
– Helen Fields, bestselling author of
Perfect Remains, *Perfect Death* and *Perfect Kill.*

'What are you doing to me, P L Kane? . . .
think my heart might be broken. Cracking thriller . . .'
– Jo Jakeman, bestselling author of
Sticks and Stones and *Safe House.*

'Riveting domestic thriller with a razor-edged twist,
courtesy of a new top talent.'
– Paul Finch, *Sunday Times*
bestselling author of *Strangers*, *Shadows* and *Stolen.*

'A dark, twisty tale with an emotional heart.'
Roz Watkins, bestselling author of *The Devil's Dice*
and *Dead Man's Daughter.*

nse and twisty! A few times I held my breath and raced
ugh the pages to immerse myself in more of the story.'
– JA Andrews, author of *Mummy's Boy.*

4 4 0 1 5 6 9 1 4   0

P L KANE is the pseudonym of a #1 bestselling and award-winning author and editor, who has had over a hundred books published in the fields of SF, YA and Horror/Dark Fantasy. In terms of crime fiction, previous books include the novels *Her Last Secret* and *Her Husband's Grave* (a sellout on Waterstones.com and Amazon.co.uk), the collection *Nailbiters* and the anthology *Exit Wounds*, which contains stories by the likes of Lee Child, Dean Koontz, Val McDermid and Dennis Lehane. Kane has been a guest at many events and conventions, and has had work optioned and adapted for film and television (including by Lions Gate/NBC, for primetime US network TV). Several of Kane's stories have been turned into short movies and Loose Canon Films/Hydra Films recently adapted 'Men of the Cloth' into a feature, *Sacrifice*, starring Barbara Crampton (*You're Next*), which sold to Epic Pictures/101 Films. Kane's audio drama work for places such as Bafflegab and Spiteful Puppet/ITV features the acting talents of people like Tom Meeten (*The Ghoul*), Neve McIntosh (*Doctor Who/Shetland*), Alice Lowe (*Prevenge*) and Ian Ogilvy (*Return of the Saint*). Visit www.plkane.com for more details.

Also by P L Kane

Her Last Secret
Her Husband's Grave

The Family Lie

P L KANE

ONE PLACE. MANY STORIES

This novel is entirely a work of fiction. The names, characters and incidents portrayed in it are the work of the author's imagination. Any resemblance to actual persons, living or dead, events or localities is entirely coincidental.

HQ
An imprint of HarperCollins*Publishers* Ltd
1 London Bridge Street
London SE1 9GF

www.harpercollins.co.uk

HarperCollins*Publishers*
1st Floor, Watermarque Building, Ringsend Road
Dublin 4, Ireland

This paperback edition 2021

1
First published in Great Britain by
HQ, an imprint of HarperCollins*Publishers* Ltd 2021

Copyright © P L Kane 2021

P L Kane asserts the moral right to be
identified as the author of this work.
A catalogue record for this book is
available from the British Library.

ISBN: 9780008372262

MIX
Paper from
responsible sources
FSC
www.fsc.org **FSC˚ C007454**

This book is produced from independently certified FSC™ paper
to ensure responsible forest management.

For more information visit: www.harpercollins.co.uk/green

Printed and Bound in the UK using 100%
Renewable Electricity at CPI Group (UK) Ltd

All rights reserved. No part of this publication may be reproduced,
stored in a retrieval system, or transmitted, in any form or by any means,
electronic, mechanical, photocopying, recording or otherwise,
without the prior permission of the publishers.

This book is sold subject to the condition that it shall not, by way of trade
or otherwise, be lent, re-sold, hired out or otherwise circulated without the
publisher's prior consent in any form of binding or cover other than that
in which it is published and without a similar condition including this
condition being imposed on the subsequent purchaser.

To Martina Cole, terrific writer and a wonderful friend.

Prologue

It was the noises outside that woke them. Woke *him*.

Noises outside the tent they were sharing, camping in the woods, part of the region known as Green Acres. Todd had woken first, sitting bolt upright when he became aware of the sounds – of someone . . . *something* out there in the undergrowth. The snapping of twigs on the ground, the swish of leaves and branches being pushed aside. He glanced across at Candice in the dimness, tucked up in the sleeping bag beside him. She was just starting to stir, though whether it was because of his movements or the ones not far away beyond the thin material surrounding them was unclear.

'D-Did you hear that?' Todd asked her, trying and failing to say it without his voice cracking.

Bleary-eyed, Candice gaped at him. 'What time is it?'

Todd had no idea. Late. Middle of the night. It only felt like he'd been asleep for a few minutes, having taken ages to drop off in the first place. Candice, on the other hand, had been fast asleep as soon as her head hit the inflatable pillow. And, in lieu of any kind of proper rest, he'd simply watched her by the light of the small battery-powered lamp before he'd had to turn it off, as she breathed in and out softly. That beautiful face, skin the colour of caramel, jet-black hair that hung in ringlets, Todd reckoned he was pretty much the luckiest man alive. And not for the first time he wondered just how he'd managed to end up with her.

They'd met at uni, both studying psychology – a class taught by one Dr Robyn Adams, who worked with the police on certain cases so was a bit of a celebrity on campus. They'd been best friends first, then it had developed into something more. And when they'd finished their course, he'd suggested this holiday because who knew where they'd end up in the future. Something cheap, because they were skint, and he knew Candice loved the outdoors. They could go on walks in the daytime, cook on an open fire and eat under the stars. Didn't get much more romantic than that.

And at night-time, snuggle up in a sleeping bag and . . . well, you know.

Hadn't exactly turned out the way he'd imagined though, had it? First, they'd spotted those creepy-looking folk out and about, when they'd been searching for somewhere to set up camp. Just two or three of them out for a walk in nature probably – but they'd all been wearing the same thing, those weird cream-coloured tunics and trousers.

'They look like they're in a cult or something,' Candice had joked, fan of horror movies that she was. 'Probably doing a bit of Devil worshipping!' But Todd hadn't found it funny. Hadn't found it funny at all and was glad when they'd passed by out of sight.

Then there was getting stung by that wasp, which apparently set a precedent. Everything that walked, flew or crawled in those woods seemed to have it in for Todd, it was like they knew he wasn't used to being out here. He was also absolutely knackered, had barely slept since they got here – and not in the fun way. Todd just found it so hard to drift off with all the strange noises around him, was too much of a city boy he guessed; and this was just such a long way from it all. The sounds of nature were louder in his own skull than the hum of traffic and buzz of people he'd grown used to. More alien to him than anything, though nothing like the noises that particular night.

'Listen!' he whispered to Candice.

'What . . . ?' she answered, looking for her phone so she could find out the time, flicking on the light. 'I can't hear anything.'

'There!' said Todd, who could distinctly hear something stumbling about outside. Maybe it was those people in tunics back again?

'It's just the sounds of the woods, babe,' Candice told him. The same thing she'd been saying for ages. 'Probably a deer or something.'

'A deer?' He was aware he wasn't really coming off as manly by this point, but the thought of something trampling their tent with them inside it wasn't exactly relaxing.

Candice couldn't keep the grin from her face. 'Yeah, you know. A deer. Don't worry about it. Won't hurt you.'

'Doesn't sound like a deer to me,' he informed her. And it didn't. It sounded bigger than that kind of animal. What if it was something else, some other kind of wild creature?

Something more ferocious.

As if reading his mind, Candice said, 'Hey, did you ever see that movie with the soldiers and the werewolves? How that started, with one of those things ripping into the tent?' She was doing this deliberately to wind him up. Candice knew he didn't care for those kinds of films, that he had a tendency to let his imagination run riot. 'Don't worry, I'll protect you.'

Might not be a werewolf – because those didn't exist, he wasn't that stupid – but what if it was something else? A nutter or whatever, a crazy cabin person living in the woods with a taste for human flesh? Or a witch, like in that old found footage movie people had thought was real at the time? This place definitely had a history. And hadn't he read somewhere it was also a UFO hotspot, out in the middle of nowhere? That there had been abductions and such? Those kinds of things he did believe in, *Close Encounters* and all that. Spoiled for choice with the options . . .

He thought about voicing his concerns, but he was already going down in his girlfriend's estimation, he realized. God, who'd want to be with such a wuss?

Then the noises came again and this time Candice looked up. Looked worried. 'Now *that* I did hear.'

Thank Christ for that, it was loud enough! Sounded like Godzilla and King Kong wrestling out there. 'What should—'

'We should probably take a look,' she suggested. 'At least see what we're dealing with.'

But what if it deals with us first? thought Todd, who'd changed his mind. He was beginning to wish this *was* a horror flick, because then he could simply switch it off. Or be safe in the knowledge that good triumphed over evil. Usually.

'Really?' he asked.

Candice nodded and took his hand. 'We'll look together.'

'O-Okay,' he said, voice cracking again.

His girlfriend led the way, unzipping the tent and peering out. After a few moments, she turned and said in hushed tones, 'I can't see anything. Can you?'

Todd joined her and his eyes searched the space in front of him. It was pitch-black out there, and he had a job even making out the shapes of trees, of branches. Maybe they should flash that phone light around, or grab the lamp? Would that attract attention? Would it be worse to see than not? 'No, I—'

He froze, squeezing her hand. The loud rustling noises were coming again, only this time he *could* see the source of it. Something was lit up, stumbling through the darkness: a figure. Todd's mind went to those UFOs again, to glowing aliens.

More alien to him than anything.

'Is that . . . Jesus, Todd – I think that's a person!' cried Candice. 'But what's . . . Is that a torch they've got or—'

No, definitely not a torch. Because the whole figure was shining with the kind of brightness not even the strongest torch would give off. And the light was coming from everywhere at once.

That was when he smelled it, the unmistakably sweet aroma of cooking flesh – similar to the smell of the meat they'd been cooking themselves on campfires. That they'd cooked earlier on the one outside, before making sure it was totally out. It was also then that Todd realized what the figure reminded him of. Not an alien at all, but a certain figure that was thrown onto the bonfire every fifth of November in this country.

Because the shape, stumbling through the undergrowth and making all that noise – looking for all the world like some kind of stuntman – was, from head to toe, on fire. Ablaze, covered totally in flames. How it was still moving was a mystery to Todd, but moving it was. Crashing on and on towards them, the noise of crackling and popping accompanying the other sounds now.

Then all of those noises, the ones that had woken them – woken him, Todd – were drowned out by something. The sound of screaming, high-pitched and blood-curdling.

The sounds of someone who'd finally realized, who understood now that they were being roasted alive.

Or, more accurately, were burning to death.

PART ONE

Green Acres is a stretch of rural land to the north-west of Granfield which encompasses farmland, woodland and even has its own set of caves. At the heart of this region is a village of the same name, which is said to have been founded as a settlement around 100 BC, although its origins probably stretch back much further. It has a rich and varied history which includes the study and practise of witchcraft. More recently, the area has been linked to UFO activity, with people reporting bright lights in the sky and even at eye level.

It is a popular area for backpackers, ramblers and campers alike, a beautiful and peaceful spot where you are guaranteed to find somewhere to unwind. Lovers of nature are bound to discover something unusual. In fact, you never know what you might spot and those who leave always find themselves returning eventually.

Chapter 1

It never failed to surprise him how quickly things could turn.

How they could escalate, go to shit.

It never rained . . . Isn't that what they always said? One moment everything might be going smoothly – as it had been in this instance, a peaceful Saturday march they'd known about the whole week – and the next . . .

PC Mitchel Prescott was on the ground floor (or should that be at ground zero?) with the troops again, where he had been for most of his relatively short career. He had seen first-hand all the things that could go wrong, knew something wasn't right.

To begin with, he'd put his edginess down to the call he'd taken before he went on duty, when he managed to finally get some signal; a garbled recorded message that had left him feeling shaken to the core.

'Everything okay, mate?' freckle-faced Tammy, one of his colleagues, had asked him, noting his reaction.

'What? Oh . . . oh, yeah.'

'You sure?'

'I said yes, didn't I?' He took a breath, regaining his composure. 'Yeah. I'm sorry, Tam.'

'Not had another falling out with Lucy, have you?'

He shook his head. 'No, no. Nothing like that. It's all good.' But it hadn't been, had it, and Tammy could see that. *Anyone* could see that. He'd had no more time to think about it though, shoving his mobile into his pocket. Heading off to the front lines of the march, supressing the thoughts and emotions which were threatening to bubble up to the surface. Memories, feelings. There was no place for any of that out here; it just wasn't professional. Keep your mind on the job, Mitch told himself, on the task at hand. Try not to think about—

This is a message for Mr Mitchel Prescott, we've been trying to get hold of you . . .

Mitch glanced around at the other uniforms who were with him then, more to take his mind off the situation than anything. Only it had done little for his nerves. Not enough, not nearly enough coppers gathered for his liking.

'Is it me, or are there more protesters than they expected?' Mitch had observed.

'Hmm, maybe.' This from another friend of his nearby, Vihaan.

'Well, just look! There clearly are!' snapped Mitch.

'All right, all right! Keep your hair on,' Tammy said to him. 'Seriously, what's got into you?'

'Nothing,' Mitch answered. 'I'm okay.'

'You sound it! Are you sure you've haven't had a marital with Lucy?' Mitch remained silent. She didn't say anything, but he could see Tammy wondering if he should even be there, as distracted as he was. Mitch was beginning to wonder himself! What had got into him, aside from anything else, was that here they all were with their arses hanging out. Wearing just their standard beat uniforms, complete with caps or helmets, the only difference being their hi-vis jackets so even if it grew overcast they could still be seen.

Mitch would have preferred riot gear, if he was being honest: full helmets and armour and round shields, like Captain America's but transparent, made of toughened plastic. But the thinking was that this just antagonized the crowds unnecessarily. For Mitch it was more a matter of taking precautions, just in case. He wasn't talking about how the French did it, tooled up like there was no tomorrow with rubber bullets on hand. Just sensible, for protection purposes.

He reminded himself nobody was expecting trouble. That had certainly been coming across loud and clear when Mitch had brought the subject up at that morning's briefing. Of how few officers would be on hand.

'But sir,' he'd protested to the Bronze Commander of this operation – a new inspector called Staton. 'That's going to leave us incredibly short-handed if—'

'We have to work with the resources at our disposal, PC . . . Prescott, isn't it?' The man with the salt-and-pepper hair knew exactly who he was; Mitch's reputation for questioning those in charge was the stuff of legend around these parts. But rumour had it the only reason Staton had risen in the ranks was the company he kept; the kind who held ceremonies behind closed doors and had funny handshakes. Certainly hadn't served his time on the front ranks, like Mitch and co. Like some of the officers Mitch could think of who had been passed over for the promotion. 'Besides, all the forecasts suggest this is due to be a peaceful protest.' Forecasts, like a bloody weather report; it never rains . . . 'We have absolutely no reason to believe otherwise. There are even going to be children on the march. No way these people would risk the lives of youngsters.'

Some wouldn't, but Mitch knew plenty of other folk who definitely would. He'd seen how certain elements could take over a 'peaceful' football match and turn it into a battleground, regardless of whether there were any 'youngsters' around or not. People who treated it like – as Frankie used to sing – two tribes going to war, irrespective of the 'collateral damage'. If you weren't preparing for a worst-case scenario, you had no business being in the force, let alone at the rank of inspector.

The orders had come down from a higher authority, so they

were told. Not that any of that would help them if it all hit the fan. Perhaps Mitch was just borrowing trouble, already rattled because of the phone message. No, it wasn't just that. He had an uncanny knack of sensing when something bad was going to happen: a copper's instinct some called it, honed over time, while others jokingly referred to it as his 'spider-sense'. Or maybe, in this instance, it was just *common* sense given the size of the crowd they'd ended up with.

So many people walking in unison to protest the latest crazy scheme the powers that be had implemented. It didn't seem to matter who was in charge of their country these days, they appeared to be determined to cock things up. Hospitals, schools (he only had to listen to Lucy's rants about this to understand the extent of the rot), the welfare system. Welfare? That was a joke! Mitch knew families on his patch who couldn't even get benefits, were having to feed their own children using food banks. And the number crunchers wondered why robberies were on the increase.

Nevertheless, this march – this protest – as futile as it seemed to Mitch, had certainly begun peacefully enough. Roads had been cordoned off in preparation, diversions put in place for traffic – directing them around Downstone city rather than through it. Placards, with general statements like 'JUSTICE FOR ALL' and 'DEMOCRACY IS DEAD' painted on them, had been raised at 2 p.m., and the sea of bodies had initially followed the police's lead. A wall of officers facing the crowd and walking backwards slowly, keeping an eye on what was happening.

In case, just in case. Because you never knew when things were going to turn, always a chance they could. Even with a march like this one, moving at a snail's pace, harmless on the face of it. Might not even be the intention, could just be hijacked by those who liked nothing better than to cause trouble.

People like the ones Mitch finally spotted, masking up by pulling scarves over their mouths and noses, tugging hoodies over their heads. Reaching inside unseasonable coats for makeshift weapons they'd brought with them, like baseball bats or rocks.

The sudden and unprovoked explosion of sheer mayhem was incredible, the noise insane. Panic from some, running in different directions – those whose only intention had been to demonstrate – anger from others at this interruption, which saw some of the ordinary members of the public turn on the ones causing the disruption. Sheer violent anarchy from the rest, including launching bottles with lit rags in them.

Mitch watched as one arced through the air, and his eyes dropped to where it would land. Not far away from one of those kids his superior felt sure wouldn't be in harm's way. He rushed forwards, ignoring the cries from Vihaan behind him to hold the line, and snatched up the boy – who couldn't have been more than seven or eight – just as the glass exploded on the concrete, splashing flames everywhere.

Ignoring the heat at his back, Mitch half ran, half stumbled away from the fire and to the side of the road. He glanced down at the lad in his arms, bawling his eyes out, but in spite of everything he seemed unharmed. There was a tap on his shoulder and Mitch almost turned and punched whoever was standing behind him. But at the last moment, he saw a skinny, bearded man in faded jeans and a T-shirt, looking terrified.

'He's . . . That's my son, officer,' he declared.

For a second Mitch wondered if he was telling the truth, but then the boy reached out for his father. He passed him over quickly, shouting, 'Get him the hell out of here! Look after him!'

The man nodded, thanking Mitch profusely for what he'd done. Then he was gone, running with his boy up a side street off to their left, keeping him away from danger. Mitch looked about him, spotted more of the troublemakers pushing forwards, shoving aside the other protesters. One had a claw hammer and was raising it, ready to strike whoever was around him – he didn't seem to care if it was friend or foe.

'Oh no you don't,' said Mitch, snarling, pulling out his baton and racing towards him. He swung and struck the guy on the wrist, forcing him to drop his weapon and cradle his arm like a baby; broken, for all Mitch knew, or cared. Reasonable force. Justifiable force. Or taking things out on him?

Then something hit him, too quickly to dodge, ricocheting off his shoulder and forcing him sideways to roll with it – but at the same time causing him to drop the baton. Mitch saw the half-brick tumble away to the ground, where it was kicked swiftly and accidentally into the tangle of legs.

He tested his shoulder; it hurt, but he could still move it, so it wasn't dislocated thankfully. Mitch was aware of someone off to his right, his senses alerting him. They were holding something else aloft. It wasn't a hammer this time, but rather a length of metal pipe. He dodged the blow just in time, but stumbled and dropped to the floor.

The figure, wearing a comedy mask, a caricature of some politician Mitch vaguely recognized, towered over him now, still holding the pipe. About to raise it and bring it down a second time.

Then he stopped, letting the improvised weapon fall from his grasp where it clattered uselessly to the asphalt, and he began to jerk around as if doing a kind of dance. It was only when the man sank to his knees with a crunch that Mitch saw the darts attached to his back, saw the wires running from that to Vihaan's Taser.

Mitch nodded a thanks to his mate. Then he scrambled to his feet, cuffing the masked attacker. This was one bastard who wasn't going to get away with his actions today. They dragged him towards the sound of sirens, of police vans that were arriving on the scene. Another Molotov exploded not far away and Vihaan raised his arm to protect his face.

'Bollocks!' he growled.

'You can say that a—' Mitch stopped in his tracks, sensing something else up ahead of him. Yes, there! A crowd gathered around a body, beating it with sticks. Kicking it. All that could be

14

seen were the feet sticking out: standard police issue. Yet somehow Mitch knew who it was. He handed off pipe man, and charged at the group – laying into them and dragging them away. Mitch was aware of something hitting his temple, but didn't care – couldn't stop. Then the mini-crowd dispersed, went off in search of more 'fun' elsewhere. Revealing who it was on the ground.

Tammy, as he'd thought. Lying there, prone, unmoving. Helmet kicked off. Face a bloody mess; no sign of those freckles now.

'Dammit,' whispered Mitch. He kneeled down and felt for a pulse at her neck. It was there, but faint. He shouted for help, but his words were drowned out by the rabble's feral cries.

Then suddenly Vihaan was beside him; Mitch didn't ask what his friend had done with pipe man, that didn't matter now. Just pointed instead to Tammy's arms, indicated that they needed to get her to a clear area. Needed to get her some urgent medical attention.

Coppers wearing actual riot gear were moving in now, somewhat too late. Too late for Tammy anyway. But they were holding back some of the most vicious 'protesters'. And there were more officers with Mitch and Vihaan, more people to assist with the moving of Tammy – to get her to one of the nearby squad cars.

And all the time Mitch was thinking to himself, how quickly things had turned. Had gone to shit.

How there was always scope for it to get even worse.

He leaned against the door to the hospital room.

A private room where Tammy was hooked up to all kinds of monitors that beeped and pinged. She'd been brought here after they'd operated on her, to stop the internal bleeding the blows and kicks had caused. Now she lay there in a coma, because of a head injury – he'd overheard the word 'swelling'. But nobody seemed to be able to tell him anything about when she'd wake up, if indeed she ever would.

Nurses flitted about around the bed, while her fiancé Zach – who'd been called in urgently – sat beside it holding her hand. Tammy's face had been cleaned up, but was still swollen – stretching those freckles now – her left eye puffed up so much it was practically a slit.

Mitch shook his head again, thinking about the last time they'd spoken. About how it might actually *be* the last time.

'Seriously, what's got into you?'

He wished he'd just told her. If only he'd got to her sooner, hadn't been preoccupied, or . . . No, this should never have happened in the first place! *None* of this should have happened; they should have had more troops on the ground. If Staton had just listened . . . He'd had a bad feeling about this one, and Mitch tended to trust those feelings. His gut instinct very rarely steered him wrong.

Watching Zach sitting there, worried expression on his face, reminded Mitch of the conversation he'd had after he'd got cleaned up himself; after the docs had stitched the cut on his forehead and checked out his shoulder, which had just been badly bruised as he suspected. The conversation he'd had with Lucy outside the entrance to A&E via video messaging on his phone.

'God, I was so worried,' she told him, her cherubic face filling the screen: those hazel eyes of hers, straight blonde locks. 'You could have let me know how you were before now.'

'We've been trying to get hold of you . . .'

And the inference was there again, a look on Lucy's face saying she'd been an afterthought. She wasn't, hadn't been. Of course she hadn't! 'This is the first chance I've had,' he replied. 'But honestly, I'm fine. No need to worry. A few cuts and grazes, I've had worse.' Could've been worse. Could have ended up like Tammy.

'You don't look fine. Are those stitches?'

He lifted the phone, angling the camera so they couldn't be seen. 'It's okay, *really*.'

'And you don't *sound* okay. Is everything all right?'

He opened his mouth to say more, about what had happened out there, about what had happened before it, about that message . . .

'Mr Prescott, I'm afraid it's bad news.'

. . . but instead he kept quiet.

Lucy sighed. 'It's all over the networks, you know. Every channel. The rioting's still going on.' Mitch knew, he'd seen it on the TVs in the waiting area. The guys in masks and hoodies jumping up and down on cars, setting those alight too. The escalation, the 'getting worse'. It had gone on into the evening and probably would do all night, frankly. They still hadn't managed to contain the situation, even though water cannons had been called in. Looting was happening now, shop fronts smashed in and people walking away with electrical goods like it was some kind of Black Friday sale. A black Saturday, for sure. Very black indeed. 'How did this happen?' she asked finally.

'Sheer bloody stupidity, that's how!' he told her, unable and unwilling to hide the bitterness from his tone. 'We weren't anywhere near prepared. I knew something wasn't right, that . . .' It was Mitch's turn to sigh. 'It's just a mess.'

'Well, just get yourself home when you can.'

'I'll . . . I'll do my best, Lucy.'

'I love you, you know.'

'I know. I love you too . . .'

Mitch returned to the present and wandered back into the visitor area, where Vihaan was also waiting. He rose from his seat hopefully, but Mitch just shook his head and told his friend there was nothing to report yet about Tammy. They'd seen dozens of officers brought in while they'd been here, the hospital struggling to cope with the influx because of the kind of budget cuts those protesters had been bemoaning. Everything going to the hot place in a handbasket. What would be left for kids like that one he'd saved back there on the street? Mitch had to wonder. The kid he'd handed over to his dad . . . .

'Mitch? Earth to Mitch?' Vihaan was waving a hand in front of his face, trying to get his attention. 'You okay? You were miles away.'

Mitch nodded slowly, suggesting they go and get another coffee. Then, the final insult. As they'd wandered through to the machine, Mitch had spotted Staton. In full dress uniform, talking to the press that were gathered. He was making a big show of being here to visit his wounded officers. Those 'resources' he'd spoken about at the briefing. Not men or women, but chess pieces to be shoved around a board in some huge cosmic game.

Mitch caught the tail end of one of the questions: ' . . . do you account for the way this march suddenly went sour?'

'Groups of anarchists, of fanatics, gatecrashed what had, up until then, been a peaceful demonstration,' answered the man with salt-and-pepper hair. 'It was a total spur of the moment thing, we've since discovered from our intelligence.' That was a joke: intelligence! 'Impossible to predict. Nobody knew what was going to happen. I doubt even they did till the very last moment.'

But I suspected, Mitch thought to himself. *I knew it . . . was at least a possibility. And those troublemakers had definitely planned this.*

'I want to praise our brave men and women who have shown courage in the face of such adversity. Now we're doing our best, with the resources we have . . .' There was that buzzword again. '. . . to restore peace to the area. And we will. In time. Those responsible will be punished, you mark my words. We will not tolerate this kind of mindless behaviour! There'll be a full press conference tomorrow afternoon at Downstone central station. But until then, thank you. Thanks everyone.'

Flanked by a few burly officers, the inspector began walking away from the gathered journalists. He blanked questions like, 'Is it true the army has had to be called in?' and, 'How can the public have any confidence in you now to maintain order?' Bailing before he could get tangled up in a tricky situation.

Mitch set off to follow him up the corridor, ignoring Vihaan's advice to leave it. The more you told him not to do something, the more likely it was that Mitch would race towards it. But he was stopped in his tracks anyway by one of those huge coppers assigned to protect the senior officer on his 'tour'. 'I want to talk to Staton,' he said, but the man – whom he didn't recognize – said nothing. So Mitch began shouting after his boss. 'Staton! Hey, Staton!'

The inspector stopped and turned. Then he nodded for the man to let Mitch by, probably so the journos wouldn't catch wind of it.

'What is it, PC . . . PC Prescott, isn't it?' Once again, Mitch knew that Staton had remembered his name – he was just being a dick.

'What happened back there, at the march. It could have been prevented,' Mitch told him.

'Didn't you just hear what I said? There was no way of knowing.'

'But I tried to—'

Staton raised a hand to cut him off. 'There was no way of knowing, Prescott. We can only go by the information we have to hand, and all of it pointed to a peaceful demonstration. The measures put in place should have been enough.'

'They weren't though, were they?'

'We only have so many resources to—'

'One of your resources is at this hospital in a coma, Staton!' he shouted.

'Would you keep your voice down, Officer. And kindly address me as Inspector Staton. Or, failing that, sir.'

Mitch looked him up and down, his lip curling. Sir? This silly sod, who'd put so many people's lives at risk . . . he wanted Mitch to call him *sir*?

'Listen, Officer . . .' He thought for a moment, searching his memory.

'Fitzpatrick,' Mitch stated, reminding him of Tammy's surname – which it looked like he had genuinely forgotten. That was how much he cared.

'Officer Fitzpatrick and her family will be well compensated. Trust me.' Trust him? Mitch would rather trust a snake. 'I understand your frustration about all this, really I do. But as I said before, those orders came from a higher authority,' Staton told him. 'Your participation in this matter is appreciated. As is your discretion.'

So that was it. Keep your mouth shut, play ball. Forget that! 'I'll talk about it to whoever I want,' said Mitch. 'Something needs to be done.'

Staton's left eye was a slit, though unlike Tammy's this was on purpose. 'Now that, Prescott, would be a very grave mistake.' He prodded Mitch in the chest as he said the words, and that was it. Mitch lunged at him, would have slammed him against the wall if he hadn't felt much stronger hands on him, pulling him away. Holding him back. 'Atrocious! Behaviour unbecoming a police officer, Prescott,' griped Staton, straightening his tie but clearly shaken. 'Nobody will believe a word you say, I'll make sure of that. You're finished in the police force, Prescott. You hear me? Finished!'

'I'll save you the trouble,' spat Mitch. 'I quit.'

'Kellerman,' Staton said to the hulking man holding Mitch, 'would you please escort *Mr* Prescott out the back way?' He emphasised the lack of rank, now Mitch was suddenly a member of the public again.

Just as suddenly, Mitch was being manhandled towards the back of the hospital, to the nearest fire exit. There he was deposited unceremoniously outside. If anything was atrocious, it was how – after risking his life on the streets – he'd been shoved from the building, like some bouncer tossing him out of a nightclub. Not only that, but the promise of being discredited as well by Staton . . . and his friends.

'I want to praise our brave men and women . . .'

Worse, things were definitely worse.

And it was then that he remembered. Still breathing heavily, he took out his phone again and stared at it. Went to his messages, the thing that had really got to him even before he was on the front line. Even before the rioting, before Tammy.

Mitch listened again to the female voice.

'This is a message for Mr Mitchel Prescott,' it began, sounding a million miles away. 'It's the hospital at Green Acres.' That name, the very mention of that place. A million miles away indeed. A million years as well. 'We've been trying to get hold of you . . . actually we were trying to get hold of your sister first, but couldn't. Mr Prescott, I'm afraid it's bad news. If you receive this could you give us a call back please?'

Mitch pinched the bridge of his nose, knowing what was coming next. Knowing also that he couldn't put off phoning them back any longer, which caused a lump to catch in his throat. 'It's about your father, one . . . Thomas Prescott. I'm sorry to have to tell you this, but he has passed away,' the quiet voice uttered.

Never rains. Isn't that what they said?

Scope to be worse . . .

So much worse.

Chapter 2

Mitch recognised that look she was giving him.

Even if he didn't, the way she was following him around from room to room as he packed his bags – a backpack and a holdall – told him everything he needed to know. Lucy really didn't want him to go. Especially as she couldn't come along; too much prep to do and meetings ahead of the new term, she'd informed him. She said she understood that he was going anyway, and yet . . .

It was just something Mitch had to do. It was his dad, when all was said and done. Even if he hadn't seen much of him over the years, it was still his dad.

And his dad – Thomas Stephen Prescott – was dead.

Mitch still couldn't really believe it. Hadn't been able to find out that much from ringing the hospital back, from trying to get in touch with the authorities in Green Acres. Just that there had been some kind of accident. That his father had died in some sort of fire.

'You mean the house? His *house* caught fire?' Actually, that wouldn't really have surprised him. His father had been getting quite vague of late – from what Mitch could tell when he phoned the man up, which admittedly wasn't nearly often enough. Mitch even suspected he might have been starting up with some kind of senility. Had trouble remembering what he'd had for lunch, or even if he'd eaten lunch at all. Couldn't recall what he'd watching on the TV the previous evening, just that he hated the presenters: 'You know, those two that are always on everything. Little blokes, they are.' That sort of thing.

It was sad to hear, especially as his dad had always been so sharp. He'd had to be, doing what he did: working for the local newspaper, *The Acre*; its very name a shortened version of the place Thomas loved so much. Wasn't to say that he ever covered anything more stimulating than a fete or a charity drive, but it kept him, and especially his mind, active. Then there was his research, into everything and anything. His conspiracy theories about this and that – don't even get him started on JFK's assassination unless you wanted a lecture that made the Kevin Costner movie look brief by comparison.

One of Mitch's abiding memories as a child was bits of paper everywhere. Folders and books ('organised chaos' his father called it . . . a bit like the riot), but also those scraps of paper his father had written things down on. Sometimes they weren't even legible, and when she'd still been alive his mother used to say that he should have become a doctor like her sister, Helen.

His mum. God, he still missed her, even though it had been almost twenty years since she'd died. Since—

'I still can't get my head around your sister,' Lucy was starting up again, folding her arms and trailing him through to the bathroom on the landing now as he searched for the travel toothpaste. He caught sight of himself in the mirror and stared, the stitching still prominent at his cropped hairline, so he brushed it down to cover it. 'This should be up to her really, she's the oldest. Why isn't *she* going?' Lucy pressed, snapping him out of his reverie.

All Mitch could do was shrug. 'Look, I don't get it either. When she was little she was always such a daddy's girl. Inseparable they were.' He used to get a bit jealous of the attention actually, because he was the youngest by a few years. But then there was that special bond, wasn't there, between fathers and daughters. How could he compete with that?

'So what happened?'

Another shrug. 'Something to do with a guy, I think. It's hard to remember.' Mitch froze, wondering if at some point in his life he'd follow his father down that road of forgetfulness. Already things from his childhood, his teenage years, were getting fuzzy and he was only in his late twenties.

'Makes sense. It's usually a guy.'

'You speaking from experience there?'

'No,' she said, a bit too quickly, before changing the subject. 'Why did *you* leave? You've never really said.'

'Things weren't the same after my sister bailed. But I guess I wanted a change of scenery as well. Something was telling me to see a bit of the world, find out what it had to offer. So I travelled a little, got it out of my system and—'

'Ended up here.' Lucy said the words like she couldn't really believe it. There were much better places he could have gone. 'Here, with me.' That insecurity rearing its head again, maybe wondering if Mitch thought he'd made a mistake.

It probably threw her back to her childhood. Lucy had told him fairly early on about being adopted, about her biological parents not wanting her. That rejection, no matter what happens afterwards, tends to stay with a kid.

'Yeah,' Mitch replied to the first statement, not getting into the second part. 'I came here maybe thinking I could make a difference. That's why I joined the police force in the first place.'

'Uh-huh, and how's that working out for you?' Lucy knew full well how it was working out at the moment. Terribly.

Her face had been a mixture of panic and relief when he told her the news about his job, that he'd jacked it in. She'd never really liked the fact he was a copper, with all the danger that entailed. But still, it was a job and the loss of his wage would hit them incredibly hard. 'Well, jumped before I was pushed,' he elaborated, going on to explain the circumstances of his departure.

'God, Mitch. You're going to go after them, though, right? Wrongful dismissal or whatever?'

'What's the point?' He told her then about Staton and his powerful friends, that they would crush him like a bug. Mitch wasn't important; he was nobody special. 'The system's more corrupt in Downstone than it was in Redmarket a few years back.'

'They cleaned up their act though. Or had it cleaned up for them, I should say.' It had been in all the news at the time, that the dodgy dealing in said town had been brought to light and straightened out. Mitch had to ask himself though, had it really? Could you ever truly get rid of a poison like that? Something rotten at its very core? 'Took people willing to stand up and be counted, but it turned itself around,' Lucy continued. 'They didn't just give up!'

'I'm not . . . Christ, I don't really want to have this conversation right now, is that okay?'

'And when do you want to have it? You're heading off to the middle of nowhere. Do you even know when you'll be back?'

'Not really,' he'd replied in all honestly. There was so much to do: find out what had happened, sort out the funeral arrangements. Things that Lucy insisted should be his older sister's responsibility. 'But it's not like I have any choice. Even if Bella was heading there too, I wouldn't just leave it all to her.'

'It's your birthday soon,' Lucy stated.

'I'm aware.'

'I thought we were going to . . . y'know, maybe do something? Spend some quality time together.'

'Lucy, my dad just died,' he reminded her, as if she needed it.

'I know, that's not what I—'

'I can't think about much else right now.' She'd looked wounded again at that. And Mitch understood her wanting to get things squared away before he left, maybe get their relationship

25

back on an even keel after all the ups and downs of late. More secure. But there was a time and a place, wasn't there?

'And what about Tammy?' asked Lucy, hitting him where she knew it would hurt. His friend was still in that coma, Zach still by her side.

Officer Fitzpatrick and her family will be well compensated.

How would that help her?

'I haven't forgotten about Tammy, trust me,' Mitch said, tears pricking at the corners of his eyes, thinking about the shitty way he'd spoken to her before everything kicked off. 'I just need to . . . to sort out all this stuff first, okay?'

'And then what?'

'How do you mean?' But he knew exactly what she meant. They'd been having money troubles before all this. Having . . . other troubles as well. Putting off conversations about where they were heading, about the future. About whether they even wanted the same things from life anymore. Like marriage, kids.

'Are you sure you haven't had a marital with Lucy?'

A marital, even though they weren't married – which was just one of the problems.

'You just lost your job, Mitch!' She looked around her at the small house they shared; the place they'd been living in together for almost three years now. Was probably wondering how they'd cope. Whether they even would.

'Listen, if it's money you're worried about, Dad had a bit put by, I think. Not a huge amount, but some. Plus there's his place, whatever might be left of it.'

'That's not what . . . You make me sound like some kind of heartless monster,' Lucy blurted out.

'No, that wasn't . . .' He couldn't do right for doing wrong, thought that would reassure her on the cash front at least. 'All I'm saying is we might not have as much to worry about as you think. Rent-wise, I'm talking about. I'm not sure how much interest Bella will have in Dad's home even if it's sold.'

Bella.

That brought things back to the here and now, snapping him out of his daze, because Lucy was once again talking about how selfish his sister was being. 'I mean, what *is* her problem? It's not like she has any ties, not like she has a proper job or anything.'

They were going round and round in circles, literally as she trailed him. And he wasn't even sure it was Bella who Lucy was upset with; not really. She just didn't want him to go, that was the top and tail of it.

'She doesn't owe me any kind of explanation, Lucy. She doesn't want to go. Simple as that.'

Lucy threw her hands up in the air, followed him as he tramped downstairs now. It had been hard enough for Mitch to get hold of the woman in the first place, finally succeeding where the staff at the hospital had failed. In the end he'd left a message for Bella at that hotel in Golden Sands where she did her turns. Her psychic evenings, if you could believe such a thing – and he didn't.

('What's the difference between what I do, and that sixth sense thing you have?' she'd said to him once when he'd visited a few summers ago.

It was different. Very different indeed. Just good instincts, that's what people said . . .)

'Regardless of anything else, I really don't think you should be alone there,' Lucy continued.

'I won't be alone. I have family still in Green Acres, remember? My aunty and uncle. It's okay, let it drop. Please.' But Lucy had got him thinking again about that strained phone conversation he'd had with Bella, who'd called him from the hotel payphone – she'd always hated mobiles. Something about her voice as she told him, 'I-I'm sorry, Mitch. I just can't.' A tremble in it, like she was scared.

Packing the last of his stuff, he left it by the front door next to his motorcycle helmet and turned around to find Lucy right behind him, still tense. 'Maybe . . . Maybe it's not such a bad thing. A bit of time away from each other,' she suggested then. A final volley. 'Like you said.'

He paused, thrown. 'I didn't say anything about—' Then he remembered, he'd mumbled something about her probably being glad he was getting out from under her feet while she worked. That was dangerous: Lucy remembered everything; read too much into the slightest thing sometimes. 'Is . . . Do you really think that?'

Lucy was close to tears, half-shook and half-nodded her head so he couldn't tell what she was thinking. Another mess.

'I *will* miss you,' he told her then, leaning in to give her a kiss, a hug. She stiffened at first, and finally hugged him back. 'We'll talk,' he promised her. 'When I get back, we'll talk properly.'

Another nod-shake, and the tears were flowing freely now. He hated leaving her like this. Felt torn in a million directions at once. But knew inevitably there was only one way he had to go. He owed it to his dad, his family. Wanted to know exactly what had happened, if nothing else.

Mitch sighed and put on his leather jacket, to match his trousers. Next he picked up his backpack, slinging it on. Then he grabbed his holdall and helmet and opened the front door. He wasn't at all surprised that it had started raining.

It was as he reached his bike parked by the side of the road, about to undo the combination lock, that Lucy called out something which made him pause one final time. Made him wonder about the real reason she didn't want him to go.

'Mitch, be careful,' she shouted. It was something she only usually told him when he was going on duty. He frowned, looked back, and said that he would.

'I'll see you soon, Lucy.'

Yet even as he strapped the holdall to the back of the Honda, put on his helmet and swung his leg over, Mitch couldn't help wondering . . .

Wondering if he wasn't the only one with a 'spider-sense' that warned them of danger.

Chapter 3

It wasn't easy to talk to the dead.

For them to talk to you, more accurately. It wasn't just the contempt some people showed for it, those who thought what she believed in was insane. Usually, she could just shrug that off, she was used to it. Had been dealing with the ridicule most of her life. No, at the moment she also had a splitting headache which wasn't helping matters in the slightest. Bella Prescott had tried everything she could think of to shift it: calming mediation, herbal teas. Had even been forced to take painkillers the previous evening, which was always a last resort for her. They dulled the mind, the senses, made it harder to hear those on 'the other side' (the departed, as she so often called them). Though anything was preferable to the thumping that was going on and had been for a day or more.

It had made it virtually impossible to sleep, tossing and turning and just not being able to get comfortable at all. Not knowing where to put herself, as they used to say. She'd found herself up and walking around in the wee small hours, padding about in the static caravan she called home. Even popping outside to sit on the steps and watch the sun rise over the ocean. It really was such a beautiful sight, tranquil and relaxing. Or it would have been if there wasn't a marching band playing inside her skull. Well, the big bass drum at any rate.

Bella knew what had set it off, *of course* she did. Talking to her younger brother Mitchel on the phone, hearing the news. They'd been trying to get hold of her apparently, the authorities at Green Acres, though nobody had said a word to her at the hotel. Trying to get in touch because she was the next of kin. She hadn't thought of herself as that in a long time, not next of anything. Not kin. Ironic really that she put people in touch with their loved ones all the time, even after they'd passed, and yet there was an overwhelming gulf between Bella and hers.

Not so much Mitch, she had to say. They'd made an effort – not a huge effort, granted, but an effort nonetheless – to keep in touch over the years. He'd even visited her, though his disdain for what she did was blatantly obvious. Yet another person who didn't take her work seriously at all. And it *was* work for her, hard work sometimes. She was as much a counsellor to the people she encountered, whether it was during her stage shows at The Majestic (a building which was anything but) in Golden Sands, or her private sessions with her regulars. Bella liked to think she was helping them, and usually she did. Not always, but usually.

Oh, she was well aware of what some people thought of her, that she was a charlatan. Downright evil, others called her. And she had to admit, there were definitely frauds out there. People who called themselves psychics or mediums, but were just con artists screwing people out of their money. Playing on their grief and their fear . . . of what came afterwards. But there were also the genuine articles like her, she'd argue, and really, there was nothing to be afraid of. If they could hear what she heard, everyone would know that. The danger never came from the dead, always the living.

Bella had never claimed to be anything she wasn't, and in most cases people found their way to her by word of mouth and necessity. Out of desperation. She didn't charge them, only said that if they thought her service was worth something then they could offer a donation. The hotel paid her for putting on the live evenings, naturally, but then she had to eat, pay the rent, same as everyone else. Every now and again, when things had been rough, she'd done part-time jobs – especially when Golden Sands was in-season. But Bella much preferred to spend her time offering comfort to those who needed it. Felt it was her calling in life, if that made sense. Resented, if she was being frank, the time spent waitressing in cafés when she could be giving some relative peace of mind.

Take Vicky here, who was sitting opposite her on the caravan's sofa today. She'd lost someone in the most tragic of circumstances the previous year, her husband Simon. Again, Vicky had come to her because she was desperate, and via a friend of hers, Jules. Julie Radcliffe, who had seen her own fair share of tragedy in her life. Bella had helped Julie, and so that woman thought she might be able to help Vicky come to terms with things too.

As Julie had explained to her friend when she first started bringing her along to the group sessions, Bella didn't channel the departed. They didn't take her over, possess her like something from a cheesy supernatural movie. They just talked, if they felt like it, and Bella listened, passed on their messages. What the living chose to do with that information was up to them.

Vicky had stopped coming to her group for a while, over the winter period – she said she'd just battened down the hatches on those long winter days and evenings, but Bella did wonder whether she'd lost her faith in all this. It was a fragile thing, easily shaken; all it would take would be a poisonous word or two from someone, a crack about Bella's voices being a mental illness: multiple personality disorder or something. About Vicky being as deluded as her if she believed in it all. But Bella needn't have worried, Vicky had returned again in the spring.

It was around this time she'd asked if she could see Bella separately, on her own sometimes. There were things to sort out with her late husband she'd prefer not to air in front of the others. Which was fine, Bella had made time for her when she could. And she knew Vicky didn't have a lot of money, so there was never any pressure about that side of things. None of this was about fleecing people, regardless of what some – Vicky's cousin, for example, some of Bella's own neighbours even – thought.

Today was one of those days Vicky had arranged to see her. Bella should have cancelled really, when she first felt the headache building. But she figured she could get rid of it; she'd never had one that lasted more than a couple of hours before. Never had been one of those people who suffered from crippling migraines that knocked them out of commission for days at a time, causing them to vomit or whatever. Those techniques she employed usually worked.

Just not this time.

Besides, part of why these people came to her was for a chat. To get things off their chest, whether their deceased relative cropped up or not. Sometimes they didn't, it was as unpredictable as the weather.

'Are you okay?' asked Vicky, finally, after being there for twenty minutes or so. She leaned over and touched Bella's arm.

Bella stared at her and nodded. 'I'm sorry. It's just . . . I'm—'

'You're really not yourself today, are you?' said the woman with the dark hair, which was only marginally longer than Bella's pixie cut. 'I can tell.'

'I . . . I'm all right,' Bella protested.

'You're absolutely not.'

'Just a bit of a headache, Vicky. It's fine.'

'Doesn't look fine. Let me make you a cuppa or something.'

'Honestly, Vicky, it's—'

'Hey, Bella, I'm doing it. It's the least I can do after everything you've done for me. Even without the . . . y'know . . . you've sat there and listened to me drone on and on about things for hours on end. You're always looking after people, I've seen you. Let someone look after you for a change.'

That would definitely make a change. Bella was usually so busy making sure everyone else was okay, she forgot about herself sometimes. It wasn't as if there was anyone around to look out for her, really. No partner. No family.

She nodded. Vicky was determined to do her kind deed anyway, so she might as well let her. 'But herbal, if that's okay? Feverfew, ginger or peppermint please.' All teas that usually helped soothe a sore head.

As Vicky rose and busied herself in the small kitchen not far away, Bella leaned back on the couch, resting the base of her skull. She was so, so tired. In fact, regardless of the headache, she'd almost drifted off when Vicky returned with the teas: ginger for Bella, which she placed on the small coffee table, moving a candle aside to do so, and an ordinary brew for herself. Vicky was quite a down-to-earth soul when all was said and done, which was why it was so flattering and so special that she'd warmed to what Bella did. If only her own brother could do the same.

'Oh, sorry. I didn't mean to . . .' said Vicky, apologizing for rousing her.

'It's okay,' Bella told her.

'So, what is it? Bad hangover? I've been there,' Vicky said with a chuckle.

Bella couldn't help letting out a little laugh herself at that. 'No, no. Never touch the stuff. I'm teetotal.'

'Then you'd better drink yours while it's hot,' Vicky ordered, smiling.

Bella had no idea whether she thought that's what it meant – that she only drank tea – or she was making a joke herself, but had a sip anyway. It wasn't that she hadn't ever drunk alcohol; actually, she'd quite liked drinking when she was younger, much to her family's chagrin. It helped to dampen down the voices that had been coming to her ever since she could remember. That she'd been too scared to tell anyone about because they'd have had her committed, that had made her wonder whether she actually should be sometimes. Whether she *was* going mad.

But now she steered clear of drink for exactly the opposite reason, to keep her head clear so she *could* hear what they were saying. Over time, and using certain practises she'd come across, she'd learned to separate them out. Only focus on one at a time. She'd also learned to tell them when to leave her alone. If you were reading a book, it was hard to concentrate on the words when there was someone's nan chatting away ten to the dozen in her head about how proud she was of little Timmy. And they respected that, the spirits. Mostly. Unless it was something pretty urgent.

'It's—' began Bella, then stopped again. Did she really want to get into this with Vicky? With someone who'd come here with her own problems today? She shook her head.

'Go on, it's all right. I can be a good listener too, when I put my mind to it.' Vicky flashed her another warm smile.

Bella's eyes brushed the floor. 'My father's just passed away,' she said.

There was silence for a moment or two, then Vicky answered with: 'Oh.'

'Yes. Oh.' Bella looked up and took another sip of her tea.

'And were you . . .' Vicky paused, obviously worried about broaching anything too personal. 'I'm sorry, I don't mean to pry. It's none of my business.'

'It's all right, Vicky. Honestly.' It was like they said in that gameshow: they'd started, so they'd finish.

Vicky sat back with her own tea. 'I was just going to ask if you two were close. I mean, you never really talk about . . . You don't talk about your family at all, actually. I just assumed, I guess I thought you were just a really private person.'

'I am,' Bella confirmed. 'But it's not that, it's just this particular . . . It's complicated.'

'I see,' Vicky responded, frowning in a way that said she really didn't at all. How could she? Bella wasn't exactly explaining herself well. Wasn't sure how to.

'We did used to be close. Mum died when I was still a young girl, you see. But then we had a falling out when I was in my teens, I can't even remember what about now and if I try to . . . I just remember the hurt, the pain. The wanting to get away.'

'Right.' Vicky drank some of her own tea. 'So you didn't really have anything to do with him after that?'

Bella shook her head. 'I still keep in touch with my younger brother. Sort of. He was the one who let me know about my dad.'

'And now you feel guilty about that?' asked Vicky, still struggling to understand.

'No. I don't know. I feel guilty for just taking off and leaving Mitch – oh, that's my brother's name. For leaving him there in Green Acres, for not being able to return with him now. But—'

Vicky sat forwards. '*You're* from Green Acres?' Bella nodded, though the action just brought fresh pain to her temples. 'Lovely bit of the world, that is.' Her visitor said that like they didn't already live in a beautiful spot by the seaside. 'We went on a holiday there once. Stayed in one of those cottages they have on the outskirts, Simon and . . .' Her voice tailed off sadly.

It was Bella's turn to reach forward now and pat Vicky's hand. 'It's okay. We're working through all that. You're working through it, you and Simon.'

Vicky nodded, tears in her eyes – and not for the first time if the subject of her late husband came up. Usually when he was talking to her 'through' Bella. 'And you can't just, y'know, yourself . . . ?' Vicky asked now.

Bella stared at her, confused.

'What I mean is, you guys didn't talk when he was alive. Why don't you try now, same as I've been doing with Simon?' She sniffed back more tears.

Ah, right. Gotcha, thought Bella. 'Doesn't work like that. For one thing they've got to want to talk to me, and I don't think my

35

dad . . . There's probably still a lot of anger there. For another, I've always had a blind spot where my own life, where my own *family* are concerned.' It was true. No one from her own clan had ever come to her from the other side, not her grandparents, great-grandparents. Not even her mother. Bella figured it was just some sort of rule when you did what she did.

'Could you not go to someone like . . . I mean, with your abilities.'

It made her sound like a superhero or something. Bella Prescott, racing off to fight evil and save the world! Nothing could be further from the truth. Bella pulled back her free hand, the one not currently employed holding the teacup, and rubbed the back of her head. 'Sounds stupid, I know, especially given what some folk think about me. But I'm just not sure I trust anyone else to pass messages on to me from my family. You know what I mean?'

Vicky's watery eyes were wide. 'I'm probably not the best one to ask that, given where I am. Given all the times I've come to see you.'

'Touché,' said Bella.

'I will say one thing, daughters need their dads. I've seen the way Mia's been since Simon passed.' Mia was Vicky's young daughter, eight now and going on eighty. An old head on young shoulders, as they were also so fond of saying. 'Oh, she says she's okay, but she's really not. I catch this look in her eye sometimes, and I know she's thinking about him. About how much she misses Simon.'

'It's not the same thing,' Bella protested, and was there just a bit of an edge to her tone? She hadn't intended that, it had just crept in.

'Yeah, yeah I know. I'm sorry, I didn't mean . . .' They drifted into an uncomfortable silence and drank their tea.

Before they knew it, Vicky was looking at her watch and standing. 'Is that the time, I said I'd pick Mia up from Jay and Jules.' Jay was Julie's son, about the same age as Vicky's daughter, more or less. The pair were best friends, the kind only seven- or eight-year-old's can be. There again, Julie had hidden that child from his father for so long, only prompted to get in touch again because of something her late daughter Jordan had said to her: 'It's time.'

Maybe it was time for her to lay the past to rest as well? Perhaps she should have gone with Mitch? Too late now. Or was it?

Her headache went into overdrive.

'Anyway, I'll be heading off,' said Vicky. 'I'm sorry if I said the wrong thing. I'm good like that.'

Bella attempted to shake her head, then gave up. 'Don't worry about it. Thanks for listening.'

'Yeah, sure. Anytime, you know that.' Vicky moved forwards now and opened her arms. The gesture was as unexpected as it was welcome, and Bella rose to accept the hug with genuine gratitude. 'You take care of yourself, Bella Prescott. You hear?'

'I will,' answered Bella, as the woman saw herself out – though she had no idea how she was going to do so. How she was even going to get rid of the pain that was threatening to crack her skull open.

Staggering across the caravan, she just about made it to the bedroom – to the bed – before collapsing on top of it. She was glad when, a few seconds later, she passed out. Glad to get rid of the pain, to embrace the nothingness that came with the dark.

Though as she descended into that abyss, all she could hear over and over on a loop were the words of Jordan Radcliffe.

'It's time,' she had said, as if the message had been meant for her, not Julie.

'It's time.'

Chapter 4

He was making good time.

Mitch had taken one break, at a service station on the motorway full of people looking like they wanted to kill themselves. End it all and be done with it. When his grilled sandwich and coffee arrived, delivered by a guy in an apron with grease stains down the front of it – dropped unceremoniously onto his table – Mitch had to admit he was beginning to see why.

The never-ending stretch of concrete which took him northwards allowed him to open up the bike, when he wasn't stuck in jams, but it was boring just heading in one direction and his legs were starting to cramp after so long. One of the reasons for stopping in the first place, apart from the fact he knew he should probably grab something to eat. He hadn't had much of an appetite, though, and the cuisine on offer at that place didn't exactly do anything to alter this. In the end, he'd taken a bite or two, gulped down the black caffeine – which was so thick you could stand a spoon up in it – and continued on his way again.

At least it had stopped raining, for now.

Mitch was grateful when he spotted the turn-off, sling-shotting from the roundabout onto the smaller, more winding country roads to head north-west. It gave him something to concentrate on, leaning one way then the other as he navigated some of the tighter bends. Something to think about other than what had happened over the last couple of days: the riot, Tammy, losing his job. Leaving Lucy the way he had, not knowing if they'd be able to fix things when he got back. If he concentrated too much on all that, it started to feel like his life was imploding. What a real mess!

Something to think about other than the reason he was coming back home, as well. The call that had sparked all this. The mysterious circumstances surrounding the death of his father. He still didn't really have the full story: his dad, killed by fire somehow. Mitch couldn't help letting his imagination run away with him.

A house fire seemed like the most obvious thing that might have happened, but an accident or something more sinister? Electrical, or had someone put something through the letterbox? A prank gone wrong? Or had his father just forgotten to switch the oven off? The authorities had been less than forthcoming, which just made him all the more suspicious. Made him suspect foul play of some sort, that and those bloody instincts he'd learned not to ignore. Something wasn't right again. But the lanes, the bends – having to watch out for vehicles that might be coming the other way on roads only wide enough for one of them at a time – took his mind off things for a while. Until he was almost at his destination.

Green Acres was a huge place, the name itself covering as much of the area as the grassland and woods did. He'd seen these from a distance – rolling hills and patches of green – even before he'd hit those narrow lanes with their passing places, spaces at the side to sneak into and avoid collisions. He'd had to do that when a tractor came speeding along to meet him, barely giving Mitch enough time to get out of the way. The man behind the wheel, ruddy-cheeked with bushy sideburns, had blared his horn at Mitch as if to say he was the one in the wrong, that he shouldn't even be on this road. Maybe he shouldn't. Maybe this whole thing had been a mistake, he couldn't help thinking. Perhaps he should just go back to Lucy, instead of getting sucked back into all this again.

Sucked into what? What did he mean by that? Mitch wasn't entirely sure he knew himself, he needed to look into this. Didn't he? Yes, of course.

The tractor's horn blared again, this time apparently to signify that it had passed by – if only it had done that as it approached! – and Mitch shook himself from his reverie again. He accelerated off once more, passing the farm that the lumbering metal beast must have come from – a path leading up to some outhouses, a massive barn and a rundown farmhouse.

Next, as the road dipped slightly, it gave him a view of the patch of water called Lake Iris; named after the kinds of flowers that encircled it, blue irises, rather than a person. A pretty name for a place so associated with ancient horrors – as it was said that witches in the Middle Ages were 'tested' here. Dunked in the lake to see if they'd drown, which meant they were innocent, or float, which meant they were in league with the Devil and killed anyway. No way to win. Another passing place of sorts. Indeed, Mitch could recall a few deaths here when he was little, accidental drownings this time which had resulted in a fence being built around the body of water, between that and the path encircling it.

Not far from this was a thick blanket of trees, popular with campers and hunters – plus a cave system just on the other side of it. That had also been popular, but with children when he was younger, especially on dares or initiations to get into gangs. So much so that they'd had to put bars over the entrances and exits to stop kids getting lost inside. Mitch suddenly remembered one such incident his dad had actually covered for *The Acre* when a team of local cavers had to venture inside to look for a ten-year-old boy who'd been in there a couple of days. It was the most excitement the area had experienced in ages, and thankfully the kid had been all right – if a little emaciated when he emerged into the light again.

As he made his way to the village which was at the centre of everything, and was actually quite tiny by comparison, Mitch couldn't help noticing a collection of buildings on a hillock that hadn't been there when he'd last been around. A collection of huts and other structures, along with a few mobile homes, which looked like it was trying to be a village as well, or the beginnings of one. He had to wonder how they'd got permission for the homes that weren't so mobile, if they even had. Though he knew from conversations with his dad that there had been rumblings about new houses being built, land sold off or whatever. Something the villagers at Green Acres weren't all that keen on, because it meant strangers disturbing the peace.

Then he spotted some people, a handful of figures all dressed the same in strange, cream-coloured smocks and loose-fitting trousers walking down towards the road. Had they come from that place? he wondered, as they watched him pass.

He couldn't help shivering at that and made a mental note to ask about the place when he got to the village. Which was about five to ten minutes later: hitting the white-washed cottages with thatched roofs on the outskirts first, complete with scarecrows in the gardens that were a familiar sight over the summer, along with well-dressings, ribbons, and the like. Splashes of colour everywhere celebrating the time of year.

Then he was in Green Acres proper, easing up on the speed. Passing the park where he'd whiled away so many hours as a child himself, its slide, swings, and roundabout still present, with benches around so that parents could look on. The small corner shop-cum-post office was next, which served the whole of the village, and the local pub The Plough which he'd been in many times – even though he hadn't been legally allowed to drink back when he lived here (that hadn't stopped him having a pint or several). It was a family pub, but then the proprietors of establishments like this tended to think the rules didn't really apply to them all the way out here anyway. Who was going to know, and seeing as police officers from the region were regulars at the lock-ins, they were hardly going to complain.

Then came the village hall, which doubled as a community centre, a meeting place for the parish council and just a general 'fulfil any need' building. It was within spitting distance of the tiny dilapidated and deserted church with its graveyard at the rear. He'd only seen a few more people dotted about here and there since he entered, but was beginning to remember that was par for the course around here. He had obviously just become used to the denser populations of cities like Downstone.

Mitch hadn't been able to help himself, he'd ridden around the village square – where there was an obelisk-like monument to those who had fallen in all the wars, planted slap bang in the middle of a patch of grass – just so he could check out the state of his dad's house. Part of him had been expecting a smoking hole in the ground, but no. There it was, intact and untouched, brown upon brown – roof and walls – with only ivy climbing the sides to break up the monotony. He let out a relieved sigh inside his helmet, glad that he didn't have to deal with the loss of his family home as well as his one remaining parent. Then the thought stuck him once more: if his dad hadn't died in a house fire, then what the hell *had* happened? It made him all the more determined to find out.

Continuing on, he turned up a side street and made for the much smaller building that his aunty and uncle had lived in ever since he could remember. They hadn't had any children themselves, so didn't need a vast amount of space. Something they were probably glad of now they were getting on in years and had both retired.

He'd tried ringing them up to find out more, his Aunty Helen and Uncle Vince, but the line had been so bad he'd given up on his third attempt. Thought it best to talk to them in person anyway, which was what he was on his way to do now, parking up the Honda outside putting down the kickstand.

Mitch strode up to the front door, taking off his helmet and tucking it under his arm, before giving a quick rap on the wood. When nobody answered after a few minutes, he knocked again. Perhaps they weren't in? He knew that sometimes they went for walks in the afternoon, keeping up the fitness regime Helen had insisted on when she'd been the GP here. And they hadn't known he was coming today, had they? Weren't expecting him at all.

He caught a glimpse of someone peering out through the front window then, so *somebody* was home. Mitch frowned at the caution, but then he had rocked up in his leathers looking like a Terminator, so . . . He backed up, leaning slightly so they could see who he was. Would they even recognize his face? He hadn't changed that much since the last time they'd seen him, surely?

The clicking of the locks and latches on the door made him start. Sounded like Fort Knox inside there. And yes, even as the door opened a gold chain was still attached. Then a balding head appeared in the gap.

'Hell-Hello?' said a tentative voice.

'Vince?'

'Who are you?'

'Uncle Vince?' Mitch tried again.

A look of understanding suddenly dawned on the older man's face. 'Mitchel? Young Mitch, is that you?'

He nodded. 'Hi there.'

The head disappeared for a second, and he heard Vince shouting excitedly to his wife. 'Helen. Helen, it's young Mitch!' The chain was swiftly removed, and the door flung open. 'My,' said his uncle. 'Young Mitch, as I live and breathe!'

Mitch couldn't help smiling at that. It had been a while since anyone had called him young. Nowadays you were over the hill if you were past twenty-five, which wasn't that much of a distant memory, but then he supposed he was still young to his Uncle Vince.

43

'Mitch,' came a female voice from inside, then a short woman in a green dress with a grey bowl cut appeared next to her husband. 'Oh Mitch, it's so good to see you!'

'You too. Both of you,' he added.

'How long has it been now?' Vince wondered aloud.

'Never mind about that, let the lad in, Vincent!' his wife instructed. She'd always worn the trousers in this particular relationship, Mitch recalled.

'I did try to get through on the phone a few times, but—'

'They're doing work on the lines here. Again! Oh,' she said then, looking past him to his bike, 'you'd better bring that round the back first, where it'll be safe.'

Mitch frowned again. Safe? It was the same thing as the locks; since when had you needed to do that in Green Acres? Then again, the bike did have all his stuff on the back so it probably wasn't a terrible idea. 'I'll go and open the side gate,' his uncle told him, disappearing from sight.

It was only now, with Vince gone, that Helen opened her arms wide and moved forwards. Mitch had to stoop to meet her embrace, but the hug was so strong she almost broke his back. 'Oh lad, it's so good to see you,' she said again. 'I wish it was under better circumstances, but anyway, welcome back . . .

'Welcome *home*.'

It wasn't long before he was sitting in the living room, being eaten alive by an enormous floral comfy chair and supplied with his body weight in tea and biscuits.

He didn't want to ask straight off the bat, in spite of the fact both these people knew exactly why he was here, so Mitch started by asking about the security stuff. The locks and the concern about his motorcycle.

'There's been a number of break-ins lately,' explained his uncle, who he could see – now that he was sitting on a more sturdy chair for his back – was wearing a shirt, cardigan, and trousers, regardless of the heat in that room. Mitch was glad they'd taken his jacket and hung it by the door. 'Thefts, that sort of thing. Better to be safe than sorry. I blame the number of newcomers around.'

'I spotted a few new buildings on the way in,' Mitch said, taking a bite of his Hobnob and a drink of tea. 'Some weird men and women in smocks or something?'

His uncle scrunched up his face. 'The Commune,' he stated, then paused before continuing. 'They claim they want to go back to nature but, well, I don't trust 'em. Things haven't been the same around this place since they began worming their way in here; no respect for boundaries, that lot. Then there's all that talk about property development. It never used to be like this, when I first moved to Green Acres.'

'Right.' Mitch had been told the story on many occasions, how his mother's sister had come to meet this man when she was about his age: a therapist by trade, they'd bonded over lectures at a medical seminar and been stuck to each other like glue ever since. She'd brought him back with her and he'd taken to life here like a duck to that water at Lake Iris. When they got going they could talk shop for England, his dad used to say. Which brought him back to thinking about his father. He shook his head, not willing to wait any longer. 'I'm sorry, I have to ask. You were here. What happened with Dad?'

Helen and Vince exchanged glances, neither of them willing to talk about it apparently. They weren't the only ones, however, and he told them so. 'Have . . . So, nobody's spoken to you about what actually happened?' queried his aunty.

Mitch shook his head. 'Only that he died in a fire. I thought perhaps his house, but that seems okay. I rode past it on my way here.'

'Oh yes, that's fine. We've been popping in and keeping an eye on things there, trying to keep the place . . .' Helen looked down sadly, then back up again. 'You really had no idea how bad things had got with him?'

'How bad . . .?' Mitch didn't have the first clue what they were talking about.

'The confusion, the . . .' Vince looked at his wife, as if asking permission to say the next bit, which he got with an almost imperceptible tip of the head. 'All right, I'll go ahead and say it then: the dementia.'

'Dementia? You mean like Alzheimer's?'

Vince nodded. 'He had good days and bad days, did Tommy. The bad ones weren't all that often, but when they happened, they were very bad indeed.'

'Why didn't . . .' Mitch shook his head again. 'You should have let me know.'

'What could you have done, love? You had your job, your life elsewhere,' said Helen. The first wasn't a problem anymore, not since he'd been canned, but yes, Mitch had to admit he did have a life in Downstone with Lucy. At least he hoped he still did. How would hearing about his father's illness have impacted on that? Probably not well. It was a selfish thought, and he'd never know now, sadly.

'You still should have told me. I could have—'

'You have to understand, he made us promise not to. Your dad never was one for a fuss.'

'A *fuss*?' Mitch couldn't believe what he was hearing, but tried to keep his temper in check. He was as mad at himself as much as anyone. He'd suspected, hadn't he? The vagueness, it wasn't anything new. But he'd just thought . . . Old people do get a little like that, don't they? Maybe if he'd visited more often, or even at all. 'Okay, so has that got something to do with what happened to him?'

A silence descended that neither of them wanted to break again, it seemed.

'Please,' Mitch prodded. 'I need to know what happened. It's one of the reasons why I'm here. That and to make whatever arrangements need to be made.'

'Yes,' said Helen. 'We know.' So she told him. About how his dad had been found out in the woods, had scared the life out of a couple of young campers.

'Nasty business,' Vince added.

'Dad was wandering about in the woods then?' Mitch asked, trying and failing to sit forwards in his chair and put his cup and saucer down. His aunty had taken this as a signal he wanted more tea and grabbed the pot, topping him up and placing a couple more biscuits on his saucer. 'But I don't understand. Why would they tell me there had been a fire?'

Another awkward silence.

'He was in a fire, they said. And—'

Uncle Vince shook his head. 'No, son. He was *on* fire.'

'What?' Mitch looked over at his aunty for confirmation, and she just nodded once. 'But I mean . . . what? How?'

'To be honest,' Vince carried on, 'nobody seems to be able to tell us what occurred. Not really.'

'So he . . . I mean, I just don't understand how—' Mitch rubbed his eyes with his free hand. Of all the things he'd been imagining since the phone call, and on the way here, this hadn't been one of them. His father. On fire. In the woods.

Absolutely crazy.

'We can only assume . . . I mean, he must have done it to himself,' Helen said then.

Mitch took his hand away and looked at her. 'To himself? You're suggesting he . . . Is that even a thing? Do people suffering from dementia do things like that?'

They both shrugged almost as one. 'The mind's a strange thing,' said Vince. 'Trust me. Who knows what he might have been seeing, or hearing at the time.'

'Is it possible he walked through a fire accidentally, those campers—'

'It was the middle of the night, their fire was totally out, Mitchel.'

'But maybe—'

'I know, I know. It's a hard thing to take in. Maybe that's why nobody wanted to bring it up over the phone.' Vince let out a long breath. 'But I'm sure they'll be able to tell you much more than they've told us, especially in your line of work and everything. All we do know is that the couple did their best to put him out. They were just too late. His burns were too severe.'

'Shit,' said Mitch.

'Language,' Helen admonished. He'd forgotten what a stickler for all that kind of stuff she was, religion and everything. Swearing. Mitch apologized, immediately feeling like a little boy who'd done something naughty.

Eventually, he spoke again. 'Okay, so let me ask you this, because like I said, you were here. You've been around him all this time. Do *you* guys think he did it to himself? Even in his state, do you think he could have done something like that? Do you think he even wanted to?'

And for a final time, neither of them spoke.

It told Mitch all he really needed to know.

Chapter 5

They'd polished the visit off – once he'd been able to detach himself from that chair – with another bone-crunching hug from Helen, a firm handshake from Vince, who'd said, 'Again, we're so sorry you had to be here under such circumstances. And with your birthday not far away.'

'Yeah,' was all Mitch could muster. It would hardly be a cause for celebration now, would it?

Then Vince put something in his hand, the key to his dad's place.

'Seems daft paying for somewhere while you're here,' Helen said to him. 'We'd love to have you stay, but there really isn't the space. We converted the spare room into a bit of a study, you know how it is.'

Mitch really didn't, he'd never been one for studies – didn't have that many books, had never written anything more complicated than an email or an incident report. But he could see how this couple would have one, same as his father. A games room with a pool table and dart board would probably be more his speed, which showed just how different he was to his remaining relatives.

Apart from Bella, of course.

'How is your sister?' Helen had asked at one point during the mammoth tea and biscuit session.

'She's . . . Yeah, Bella's good,' he'd replied. As far as he knew, she was.

'Still doing the whole . . . you know what?' asked his aunty, like she couldn't bring herself to say the words psychic or medium. As if she was on the game or something. Mitch had nodded. 'Stuff and nonsense, the lot of it!' But then he wouldn't have expected anything less from a woman of science. Except there was that whole religious aspect to Helen, wasn't there? A staunch believer. She'd explain that away, of course, by saying medicine came from a higher power, not human beings. Yet she couldn't bring herself to believe in Bella's skills. Not that Mitch could talk.

'Just a different form of therapy,' Vince chipped in, coming to Bella's defence. 'People deal with their grief in different ways, don't they?'

'I suppose,' Helen had agreed. 'And it would be nice to see her again. It's been an age.'

'Yeah,' Mitch said. 'Definitely.'

It made him wonder, as he was wheeling the bike back round to the front, his aunty's words still ringing in his ears about 'leaving him to settle in' and knowing 'where we are if you need us', exactly how Bella was dealing with her own grief over this. Perhaps she wasn't. Her refusal to return would seem to back that up, but . . . He should give her another call, if he could get through to her, that was. Golden Sands and Green Acres had that in common anyway, both black holes where communication was concerned. Not even the landlines were working properly here, so he was surprised when he got outside and found he had a message on his mobile from Lucy.

'Hope all ok,' with a couple of kisses, it said. He sent a quick one back to say he'd arrived, how he'd spent the afternoon and where he was going next, kicking himself that she'd had to be the one to get in touch first.

As he put on his helmet and got on the bike again to travel the short distance back to his dad's place, he couldn't help thinking that generally speaking he really didn't know where he was going. He'd come here for answers, but instead his head was filled with even more questions that he *couldn't* answer. About his father, about what had happened to him.

'Do you think he could have done something like that? Do you think he even wanted to?'

Thomas Prescott wasn't the sort of man who'd ever contemplate suicide, he was far too stubborn for that, regardless of any diagnosis – which he probably didn't trust anyway. Not even when he'd lost his wife had he thought about calling it a day, even at his lowest ebb. Sure, he drank a lot more than usual – but as Vince had pointed out, people handle grief in their own way. There had definitely been no talk of razor blades or sticking heads in ovens – that Mitch knew about anyway. Then again, he had been very young; he'd have been shielded from it all if there had been. No, Bella would have said something to him about it afterwards, when he was older. Would have needed to talk about it, if he knew her, and only with someone close.

So, the dementia. Something that could make you set fire to yourself? Mitch didn't – couldn't – buy it. Admittedly, he had a limited amount of experience where this kind of thing was concerned. But wasn't there an in-built survival instinct in human beings, to prevent this sort of thing? He'd read somewhere in a magazine article, probably while he was at the dentists or somewhere, that the instinct to jump when you're looking down in a high place is your mind wanting to take the next step – literally. Carry on moving forward, even if it meant you splattered all over the pavement. But setting yourself on fire? One of the most horrific things you could do to yourself. Come on! Even animals steered clear of fire, that's why cavemen had lit fires at the dawn of time, hadn't they? His aunty and uncle had more experience of the disease Thomas apparently had, but the fact they'd remained silent when he asked them if it was possible his father had done this to himself spoke volumes.

That just left one other alternative: someone had done this *to* his father.

But who? And why?

Perhaps he'd find some answers at the family home? But Mitch spent ages just parked outside it, sitting on the bike and staring at the house, the front door. It was only when he began to draw strange looks from a family, a couple with children passing by, that he got off. The last thing he needed to contend with today was the police, called to investigate a person loitering outside the place. Although sometime soon, he needed to pay them a visit, maybe even arrange to see the body. It was too late today, however, Mitch decided. Or perhaps it was just another thing he was putting off?

Remembering what his aunty and uncle had said about safety, he'd wheeled his bike around the back – locking it up securely and grabbing his stuff before returning to the front.

Even then, he'd dawdled with the key in his hand. It just didn't feel right to be doing this, but then who else could? He and Bella were the only ones left to sort all this out: the house, and whatever else *needed* sorting. Gritting his teeth, he put it in the lock and turned it. The door opened with a loud creak; it sounded like the hinges hadn't had any attention in aeons.

Regardless of the fact it was only late afternoon, it was dark inside the house. And cold, in stark contrast to how it was outside and how it had been at the previous home he'd visited. Mitch half expected to see his breath turn to mist in here. It was as if the spirit of the person who'd owned it had kept it warm, and now that he'd gone—

Yeah, he'd been warm all right. At the end.

Mitch blinked away the images that were forming in his mind, the horrible pictures of his father alight, staggering through those trees at night-time, his flesh turning black and . . .

Dumping his stuff in the hallway, dropping his helmet on top of that, Mitch closed the door behind him with a slam. Then he leaned against it, summoning the strength to continue with this task. Eventually, he pushed himself off and made his way through the hall, wooden beams guiding him along.

With every step, memories came rushing back. Of running up and down that hallway as a nipper, bounding up and down the stairs that were on his left a bit further in. So full of energy he couldn't even begin to imagine doing that now; it was like the world out there, and what had happened, had conspired to suck all of that out of him. At this moment in time, he would have given anything to be that age again. God, he was far too young to be so jaded, wasn't he? So cynical? What had happened to him?

Life. Just life. Getting older and the consequences of that, of his experiences – especially recently.

The door to the living room on his right was open and he glanced inside, taking in its faded maroon sofa and a couple of chairs (one wingback), bookcases lining the walls, a fireplace with its mirror hanging above it, the small TV in the corner on which Thomas used to watch those programmes he'd bitch about. Every presenter must have looked tiny on that!

He ventured upstairs next, taking the steps slowly and using the wooden handrail – so much of this place was wood! – ending up on the landing. In front of him were the two rooms that made up the toilet and bathroom, separate in case someone wanted to use the loo and another person needed a bath or a shower, which were actually one and the same combined. On his right was a corridor that led off to two bedrooms opposite each other, the first of which had been Bella's when she'd lived here and the furthest away had been his. Neither had changed very much, he noted when he looked – but then there wouldn't be any cause to. Single beds in each, a wardrobe, dresser, desk for doing homework on.

At the other end of the landing was the master bedroom, where his mum and dad had slept when she'd still been alive – and his father had done the same on his own for all those years after she passed. A double bed in here, the covers still rumpled from the last time it had been used. Mitch pulled a face at the thought of kipping in there, but then he didn't particularly fancy sleeping in a single bed again after all this time. He'd just change the sheets in a bit, he told himself. That should help.

Returning downstairs, he came across the study he'd been thinking about earlier. It looked like there had been some attempt by his aunty and uncle to keep things tidy, but there were still books and papers scattered about everywhere, especially on the desk and chair Thomas used to work at. If Mitch knew his dad, he would have fought any kind of intrusion into this inner sanctum, and might have messed things up again afterwards even if they had been inside. Then again, maybe the disorder in here had been part of his father's affliction? No, he'd been this way even before he started to become vague. Mitch *remembered* it being disorganised.

Continuing on to the kitchen, with its large wooden – more wood – table in the middle. They used to eat on that. Never in the living room, that wasn't allowed, always at the table like civilized people. Mitch had been told the cupboards and fridge-freezer should still be well stocked, enough provisions to last him until he could get to the shop. There was tea, he was assured – his aunty and uncle were obsessed with that particular drink – and long-life semi-skimmed milk, and the kettle was in full working order, so that was all right. Get your priorities straight. He checked a few cupboards, finding tins inside them, and in the one they'd used for medicine: plasters, bandages, paracetamol, and so on. Only now there were also prescription pills for various other ailments, many of which he didn't recognize. Some of which were probably for the dementia, Mitch figured. There were so many that it was a wonder Thomas Prescott didn't rattle when he walked. If he took them, that was.

Mitch was turning to head out again and fetch his stuff, when he froze. Saw the door there on his left, ajar. The door to the only part of this house he hadn't revisited yet. Mitch swallowed dryly.

It had always given him the creeps, that bit of his old home. But then they did with most people, didn't they? Those sections of any house. The very top bit, the attic (which thankfully this place didn't have), and the very bottom. The underneath of the house.

The cellar.

Both similar kinds of spaces, meant for storage primarily. Places of ladders and slatted steps, of cobwebs and insects. Full of dark nooks and crannies where a child's imagination could run riot. He'd never been brave enough to go down there on his own, had never really had any cause or desire to. The thought alone was enough to send a chill up and down his spine, along his shoulders, to tickle the back of his neck.

Quickly, Mitch went over and closed that door shut. Then he continued out of the kitchen, without looking back.

Once he'd unpacked some of his stuff, turning on a few lights throughout the house, he thought about heading back into the study to have a poke around.

But, after surveying the scene once more, Mitch became so depressed with the thought that before long he'd need to sort out *everything*, not only in this room but in the whole house – possibly alone, unless he could convince Bella to come – that he just shifted the detritus and sat down in his dad's chair, staring at the computer screen which looked like it had seen better days back in the '90s. It was like there had been some vague attempt to move with the times, but only a little. Christ alone knew what kind of operating system that thing used, the tower looked like it was carved out of granite or something.

There were several sets of drawers on either side of that desk, however, and Mitch found himself opening a couple and rooting around inside them. One was filled to the brim with old copies of *The Acre*, another with journals and periodicals. In the very bottom one there were more piles of papers, a few boxes of staples and paperclips. But underneath all that, something else. Mitch's fingers recoiled at first, because he wasn't expecting glass. Then he looked properly and he found most of a bottle of eight-year-old German brandy tucked away inside. He couldn't help smiling at that.

'Good old dad,' he said out loud, determining to have a drink or several in his memory that evening.

More searching, and in another drawer he found a stack of photo albums. Mitch opened the first, only to be confronted with a picture of his mum and dad who looked even younger than he was; than his aunty and uncle had been when they met and she brought Vince to the village. They were standing in the square, the photo light but still in colour, when colour must have been quite new. The couple – were they even married at this point? – appeared so happy. Smiling and holding each other like he and Lucy were doing in quite a few early photos – for dates, special occasions . . . birthdays – on his phone, and stored in the cloud. He wondered then, as so often he did, what would happen if technology suddenly failed one day – say after some kind of huge EMP? Would all those digital memories be lost forever? (Would there ever be any more photos of him and Lucy like that?) Were the ones he was holding any better: they could fade; they could rot. They could be destroyed.

He flicked through more pictures, a whole history in just that single album. More in the others, some of Bella when she was only a baby, when she was a toddler. Mitch grinned again, decided to take these into the living room along with the brandy and make a night of it.

So, he carried the photos through, grabbing a glass from the kitchen for the alcohol – of which he poured a generous measure as he sat down on the couch. He considered lighting the fire, with yet more wood – because it was still quite chilly in here – but knew the brandy would soon warm him up. Sucking in air through his teeth at his first taste of the drink, the brown liquid simultaneously fiery and smooth, he flipped through page after page of photos. They showed not only the history of their family, but Green Acres itself, although it had to be said that hadn't changed as much as the people who resided there.

Mitch had never really thought about why they were so resistant to change, but looking at the buildings, the scenery in the background, it was pretty obvious. There was not only a rich tradition here of communal celebrations – from harvest festivals, to winter carol services – dating back generations, but also it was just such a pretty place. Compare it with the likes of Downstone, Hannerton, and Granfield, with all their glass, metal and concrete, and it wasn't hard to see why the folk living here wanted to keep the outside world at bay. Where some might argue it belonged.

Now the outside was creeping in, wasn't it? The thefts that his aunty and uncle were talking about, the housing developers sniffing round – it was only a matter of time, all that land out there – and just a sense of life speeding up and spiralling out of control.

Imploding.

Pouring more and more brandy, Mitch pored over more and more photos. Coming at last to one of his father, middle-aged, standing proudly outside his home, leaning on one of the walls. He had no idea who'd taken it, a neighbour or relative, but Mitch fished it out and held it up, then put down his glass and traced the edges of his dad's face with a shaking finger.

He hadn't cried, not in all the time since he'd heard the man was dead, but now those tears came. And they came in abundance, wracking Mitch's body as he sat back on the sofa still holding the photo, only gradually letting it fall to his lap when it felt too heavy for him.

Heavy, just like his eyes – the stinging saltwater making them sore, making them want to close and stay closed. Suddenly he was very tired, too tired to fight it anymore. His body was crying out for the sleep it had been denied since he'd found out his father had died.

Since his father had been killed?

No, don't think about that. Just think about how warm it is now in here, how comforting that blackness is since you've shut your eyes.

How it feels to rest. To be at rest.

But that feeling of contentment soon drifted away, as Mitch began to dream. A dream not of darkness itself, but a descent into darkness. Going down one step at a time when he couldn't even see them, having to gauge where he was as he went further down and down. Suddenly stopping, hearing a noise and seeing something. Shapes in the blackness. Outlines really, figures moving about. Then shadows, flickering shadows. Monsters, even though he knew they didn't really exist. Monsters who were going to—

Mitch jerked awake when he heard the scratching sound, his whole body tensing. Used to living on his nerves, he hadn't been able to ignore the sound once he'd registered it, however faint. However far away it seemed.

Shaking his head, attempting to clear the fog, he looked first from the bottle of brandy in front of him – which was almost empty now – to his watch, which told him it was the early hours of the morning. He'd been asleep some time, and wondered how long that scratching might have been going on before he noticed it. Clearly he'd been deeply asleep.

Mitch started to rise, his legs feeling like jelly and hardly able to support him. He just about managed to stop himself from crashing back down into the seat again, rolling over to use the arm of the sofa to lever himself up.

There it was again: a scratching, creaking sound. What *was* that? Burglars trying to get in? Maybe someone had heard the place was empty and decided to try their luck, those newcomers his Uncle Vince had been so worried about, that he didn't trust? If so, they'd definitely picked the wrong night to do that. If he could just get to his feet properly, he'd give them the pummelling of their lives!

Oh, who was he kidding? They'd flatten him in this state.

So he glanced around for a weapon he could use, spying the poker on the hearth. Mitch tottered towards it, trying desperately not to topple into the fire itself. It wasn't lit – just how do you

accidentally set yourself on fire again? In a drunken stupor maybe?
– but it still wouldn't do him any favours. Snatching up the iron
rod with the jagged end, he nodded to himself. It felt like a good
replacement for his baton back when he was on duty. Could potentially do more damage than that thing if used in the right way.

Okay, right. Time to go and see what that blasted noise
was. Mitch swayed as he made his way out through the living-
room door, cocking an ear to work out where the scratching
and creaking was coming from. His right he decided, along the
corridor and into the kitchen. Listening again, just to make sure,
he set off in search of those burglars to wallop them.

But when he arrived in the room, the lights still on in there
too as he'd left them, he found it eerily empty. And didn't a part
of him feel worse because he was on his own in there? Especially
when that noise came again, louder than ever.

It was coming from the door, also on his right.

The cellar door.

Mitch's hands began to shake again. No, *anywhere* but there!
The scratching came again, more urgently. Definitely from inside.
Good Christ! He had to check it out, what other option did he
have? He wasn't just going to curl up back to sleep knowing there
was someone down there. Someone who might come up while
he was asleep and—

Swallowing even more dryly than before, possibly because of
the dehydration, he stepped forwards gingerly. To be fair, it was
the only way he *could* step forwards, because the room was spinning. *Fuck!* Why had he drunk all that brandy in the first place?
Toasting his dad.

Poor choice of words. Very poor choice.

Mitch shook his head and raised his free – still shaking – hand.
Reached out for the handle of the door, though it was the last
thing in the world he wanted to do. Time stretched out to match
his fingertips, which were now brushing the edges of that handle.
Was it his imagination, or was it hot? Burning even?

It didn't matter, he needed to get that door open. Steeling himself as best he could, holding the poker high in his other hand, readying to strike.

The noise had stopped. The scratching and creaking. Now there was nothing, and he began to wonder if he'd simply imagined the whole damned thing.

Then the door itself banged, loudly, as if something was trying to force it from the other side. Mitch leaped backwards, nearly tripped and fell over, but righted himself at the last minute by grabbing the edge of the wooden table. A good job too, because if he'd fallen over he might not have gotten back up again.

The thumping against the door reminded him he still had another problem to deal with, a very real one on the other side of that barrier.

'Sod this!' Mitch muttered. Rushing forwards, he grabbed the handle, the poker up and primed for action. Pulling on both the handle and the door, it swung wide open, revealing the absolute darkness inside.

He immediately regretted his decision, wanting to slam it shut again – but it was too late. Mitch was already staring into that particular abyss. What's more, it was staring right back at him. Whether it was the nightmare he'd just had, the brandy, or something else, he was seeing those figures moving, those flickering shadows again. Those monsters in the cellar. And he wanted to descend, that part of his mind making him move forwards off the edge even though it was dangerous, even though it might kill him.

'W-Who's there?' he asked, unable to keep the flicker from his own voice. 'I said who's—'

Suddenly there they were: eyes. Bright eyes in the darkness, the thing he'd felt staring back at him. Glowing orbs, boring into him. Rushing at him as swiftly as he'd rushed at the door and flung it open, eager to face whatever was behind it – or not.

Shadows, outlines, barrelling towards him, and Mitch swung the poker to meet them, causing a swishing sound as it cut through the air. Causing him to almost drop forwards and topple down the cellar steps he knew must still be there – even though he couldn't see them for love nor money. He'd be descending quicker than ever then, wouldn't he? A broken neck putting paid to any chance of tackling whatever it was that had been scratching and banging.

Whatever was coming at him, ferocious and angry. He just about caught a flash of something cream before gravity took him, dragging him backwards rather than forwards this time, the poker flying out of his grasp.

He fell flat on his back in the kitchen, all the air from his lungs exploding out of him. Knowing that he needed to get back up again, or at least sit up because something was out here with him, he attempted to move and regretted that instantly as well. If he felt like this now, imagine what it would feel like in the morning when the alcohol wore off. If there was a morning. If he *made it* to the morning.

Even if this was only an intruder – intruders? – then they could still do him some damage while he was down and out like this. Could still mess him up if they found that poker he'd dropped and used it on him, just like he'd intended to do to them. But those eyes – bloody hell, those eyes! They hadn't been anything approaching human, had they?

No. They hadn't.

Because, as he used his elbows to roll himself and looked over in the direction the monster had gone, he saw it now clearly. As clearly as someone who'd had a skinful could.

Saw it there, still staring at him. Ready to spring again, those creamy claws out. Ready to finish the job it had started. Only something made it pause and wait. Some kind of recognition that he wasn't really a threat. That he'd only been on the attack because Mitch thought he was being threatened himself.

Then the monster opened its mouth, revealing razor-sharp teeth.

And it let out a meow.

Chapter 6

She saw them, the monsters in the darkness.

The shapes, the outlines: the figures. Had heard the noises first, not just the scratching and shuffling – the banging. But also voices, the low mumbling that she couldn't understand, but which terrified her.

She'd descended, seemingly into the bowels of Hell itself. Lower, lower, drawn – no, led – down here. Somehow hadn't been able to resist no matter how hard she tried. It was like her limbs felt too heavy, like she was drunk.

There they were, the flickering shadows. All gathering, all talking – all those voices overlapping. Why couldn't she separate them, understand what they were saying? What they were trying to say to her? Usually the voices she heard *wanted* to communicate something to her, or to others. Why were they making it so hard?

Why was she seeing all this in the first place?

The noises were getting louder the closer she came, and the closer she found herself, the more she didn't want to see. Was scared to witness what the shadows were doing, because—

She should turn away, run. But couldn't. Something was stopping her, some*one* was stopping her. Somebody behind her, hands on her shoulders holding her in place. Strong hands, firm, digging in. A feeling she'd felt before, but hated with every fibre of her being. The helplessness, the notion that her body wasn't under her control, but someone else's.

Suddenly she could make out one voice in the darkness, not low or mumbling, but crystal clear: 'Wake up!'

What?

'Wake up!' it repeated. If she couldn't run, get away, then that was the only thing to do. The only way of stopping all this.

'*Wake up!*' it virtually screamed at her this time. 'Bella, you have to wake up!'

It was then, and only then, that she recognized the voice.

Recognized it as her own.

Bella sat bolt upright in bed.

She was dripping with sweat, had kicked off the covers because she was so hot. Felt like she was melting, burning up. Her breath was coming in quick gasps, and she struggled to slow it down, calm herself.

A dream. Just a dream.

No, *that* had been a nightmare. Pure and simple. In her experience, when they were so intense they were usually trying to tell you something. Warn you about something. Her head was pounding again, that now familiar pain she'd been living with for a few days and couldn't shake. It had only grown worse, nothing shifting it – not even the really strong over-the-counter painkillers she'd had no choice but to buy and take, even though it went against everything she believed in. Poisoning her body.

It was starting to affect her life now, her livelihood. She'd already had to cancel her upcoming event at the hotel because she didn't think she'd be well enough. No, not just that; she couldn't hear the voices anymore because of it. Couldn't hear them unless—

They were mumbling in her dreams apparently. The dead? Or were they? She couldn't tell. Couldn't hear anything clearly except her own voice, yelling at her to wake up – perhaps in more ways than one?

And why was she thinking about Mitch?

Understandable to some extent that he'd be on her mind, as he'd gone back to their home. Gone back alone. Particularly at this time of year.

It was then that she heard the noise, the shuffling movement not far away. The creaking. A carry-over from the nightmare, from the things in the darkness, the shadows and figures and . . . monsters? No, this was coming from the main part of her caravan, just through the bedroom door ahead of her. Ignoring the throbbing at her temples, the feeling that someone was crushing the back of her skull, Bella crawled down the bed – there wasn't a vast amount of space on either side of her double in here – and reached for her nightgown which she'd left there. Wrapping it around herself, she clambered out and made her way towards the door.

'Who's out there?' she asked in the most confident voice she could muster, sounding like she meant business.

No answer. But the noises continued.

There was no choice but to *go* out there and confront whoever was in her caravan; for one thing she couldn't afford to be burgled. Didn't have any insurance on this place, the site rental was expensive enough all year round. And people thought *she* was creaming money off the vulnerable? Pah, if they only knew!

'You'd better get out of here!' she barked, making her way into the caravan proper. 'I mean it! You'd—'

She paused, seeing the outline, the shadow there. A single figure that should have been left over from the nightmare, but wasn't. It was in here, with her. Had invaded her own private space.

A monster.

If this had been a film or TV show, she'd have woken up again and it would have been a double bluff. A dream within a dream, like that movie she'd seen at the cinema with that dishy *Titanic* actor, where they could enter people's dreams and implant ideas. Extract them too. If only!

It turned, this shadow, to stare at her. Bella wanted to scream again, not at herself to wake up – because she was already awake – but for it to get out of her home. Get out and never, ever come back! But she just couldn't get the words out, felt that heaviness in her limbs once more. Felt drunk, even though she hadn't had an alcoholic drink in such a long time.

Then the shadow was moving towards her, rushing at her. Attacking her! She saw it. She *felt* it.

The monster in the darkness.

Chapter 7

'Come on then, you little monster.'

He'd made a friend, it seemed. Mitch wasn't sure when or how, but his father appeared to have adopted a cat. A stray, clearly – because it didn't have a collar or anything – but for it to be in his house, it must be used to just coming in and making itself at home. Either slipped in the last time his aunty and uncle were here, or when he himself had entered, because Mitch couldn't see any other way it could have got in. There were no windows open anywhere, certainly wasn't a cat flap.

Looked like a stray, as well, its black fur clumpy and matted. But it also looked pretty well fed, which meant that either it was extremely good at hunting and killing or his father had been feeding the thing for a while. They were creatures of habit, cats, returned to the places where they felt welcome, especially where the food was plentiful. He'd had a friend once on the force who'd got a ginger tom, but his then girlfriend had mistreated it; used to kick it, shout at it. In the end, as much as it had loved its owner, the cat had buggered off and found a home elsewhere. That's what they did.

That's what this runaway had done as well, apparently. Found another home, just like Mitch had done eventually when he left here in the first place. The jury was still out as to whether that had been a good decision or not, but this particular beast seemed happy with the way things were. Perhaps it had sensed Mitch was related to Thomas Prescott, but regardless of the way the pair had met – Mitch swinging that poker around like a maniac, freaked out by this clichéd jump-shock from a slasher flick – it hadn't taken long for them to bond. If nothing else, and he had apologized regardless of whether the creature could understand him or not, the tin of tuna he'd found in the cupboard and put down on a saucer for the animal had seen to that.

Then, when Mitch had retreated to the living room again – shutting the cellar door, so the cat couldn't get trapped in there like it had earlier – it had followed once it had finished the fish. After thinking about it for a few moments, it had hopped on the other end of the sofa and curled up, spending the rest of the night there with the interloper, having decided that actually he was okay.

Now, the next morning – and nursing one hell of a hangover – Mitch had woken up to find the cat gone, and even though he'd called it there was no sign of the thing. It had obviously found somewhere else to hide out.

However, when he'd started to prepare breakfast for himself (he couldn't face anything more elaborate than dry toast, and that was only because he didn't want to take paracetamol on an empty stomach) he'd heard that distinctive meowing again, the cat waiting at the back door.

'Abandoning me already?' But all it had wanted was to pop out and find somewhere to go to the toilet; it soon came back in again after he left the door open on the off chance. Now it wanted more food, so he dug around in the cupboards for something else to feed his companion.

Sardines in oil (there was a lot of fish in, which again tallied with the sudden adoption of a cat), which he'd placed on another saucer – and the living shadow had appeared as if by magic in the kitchen doorway. 'Come on then,' he said to it, putting down the saucer and grinning as it lapped up the tasty treat. 'Don't get used to it, mind. I'm only visiting. There'll be new owners here at some point.'

Or would there? Hadn't he been thinking last night, as he'd gone through those photos, that Green Acres might be quite a nice place to settle back down in? Crazy idea, because he was settled with Lucy already and she had her job in Downstone. But he was at least here until he untangled what had happened with his father's death, then Mitch still had to go through the man's belongings and such, organize the funeral . . .

The death first, then the rest. Which meant a trip to see the local plod, their station on the far side of Green Acres village, if Mitch remembered rightly. As he'd got himself ready to leave, the cat had found him again and started curling round his legs. It was more that it was marking Mitch out as its property than anything approaching affection, he knew, but again he couldn't help smirking. 'So, are you staying in here or heading out too?'

He got his answer when it turned its back on him and made for the stairs, sprinting up them. Probably where it had been when he woke that morning, nestled on one of the beds or something. If it was staying inside, and he'd shut the back door again by now, then he should probably put something down for the cat to use as a litter. He found a tray in one of the cupboards that had been used for painting, and filled that with old newspaper, making a mental note to buy some actual litter and proper cat food if his guest was remaining – and a large part of him hoped it was. Took the sting out of being alone here, to have another living thing around. Even gave him something . . . someone to talk to, now he didn't have Lucy. He should really give her a call . . . Later. He'd do it later.

'Okay, see you in a bit then,' he called out – even though the cat was long gone – proving his point.

Though it was pretty hot again outside, Mitch hauled on his leather jacket and did up his helmet, glad when he saw his bike was still where he'd left it around the back. He wheeled the vehicle to the road, climbing on it and starting it at the same time. There were a handful of people dotted around, walking mainly, but not many – same as yesterday. They stopped and watched him, a person on a motorcycle like his obviously some kind of novelty in these parts. An ordinary cycle, yes, but his contraption . . . ?

Pulling away from the curb, he guided the Honda along the street, heading back in the direction of his aunty and uncle's, but instead of taking a right into that side street he carried on down the main drag. Wasn't long before he came upon his destination, a converted stone house that hadn't changed a bit since the last time he'd seen it as a child, with its blue door and light outside that helpfully announced: 'POLICE'. He remembered how he'd spent a long afternoon in here waiting for his father to come and pick him up, after being caught scrumping for apples in Mr Patterson's orchard. Hadn't been his idea, but his mates had cleared off when they heard the man approach and he hadn't been quick enough to get away.

Bloody hell, Mitch thought. He'd forgotten all about that till he saw the place again – probably blocked it out because of the bollocking he'd received from his dad afterwards. Flinging words like 'respect' and 'the law' at him, while little Mitchel stood quaking at his wrath. Looking back, it had probably just embarrassed Thomas in front of his neighbours in the village: a man of his standing in the place, with a troublemaking son. Not that Mitch had been, of course. No more than any other boisterous kid.

Mitch turned off the engine, took off his helmet, and parked the bike up outside the building – which had a living quarters for whatever officer was on duty upstairs, he seemed to recall. It should be safe enough, outside a police station, but he put his lock on the bike anyway, just to make sure. He could afford to lose neither the bike itself, nor the time it would take reporting it stolen and going through the motions. If there was one thing he did know, it was that it took an age to get anything done around these parts. Apply for a marriage certificate here and they'd be burying you together in the cemetery before it arrived. Assuming your death certificate had arrived, that was.

An exaggeration, perhaps. Both his parents and his aunty and uncle had got hitched here without a problem, though only one of those couples were still around. The other . . .

It was why he was here. To find out about what had happened to the last remaining half of that particular married couple, only when he tried the door he found it was locked. Mitch knocked several times, but no one answered. He'd be screwed if it was an emergency, wouldn't he? Mitch checked the times on the door – and yes, it should definitely be open.

So, taking off his jacket as well, he decided to wait, sitting on the bike until someone showed their face. That was about forty minutes later, when a police car which looked like it should be in a museum pulled up behind him. The door opened, and out of this climbed a uniformed officer who looked just as ancient. A sergeant, judging from his stripes: a man who for all the world looked like Santa Claus, but with a blue outfit instead of red. With white hair and a massive, white curly beard, and cheeks as ruddy as the farmer who'd nearly collided with Mitch on the way here. He also had a belly to complete the look, the one his lookalike could allegedly shake like a bowl full of jelly when he laughed.

This man wasn't laughing. Looked like he never cracked a smile, let alone chuckled. He glared at Mitch suspiciously, eyes narrowing as he put on his peaked cap – jamming it on so tight Mitch thought the material at the top might split. Then his eyes dropped down to the bike, before slowly travelling back up to Mitch's face, never widening once.

'Hi,' Mitch called out, raising a hand in greeting and pushing himself up from the bike's seat.

The man nodded. 'Mornin',' came his own reply, and it was as if the fellow's speech had been recorded and slowed down, like kids used to do when they were mucking about for fun;

dragging out the word until it sounded like it was three or four syllables. Then he ignored Mitch completely and closed the car door, locking it manually with a key – rather than simply blipping it with a fob – before making his way slowly to the station door. There he stood for a moment or two, examining the other keys on his ring, before selecting the correct one and shoving that into the door to open it this time. A few moments after that, he was inside – without even asking what Mitch wanted or what he was doing sitting outside his nick.

Mitch sighed, head drooping. And, carrying his jacket and helmet, followed the sergeant inside . . .

Which was just as he remembered it, as well. Maybe a lick of paint since he'd sat on the slatted bench to his right, waiting for his dad, but nothing more. Now he used that bench as somewhere to put his jacket and helmet. The counter on his left was still the same, even some of the leaflets looked like they were from that time so long ago. Mitch frowned, because the sergeant appeared to have vanished – just like the feline at home (his *dad's* home) had a tendency of doing – another magic trick. It took him a second to realize he'd gone through the door ahead of Mitch, closing that behind him, and was coming into view round the corner. Mitch waited. Then he waited some more . . . For the sergeant to take his place behind that desk, arms wide apart, leaning on and gripping the edge of it where for a brief moment Mitch could have sworn he saw indentations. Like he'd been wearing the wood away for decades and had got it just right.

It was only now that he looked up, evaluating Mitch once more and finding him lacking. 'Aye?' he asked in that strange sloweddown way, as if he existed in a different time zone to everyone else.

'Yeah, hi. Hello,' Mitch said again, which elicited no more response than it had outside. 'My name's Mitchel Prescott.'

That did get a response, a slight twitch of the eyes he was so fond of narrowing. 'Prescott,' said the policeman in those deep tones of his. Then he surprised Mitch by saying: 'Apples.'

Could it be . . . No, surely not! But it was. Now that Mitch cast his mind back to sitting in here, he thought about the copper who'd nabbed him in the first place. The one who'd brought him back here and rung for his father to come and pick him up. Almost twenty years had passed, but yes – the same beard, just shot through with grey back then instead of snow white. The same judgemental eyes. Good God, this man had a memory! But then Mitch had to wonder how many criminals passed through here on a daily basis anyway. Just had the single cell in the back that he was aware of, and he only knew that because his father had threatened him with it after the scrumping affair. 'I've a good mind to let them stick you in there to cool off, lad! You need to be punished!' Over apples. Bloody apples! It had lodged in this guy's mind, obviously. Though according to his aunty and uncle there was a veritable crime wave happening at the moment, with regards to robberies at any rate.

Mitch gave a nervous laugh, then wished he hadn't. This guy didn't possess anything approaching a sense of humour, would not find his antics as a boy funny, and the subject he himself was here about was definitely no laughing matter. 'Yeah, I-I'm sorry about that. It never happened again, if that's any help?' Apparently not. 'Turned into a fine, upstanding citizen, as it happens.' He thought about adding that it was all down to him, then decided it was overkill. Again, poor choice of words. 'Actually, I'm a copper myself.'

Those eyes were narrowing again. 'That a fact?' said the old man in his strung-out drawl. In the absence of any kind of inflection, it was hard to tell whether it was a statement or somehow this guy knew that wasn't the case anymore. That Mitch was so fine and upstanding, he'd been drummed out of the constabulary. For insubordination, no less. No, that wasn't correct – Mitch had quit. *Before* they'd had a chance to drum him out for insubordination.

He figured it was best to just nod, since he couldn't be sure this bloke wasn't a human lie-detector.

'You'll be here about your father, I suppose?' the sergeant said next, though it took him about a week to get it out. If he was sympathetic to Mitch's plight, or sorry for his loss, he didn't show it. This might as well have been a robot talking to him, there had been more emotion from the cat.

'I am, yes, sergeant . . .'

He waited for the man's name. Waited a while before he got it. 'Wilkinson.' Another wait as the sergeant shook his head and offered: 'A nasty business.'

'Yes,' Mitch agreed. 'I wasn't told much about what exactly happened when they phoned me up. I've found out a little more since, but I was wondering, I mean, could you shed a little light on things for me?'

'A little light?' repeated the man, who sounded like he hadn't understood the question.

'Yeah,' Mitch continued. 'You know, the hows and wherefores. What exactly happened to him, all that.'

'He died,' the sergeant said, as if it would explain everything.

Mitch rubbed his forehead, could feel the paracetamol wearing off – the effects of the hangover returning with a vengeance. 'Yes, yes I know that. I mean, *how* he died. The fire.'

The sergeant nodded now. 'He died . . . because of the fire.'

God, thought Mitch. It was like pulling teeth. 'No, I know that. I just . . . The people who found him, campers weren't they? Did they have anything to say? I'm assuming they were interviewed? Are they still around?'

Wilkinson shook his head. 'Sent them on their way.'

Right, of course he had. Perfect. 'And . . .' Mitch nodded, waiting for more. The sergeant was frowning, obviously waiting for Mitch to carry on with his sentence first. 'And what did they say in their statements?'

'Oh, I can't tell you that.'

'But I just told you . . . Look, I'm a policeman myself. Even if I wasn't, I've got every right to know what—' This was getting

73

him nowhere, so Mitch changed tack. 'The body then. Where's the body right now? Still at the hospital?'

'In the morgue,' Wilkinson answered eventually, giving a single nod.

Mitch nodded back, gestured with his free hand. Nothing. Okay, fine, if he needed it spelling out: 'Do you think I can see it?'

Wilkinson thought about this, before asking, 'Why?'

Because I'm having a barbecue this weekend and I'm looking for cooking suggestions, why do you think? 'Has he been formally identified?'

'There . . .' Wilkinson began, then thought about his next words carefully. He thought about all of his words carefully. 'He wasn't in a good way.'

No? Really? He'd been on fire and not in a good way, imagine that? Didn't he want *a tan or something?*

'They used dental records,' Wilkinson said finally.

That would make sense. He would have been a complete mess after all that, it had probably taken a while to even work out who he was. 'I'd like to see him,' Mitch stated sombrely and in a tone he hoped conveyed the message that he wasn't about to take no for an answer.

Wilkinson's eyes narrowed again, then opened wide. 'You want to see him?'

I thought that was what I just said! 'Yeah. I want to see him. *Please.*' He added that in case it was his lack of manners standing in the way.

Sergeant Wilkinson nodded one final time. 'All right then, lad,' he said in that peculiar way he had of speaking. 'If that's what you really want.' Mitch thought about chipping in – let's face it, he had bags of time to do so – saying that yes, absolutely that's what he wanted (even though it was really the last thing in the world he actually did want), but in the end didn't need to.

'Then I suppose I'd better take you myself,' the old man completed.

Chapter 8

If he wasn't careful, he'd develop a problem.

Mitch had promised himself he wasn't going to have a drink tonight; for one thing most of the brandy was gone, and for another the hangover that morning had been vicious. He needed to keep a clear head at the moment; needed to be sharp, at his best.

There were some officers on the force who swore by it, of course. Took the edge off, they said. But he wasn't on the force anymore. Hadn't succumbed when he'd been working the job, just the odd celebratory one or few after a big case (the rounds were usually on the senior officers then, so it seemed rude not to). Lucy's disapproval was enough to make sure it didn't become a habit at home, no matter what he'd seen or encountered that day.

Lucy was miles away at the moment, however.

Speaking to her via video messaging didn't really count. He'd done that back at the hospital again, when he'd come out from seeing his father – finally called her up. Had needed to see her, hear her . . . hear someone familiar's voice. Thought it might be enough to carry him through.

Mitch had ended up hiding how he felt once more, though, didn't want to lay all this on her. And so the conversation had been more than a little stilted, awkward. Sticking to the basics.

'How are you?'

'I'm doing okay, Lucy. You know? As well as can be expected.' Whatever that meant.

'Uh-huh.'

He certainly hadn't gone into the details of what he'd seen after he arrived at the small hospital a short distance from Green Acres village. He'd been driven there by Sergeant Wilkinson – as fast as he talked. But he'd been grateful to the man for taking him, for coming with him, and by the time all this was over the guy was actually quite growing on Mitch. His heart was in the right place, at least, which was more than you could say for people like Staton.

'Through there, lad,' he'd pointed as they entered the tiny facility, but Mitch recalled where everything was from the old days. The days when his Aunty Helen had her surgery here, before she retired. 'I'll give you some privacy.'

The lone, middle-aged receptionist with straight brown hair, who'd been reading a battered paperback when he got to the desk – possibly the woman who'd phoned him up – pointed him in the direction of the morgue: one of only a handful of rooms they had here. He'd have been able to find it himself simply by trying each door, would've taken minutes.

He was glad there was someone around when he entered: a doctor who introduced himself as Larson, standing up from his position sitting at a side desk and shaking Mitch's hand. Larson had one of those smug faces and grins that you really wanted to just slap, looking at Mitch over his thin-rimmed spectacles, but was actually all right. He spoke quicker than Wilkinson, which was something, and actually turned out to be the most helpful person Mitch had encountered since returning.

'Ah yes, the Prescott incident.' That's what he'd called it, an 'incident', not case. 'Nasty business,' the doctor told him, echoing his uncle's and Wilkinson's words.

'So I'm told,' Mitch couldn't help saying. 'I'd like to see him, if I can.'

Larson's brow creased, had the same look as Wilkinson back at the station. 'Are you quite sure? I mean, he is . . . was your father.'

'That's why I have to see him,' Mitch insisted.

'Fair enough.' Larson escorted him to the quartet of drawers in the chilled metal cabinet where they kept the recently deceased, explaining that Thomas Prescott was the only resident at the moment. 'There aren't that many at any given time,' he went on to explain.

The inside was even colder when Larson opened up the drawer itself, the exact opposite of the extreme temperature that had killed his dad in the first place. Mitch shivered, regretting having left his jacket behind. The body was covered over with a sheet, just a misshapen lump resting on the drawer which slid out. 'Now, are you certain about this? It's not a pretty sight.'

Mitch nodded emphatically. What was it with these people trying to stop him from seeing his father's remains?

Then Larson had pulled back the sheet, and he had to admit they may have had a point. It wasn't that Mitch hadn't seen dead bodies before, in fact – contrary to popular belief – PCs actually saw more of those than senior officers, because they were often the first on the scene. He'd seen stabbings, hangings, gangland executions, and, yes, deaths by fire before. It was just that the patchwork of charred blackness, of pinks and reds in front of him, was his dad. Making that mental connection was enough to turn his stomach and force him to look away again.

Larson had obviously seen this before and was ready with a plastic bowl. 'I'm okay. I'm all right,' Mitch assured him. He thought of saying that it wasn't seeing his parent like this, it was the hangover finally catching up with him, the queasiness from all that brandy. But it would have been a lie – and why did he need to act the tough guy here?

It. Was. His. Dad.

Had been. And even though he'd only seen the body for a few moments, every single inch was etched into his memory now:

his mind flipping between the disfigured form and those pictures he'd found of his father back home. Re-enforcing that connection.

Larson had patted him on the back, telling him he understood. 'Incredibly hard. Very difficult,' he said.

'I just can't . . .' He looked up at the man, who appeared no less smug than before in spite of his words; it was a good job he was a decent human being. 'What happened, Doc? I can't get any answers out of anyone. What does the coroner reckon?'

'Well, I sort of double up as that.'

'Pathologist, then?'

'Again . . ?'

Mitch sighed. 'I just need to know what you think.' When Larson looked uncomfortable, like he shouldn't even be discussing this with him, Mitch informed him that he was police himself, and whatever he said would go no further. Asked him if he thought it was an accident, given his father's previous medical condition.

'I don't really want to say for definite, but . . . Okay, all right, what I can tell you is it looks like there was some kind of accelerant involved, probably petrol. We'd have to run some tests to confirm that, obviously.'

'And has the go-ahead been given for that?'

'We're still waiting for the green light,' he said. 'You know how it is around here.'

Mitch knew, but this was his dad for Heaven's sake! 'Who's the SIO on the case?'

Larson looked at him blankly. 'I don't think they've . . . Isn't Sergeant Wilkinson handling all that?'

Handling it? Not so's you'd notice, thought Mitch. 'But in your professional opinion, this was most likely done *to* him? It could be murder we're looking at?'

Larson shook his head. 'Now, I didn't say that.'

'Someone could have lured him out to those woods, poured petrol all over him and—'

'People have been known to do this to themselves, you know.

78

That Buddhist monk from the sixties, if memory serves, the Tunisian fellow from a decade or so ago.'

Mitch struggled to recall the examples from history Larson was talking about. 'They were both protests, weren't they? Catalysts for change or something?'

'Well, yes. Indeed. All right, that fellow outside the White House not so long ago then.'

Mitch had definitely read about that at the time, someone who'd been out of his tree on drugs – K2 laced with PCP, wasn't it? They'd called him the 'Zombie' man, which was why it had stuck in his mind, and they'd never worked out why he'd done it other than he was probably hallucinating. Eyewitnesses had described him as a 'human torch', like that guy in the comics. Had that been what his father had looked like, thought Mitch – and again flashes of the man before and after sped through his mind. He'd shaken his head to clear them. 'You're saying my dad could have been suffering from hallucinations at the time? That they caused him to do this to himself?'

'I'm saying anything's possible, Officer Prescott.' That title sounded weird now, and Mitch couldn't help wincing just a little, though if Larson noticed it he didn't say anything. 'In my line of work you end up saying that more than you'd like to.'

Anything's possible.

He'd thanked the doctor, and they'd exchanged numbers – mobiles and landlines – to keep in touch about what was happening.

The journey back with Wilkinson, after the talk with Lucy, was just as enlightening as the one there. For every question Mitch asked, the old policeman would think about it forever, then answer slowly without actually answering at all, sounding a lot like that Ent from *The Lord of the Rings*. The only thing he really managed to get out of him was the exact location where the 'incident' had taken place, a spot in the woods between the caves and the lake.

Until they passed what his uncle had called 'The Commune' again, and Mitch spotted a few more of those people in cream smocks dotted about. Started to get that strange shivery feeling again. 'What's your take on those guys?' he'd asked, and Wilkinson had briefly looked up and over. Couldn't help sneering when he saw them. 'Not a fan, eh?'

'You want to leave them well enough alone,' he said in his slow drawl.

'Is that right? Any particular reason?'

No reply. In fact, he couldn't get another word out of the man after that.

When they arrived back and got out, Mitch had thanked him, retrieved his jacket and helmet from inside the station, and headed back off on the bike again. He made for the small shop that served the village, ostensibly to get that cat food for . . . he realized he hadn't named the thing, but Cat seemed to suit it somehow. Also, however, with one eye on the fact that night-time would come around all too soon and he was pretty much out of brandy back at the house. Mitch told himself he might fancy some later, that he'd developed a bit of a taste for it (yeah, right, in one day), when the truth was his actions were being fuelled by those images of his dad again.

Before: the photo from last night.

During: human torch.

After: blackened husk.

Too much, it was; *would be* too much tonight. Certainly, brandy would help him sleep and he'd need to rest if he was to get to the bottom of all this.

The shop itself was not much bigger than his dad's living room, with three aisles you could walk up and down in a couple of strides. On the inside left when you came in were racks of magazines, with newspapers arranged at the foot. He spied the green logo of *The Acre* straight away; the headline 'Proposed Housing Development Scheme!' was in huge writing on the front, a small picture of a new-build house accompanying it. He could well imagine the slant that paper had given the piece, making it sound like invaders coming over the horizon.

At the back was a glass booth with a hand-painted red sign attached to it proclaiming it was the 'Post Office'. It more closely resembled one of those fortune-telling machines you might find on Golden Sands pier, but instead of a plastic man with a beard, the booth here was currently unoccupied, its chair empty. Mitch guessed that if you wanted stamps or whatever, you'd have to wait for the teenager who was manning the main counter to put on his other hat and open up the booth. Reading between the lines, the acne-riddled youth was probably the son of whoever owned the place now and they were keeping him occupied during the holidays, while simultaneously saving money by not having to hire someone to man the fort.

When Mitch had been about his age, the owner had been a fearsome old battle-axe called Mrs Cooper, a widow whose husband had probably passed away from a case of terminal nagging. Had the woman had children herself? He couldn't remember. But the lad did sort of look like old Coop, so maybe he was a grandson or something? That was how things worked in Green Acres, stuff got handed down through generations and it took a while for them to accept you as one of their own.

He found the litter and dry cat food with the other pet stuff, tins of dog meat and the like, picked up a few microwave meals for himself, then took them over to the young boy. Mitch craned his neck, perusing the bottles of booze behind the counter, thought about asking what kind of brandy they had then decided he wasn't that fussy, and just asked for a generic brand.

'Pay by card?' he said to the lad, who definitely wasn't old enough to be selling the hard stuff.

The youth, whose face was a landscape of pockmarks and pus-laden spots, shook his head emphatically. 'Cash only.' Mitch saw when he opened his mouth that he also had a brace. The poor devil. Mind you, he'd probably come out the other side of it looking like some kind of model.

Mitch checked his wallet and found he only had a couple of

notes left, and the brandy would wipe most of that out alone. Luckily the rest of it didn't come to that much. 'Is there anywhere around here I could draw some more out? A hole in the wall?' he asked, and the boy looked at him as though he was mad. 'Never mind, I'll figure it out.'

Thanking him, he took the plastic bag and strapped it to the back of his bike – then clambered on again and went home.

After parking the Honda round the back and locking it, he entered the house via the front, still half expecting to find his dad inside waiting for him. That was never going to happen, not now, and the thought of it made him want to open that brandy right away.

What stopped him was the sound of the cat padding along the landing, then down the stairs again, yawning as it went. 'Hey,' he said to it. 'I hope you've had a more productive day than I have.' The black feline reached him and began to rub up against his legs again, probably in anticipation of more fish. 'Not today. Today you've got . . .' He took out the packet of dry food and read from the side: 'Chicken-flavoured chunkies. Hmm, doesn't that sound appetising?' He exchanged glances with the cat, who didn't appear impressed.

It – because he still didn't really know what sex the animal was – looked even less keen once he'd ripped open the packet and put a sprinkling into a cereal bowl, before placing it on the floor. It took one sniff, then walked off. 'Please yourself,' said Mitch.

He had to admit, he felt the same about his lasagne – which he nuked in his dad's old microwave. It looked like it had been manufactured by the same people as his computer. The finished meal didn't resemble what was on the box in any way, shape or form. Indeed, all it served to do was remind him again of the sight in that morgue, the burned edges of it especially. He jumped when he felt the cat winding itself round his legs under the table.

'Bloody hell! What, you want this?' He put the plate on the floor and the creature went straight for it. 'Knock yourself out, mate.'

At least one of them would eat well that teatime. Mitch resisted the brandy for the moment, which was staring at him from the side where he'd dumped it, and sorted out the litter – chucking the used newspaper – then wandered through to his dad's study once more.

'Organized chaos,' he said to himself, as he looked around again. But in here there might be a clue as to who'd want to cause his father harm. It was worth having a look, especially now that he'd moved all the photo albums out of the way. Thomas Prescott's bookcases, of course, contained tomes covering all sorts of topics – mainly stuff about those conspiracies he was so fascinated with. Had one of those old investigations landed him in trouble? Got him on the radar of someone he shouldn't have been? But how to narrow that down? The old man's interests were so wide-ranging.

Mitch decided to try powering up the old computer first. Maybe there was something on that which could help, an article he'd been working on? A book even? He'd always talked about writing one when he had the time. Mitch pressed the on button, a big round thing on the front of the tower, and sighed when nothing happened. He was just about to use the tried and tested method of giving something a good old whack when it didn't work, and he noticed it wasn't even plugged in.

Rectifying this, Mitch tried again and was successful. He even got the monitor to come on, which was a square button this time. But he was celebrating too soon, because it blue-screened and he had to reboot the whole system to get it to work. Then he discovered it was password-protected. Mitch sat back in the chair, playing with his bottom lip. He leaned forward, tried a few of the obvious ones. His mother's maiden name, 'Green Acres', the name of the brandy he'd found in the drawer and had been drinking the previous night. Then he tried some date of birth stuff, his dad, his mum, even his own . . . The last one he tried had been his sister's, which worked – and it made him think that he really did need to ring her up and fill her in.

But not just yet. Now he'd broken in, he had work to do.

Bella could wait a little while longer.

Chapter 9

Bella had waited there for ages.

Sitting in Golden Sands station, waiting to see her friend. No, not friend really: acquaintance. Someone she'd met last summer when he'd been working a case she'd accidentally become entangled with, sort of at right angles. Without meaning to.

She'd sat there most of the morning, after she'd woken up on the floor of her caravan. She'd felt battered, had obviously been knocked over, knocked unconscious in the middle of the night by that person in her home. The intruder, the one she'd thought of as a monster. She still couldn't say why that description sprang to mind. Her first thought had been to call the police, but of course she had no phone at her place, not even a mobile. Those were pointless here anyway; there were whole areas of Golden Sands where you couldn't get a signal at all, the caravan park being one of them.

The payphone then, up in town – but she thought to herself if she was going up there anyway, she might as well go straight to the horse's mouth, so to speak. To someone who owed her a favour, who she'd given a heads-up to in the past.

So she'd got dressed, head still thumping – but strangely a bit easier – and climbed into her lime green Beetle, starting her up and driving to the police station here.

She'd asked to see the man in question, said it was important, and been told in no uncertain terms that she'd have to wait. That's what she'd done, waited and waited. And the more she'd thought about it, the more she wondered whether it was a good idea to even report this at all. A lot of people thought she was a weirdo anyway, that she saw things which weren't there (actually she just heard things, but it was splitting hairs), and others might think she even deserved it.

Eventually, as she was about to give up and head off again, rising to make for the door, he'd appeared. He was younger than her, maybe only slightly older than Mitch, but the events of last summer had definitely caused him to grow up somewhat. Had turned him into a man, if you wanted to use such an outdated phrase. Not only had he helped take down a murderer, he'd also found love. Whether that love was reciprocated was another matter, and one of the reasons – Bella suspected – that Detective Sergeant Ashley Watts looked like he had the weight of the world on his shoulders.

As he opened the desk and came through to the waiting area, he brushed back that flop of hair he thought was so stylish, but which actually made him look like a reject from the '80s. All he needed was the white or silver suit and he'd fit right in on the set of *Miami Vice*: a show she remembered watching on reruns with Mitch when they were young.

'Bella?' he'd asked as he drew nearer. 'I haven't seen you since . . .' He looked down, obviously recalling the disastrous incident all too clearly. She'd been assaulted that night, as well, by the object of Ashley's affections no less. Though the woman had been practically paralytic at the time, and had a real problem with her particular profession. 'I'm sorry to keep you waiting, we're flat out working on this forgery ring that . . . Doesn't matter, DI O'Brien's keeping me busy, let's just say. Now, what's all this about?'

'I didn't mean to bother you, DS Watts, but—'

'Ashley, please. Or Ash if you like.'

'Ashley then. I just didn't know who else to turn to. You see, I was attacked last night.'

'*What?*' He said it a little too loudly, drawing the attention of everyone else in the waiting area. Watts could see by her face that she didn't want this spreading around everywhere, so he pulled her off to one side where they could talk privately. 'You what?'

'I was attacked,' Bella repeated. 'There was someone in my caravan. My home.'

'Have you reported it? Officially, I mean?'

'I-I don't want to make a fuss. Can we just keep it between us for now?' She didn't know why, but for some reason that was important.

'I guess, if that's what you really want. Were there any witnesses to it?' he asked next.

'No, I was alone. I live alone.'

'Yes, right. Okay.'

'I thought maybe you'd be willing to come and have a look.'

Watts checked over his shoulder, as if waiting for his boss to pounce on him. Bella knew all about DI O'Brien. She also knew the woman was a lot nicer than she preferred people to think, that she wouldn't mind Watts taking a break to help an old . . . friend.

'I figured that seeing as I helped you out that time, put you on the right track last year, that—'

'Yes. Yes, all right. I do need to return that favour, Bella. Especially as you never pressed charges against . . .' Watts nodded, went back to the desk and told the uniformed police officer on duty to relay a message to his inspector, that he was taking an early lunch.

Then he'd accompanied her back to the caravan to cast an eye over it. The first thing he'd done was check the door and the windows. 'No sign of forced entry anywhere, but really we should be getting people to come and take a look at this, Bella. There could be—'

'Just you, Ashley. Please.' Bella still didn't know why she was so insistent on that. But for some reason she needed to keep things between them, and she trusted Watts.

'Okay, if that's what you really want,' he said again. 'And nothing was taken? You're sure?'

'I don't think so. I really don't have very much *to* take.'

'So, tell me again, you woke up and heard noises. Came out into this bit of the caravan and . . .'

'There was a shadow, a figure in here. I could see the outline, its shape.'

'Outline?' His voice said that he was struggling to believe her version of events. Then he looked left and right, trying again to work out how they might have gained entry to her place. 'What were you doing just before you heard the noise?'

'I was asleep,' Bella admitted, and she looked down as she remembered the dream.

'All right. So, is it possible you were a little groggy? We're all a bit like that when we first wake up. God, I can barely open my eyes – they're practically glued together. Need my first cup of coffee of the day before I can even . . . I'm rambling, aren't I?'

She nodded, then winced. The thumping in her head was intensifying once more. 'I didn't imagine it, Ashley.'

'Not saying you did, Bella,' he told her, but there was a hitch in his voice that said otherwise. 'I'm here, aren't I? I'm just not sure—' Wincing again, she leaned against the side of the caravan for support. 'Hey, hey, you don't look so great. I think maybe instead of coming here we should have got you to Golden Sands General.'

'It's not from the attack.' She hadn't told him about the blackout, about the time she'd lost – and didn't now. There'd been no blurred vision, hadn't even been much of a bump. That wasn't the important thing, it would just distract him. Make him question her judgement even more. 'I've been having these headaches recently, even before all this and—'

'Listen, you sit down and I'll put the kettle on. Make us both a brew. That usually helps with everything.'

'I'm good,' she said to him. 'I just want to know who did this.'

Watts sighed deeply. 'Well, that's going to be a bit difficult – especially if you won't let me bring anyone else into it. I'm good, but not *that* good.' His laugh told her that he didn't really believe he was that great anyway, his insecurity still shining through.

'But what if they come back?'

Watts rubbed his own shoulder, not really sure what else to say. 'If it's any comfort, I doubt they will. They had every opportunity to burgle the place and didn't. Like you said, there really isn't anything much to pinch. No offence.'

'None taken.'

'And I'm assuming they didn't, you know, do anything to you, because you would have said. Wouldn't you?'

'They didn't,' she assured him, finding his coyness quite sweet.

'So that wasn't the motivation.' He shook his head. 'I'm struggling here now.'

Bella was too. The more Watts talked about it like this, in the cold light of day, the more she began to question what had happened herself. What possible reason could there have been for it? Pure malice? She had no idea – but still, it had happened. Hadn't it?

'I'd love to put someone outside to keep an eye on the place tonight, but we're a bit stretched. What am I saying, we're *always* stretched!' Another laugh, this time at the limited resources of Golden Sands police. 'But I could stop by later on, if you like. Check on you. Or, y'know . . .' He was eyeing the couch, as if working out how comfortable that might be to sleep on. 'I live alone as well, nobody would miss me for a night.'

It was tempting, but Bella shook her head. She liked her privacy too much, didn't even know her neighbours here at the park that well – the ones who were permanent residents, not the holiday-makers. Wasn't sure they wanted to know *her*. And Bella could stand people in her van for short bursts, but all night? Not to mention a guy. 'I don't think Robyn would be too impressed, do you? She'd probably deck us both if she knew you were even here talking to me.'

Watts shrugged. 'Who knows! I haven't heard from her in a while.' He looked so sad then, heartbroken, even at the mention of Dr Robyn Adams. The psychologist who'd blown into their lives the previous summer, to help her cousin Vicky; a woman Bella was still helping. Watts had fallen for Robyn in a big way, only for her to return to the city she came from: Hannerton. Back to her uni teaching and police consultancy. A woman who'd drunkenly hit Bella, though she hadn't taken the matter further.

Bella patted his arm. 'She'll be back in touch, trust me.'

Watts looked hopeful then, in spite of himself. 'Is that the whole . . .' He tapped his temple, more usually the symbol for people being crazy, but she guessed in this instance he meant her 'abilities', as Vicky had called them.

Bella shook her head, though it pained her to do so. 'It's a bit on the fritz at the moment, I'm afraid. Call it woman's intuition, Ashley. You're a good guy, she'd be mad to let you go.' They exchanged a look then, and Bella broke it off first, dropped her hand from his arm. *Definitely* a bad idea for Watts to spend the night.

As there really wasn't much else he could do – Bella wasn't sure what she'd expected Watts to do in the first place: come in like Sherlock Holmes and announce the names of the intruders because of some minute clue she had missed? – she thanked him and drove him back to the station.

'Call me if you need me, okay?' he said. She didn't tell him she had no way of doing that, even as he gave her his card with all his numbers on.

So now she sat here again and waited, in her home. Her head throbbing more than ever. Waiting here to see if the shapes, the outlines, would return.

Waiting all alone.

In the dark.

Chapter 10

Even with all that information, even after everything he'd learned, he was still as much in the dark as before.

After gaining access to his dad's old computer, Mitch had trawled through his files – gravitating towards the ones that had been accessed in the last few months first. The topics Thomas had obviously been most interested in. Somewhere in those, Mitch felt sure, there would be a reason for why he'd died. Why he'd been killed?

He'd narrowed it down to three, the initial two subjects not a huge surprise because of their links to this location. The first was increased incidents of lights, both in the sky and in the woods at Green Acres. Lights that may or may not have been UFOs. Mitch had been aware of this area's connection to flying saucer sightings since he was old enough to be aware of anything. Reports of strange glows, ramblers disappearing – some came back and said they'd lost time, others didn't and were still missing. His father was compiling some sort of database on it all, it looked like. Fascinating stuff, and something he could definitely have got a book out of, if his mind hadn't started to deteriorate, that is.

Mitch wasn't sure he held much stock in such things himself. Bug-eyed monsters coming down from Planet X to suck your brains out? It was the territory of '50s and '60s sci-fi movies featuring men in rubber suits. Yet there was a lot of evidence out there that could, as Mulder and Scully might say, make you 'believe'. Project Blue Book, Area 51, and all that. The government, especially in the US, historically went to great lengths to keep it all under wraps, allegedly even bumping people off. But here, in Green Acres? Mitch found that very hard to believe.

The next topic was witchcraft. The inspiration for low-budget horrors now instead, kids out in the woods screaming at twigs! Though again, Mitch couldn't deny the long history Green Acres had with it all, especially back in the Middle Ages when witches were hunted and killed by the likes of Matthew Hopkins, the notorious Witchfinder General. Back then, they'd thought witches – and warlocks, let's not forget the male counterpart – were in league with Satan himself, even worshipped him at ceremonies called Sabbats which made a mockery of the Christian religion. Things like witch's marks, which often were created by the hunters themselves via a method called 'pricking', dunking, and torture were prevalent. Most of the victims were just innocent women, some of whom used natural remedies to cure all sorts – though that was hardly grounds to execute them.

A couple of things in his dad's writings caught Mitch's attention, however: the sections about familiars, for starters. How they would be animals like birds, hares or, more commonly, black cats. He'd scratched his stubbled chin at that one, cocked an ear out for the animal which fitted that description currently sharing the house with him. Nothing. Familiars would keep an eye on their masters, warn them of danger and generally protect them. It was a ridiculous notion, but what if that stray had appeared to try to warn his father about impending doom?

Mitch shook his head, even batted away the thoughts physically with a hand. That someone might think his dad was, what, a warlock? But there was that talk about Bella, wasn't there? Communing with the dead was one of the skills of a witch, wasn't it? And there was no doubting that if she'd existed a few hundred years ago, Bella might have been burned at the—

The second thing to make him pause. That method of execution favoured by witch hunters both here and abroad, whether it was tying them to a stake on a bonfire or just catching them and setting fire to them on the spot, he couldn't just dismiss the way his father had died as a coincidence. This wasn't about whether Mitch believed in such things such as witchcraft or whatever, it was about whether someone else did and had acted accordingly. Someone insane. Someone dangerous. Someone who, if he kept looking into all this, might start to see Mitch as a threat as well.

Good, he'd thought. *Come at me – I prefer to see who I'm dealing with!*

Who I'm fighting.

Moving on, he'd discovered the next thing his dad had been obsessed with. A folder all about cults and the formation of them. Interestingly, he seemed to be doing this research because of the Commune that had got a foothold in Green Acres, something that made Mitch raise an eyebrow. Did his death have some kind of link to those people up there? Thomas had certainly done some digging into the matter, noting that it was a loophole that had enabled the collective to set up a presence where they had; something to do with old family ties. Returning to the area. It was clear that his dad didn't care for the group in the way that he wrote about them, but had that caused his demise? Did they see him as whipping up trouble for them? According to his Uncle Vince, the recent crime spree in Green Acres itself was well and truly down to them – though there was little or no evidence to back that up.

'I don't trust 'em . . . worming their way in . . .'

'No respect for boundaries.'

One thing was for sure, there'd be more strangers around these parts soon if property developer Neil Sheldon got his way.

There was a document inside that folder talking about how the man was targeting specific parts of Green Acres to build luxury houses and apartments, aimed at people who had more money than sense. Mitch wasn't sure what his father was trying to say here, if anything. Perhaps just the general distrust of outsiders again, or maybe that Sheldon was one of those people with a cult of personality? But he'd already decided to look into this, along with everything else he'd found on here, more closely.

Mitch had attempted to print some of the stuff off, but either his dad's old printer had run out of ink or it was just plain knackered – not surprising given the amount of printouts scattered about the room. So he'd jotted the most relevant points down on a nearby notepad, then turned the thing off.

Searching around the study, he quickly found books pertaining to some of those topics; indeed, there were a handful on the pile he'd shifted from the chair. Mitch had gathered these up and taken them into the living room, the same as he'd done with those family albums the night before. That's when he'd caved and fetched the brandy, figuring it would help him not only to forget the things he'd witnessed that day, but get through some of this dry research. Mitch wasn't his father, didn't enjoy looking into all this rubbish. He liked finding clues, following trails, but sifting through pages and pages of text about the Salem Trials or the Roswell Incident? It really didn't float his boat. A necessary evil, he realized, if he was to figure out what had happened here.

As the night wore on, though, and the more he drank, the harder it was to stay awake. Mitch considered heading upstairs, but even in his drunken state he remembered that he hadn't changed the sheets on his father's bed.

A picture of that sheet in the morgue flashed into his mind at the very thought of it, being pulled back to reveal . . .

Charcoaled flesh: black, pink, and red.

He reached out for the bottle of brandy and poured himself

another large one. Knocking that back proved to be the final straw, his eyelids giving way at last.

Pitching him once more into darkness.

Returning him to the dream, to the blackness there and, yes, the figures. The outlines, people gathered around. Not total darkness then? And, unlike the previous night, he could hear them talking – though he couldn't understand a word of what they were saying. Muttering and mumbling, faces concealed: heads bowed, but also covered. Did they even *have* faces? Just blackness, more darkness.

Mitch was aware that he was shaking, terrified of what he was seeing. What it meant, though, he had absolutely no idea at this time – just that it was very, very bad. That it had something to do with what had happened to his father.

What *had* happened to him? What did Mitch even mean by that? In the dream it didn't really matter; all that mattered was what was going on in the darkness, the flickering revealing more and more. Details he'd missed previously, like the gloved hands of these figures going about their business. In secret, in hiding. Something he shouldn't really be spying on, in case he got caught. And what then? What would they do to him, if he saw?

Nothing good, that was for sure.

So, he should probably get out of there, right? Out of this space – wherever he was – and away. Run. Except they'd spotted him now, hadn't they? Were all turning towards him and staring in his direction, their eyes glowing like the cat's had. The cat? What about the cat? That had happened when he woke up, hadn't it? And he was asleep now. Dreaming.

Hearing the mumbling, the *chanting*.

The noise as they moved, heading in his direction. Heading for him, reaching for him with those gloved hands. Figures, only they couldn't be human because he couldn't see their legs at all. How were they moving then? Floating? No, they wouldn't be making that shuffling noise if they—

Scratching, like claws on wood. The cat. It was the bloody cat again, wasn't it?

Mitch was frozen with fear, couldn't even shiver. Locked inside his own body, unable to move. As they surrounded him, engulfing him. These . . . these things, whatever they were. Their voices, their strange words deafening him.

Until he couldn't take it anymore. Not able to move, but about to scream maybe? Yes, his jaw was working at least, his mouth opening. Forming a word, a name. Shouted out loudly, a cry for help:

'*Bella!*'

And suddenly he was—

Awake.

Almost falling off the sofa, scrambling to stay on it.

Darkness. Even though he'd left the lights on, everything was in darkness. Black. Mitch blinked once, twice. Objects flickering ahead of him: bookcases, fireplace—

Figures. People.

The people from the dream, the nightmare? No, these were here. They were real. In the house, in this room with him!

Now Mitch was scrambling to get off the sofa, to form words again: 'Who . . . ? What the hell are you . . .' He was aware he was slurring, the effects of the brandy still apparent. The figures – were there two, three? It was hard to tell – were rushing at him. But this wasn't like the nightmare, they weren't floating, they had legs all right. They had heads, covered by caps this time.

What had he done with that poker? Where had he left it after the cat? In the kitchen? Fuck it!

Mitch took a swing at the closest figure, aiming for where he thought the jaw was. But it was a sloppy, clumsy affair, hitting nothing. His opponent, however, was far from inept. Mitch felt the punch to his side, in the ribs, and let out a howl. There wasn't enough brandy in the world to drown out that kind of pain.

Next he was being shoved backwards by another set of hands,

back onto the sofa where the momentum took Mitch and the furniture over. Pitching him on the ground near the front window, accompanied by the books he'd been going through. He thought he heard voices then, someone saying they should get out of there.

Mitch tried to rise, before they got away – what he could do about it was anyone's guess – but everything felt too heavy again. Easier just to let go. Drop back down to the floor.

When his eyelids closed this time, there was darkness again. But he didn't dream.

And for that he was grateful.

PART TWO

The most famous example of witchcraft in and around the region of Green Acres is the Apple Hill Coven – notable members included Madeleine Turner and Elizabeth Croft – who operated in the late sixteenth century. Responding to calls for help, witchfinders visited and rounded up the culprits to interrogate them and determine their guilt in the eyes of the Lord. The most common accusations levelled against the magick-users were 'unsanctioned gatherings and worship', 'uncleanliness with men and devils', 'theft of sundry items from the village', 'harm to children', 'poisoning', 'flight and invisibility', and various undisclosed 'abilities'.

Though they always proclaimed their innocence, stating that the herbs they used to 'cure' were only for medicinal purposes, and nothing at all to do with the black arts, in time all the members of the coven were executed for their practices.

Chapter 11

'A bit of a state.'

The words were slow and drawn out, as he'd come to expect from Sergeant Wilkinson. What he couldn't tell, however, was whether the policeman was referring to the house or Mitch himself. It would have been applicable to both.

He'd been roused that morning by the cat, meowing loudly in his ear and licking his cheek. 'Wha . . . what?' Mitch had said, jerking and scaring the creature enough that it backed away from him for a moment. Then returned, nuzzling into him. 'Urgh,' he said then, feeling the pain everywhere. Feeling beaten, because let's face it, he had been – in more ways than one. Feeling like he'd been struck in the ribs then pushed over a sofa; he was lucky it hadn't tipped completely over and landed on him. That particular morning, a hangover was the least of his worries. Mitch looked over at the cat, the blurry bundle of fuzz gradually coming into focus. 'Some protector you are,' he managed.

When he felt able, he'd got to his knees, clutching his side. Then he'd used the windowsill to drag himself up, to get shakily to his feet, Cat meowing at him loudly. Probably wanted feeding or its litter changing. That would have to wait today.

Mitch had staggered to the door, taking in the books that had been thrown from the shelves in the living room, the tipped-over chairs. The missing TV. Then out into the hallway, his jacket on the floor, his wallet tossed there. Hadn't been much in it apart from his cards. Heading to the kitchen, pausing to look inside the study – which was in even more disarray than usual. Papers and books everywhere, as if a tsunami had hit the room. The monitor was still there, but its screen was cracked. Of the tower there was no sign. Mitch let out a weary sigh.

It was the same story in the kitchen, food everywhere and the microwave missing. The back door was wide open, obviously the way they'd gained entrance. He poked his head out, relieved when he saw that his bike was still there and hadn't been vandalized – that he could see. He didn't have the heart to go upstairs and see what was missing from there. He probably wouldn't know anyway, he'd hardly had time to catalogue anything in his time here. So he'd made his way back out to the hall to use the phone, only to discover they'd yanked the landline from the wall, ripping out the socket in the process.

His mobile, he'd call the cops on that! Except he couldn't find the thing either when he returned to the living room. 'Christ alive,' he muttered, thinking absently it was a good job his aunty wasn't here or she'd tell him off.

There was no choice but to open the front door and stagger round to his neighbour's house to use their phone. Even then, he'd had to knock several times before they answered, through the letterbox initially. Though given what had just happened, Mitch was beginning to see why folk were so uptight around here lately.

'What do you want?' the disembodied voice had asked; like the cat, he couldn't really tell whether it was a male or female. Mr Tattersall had lived in this house when Mitch had been next door, but he'd been knocking on for a hundred back then. People lived to a decent age around here, but that would make him some sort of superbeing if he was still around. Maybe a son or daughter?

'Hi, my name's Mitch Prescott,' he'd told the person, bending – though it hurt like a son of a bitch. He explained the situation, what had happened, and said that even if the neighbour wasn't prepared to open the door could they please ring for Sergeant Wilkinson to come. The letterbox had snapped shut without even a goodbye, so Mitch had no way of knowing if his request had been granted. Not until he heard the police car eventually coming, that was – sirens on, as if it was some kind of emergency. Wilkinson was a few hours late for that.

That's when the police officer had entered, looking around and tutting. He checked out the living room, face souring when he saw the half-empty bottle of brandy. That's when he'd uttered those drawn-out words, 'A bit of a state, aye.'

'That's one way of putting it,' Mitch said to him. 'Any chance of getting some forensics people out here or whatever, dusting for some prints?'

Wilkinson gaped at him like he was speaking Chinese. And instead of replying, he wandered through to the kitchen, peeking into the study briefly and tutting again. Mitch trailed behind him, as the man nodded at the back door. 'That's how they got in.'

Yeah, thanks, Columbo, he thought. *I'd figured that much out myself.*

Then the man was examining the lock. 'You left it open.'

That Mitch hadn't realized. 'What? No. I locked it up, I'm sure of it.' But was he? Had he locked up after sorting out the litter? He couldn't remember now, and the hangover, the pain, wasn't helping with his memory. The cat had been distracting him again, so maybe . . . The cat. There was no sign of it now. Was it upstairs or had it gone off in search of food elsewhere? Would it even come back?

The man with the white beard was pointing at the lock, which was indeed undamaged. Damn! Even if his dad had insurance – and Mitch didn't know whether that had been renewed or not – his carelessness would probably bollocks everything. Good luck making a claim when you'd basically left out the red carpet for the burglars.

Though the more he thought about it, the more he'd been thinking about things in the time it had taken Wilkinson to get there – hell, in the time it took the guy to say his first sentence – the more he was growing suspicious about the reasons for this 'break-in'. Yeah, sure, things had gone missing. The TV, microwave – though how much they'd get for those was questionable: about three groats? – and of course he hadn't checked upstairs (had any of his mum's old jewellery gone? He really hoped not, because it was his negligence that was to blame), but the mess that they'd caused . . . Organized chaos? The stolen tower with those files on he'd been looking at last night. Maybe he was just reading too much into it all, perhaps they'd simply been trying doors and he was the only one who'd been stupid enough to leave his bloody back one open for them to get in! He still couldn't believe he'd done that. Holy shit!

'Is there any CCTV coverage in this part of the village?' Mitch asked then, clutching at straws. Sergeant Wilkinson continued to gape at him. 'Don't worry about it.' They'd got in through the back anyway, he doubted there'd be any cameras covering that area.

'Mitch? Mitch, sweetheart, are you there?' Definitely a female voice this time, one he recognized immediately.

'In here,' Mitch called through to his Aunty Helen, berating himself for leaving the front door wide open this time, not that there was much left to take at this point in time. Then she was in the room, Uncle Vince trailing behind; the jungle grapevine was on top form today, it seemed. 'Oh my,' said the woman, having seen the devastation on the way in, and now inside the kitchen. She went over to Mitch, giving him another one of her famous hugs, only standing back when he winced.

'You're hurt, love,' said Helen.

'They got in a lucky punch to the ribs,' he told them.

'Show me,' the woman said. It wasn't a request.

'In a moment.'

'*Now*,' she ordered, practically pulling his shirt up to see what the damage was. At the same time, Wilkinson was making noises about leaving them to it.

'Is that it? You're not going to do anything else?' asked Mitch.

The old sergeant looked at him again, then he returned to the back door and held up a finger for them to watch. Next, he shut the door and locked it. He nodded, as if to say, 'That should do the trick!'

The copper really did leave then, with another nod. 'Thanks,' said Mitch, waiting for him to be out of the room fully before adding, 'for nothing.' Then he started giggling. 'That tickles!'

'Sorry dear,' said his aunty. 'But it doesn't feel like any of those ribs are broken.'

'Always a good thing.'

'What happened?' asked his uncle.

'I woke up in the middle of the night. I'd nodded off on the couch doing a bit of research and—'

'Research?' asked Vince.

'Oh, just looking into some of the stuff Dad was working on before he was . . . Before he died.' The pair in front of him exchanged glances then, but said nothing, so Mitch continued, 'Actually, the noise they were making woke me and, well, we got into a bit of a scuffle.'

Helen sniffed the air. 'Had you been drinking, Mitchel?' Not Mitch now, but his full name. He didn't see what that had got to do with it, but said he'd had a brandy or two.

'It's how they got the better of me, really. If I'd been with it then . . .'

Vince nodded sombrely. 'Ruffians. I warned you about them, didn't I?'

'You did, yeah. I hadn't realized things were quite so bad here.'

'They aren't,' said Helen.

'They *weren't*,' Vince clarified. 'Strangers,' was all he needed to add. It was clear they put everything that was wrong in the area down to this incursion from outside, and at the moment Mitch would have trouble arguing against that. People didn't used to get attacked in their own home when he had lived here before, and it was not the only thing that had changed. What he'd seen out there in the world was slowly encroaching on one of the few untouched parts of the country, maybe even the world. *Progress,* he thought to himself.

'I was thinking, maybe all that had something to do with what happened to my dad, do you think? He was looking into the Commune, the development schemes – among other things.'

'Who knows,' Aunty Helen said, giving a half-shrug. 'Thomas always had his obsessions, and he was getting very strange by the end. Paranoid, you know? Fixating on things. That happens with people who've got what he had.'

Mitch gave a small nod. '"Just because you're paranoid, doesn't mean they aren't after you." Kurt Cobain.'

'Actually, I think you'll find it's Joseph Heller in *Catch-22,*' his uncle pointed out.

'Same sentiment,' Mitch said.

Aunty Helen looked around again. 'How about we give you a hand to tidy up,' she said to him.

'That would be . . . Hey, shouldn't we take some photos before we start? For the insurance, I mean. Did Dad even keep up with all that?'

'I-I've absolutely no idea,' Helen admitted. 'Maybe there are some papers in the study, or upstairs?'

'Fu—' Mitch began, then remembered he'd been told off the last time he swore in front of this woman. 'Fudge. I haven't even been upstairs yet, and Wilkinson didn't even seem to give a . . . toss. Who knows what kind of a mess they've made up there!'

'Let's take a look then, shall we, lad?' Vince suggested.

Mitch nodded, following him. Only stopped when his aunty shouted after them: 'And I'll get the kettle on, make us a nice cup of tea.'

As it happened, the burglars had been everywhere *but* upstairs.

Perhaps they'd been disturbed before they could ransack the bedrooms, but Mitch couldn't help thinking again that they'd been in the only places they wanted – or needed – to. That the kitchen, the living room, had been a misdirection. That the main target had been the stuff he'd been looking into last night, and was now gone. Apart from the books he'd brought in with him the previous evening.

'Someone's been in here, mind,' said Helen when she saw Mitch's bedsheets had been rumpled in his old room. 'Is this where you've been sleeping?'

'Oh, no. That'll be the cat,' Mitch told her.

'Cat? Your dad didn't have a cat.'

'To be honest, I think the cat had him.' Mitch smiled and shook his head. 'It seems quite at home. Or rather I think it's a stray from another home. Doesn't have a collar on, though.'

'I wondered what that tray was doing down in the kitchen,' offered Vince.

Helen's face scrunched up. 'Not very hygienic, that.' Ever the doctor.

'He . . . she . . . *it's* good company,' Mitch argued, realizing he hadn't even seen the animal since first thing that morning; his relations weren't the only ones who didn't like strangers.

'Filthy animals, cats. Can't abide them!' Helen had informed him, insisting on changing the sheets on *all* the beds upstairs.

They failed to find any insurance papers, but Mitch needed to get in touch with places like the solicitors anyway about his father's estate so he'd make some enquiries then. As it was, Vince managed to persuade the neighbour who'd alerted the police (male, it turned out) to let Mitch in so he could cancel his cards and report his phone as stolen, which were the real priorities. The best his bank could do about replacements was send out debit and credit cards to his home address in a few days, or he could call in at his nearest branch – which was miles away from Green Acres. He'd have been better off losing it abroad, they told him helpfully. As for the phone, maybe get a 'pay as you go' in the meantime, though his aunty and uncle didn't hold out much hope he'd be able to buy one from the local shop. They never really bothered with those things themselves, Vince told Mitch.

However, with the three of them working on the tidying up operation, and constantly supplied with cup after cup of tea (seriously, his Aunty Helen was obsessed!), they soon had the downstairs looking much better. It was well into the afternoon by the time they were done, however – and it was only then that Uncle Vince mentioned eating. 'We'll head off to The Plough, get some dinner inside you. I bet you've not had a decent meal since you got back, judging from that ready meal box in the kitchen.'

It was hard to argue with that, and Mitch was starting to feel hungry now. Helen shot Vince a look that said, 'Is the pub really such a good idea?' Probably had Mitch down as some kind of raging alcoholic, but then if you couldn't drink when you found out your dad had set himself alight (been set alight?) then when could you?

Like father, like—

Before his aunty could say anything about it, Vince was fetching coats and leading them off down the road. 'The hub of any community,' was his argument.

As with the police station, and the hospital, nothing much had changed inside this place either. Mitch felt the familiar twinge of nostalgia he'd experienced so many times since he'd returned. Seeing the sepia-toned photos on the wall of farmhands working the land, pushing those ploughs the pub was named after – it had been established a few hundred years ago to cater mostly to that clientele – made him long for a simpler time.

It wasn't very crowded so they soon found a booth, sliding onto the benches and grabbing menus. 'The rib-eye of beef is very nice,' Vince told him, and Mitch almost immediately felt his mouth watering. He decided instead to plump for the traditional beer-battered fish 'n' chips – his favourite dish – knowing that he'd probably be trying most things on this menu before his time was done here.

'I'll have to owe you,' Mitch said as Vince rose to go and order – adding a Diet Coke to go with the food.

'Nonsense,' his uncle told him, flapping a hand. 'This one's on us, son.'

When Vince had gone, Helen said, 'And we'll give you some money to tide you over for a bit.'

'You don't have to do that. I did ask about a cash machine yesterday, but . . .'

'They used to have a standing one inside the shop a while back, but it broke,' Helen said. 'Had to go in for repairs or what have you, and never came back. Kept giving people the wrong amounts anyway.'

'I'll try the post office there, see if they can sort me out with—'

'It'll be quicker, and easier, for us to just lend you some. You can pay us back as and when. Your mum would have wanted us to look after you,' Helen told him. Not his dad, his mum. But then the woman had been her sister, he was Helen's nephew on her side – and he wondered then how close his aunty, or both of these two really, had been to his dad. Had their loyalty to him just been about who he'd married so long ago? Or the way they'd looked out for Thomas medically just been about Helen's former profession? That he would have been her patient if she hadn't retired. Not for the first time, Mitch realized there was so much about his family he didn't know, that couldn't be found out just by looking at old photos in an album. Maybe he'd discover more while he was here, get to know these folks a bit better. Reconnect. Introduce Lucy to them at some—

Oh God, *Lucy!*

He should have rung her when he was using the neighbour's phone, but it had taken so long to get through to the bank and phone company. In all honesty, he hadn't really thought about it: about how she might be trying to get through to his mobile and failing. Mitch was about to get up and ask to use the phone in the pub, when Vince returned with the drinks – an orange for himself, tea yet again for Helen – and it wasn't long after that the meals arrived. They were probably the only people in the entire place eating, which explained the quickness. Brought over by a burly man Mitch didn't recognize, who could have been the cousin of the guy from the service station, complete with apron, Mitch soon began hoovering it up. He hadn't realized quite how starved he was and being in a fight, however brief or half-hearted, had really given him an appetite.

Vince had plumped for the rib-eye and let him try a bit, while Helen had just gone for a shepherd's pie. She smiled when she saw how quickly Mitch was eating. 'Nice to see a growing boy enjoying his food,' she commented.

'I'll be growing outwards at this rate,' Mitch said, swallowing down another mouthful.

'Tuck in, you've earned it.'

'It's all home-cooked on the premises,' Vince added. 'That's what makes it so tasty.'

'Because it's cooked by someone else?' said Helen, then looked at her husband seriously – before laughing. 'Relax Vincent, food always tastes better when you eat out and someone else is doing the washing up afterwards.'

'Truer words have never been spoken,' said Vince.

The conversation had flowed quite easily after that, doing the reconnecting thing Mitch had been thinking about. But also finding out more about what his father had been going through in the last few months of his life.

'You'd pop in and find that he'd left the taps running in the bathroom, or the oven on or something. We did our best to keep on top of it, but it was getting to the stage where he was going to need help twenty-four hours a day.' Helen sipped at her third cup of tea while they'd been there. 'But you know how obstinate he could be. Getting him to agree to something like that would have been like . . . Well, it would have been hard. And I didn't want to be the one who signed off on that, doctor or no doctor.'

'I can see where you're coming from, but surely if he was that bad . . .' said Mitch, still nursing his first Coke.

Vince nodded. 'I suppose we just didn't want to admit it.'

'I really wish you'd let me know sooner,' Mitch told them again. 'I'd have come straight away.'

'But your job, your life,' Helen reminded him.

'I'd still have come.' Mitch began picking at a beermat, tearing little bits of cardboard from the edge. 'Actually, look, I didn't want to tell you this when I saw you the first time, but, well, I kind of lost my job.'

'Oh no!' said his aunty. 'Are you all right, love?'

'What happened?' asked his uncle, so Mitch gave them the broad strokes. 'The world's such a violent place, isn't it?'

'You poor thing,' said Helen, rubbing his arm. 'That's awful.'

'It'll be okay, I'll figure something else out. Security, maybe?' He stopped picking the mat and laughed. 'Although I should probably remember to lock the doors if I'm going to go into that line of work. Not the best of starts, is it?'

His uncle shook his head, but he was actually disagreeing rather than agreeing. 'You'll be fine, son. I can see big things in your future.'

Mitch laughed again. 'Bills probably.'

Vince couldn't help laughing at that one. 'No, although those don't stop coming, do they? What is it they say, taxes and—'

'Death,' said Mitch looking at him. 'Death and taxes.'

That killed it stone dead, literally. But then Mitch was good at doing that. Could ruin a fun night out in seconds, so Lucy had told him . . . Lucy, he really should let her know what's going on.

His aunty and uncle had headed off not long after that, though Mitch said he'd hang around for a little while. Didn't fancy going back to his dad's just yet – not after everything that had happened there overnight. 'All right, just don't drink too much, okay?' said Helen, shoving notes into his hand. It felt like he was getting pocket money again, and no one had monitored his drinking since he was in his teens.

As Vince held out a hand, letting Helen go first, he winked at him and whispered, 'You do what you want, young Mitch. Have one on me.' The man slipped him another couple of notes, then clapped him on the arm.

When he'd woken up, the last thing on his mind was having another drink – not after two nights on the trot. But, sitting there these past few hours, and watching as more people filtered in, the evening crowd he guessed, Mitch had suddenly started to fancy a drop or two of the real ale here. His taste for booze returning.

Plus, as his uncle had said, this was the hub of any community. The longer he hung around, the more he might find out. Perhaps he could even sniff out the culprits from last night, get a lead on them?

Just take it steady, he told himself. *Dull the ache in those ribs, if nothing else. Take the edge off more than a beermat. Just don't get into another state.*

Oh, all right, he thought. *Maybe just a little bit.*

Chapter 12

She looked in a right state.

That's what his old mum would have said if she'd seen this woman: hair in disarray, black bags under her eyes. If anything, Bella looked even worse than she had the day before, like she'd aged about ten years.

Watts hadn't been able to get her off his mind all evening, all night. Had had about as much sleep as Bella, judging from her appearance. What had she done: waited up in case those people who'd broken in had come back? If there even had been anybody. He was beginning to wonder whether it had been a good idea to check up on her, though, during his lunch hour – because this was doing very little to put his mind at rest. Watts was more worried than before about her now that she'd answered the door.

He'd knocked several times, after pulling up outside the caravan park itself and heading in on foot; Watts wasn't sure whether he'd be able to park inside, there only seemed to be one space and that was currently occupied by Bella's lime-green Beetle. Which was how he knew she was in, or should be.

It had taken ages to get a response, however, and when Bella appeared in the doorway it was as if she was emerging from hibernation, or she'd been in a coma. Except she didn't look as rested as someone who'd been asleep for the winter, not by a long chalk – dressing gown pulled tightly around her like a shield. The first thing she'd done was yawn, before either of them could get any words out.

'I . . . hey there. How're you . . . Are you okay?'

Bella gazed at him like she didn't recognize who he was, and it had been less then twenty-four hours since he'd seen her last. 'Ashley?'

'Yeah. Are you—'

'I'm okay,' she told him, though not even she seemed to believe a word of it. 'Just this headache, you know?'

'You've still got it?'

She nodded, then winced. He couldn't help peering into the caravan behind her, which looked in just as much of a state as the woman who owned it. How had it got in that much of a mess in a day? It had been fine when he'd been here last. 'I'm finding it hard to concentrate as a matter of fact.'

'Do you mind if I come in?' he asked her, not wishing to be pushy but his detective's radar was kicking in and he really wanted to see the place.

Rabbit trapped in the headlights didn't even begin to cover it. 'D-Do you fancy a walk instead, maybe down on the beach? It might clear my head a bit.' She was waking up apparently, enough to work out a way around him seeing inside the caravan proper. Enough to stall him, by getting him to wait outside while she ducked back in to 'get changed', as she told him when he agreed to the walk.

Watts heard the banging around inside, her clearing things up – clearing things away, possibly in case he wanted to call and look inside upon their return. Just what the hell was she doing in there? he wondered. But before he could knock again, there she was at the door, wearing trainers, shorts and a sweatshirt. Dressed for the beach, which was more than Watts was in his suit.

As they'd taken the steps down to Golden Sands beach, and walked alongside the ocean, he'd loosened his tie and slung his jacket over his shoulder, though not before rolling his sleeves up.

Neither of them had spoken to begin with, Watts stopping to pick up a pebble or two and skimming them into the water. He'd always loved the sea, but then he would do having lived here all his life. Watts wondered then about how long Bella had been here; he knew she hadn't been born in this area but not a lot else. He was just about to ask her, for something to say more than anything, when she stopped and turned to him.

'Ashley, do *you* think I'm crazy?'

'What? Why? Because of the whole medium thing?' He recalled tapping his temple the last time he'd seen her, had kicked himself afterwards – even if he didn't really believe as such.

'That wasn't . . . But, yeah, I guess. Usually I don't care about what people think of me. Or what I do. I'm just trying to help folks, you know? Lately, though, I'm starting to wonder if . . .' She shook her head. 'Oh, I don't know what I'm trying to say. I'm thinking that I might be losing the plot.'

'You don't, I mean forgive me for saying, but you still don't look that well.' Should he say something? He figured he might as well. 'Actually, you look worse than yesterday, Bella.'

'Thanks a lot,' she said.

'Hey, you look great to me, I just . . .' He gave a nervous laugh. 'God, I'm not coming across very well, am I? I just meant you look very tired. Did you get any sleep at all?'

'Yeah. A bit. But it was difficult with all the—' She stared at him. 'After what happened.'

'I get that, people in your situation. It's bound to destabilize you, make you question things. As for whether I think you're crazy.' Watts shook his head finally. 'No, I don't think that at all.'

'I'll bet Robyn does.'

He frowned. Why bring Robyn back into it? Bella knew what that woman thought about her. It wasn't how he felt, though. 'And does that matter to you?' Watts asked, turning it back on Bella.

'No. Not really. I was just trying to help her before. That's all I ever try to do, help people, Ashley. Same as you.'

'Right. I know that. You're a good person, Bella. You did help Robyn. You helped me, that's for damned sure.' Watts took the jacket off his shoulder and put it over his arm. 'I thought about coming to see you, you know. When things died down a bit.'

Bella laughed sadly. 'I bet I know why. Look into the future and tell you whether Sergeant Watts and Dr Adams will live happily ever after.'

'No, I—' he began to protest, but couldn't. Watts would be lying if he said that hadn't crossed his mind, as silly as it sounded. Something, anything, to give him hope.

She'd be mad to let you go.

'Doesn't work that way, I'm afraid. Doesn't work at all at the moment, not with this bloody . . .' She rubbed at her head, hand going from the front to the back.

'I really wish you'd let me take you to the hospital, get you checked out, Bella.'

'It's not like that. I don't know how to describe it, except it's like there's a door in my head that's shut and something keeps on banging on it. Something that needs to be let out. It started when my dad died.'

'Oh wow, your dad died? When was this?'

Rabbit, headlights again. 'The other day,' Bella finally admitted.

'Why didn't you tell me?' Watts had no idea why he was asking that, it was really none of his business.

Bella stared out at the ocean, at a boat on the horizon. Disappearing over it. If he was a betting man, he would have been willing to place a significant amount of money on her wishing she was aboard that vessel sailing away to who knows where. 'We hadn't seen each other for quite a while.'

'Okay,' said Watts. 'Listen, I didn't mean to overstep the mark.'

She turned her head back and regarded him. 'It's all right. No big secret. I'm just not very good at the whole sharing thing.'

It was his turn to look over the horizon, suddenly wishing for a taste of that freedom himself. 'Yeah, I know what you mean.'

'My brother went back home, to Green Acres.' *Well, that answered that question*, he thought to himself. 'He rang me the other day, wanted me to go back with him but . . .'

When Watts faced her again, she was crying. 'Hey, hey, it's okay.' He thought about opening his arms to give her a hug, then decided against it. He barely knew this woman when all was said and done, even as a friend. Though she seemed to know everything about him.

Call it woman's intuition, Ashley. You're a good guy.

'You can tell me anything, you know. I'm kind of like a priest in that respect. Erm, well, maybe not a priest. I'd probably fail the medical.'

She laughed then and he laughed with her. 'I'm sorry,' Bella said, 'I'm just trying not to picture you with the dog collar now. That one's going to stay with me.'

He gave a mock frown. 'I really hope not.' The last thing he wanted was for her to think of him as some stuffy religious figure, and she smiled. It was a sweet smile.

No, he really shouldn't go there. Extremely bad idea. Of course, he was attracted to Bella, he'd have to be blind not to be. She was gorgeous, and that was after a couple of bad night's sleep! But there was no getting around her line of work, the fact she was more than a little . . . odd. Watts still wasn't quite sure what he thought about the whole psychic thing, really. He believed Bella believed in it. And she *had* given him that heads-up last year which he'd followed through on, leading to the eventual arrest of a killer. More police forces could probably use someone with Bella's talents . . . hunches? Yet it also made him feel uneasy, although that might just be because he wasn't used to it. Didn't know what to make of it. For people like Bella, for the people who went to see her – both privately and at her stage show at The Majestic – it was a fairly commonplace thing, he guessed.

Then there was Robyn.

She hated Bella, still blamed her for putting a spoke in the wheel where it came to her and her cousin, Vicky. As a psychologist, Robyn came at things from a very scientific point of view and thought folk like Bella were charlatans. That they had an angle, usually money. He'd found it best not to get her started on the subject, because once you did . . . Then again, did he really care what she thought anymore? He hadn't heard from her in weeks, but he'd kinda got used to that by now.

'You know what it's like, Ash,' she'd say. 'Work's just busy.' And she did juggle two jobs, it was true, which didn't leave a vast amount of time for a personal life. Working for the university as a lecturer, but also as a consultant for the police. With that guy, DI Cavanagh. Cav, as she called him, a bloke he hadn't even met but was jealous of even though – as she kept pointing out – he was happily married with kids. Not that Watts thought anything was going on with them, he was just jealous of the closeness they had working on cases together, he supposed. Watts had felt like he'd got a glimmer of that when they'd been working together here at Golden Sands, but that git *Cav* (*not fair, you don't even know him*) got to do it all the time. Working the cases, working those high-profile cases, catching serial killers and the like.

While he was stuck here, taking down forgers and petty thieves. Smugglers, drug dealers. It was worthwhile work – helping people, as Bella had said – but something was definitely missing. Job satisfaction, a long-term relationship? If he moved to be closer to Robyn, he might get both of those. But, of course, Robyn being Robyn, he still had no idea where she was in this. As non-committal as she had been at the start of . . . whatever it was. There'd been a spark, definitely. And he'd been to visit her a few times, which had been lovely as far as he was concerned – but apart from a kiss or several, nothing had gone any further. He'd always respected her privacy, stayed in a hotel in Hannerton so's not to pressure her.

And Watts couldn't help wondering if it was down to that first time they'd almost . . . When he'd asked Robyn if she was sure, because she really hadn't been before. She'd been drunk and he'd done the gentlemanly thing, the respectful thing. Robyn had been in the state that time, drunk and maudlin. Staying at The Majestic after she'd rowed with Vicky, that had been the evening she'd lamped Bella as well. Because she hated her.

Imagine if Robyn knew they were becoming friends. If that's what was happening. *Were* they becoming friends? When Bella was keeping him at arm's length now, after she'd come to him for help in the first place? Was his usual luck with the opposite sex kicking in?

No, there was more to it than that. He knew there was.

New friends, old friends. More than that? Right now, he just wanted to help Bella – make her feel better somehow.

She was looking out at the sea again, gazing across the water. 'Do you ever just feel like walking into that, and never coming back. Not having to feel anything at all?'

Watts' eyebrows knitted together again. Of all the things he'd expected her to say, that hadn't been one of them. Suddenly he was more worried about her than ever, though he really had no right to be. This woman, who spent all her time talking to the dead, was she seriously considering joining their ranks? He realized he hadn't answered and thought he'd better say something. 'N-No. Not really. Where there's life there's hope, Bella.'

'Your gran used to say that,' the woman beside him replied without missing a beat.

He opened his mouth to answer, and closed it again. Then told her, 'My mum, actually. She's always said it.'

'She got it from her mum,' Bella stated simply as if it was just a fact. And it probably was as far as she was concerned; that 'talent' of hers hadn't abandoned her completely then, headaches or no headaches. 'Quite right too.' Bella took his arm, slipped hers thought it.

New friends.

Then she started walking again and Watts walked with her, in silence.

Chapter 13

'To old friends.'

She held up her glass and he chinked it. Old friends. *An* old friend. And more. 'Old friends,' Mitch repeated.

He hadn't spotted her until he'd gone up for his next pint, having discovered a local brew he was growing particularly fond of. She was part of the shift change, obviously, as it got busier. Actually, he hadn't taken much notice of her even then, just asked absently for another 'Traditional'.

'Nice, that one, isn't it?' she'd said, and he'd looked up then to see a barmaid with strawberry-blonde hair and red lipstick, wearing a white blouse and black skirt – broken up with a chunky belt and buckle.

'Hmm,' Mitch had answered. He'd never actually tried it before, though he recalled regulars here going on and on about it. A generic lager had been his tipple back then, still was when he went out with mates or colleagues from work.

As he'd paid her, he felt the woman's eyes on him. Boring into him almost. It had made him feel a little uneasy, if he was being really honest. And more than a little bit guilty, not that he was doing anything wrong – she was looking at *him*! Nevertheless, he'd felt bad enough to finally head to the phone now he had some change. Placing his pint on a shelf, he dialled the number from memory.

'Mitch! I've been trying to get hold of you all day!' He hadn't been expecting quite the level of panic he heard in that voice, but then this was Lucy when all was said and done. She'd turned worrying about him into an art form.

He told her what had happened, how there'd been a break-in and his phone had been one of the things they'd taken. 'My aunty and uncle helped me clear up the mess,' he told her.

'And this is the first chance you've had to let me know?'

There was a hesitation then, because of course it hadn't been. He'd just prioritized the bank, the phone company. Lunch. Pints of Traditional. 'I—'

'What's that noise, where are you ringing from? Are you in a pub, Mitchel Prescott?' He was in real trouble now. 'How long have you been in there?' She might as well have been asking how many he'd had. Bloody hell, first Helen, now his girlfriend!

'Maybe it's not such a bad thing. A bit of time away from each other . . . Like you said.'

'Uncle Vince brought me, him and my aunty paid for a bite to eat.'

'Sounds like you've been having a nice time.' Mitch knew what she meant: he had been here while she'd been sitting in Downstone not knowing what was going on. Ringing him and not getting an answer.

'Well, apart from tackling intruders in the middle of the night. Yeah, a fantastic time!'

'Tackling? Were you hurt, Mitch?'

'I . . . Not really.'

A pause down the line. 'What does that mean, not really?'

'It means . . . Look, it was nothing I couldn't handle.' Nothing he would have been able to handle if he hadn't been legless.

'I see. Okay.' Another pause. 'And where are your aunty and uncle now?'

He'd thought about lying, saying they were still sitting in the booth where they'd been earlier, tucking into their rib-eye and shepherd's pie. But there was always a chance Lucy would find out. Women, in his experience, usually did. 'They went home,' he told her.

'Right. I'd better leave you to it, then.'

'Lucy, don't be like that.'

'Like what?' The edge hadn't left her voice in the slightest.

'You have no idea what it's been like coming back here. My dad, and then last night—' His pips started to go, and he fished around for more change but found he didn't have the right coins. The line went dead.

Shit! She'd probably think he'd hung up on her now. From a pub. Moaning about the fact he'd come back here, when she didn't even want him to in the first place! Mitch grabbed his pint, took a pull on it and went back to the bar. He'd been intending to get more change, break into a fiver, but when he arrived there the barmaid was still staring. 'Can I do something for you?' Mitch asked.

She grinned, and when she did, dimples appeared in her cheeks. 'You really don't remember me, do you?'

Mitch thought about saying, 'Should I?' but that would have been rude. Instead, he racked his brains trying to recall her face, her name. Was definitely struggling and she could see it.

She laughed. 'Made that much of an impression, did I?'

Mitch shook his head. 'It's not that, I—'

'Denise? Denise Kelly? We were at school together. That's assuming you're Mitchel Prescott, and I reckon you are.'

Denise . . . Denise. Oh, *that* Denise! Mitch couldn't help grinning, couldn't believe he hadn't recognised her. 'Denise, of course! How are you?'

She smiled again. 'I'm good, thanks.'

'What're you up to these days?' Mitch thought about how stupid the question sounded even as he was asking it, as she was waving her hand around to show what she did for a living. Some copper he was. 'I meant, you know, how're things in your life?'

'Am I still on my own, or do I have a string of husbands behind me and a bunch of kids back at home?' She chuckled. 'Still young, free and single. There was someone, for quite a while as it goes. But it didn't work out.'

He hadn't actually been asking anything that intimate, but then Denise had never really been backwards at coming forwards, Mitch thought to himself. Never got embarrassed talking about all that stuff. Yeah, bits and pieces were coming back to him now. 'I'm sorry,' he told her, and genuinely meant it.

'And you?'

'It's a long story,' was all he'd tell her at that point.

'I figured I'd . . . we'd see you back here before too long. What with what happened to your dad and all.'

'Yeah.' He let out the word as a long, drawn-out sigh.

'It was a—'

'Nasty business. Yes.'

Denise offered a sympathetic smile, showing those dimples once more. 'I was going to say such a shame. I liked Tommy. Used to come in here all the time.'

Mitch shook his head apologetically. 'Sorry, it's just that people have been saying that to me since I got home. Got *back*,' he clarified, because this wasn't really his home anymore. Hadn't been for a long time – probably since the last time he'd seen this woman – and that had been his own choice.

Nodding slowly, Denise had asked him if he wanted another drink. 'I still have half of this one left,' Mitch replied.

'That won't take you long, big strapping fellow like you,' she said with a wink. 'All grown up and everything.'

Mitch could feel his cheeks turning red, nodded just so she'd focus her attention on something else. But Denise kept her eyes on him all the while she was pulling the pint of Traditional. 'Tell you what, it's on the house. Because of your dad.'

'Oh, right.' He felt weird accepting it, even though it was a nice gesture on her part. 'Only if you let me get you one in return,' Mitch told Denise. That way they'd be even, right? He wouldn't owe her.

'All right, ta. Very kind of you.' She pointed at the spirits on the back, to see if that was okay and Mitch nodded again. Denise helped herself to a gin, adding some tonic to it. Seemed like they had no problem with the staff here drinking while they were working, because that's when she'd proposed the toast. 'To old friends.'

Except they hadn't just been friends, had they? They'd been a bit more than that. Had even 'gone out' for a little while, in that way you do when you're kids. A snog behind the bike sheds, a fumble or two out in the woods. That kind of thing. Yes, it was *all* coming back: Denise had been the one who'd set him on the road to being 'a man', if you could call it that. Hadn't popped his cherry, that had been a girl a long way away from here, when he was on his travels before settling in Downstone. Before Lucy even.

Crap! *Lucy!*

He remembered the phone call, what he'd been doing when he came back to the bar – getting change so he could ring her back. Mitch checked his watch: about half an hour had passed. Jesus, even if he rang her now he'd get so much shit. Might be better to just leave it till the morning, find a phone box in the village somewhere because the one at his dad's was screwed.

But before he could do anything at all, he was getting a strange feeling. Not his 'spider-sense' as such, but a shift in the atmosphere, a hush. The calm before the storm. Suddenly there was shouting coming from the other side of the pub. Mitch looked up and across, saw a handful of people gathering to watch.

'Mitch,' he heard Denise saying – couldn't be sure whether she was trying to get him to stay where he was, or wanted him to help.

In the end, it was simply reflex; he was leaving his pint behind and drifting over to where the disturbance was. Gravitating towards it. In the middle were three men: one a thin, craggy-looking fellow he vaguely recognized, leaning heavily on a stick; another a bloke dressed in quite a sharp suit, looking out of place in a country pub – and that had to be his wife or girlfriend sitting at the table he was standing next to, because she was in a teal silk dress with her hair up (together they looked like they were ready for a night out at the Savoy or the Ritz). Which just left the other guy, who Mitch definitely knew straight away, because he'd nearly run into his tractor.

The farmer with those huge sideburns – dressed like he'd just come from work, in a ripped jumper and dirty dungarees – was more ruddy-faced than ever, temper colouring his cheeks even as Mitch felt the colour draining from his own.

'Bloody parasite!' the farmer barked at the well-dressed man. 'Worse than those hippy trespassers, you are! Why don't yer just fuck off back where you came from and leave us all in peace!' It didn't sound like a request.

'Well, my grandparents were from this area originally, albeit many moons ago, so . . .' answered the smartly dressed man.

'Gentlemen, gentlemen.' This was from the man with the stick, an effort to try to keep the peace. It would take more than that soon, if Mitch was any judge. 'Please.'

'This isn't one o' yer fancy council meetings, Nuttall. The time for words is past.' Another snarl from the farmer. 'An' I've always been a man of action anyway!'

'Except when it comes to acting in your best interests, Mr Granger. The best interests of this village, this entire region.'

'Piss off, Sheldon!'

So the sharply dressed man was Neil Sheldon, thought Mitch. The man he'd read about in his father's notes. Property developer Neil Sheldon.

'If you'd just stop being an idiot and—'

That was it. The moment things turned, and farmer Granger lunged across for Sheldon. The moment that Nuttall guy with the stick got in the middle of the fight and was elbowed away. The blow would have seen him on the floor if it weren't for Mitch stepping forwards and catching him, righting him. 'Are you okay?' he asked the man, who nodded.

Now it was Mitch's turn to get in the middle of things. He had plenty of pent-up anger himself left over from the previous evening, and he hadn't had nearly as much to drink today. Some might say he hadn't had enough. Mitch would have disagreed, he'd had just the right amount for a rumble.

Granger had Sheldon by the scruff of the neck, was pulling the man towards him as the woman in the teal dress let out a yell. The big farmer's fist was drawing back to punch his opponent, and Mitch was there to stop him. He grabbed that arm and yanked it, spinning a furious Granger to face him. It was only now that Mitch began to wonder if he'd bitten off more than he could chew. Not only did he not have his baton, pepper spray or anything else he usually relied on when breaking up a fight like this – including handcuffs for after the perp was incapacitated – but he didn't have backup either. Which was more than might be said for Granger. For all Mitch knew, half the pub could be on his side in whatever row this was.

Sheldon forgotten about for the moment, Granger set his sights on Mitch, taking a swing at him instead. Mitch ducked, avoiding the blow, but his ribs protested. He really shouldn't have been getting into a scrape this soon after his last one, wasn't his business until he *made* it his business. But he was trying to stop it from escalating, was probably the only one present with the training to take down Granger with the minimum of fuss – supposedly.

Gritting his teeth, Mitch skirted round the back of the big farmer and grabbed him – under the armpits so he couldn't shake him off. Holding him in place, even though it was just about killing Mitch, the old injury in his shoulder protesting too.

'Enough!' someone bellowed. 'That's *enough!*'

It was the fellow in the apron who'd served them their meals earlier, wading in to settle this once and for all. The owner, perhaps?

'Talk to *him!*' shouted the man in the suit, pointing at Granger. 'We only came in here for a quiet drink.'

'It's true, Granger here started it,' Nuttall confirmed.

'All right, all right. Settle down Cam,' the owner said to Granger. 'And you, yer can let him go now, mate. He won't cause any more bother, will ye?'

Granger gave a non-committal shake of the head. Mitch wasn't hugely convinced, but when he felt the man he was holding loosen up, he had no choice but to step back and hold his hands in the air – still tensing, ready in case Granger should turn and want round two. The big man grunted, shrugging off hands that were not even there any longer. Keeping up the pretence of the tough guy. He gave them each a glare in turn, Sheldon, Nuttall, and then Mitch, before breaking through the crowd and heading for the exit. Leaving The Plough with a slam of the door.

'What a psycho,' said Mitch when he was gone.

'He doesn't mean any 'arm,' the man in the apron assured him. 'Just gets het up about things.'

'Doesn't mean any . . .' But the man wasn't even listening to him anymore, and the onlookers were dispersing – as if this was something that happened every night in the pub. No more unusual than a game of dominoes. Was it his imagination, or had this place got rougher too in the time since he'd last set foot in it?

A hand was on his shoulder and Mitch flinched, almost turned and took down whoever that was as well – when he saw it was the older man, still leaning on his stick. 'Oh, I'm sorry, lad.' He offered his free hand now for Mitch to shake. 'Appreciate the catch, I wouldn't want to bugger up my other hip! Councillor Nuttall.'

Mitch shook the hand. That's right, Nuttall. He recalled this man having something to do with politics back in the day, but that hadn't really interested Mitch at the time. 'Prescott. Mitchel Prescott.'

'Ah yes, Tommy's boy,' Nuttall said, raising an eyebrow. 'Very pleased to see you.'

'I'm glad someone is.' And now Mitch was thinking: a councillor, and he knew his father? Didn't hurt to have one of those owing you a favour, especially when you were looking into the things he was. Might even be more use than bloody Sergeant Wilkinson, could get a DI here or something to help.

'That makes two of us,' said another voice. Then there was a cough from the seated woman, and Sheldon changed it to: 'Three, I mean. Neil Sheldon, Mr Prescott. Thanks for stepping in. I think I should probably buy you a drink or several.'

'Oh, no. That's okay, I've got—'

'I won't take no for an answer,' said the man.

Nuttall caught the bloke in the suit by the arm. 'Neil, I can only apologize for Granger's behaviour.'

'He needs locking up,' said Sheldon's companion. Mitch couldn't agree more.

'If he signs over that land on the lower fields, I'll forget it ever happened.' Sheldon smiled then and he looked more like a predator than Granger had, even during the fight. Nevertheless, Mitch accompanied him and his girlfriend – wife? – back to the bar again. Back to Denise, who'd been watching the whole thing from a distance.

'Give this man whatever he wants,' Sheldon told her.

Mitch picked up his full pint. 'Like I said, I have one here waiting.' He tipped it again in Denise's direction, thanking her once more.

'His next drink then, and the next couple after that,' said the property developer, handing over a crisp note to the barmaid – who looked incredibly impressed. 'You've got skills, my young friend. You're trained. What are you, police?'

Mitch didn't see any reason to lie about it now. 'Until recently.'

'Right. Okay. So you're at a bit of a loose end?'

'I wouldn't say—'

'Have you ever considered any private security work, body-guard, that kind of thing?' asked Sheldon, and Mitch thought back to the conversation earlier where security work had cropped up in passing.

'I hadn't really—'

'Well, when and if you ever do, give me a call.' He handed Mitch his card; he didn't think it was worth telling Sheldon he didn't actually have access to a phone in his current circumstances. He just thanked him, and Sheldon clapped him on his back – then headed off with the woman in the silk dress.

'I think you've just made a new friend,' Denise said to him.

'Yeah.' But Mitch couldn't help thinking about that farmer, Granger. Who in the pub might be mates with him, on his side. Couldn't help thinking . . .

He might just have made a few enemies as well.

Chapter 14

He'd thought about walking, rather than the bike.

After all it was such a nice day, the sun up there in a relatively cloudless sky, the beautiful surroundings. It was the kind of day people came here to experience, to revel in: those who hired cottages or camped or just walked out there on the moorland. Seemed a shame to wrap up in leathers and plonk a ruddy great helmet on your head; for one thing it was really hot today. Had been getting hotter since he arrived from Downstone. But Mitch had a lot to get through and his ribs were still aching – especially after the scuffle last night.

With a couple more rounds ahead of him and paid for, he'd stayed in the pub and got chatting to Denise. That is, he listened as she told him more about the people who had been involved in the altercation – Nuttall, Granger, and Sheldon – and how this had been going on for a while. 'Tempers have been running a bit high ever since Mr Sheldon moved into the area,' she'd said to him.

Mitch could imagine; he'd read the stuff his dad had written about the man wanting to purchase chunks of Green Acres to build on, then eventually sell off. He couldn't imagine anyone being okay about that, most locals had his aunty and uncle's view of new people coming in causing disruption. All right, it was inevitable that some outside people would marry into families here – his

Uncle Vince for one – and you needed a bit of new blood every now and again, or things stagnated. But the villagers liked their traditions here, their beer was even called 'Traditional', for Heaven's sake! Things were changing though, fast, and that was not going down well. Hardly surprising, when the result was break-ins and vandalism, the kind he'd witnessed first-hand himself.

'Oh, they're blaming a lot of that on things like the Commune,' Denise had explained. 'One step off gypsies and homeless people they are, but I guess we're stuck with 'em.' That loophole his dad had 'mentioned', the old family connection – and Denise's opinion was probably the majority of people's. The folk here made the NIMBY crowd look like amateurs. At least the kind of clientele Sheldon was talking about bringing into the fold had money, could afford the kinds of luxury and exclusive houses he was going to stick on this land. It was just a shame that in order to do that, the beautiful landscape had to change. But such was the way of all things, Mitch supposed. The Commune was what interested him most, however. Granger's 'hippy trespassers'.

His uncle's words:
I don't trust 'em.
Wilkinson's reaction:
You want to leave them well enough alone.
Always a dangerous thing to say to Mitch. Made him want to poke his nose in even more. Like a red rag to a bull. His father had been looking into them as well, and he decided maybe it was time he paid them a visit. See just what kind of a 'cult' they were really dealing with.

Once he'd finished his drinks, Mitch decided to call it a night and head back. He wanted to stay relatively compos mentis in case anything happened at the house again. Denise had offered to walk back with him when she finished her shift – shouldn't it have been the other way around? Or was *he* being old-fashioned? – but Mitch didn't want to give her any ideas. No more than the ones she was already getting anyway.

But once he stepped out and with the walk across the square ahead of him in the dark, Mitch began to regret that decision. He could definitely have used the company, the shadows between buildings – where the streetlamps couldn't reach – certainly seemed to be getting longer with each step. Seemed to have things (people, monsters) hiding in them. It was like he'd inherited that paranoia his aunty and uncle had talked about from his dad, though he had been in yet another fight tonight, he reminded himself. What if Granger had waited around to take his revenge, or worse still, gone and gathered a bunch of mates to leap on him as he made his way home?

Thankfully that hadn't happened, but Mitch would've been lying if he'd said he wasn't glad to get to the front door. To put the key in the lock and turn it. Only to jump again as something touched his leg. Something else outside in the shadows; that looked like a *living shadow*. His very own little monster, which meowed again and began curling around his legs.

'Well, hello! You're back again, are you?' Mitch bent and picked up the cat, which immediately started to rub itself against his face. He laughed, the fur tickling his cheek. 'I guess you're my friend, aren't you? Or is it just conditional on the amount of fish I can feed you?'

Mitch had toed open the door, placing Cat on the floor again – and as if to prove him right, it headed off in the direction of the kitchen. Closing the door behind him, remembering to lock it, Mitch followed the creature. 'My aunty reckons you're a filthy thing,' he told the 'pet', who looked over its shoulder at him and let out a meow of complaint. 'Her words, pal, not mine. All right, all right, let's see what we've got for you tonight. I'm guessing I can't interest you in any more of that dried food.' The short, sharp meow he got in reply said it all. And digging into the back of the cupboards, he managed to find some tinned spam that was in date.

Making sure the back door was still locked – it should be, he hadn't touched it since Wilkinson had demonstrated how it 'worked' earlier, and the litter had already been changed as part of the tidy-up so there was no need to unlock it – he'd hit the sack, heading upstairs this time. Contemplating the double bed for a moment, Mitch still couldn't bring himself to spend the night in his mum and dad's old room, no matter how much more comfortable he might be. It just wouldn't have felt right.

So, he'd taken to his old bedroom, crashing in there for the night – and hadn't been surprised when Cat joined him not long afterwards. He couldn't work out whether it was glad or pissed off he was in there too, taking up space. But in the end it snuggled up to him and he figured it was quite pleased to share the bed with him. The feeling was mutual.

Even with all his good intentions, he'd still overslept – probably because he didn't have a phone to set an alarm on, instead relying on the sunrise to get him up. Which he'd slept through. There'd been no sign of Cat that morning, but it had showed up again for breakfast. 'I'll soon be running out of things from the cupboard to give you,' Mitch told it, doling out the rest of the spam, while he stuck to his toast; the toaster was something else the thieves were apparently not bothered about. He'd made a few cheese sandwiches for later and changed the litter again, securing the back door once he was done, and got ready to scoot off.

Cat had followed him out today, perhaps also wanting to make the most of the sunny weather. 'Right. See you later, then,' he called out to it, suddenly feeling foolish for talking to the animal in public, particularly when it was taking not a blind bit of notice.

And he was on his way, fetching his bike, donning his helmet and setting off back along the road he'd used to enter the village.

Pointing his Honda in the direction of the Commune he'd seen that first day.

Denise's description of a kind of gypsy encampment was quite far off the mark.

Yes, there were some mobile homes here – in the dusty yard slap-bang in the middle of the greenery – and a couple of caravans, though nothing approaching the size of the one his sister lived in. (Would the people in Green Acres have considered her a gypsy now too? he wondered.) But in the main these people lived in wooden structures they looked to have put up themselves; simple buildings, some square and others longer, rectangular. They looked relatively new, however – nothing like the buildings down there in the village itself, which had stood the test of time. And they looked temporary, which also made Mitch wonder how long they expected to be here.

As he rode in and parked up, he spotted chicken runs – a couple of people in them wearing very simple cream tunics and trousers, collecting eggs – and a few goats tethered, which the Commune probably used for milk. One of the figures, a woman, placed a hand against her brow, shielding her eyes from the sun so she could see who was visiting. Beyond her were stretches of land that looked like they'd been farmed, albeit on a small scale. Patches where he could imagine vegetables might be growing like in an allotment or something.

There was also a small bonfire burning not too far away, people tossing things onto it, getting rid of their rubbish; well, it wasn't as if the bin men made it all the way out here, Mitch supposed.

As he climbed off the Honda, kicking down the stand, locking the vehicle and taking off his helmet, more people dressed the same way appeared seemingly from nowhere. Dozens actually. A few stood out: one man with ginger hair, verging on red; another completely bald with fleshy lips; and another, this time a woman, with terrible acne like the lad from the shop . . . or were those burns? No way of rocking up here unnoticed then, Mitch mused. And he also pondered absently how many hidden figures might be watching him, training their telescopic sights on him, pointing the barrels of their machine guns. But this was England, he reminded himself, then also remembered he knew plenty of people who could get hold of that kind of weaponry on the streets. Where there *were* actual streets, of course, and not dirt tracks.

He decided to take his chances and go to meet them anyway; Mitch needed to talk to these people whatever the consequences. Whatever he discovered.

A tall man with thinning hair, a broad chest and skin the shade of tanned leather approached him, holding up a hand. Whether he was telling Mitch to halt or waving in greeting was unclear. Either way it was enough to get Mitch to stop, waiting for the guy to cover the distance between them.

'Hello, brother,' he said. His voice was kind, warm, but strong at the same time. Could command respect, thought Mitch. Command *people*? 'What brings you to our humble home this day?'

Mitch hesitated, not sure what to say now that he was here. He decided to start with, 'I'm investigating a crime that happened not long ago, and not far from here.'

The man nodded. 'You're with the police, then?'

Again, Mitch wasn't sure how to respond to that. Thought it best to nod, since he'd started down along that path – in more ways than one.

'You won't mind if I ask to see some identification?'

Not only did Mitch no longer have his police ID, he didn't even have his cards in his wallet. He thought about telling this man all his methods of identification had been stolen, but that sounded lame even to him – regardless of the fact it was the truth. 'Okay, okay. I'll level with you.' Mitch said this in the hopes he might get the same back. 'This isn't an official investigation, although I am in touch with the local authorities.' That kept it nebulous enough, he figured. They could take it that he was still with the force, he wasn't saying otherwise. And the authorities *had* been in touch with him – or he had been with them – since the start of all this. He'd been in touch with Wilkinson, too, for all the good it had done him. 'My name's Mitchel Prescott and this is about my father, Thomas.'

The man gave another nod, but if he'd heard the name before he gave no indication. Instead, he said: 'My name is Daniel.' That was it, no surname. Just Daniel. Not even Danny.

'Right, well, pleased to meet you, Daniel.' Mitch hedged his bets, nodding a hello to the others behind him who were forming a wall between them and the buildings. None of the group nodded back. If the villagers didn't like their kind 'trespassing' on what they saw as their land, then it looked like the feeling was mutual. And for people who didn't adhere to boundaries, they seemed pretty keen on protecting theirs.

'You say this is about your father?'

'Er, yes. He died, oh, about a week ago now. In suspicious circumstances.'

Daniel pursed his lips before asking, 'What kind of suspicious circumstances?'

'He burned to death in the woods.'

There was no shock, no surprise at this. Daniel simply nodded again. *If he bloody well says it's a nasty business, I won't be responsible for my actions*, thought Mitch, but the man remained silent. He had the air of a monk about him. One of those monks you see in movies who've taken a vow of pacifism, but could actually snap your neck like a twig. Definitely the air of a leader about him. That cult of personality he'd read about; could probably do with reading more about.

'Do you mind if I ask you some questions?' Mitch prompted.

'That depends on what the questions are!' came a voice from behind Daniel. Male, but Mitch couldn't tell who'd spoken in the crowd.

Daniel turned. 'James, please.' There was a mumbling, but Mitch still couldn't tell who it was – only that the tanned man had caused them to shut up. A woman joined Daniel now, about the same age as him – in her forties – and stood at his side. 'This is my life partner, Leah.'

The woman, whose grey-black hair was tied back in a ponytail, nodded to Mitch. 'You won't find what you're looking for here, Mitchel Prescott,' she told him.

'You seem pretty certain about that,' he replied.

'We don't mean anyone any harm, in spite of what you might have heard elsewhere.'

'And what might I have heard?' *That sometimes you guys make your way into the village, especially at night-time? Did you make your way into my dad's place the other night?*

She smiled, going for sweet but just coming off as creepy. 'People fear what they do not understand. Always have.'

'They look for scapegoats,' Daniel added. 'When they should look to their own.' They weren't wrong, the people in Green Acres were definitely afraid of newcomers, of change. Were searching for people to blame for the spate of crimes that were happening, if nothing else. Who was to say it wasn't kids doing all that, people's children? Brothers, cousins or whatever?

'My dad was a journalist.' Mitch almost said investigative journalist, which would have made him sound like someone from *The Daily Planet*. 'He was poking around into a few things. One of them was this Commune.'

'Why?' asked Leah.

Mitch shrugged. 'I was hoping you might be able to tell me.'

Both Daniel and his life partner looked blank. It was the latter who answered, perhaps the real power behind this throne? 'I can't think of a single reason. Unless it was to write about our unique lifestyle.'

'Unique?'

'We used to be like you people. Like you,' Daniel corrected himself, probably because it made them sound like some sort of separate species to the rest of humankind. 'Believe it or not, I used to be in telemarketing. A manager, no less.' Mitch could definitely believe it, now he'd said it; could picture Daniel in that setting more easily than he fitted into this one. 'My whole life was about deadlines, profits, hitting targets. I worked hard and I drove my workforce hard as well. Some of them even had breakdowns.' He shook his head. 'Can you imagine, being such a bas— Being someone who'd do that to another person?' Mitch's aunty wasn't

135

the only one who didn't like swearing then, though Daniel still had to fight against the habit. It meant there was probably a religious aspect to this Commune as well, didn't it? Or was that just a front? 'I ignored my health, my family, ignored Leah.' He looked to his left, smiling sadly; Leah smiled back. So she'd been his 'wife' back in the real world as well? 'Then we had a revelation. Were shown a better way. A more humble way.'

'The only way,' said Leah, before quickly adding, 'for us at least.'

'So you went from pension schemes and portfolios to chickens and goats,' said Mitch, barely able to conceal his smirk. A fad, nothing more – and they'd clearly managed to convince a bunch of other people to go along with them. Loyal followers by the looks of them. People who'd fight for their right to, as they'd called it, live their unique lives.

'If you like,' said Daniel, obviously not caring for the way Mitch had put it.

'Shunning society.'

'To be honest, society could do worse than take a leaf out of our book,' stated Leah. 'Maybe start again afresh.'

'Right, yeah. And you put all your money . . .' He looked behind the couple, meaning everyone present. 'Into this endeavour?'

'We obtained the land legally, yes,' said Leah.

'But not exactly welcomed with open arms, right? Into the lion's den, Daniel?' They weren't the only ones who knew a bit about religion.

'My namesake escaped that predicament because of his previous kindness, because he helped,' said the tanned man. 'We can only strive to be as kind as he was.'

'Okay, okay. So you don't know anything about my dad, about what might have happened to him?' What had Mitch been expecting, someone to confess right there and then to setting him alight? Maybe he'd stumbled on a weird ritual here at the Commune and paid the price for it?

Leah shook her head emphatically. 'No. Certainly not.'

'But we *are* sorry for your loss,' Daniel told him.

'Thanks.'

'We too have suffered losses of our own,' said the tanned man.

'Excuse me?'

'Oh, I merely meant that we know what it is like.'

'You've suffered . . . Are you talking about here? People going missing?' asked Mitch, remembering what it had said in those reports about people disappearing. The abductions. He had no idea what it might have to do with this, but saw no harm in following that line of enquiry.

They exchanged looks, but said nothing.

'Hey, if any of your Commune have gone missing since you've been here, you need to tell me,' Mitch said, stepping forwards. He noticed the wall of people behind the pair move forward as well, and stopped.

'I think perhaps you should look for answers to your questions somewhere else,' Leah told him.

'What, no tour of the place? Don't they usually do that in situations like this, to prove they've got nothing to hide.'

'Do they?' said Daniel, but didn't offer it as an option.

And wasn't this the part where Mitch would say he'd be back with a warrant to search the place, except he had no idea how he'd obtain one of those. 'Look, I'm just trying to get to the bottom of all this. Get things straightened out.' But maybe that was something they really didn't want him to do.

'Good day, Mitchel Prescott,' said Leah, extending her hand in the direction of the bike for him to leave.

'Yeah, yeah,' said Mitch, then waved a hand himself over to the side saying: 'Nice fire you've got going there, by the way. You guys like fire, do you?' A couple of the Commune members stepped forward threateningly, and Mitch turned away. 'Don't worry, I'm going, I'm going.' Then thought to himself:

But don't be surprised if I come back.

Chapter 15

'So he hasn't come back yet?'

What *was* this woman's problem? 'No, no he hasn't. But then again I wasn't really expecting him.' *And, to be honest,* she thought, *I'm not sure if I ever want to see him again!*

That wasn't true. That would never be true. Of course Lucy wanted to see Mitch, she missed him like crazy. Had been worried sick when she couldn't get hold of him on the phone, when no one had let her know what was happening. Not until that call the night before, another afterthought. A rushed and strained affair from a pub. A pub of all places! Where his aunty and uncle had taken him, spent the best part of the day with him. Wasn't there just a bit of her that was jealous about that? Not to mention jealous of whatever else might have been going on after he'd hung up – yes, bloody well hung up! – on her.

What, was she worried he was making time with some local girl, having a roll in the hay or something? Wasn't like she didn't trust Mitch, it was more the other girls. Girls from his past, who still lived where he came from. People who might understand him better?

Bullshit. Mitch was a city boy, had been for a long time now. Since he got out of that place, went on the road, and finally settled in Downstone. With her. (Settled *for* her?) A city girl. Lucy had been raised here when all was said and done, had been waiting for Mitch all her life, had known as soon as she saw him that he was the one.

Except he'd hung up on her, hadn't he? She didn't know whether to be worried again or furious. To be honest, it was a bit of both.

Probably shouldn't have said they needed some time apart then? She wished that she hadn't now, didn't even know where it had come from! One of those stupid things that come out when emotions were all over the shop. *Of course* she didn't want that, she wanted him here. With her. Knew all the reasons why he had to go, why she had to stay, but – like him – was torn.

At the end of the day, she loved him. He was special, what they had was special . . . wasn't it? To her anyway. She just wanted to look after him, and not in some stupid '50s housewife kind of way. Just wanted to, needed to. Her feelings ran so deep.

All day long she'd been staring at papers, sitting at their kitchen table trying to force the letters, the information about the new syllabus next term to sink in. She couldn't afford to waste days like this, just gazing at bullet points but not taking them in. It was one of the reasons she hadn't been able to go with him herself (to keep an eye on him, eh?) because she had duties here. Had to stay here. But that didn't mean she had to like it, imagining what might be going on all those miles away.

Who he might be with.

Jealous.

Whether he'd been in any more scraps. Jesus! Better than being on the front lines in a riot, at any rate. Her pacing the living room because she thought he might get stabbed or shot or—

You don't have to worry about that anymore, though, do you? Now he'd been sacked. All right, quit before he was sacked for bad behaviour. Didn't matter. That didn't matter now, did it?

Lucy had thought about calling up Helen and Vince, getting

more information about what was going on. They were the ones who'd been around, after all. Were . . . close to him. But she didn't want to give Mitch the idea she was checking up on him. Clingy, just sitting here thinking about him, when of course she was spending all her time . . . sitting here thinking about him.

Only, come the morning when she still hadn't heard anything, she'd done exactly that. Rung up the number she had for them, tried to get through, except an annoying electronic voice kept telling her they were having trouble connecting. No shit. Her and Mitch were having the worst time imaginable trying to connect. Although had it been any better when he'd been at home?

So, after not being able to get through, staring at those papers – the text swimming on the pages – caving and hitting the wine in the cupboard, the last thing she'd needed in the world was a call from Mitch's sister, Bella.

'D-Do you know when he'll be coming back?' she asked next.

'No. No, I don't.'

'When are you expecting him?'

Lucy closed her eyes and opened them again slowly. 'I'm not. Not yet. He hasn't told me, Bella. What's all this about anyway?'

'I really feel like I should speak to him. And I can't get through on the old house number. I-I just need to talk to him. It's important.'

'Oh, *now* it's important to speak to him, is it?' The words were out before Lucy could prevent them. The accusation out as well. You abandoned him. Again. Useless woman, Lucy really couldn't stand her.

'No, well I-I just . . . I'm sorry I couldn't go with him, if that's the . . .' *Your words, not mine*, thought Lucy. 'It's difficult for me, I—' She sighed down the line, or was she crying? 'I just have this horrible feeling, like he's in trouble or something. I mean, I can't really rely on it or anything, but I think that—'

'Bella, I don't know what to tell you. He's not here. I haven't heard from him in nearly a day.'

'And what did he say then?' she persisted. Cheeky bitch!

Lucy folded one arm over her chest as she replied. 'If you must know, they'd . . . he'd had a break-in at the house.'

Silence. Then, in a weak voice: 'A break-in?'

'That's what I said, yes. Unfortunately, we got cut off before he could tell me any more.' Lucy didn't want to give this woman any hint that Mitch might have hung up on her, that they might have argued. Again.

'A break-in,' Bella repeated. She sounded really strange now.

'Listen, I'm really busy today, getting ready for the new school year. Maybe you could—'

'Yes,' said Bella, her voice growing stronger. 'Yes, of course. Sorry to have troubled you, Lucy.' She hung up without even saying goodbye, leaving Lucy to gape at the phone, calling her all kinds of names under the sun. Wondering just what that woman's problem really was.

Chapter 16

What exactly was their problem, what were they hiding?

On the surface they seemed harmless enough, had just wanted to leave all the stresses of the rat race behind them, live a simpler life – so they said. Stay out of people's way, keep their heads down and live off the land. But something was going on behind the scenes, Mitch was certain of it. Maybe they were producing more than just vegetables there, a front for something criminal?

And that talk of losses? Had members of the Commune been taken? he wondered. If so, had they come back again or were they gone for good? Had they even bothered to report it to the police – and could Mitch really blame them if they hadn't? Wilkinson was absolutely useless.

So, what if they'd decided to take the law into their own hands? An eye for an eye, wasn't that what the Bible said? You take one of ours, we set fire to one of yours? Perhaps even his father. Didn't mean Thomas Prescott was involved in anything; just happened to be wandering around in the wrong place at the wrong time – not really knowing where the hell he was. Or had they mistaken that for snooping into their business, thought the old man might have seen something he hadn't? And he'd just bloody well confirmed as much to them, that his father was looking into their 'unique lifestyle'.

Had Mitch just put a target on his own back? Or maybe it had been members of the Commune who'd broken in the other night, ahead of all this, wanting to trash anything they thought his dad might have compiled on them? Indeed, now he thought about it, hadn't he spied a couple of members of that cult wearing caps? Not unusual, it *had* been quite sunny. Just a coincidence? Changed out of whatever dark clothes they'd been wearing – cream was no good for breaking and entering at night – but forgot the caps? Or just didn't give a shit?

Something fishy was going on here, so fishy Cat would be curling round his legs in anticipation of eating it. Mitch just didn't know what it was – yet. He didn't need that weird spider-sense of his, which seemed to be on a bit of a go-slow itself, to work out something was amiss.

Thinking about it all, as he sat on his bike on a quiet stretch of land and ate his sandwiches, reminded him about his next stop on this long day of his. The place he needed to visit afterwards, and indeed set off for on his bike once he'd washed the bread and cheese down with water from the fridge he'd also brought with him. But once he got a bit closer he realised he wouldn't be able to get to the exact spot on that particular mode of transportation. Not with all those trees.

So he'd been forced to leave it – against his better judgement – on the outskirts of the woods, at the treeline, tucked away behind the trunk of one and hidden as best as he could. Had to believe that in such an isolated spot no one would see it, let alone steal the thing. It'd probably be safer than round the back of his house actually, but Mitch had locked the motorbike up anyway just to be on the safe side. It was a habit he'd got into in the city anyway, and definitely needed to keep up with here in Green Acres. He wasn't about to lug the helmet in there with him, though, so had to leave that hanging from the handlebars.

The woods looked quite dark, so Mitch was glad that he'd brought along the small torch that lived on the back of the bike. The number of times he'd had to fix the machine, or even a tyre, while he'd been out in the middle of nowhere had taught him to be prepared. However, as he entered he found that it was lighter inside than it appeared – so he tucked the torch away in his jacket pocket for now.

Mitch hadn't brought a map, it would do him no good anyway – just show an area of woodland – but he was confident that he could find the spot he was looking for easily enough working from memory. Sadly, it wasn't long before he was completely lost, one bit of the woods looking very much like another around these parts.

Then he spotted it, something that marked the exact location. Wilkinson had at least done that, cordoned off the area with blue and white tape; wrapped around three or four trees, creating a perimeter of sorts. Mitch froze when he saw it, unable to approach for a little while. Needing to screw up his courage, knowing that he had to see the place where his dad had met his horrific end.

Slowly, carefully, he stepped up to that tape. Could see even as he did so, that someone had already broken it on the far side to gain entrance. He sighed, but it probably didn't matter. The police here seemed to think that CSI stood for Can't See It. As in, can't see it happening. As in, can't see the hand in front of their faces, more like, or what was going on under their noses! Which was why Mitch was out here in the first place, when he shouldn't have to be. God, there should be someone out in these woods guarding the crime scene at the very least, with an active investigation happening – and he used the term 'active' very loosely. Hadn't he himself spent hours in Portakabins guarding scenes just like these? Making sure no one mucked anything up, patrolling the area, and that was after the CSIs had done their jobs in the first place. To his knowledge nobody apart from Wilkinson, and perhaps Larson – the closest thing they had to forensics, the only person he'd met who had half a clue – had even been near the place.

Mitch took in the blackened area, almost a perfect circle, where his father must have stood. Where he'd dropped to his knees and keeled over, as the flames had lapped over his body.

Again, he saw that lump in the drawer Larson had shown him: the blacks, the pinks and reds. Identifiable only from its teeth, from dental records, because it had been in such a mess. Not even closing his eyes blotted out the images, only made them worse in fact. More vivid.

His eyes snapped open again, and he looked away. Looked around for the area where the tent must have been, though the flattened grass and undergrowth would probably have returned to normal by now. Mitch could only imagine what those campers had thought – waking up in the middle of the night to that sight, a human bonfire crackling and popping out there in the trees. He could only imagine because he hadn't even been allowed access to the statements they'd made, let alone knew who they were. Not that a civilian – which he guessed he was these days – should have access to such material, even if they were related to the victim. *Especially* if they were related. Mitch could also imagine the reaction from some of the detectives he'd worked with if they were told they had to keep relatives in the loop when they were trying to crack a case.

One guy he'd come across over the years, Channing his name was, Mitch remembered (too many teeth, speaking of dental records), liked to tell the story of how when he'd been working in Redmarket a distraught father had muscled his way into the investigation. 'Blasted nuisance he was. Sticking his oar in left, right, and centre! It was because of him I had to transfer in the first place, stirring things up.' It had been around the time they'd found all that corruption going on with the mayor so he'd made that connection – Mitch had been talking about it with Lucy before he left just the other . . .

Shit! *Lucy!*

It was only now that he thought about how he'd left things with her again. The way the phone had cut off and how she might think he'd hung up on her because of how things were with them. But then there'd been Denise, the fight, Sheldon, Denise again . . .

Instinctively, he reached for his mobile in his pocket then

caught himself, suddenly remembering that it had been stolen. Mitch leaned against one of the trees with the tape on it. He would have – should have – been in touch with her all the time under any other circumstances, though even when he'd had his phone there hadn't been as much contact as usual. Why was that?

Cut yourself some slack, your dad just died, you saw the body – no, don't got there again. You've been in not one, but two brawls (if you could even call the first one that). And she hadn't been here, that was her decision. Not that he wanted . . . Too busy, even though she could see how upset you were. Just like Bella, couldn't be bothered to—

He stopped. Mitch hadn't thought about his sister in ages either, had been meaning to give her a call as well. She didn't even really know the ins and outs of how their dad had met his end. In front of him, on this patch of grass, surrounded by these trees.

Bloody hell! Why was it down to him to keep everyone updated, that wasn't his job! Why did he have to keep reporting back to them, why weren't they here? Why wasn't she – Bella – here? With him, going through all this?

Why was the only friend he had in the universe right now small, black, furry, and wanted fish or meat all the time?

You don't choose cats, they choose you – hadn't he heard that somewhere? The feline in question had chosen his dad, then him. Something in the family line, perhaps? Some kind of—

Bella's 'gifts', being able to talk to the dead – if you believed in all that bollocks – his senses. Just a policeman's eye, putting together clues. Knowing when things were about to turn sour. *Common* sense. That's all. But trusting it. Being self-aware, knowing your surroundings. Knowing when—

When you were being watched.

Mitch looked up and across, caught sight of the figure which ducked behind a tree. There was a rustle of leaves off to his right and he twisted, saw another. Off to his left, a third. 'Hey!' he shouted, before he'd had a chance to even think about it.

About maybe having the element of surprise, though if they were following him that would have been out of the window straight off the bat, wouldn't it. Had they been following him since the Commune? Come *from* the Commune?

Mitch set off, aiming for the middle figure he'd seen. The one that was hiding behind the tree ahead of him. 'Hey! Hey you! Stop!' He almost said 'police', needed to keep reminding himself that he wasn't anymore; wasn't here in any kind of official capacity. But he could make a citizen's arrest, right? Like last night in the pub. Only what was he going to say these people were doing? Loitering with intent in the woods? He was doing that himself, for Christ's sake! Used to do it as a kid. And loitering to do what? Get the jump on him? There were three like the other night at his dad's place, dressed in dark clothes the same way. Were they wearing caps? Was it them? Members of the Commune, or not? Or was this Granger and his mates, like he'd imagined might be waiting for him outside the pub or on the walk back?

Needless to say, whoever this was didn't stop, and by the time he got to the tree in question the figure had vanished. Mitch whipped his head left, then right, searching for signs of the other two. Nothing.

A snap of bracken, and he saw the original one he'd been pursuing ahead of him. Saw he was wearing a hoodie rather than a cap. 'Gotcha,' Mitch whispered under his breath and set off again. He lost that guy minutes later, but picked up the scent of the one off to his left, changing course immediately to run after him. His ribs were still throbbing, but he put that out of his mind, concentrated on catching up with these men – catching at least one of them. Wasn't thinking clearly, or might have been worried about what they'd do to him if they turned suddenly and ganged up. Three against one, not great odds – especially when the 'one' in question was already injured. Another lucky punch to the side and he'd be on the floor, theirs for the taking.

Shit! Mitch lost sight of his target, but spotted the figure from the right briefly, running through the trees. Off he went again, cutting across diagonally, but all the time moving forward. Heading away from . . . being *drawn* away from the crime scene. Was that the intention in the first place?

In any event, all three of them seemed to be coming together. Heading for somewhere rather than away. Then Mitch saw where they were going, their destination all along. Of course! Mitch spotted the person he was trailing just as they slipped in through the entrance – the bars there prised away, allowing one person at a time to squeeze through. Had there been time for all three to go in there? Maybe, probably. One of them was inside, that was for damned sure! Which meant he had to follow; couldn't risk losing them. Losing a lead. No way of calling for anyone else, for help – his quarry would be deep inside and out the other end by the time he did that anyway – plus what help would the likes of Wilkinson possibly be?

No, he was on his own. Like he had been all along with this, not even the cat here to keep him company this time. His, what, familiar? Mitch was beginning to wish he did have bloody magical powers, like those cops in that book he read once. No, not the cops, the people they were after in that alternate universe.

Didn't matter, he *had* no such abilities.

Swallowing dryly, Mitch reached the entrance to the cave system. The one all those people had got lost in: the one that kid had got lost in when Mitch was younger, resulting in those bars, though they'd got rusty and weakened in the intervening time.

He had no choice but to go in. Disappear, as those figures had done.

Into the darkness.

One of the first things Mitch had done inside the cave was reach for his flashlight, switching it on.

He swung it around like a lightsabre, wishing it was such a weapon – but expecting at any moment to encounter Darth Vader blocking it with his red one. Yet there was nobody, not even the person he'd followed in here. Though when he cocked an ear, Mitch could hear the echo of footfalls in front of him.

'Hey!' he called out again, and now that echoed as well, rebounding off the walls and coming back at him tenfold. Unsurprisingly, there was no reply. He pressed on.

The walls of the cave were dry to begin with, but the further inside he went the wetter they became. No great shock, when you weren't that far from the lake and were going lower now, and still lower. Mitch hesitated, shivered – feeling the coolness as he descended.

Lower, like a descent into—

He shook his head, continued on, continued to swing that flashlight left and right. Seeing patterns on the cave walls, weird swirling shapes that might have been natural or man-made, he couldn't tell which. On he went, and down. There were even makeshift steps, almost unnoticeable at first, then more ridged. Deeper, more slippery.

Mitch lost track of time in there, just as he'd lost track of the figures he'd been hunting. There was no sign of them at all now, not even sounds ahead of him. Then he got to a fork in the caves, one tunnel going off to the right, one to the left. They could have split up, or all gone in one direction – he had no way of knowing.

'Fuck me!' shouted Mitch, frustrated, and once more the words came rushing back at him like wind. He had to choose, left or right.

Life or death.

He had no idea where that thought came from, but it didn't exactly set him at ease. Was one the way where he'd become lost and trapped, doomed to die in here? Nobody even knew he was *in* here! Now would be a really great time for those super senses that he didn't really call super senses to pipe up.

Left. Maybe. No, definitely . . . left. Mitch ploughed on, even when the tunnel seemed to zigzag. Something was telling him if he just kept going forwards at some point he'd hit the centre of the cave, and then—

He slipped, toppling sideways into the wall. Dropping his torch on the hard floor. It clanked, clacked, and then cut out. Utter darkness, like the darkness he'd stared into at the mouth of the cave – at the door of the cellar – and Mitch began to panic.

Why the hell had he followed those idiots inside? He didn't even know who they were, only that they'd run when he shouted at them. Who wouldn't, with a madman screaming for them to stop? Whoever they were, they clearly knew this place better than he did. Might even be able to find their way around in the dark. Which was more than he could.

He couldn't even find—

Wait! There it was. Scrabbling about on his hands and knees, Mitch was feeling around in front of him, and his fingertips had brushed the edges of the torch. But he'd knocked it away again, sent it sprawling out of reach. Mitch's breath was coming in quick gasps, his hands slapping the floor of the cave and feeling around for that torch again. It felt like he'd put his right hand in something soft and pulled a face, yanking it back out again.

Mitch heard a scratching sound, shuffling.

Jesus! What the hell was that? Something brushed against his shoulder – something passing him, behind him? He had no idea! Sweat was streaming down his face – it was now simultaneously hot and cold in the corridor – and it was running into his eyes, stinging them. Not that he could see a bloody thing anyway, but—

The torch. The fingers on his right hand found it again, snatched it up quickly this time (he learned from his mistakes, Mitch) and pressed the button.

Nothing happened. Still just blackness in front, to the sides, behind. What had touched his upper arm? Were there bats in here?

He kept flicking the button: on, off, didn't matter, it was completely broken by the 'looks' of things. Or maybe loose, the end where the bulb was might be, the bit you unscrew to change the batteries. He checked, and it was. So he screwed it up tightly, tried the button again and said a silent prayer, though he didn't really believe in all that.

Nothing happened. Again. The prayer had failed, maybe because he didn't really trust anything like that. Guardian angels or whatever. Didn't even believe in those voices Bella heard, guiding people. Telling them what they wanted to hear. Warning them.

She didn't warn you, did she? Didn't say, 'Whatever you do, don't go back home, don't leave the back door open, don't get into those fights.'

Don't. Go. Inside. The. Sodding. Cave!

Shouldn't have needed a warning, should have been common sense again really. Caves? Give that one a miss, because you might never find your way out again. Might end up starving, or—

Water. That was the main one, wasn't it? You could last a lot longer without food – and right now those cheese sandwiches were fighting back, threatening to come up again as his stomach tied itself in knots. *Can't afford to lose your lunch, because that's all you have inside you, and you'd also lose . . . Water.* Mitch would be dead in days without that, as opposed to weeks without sandwiches.

Crap, was he getting delirious already? Surely not? But then how long had it been, how much time had he actually spent in this place? Now it was pitch-black, and he couldn't see his watch, it was even harder to figure out the passage of time. Or where you were. *On the ground, on your knees. That's where! Get up. That's the first step, bats or no bats.*

Mitch grabbed the wall again, steadying himself as he rose. Leaning against it and feeling his way along. Breath coming in gasps, dread rising within him. He was still holding the torch, still living in hope that it might suddenly come on and illuminate the whole place, give him a fighting chance against whatever evil was lurking inside.

This must have been what it was like for the boy years ago. He could relate. That had been a lad, though, didn't know how to keep himself calm, level-headed. *And that's what you're doing, is it? Could've fooled me!* No matter how much we kid ourselves we've grown up, that we're adults, Mitch knew that inside everyone was a small child, especially when the trappings of society, as the Commune called it, were taken away. They didn't seem to care, might not care if they were here in this cave, in the dark. Which could offer a clue as to the identity of those—

Then he heard it again: scratching, scuffling. Ahead of him; ahead and down. His first instinct was to go in the opposite direction, but he knew he had to face this. Mitch felt along the wall, his only anchor in the black, moving towards the noise. Where he *thought* it was coming from; it was still hard to tell because of all that echoing. Twisting and turning, impossible to fathom where he was going or be able to find his way back.

Down and down. Down those steps in the . . . dream. Was he dreaming? Down those steps into the . . . cellar at his dad's, the one he'd always been afraid of because little kids always are. Cellars, they're another no-no, right? Cellars and—

Caves. Tunnels. Tunnels with flickering lights at the other end of them. The light at the end of the . . . Usually a train, in his experience. Something that hit you slap bang in the middle of your—

A space ahead. Flickering on the walls.

Walls that Mitch could now see were covered in paintings, etchings, the markings leading to them all along. Faded, because they'd clearly been here oh so long. Centuries maybe? Mitch was no expert on that kind of thing. No historian, no archaeologist. No Indiana Jones! Couldn't read the language, it made no sense to him, but the pictures, they made all the sense in the world. Figures, dark figures, hooded figures in a circle with what looked like a yellow light in the middle.

Made sense, not least because he could see the live version up ahead in that space. See those three . . . no, *more* than that, four, five, figures that were in this opening. They'd joined their friends. Standing, chanting, dressed in strange robes. The Commune's other more serious, more disturbing 'uniform'.

Holy mother of . . . Had he stumbled upon the crux of the entire thing? Why they had come here, come *back* here, what they were doing? What they were worshipping in these caves? Trying to summon something, destroy that society which could do with taking a leaf out of their book? Start again, start from scratch. And had his father stumbled onto it too, perhaps without even knowing it – or remembering it, given his condition? Stumbled onto it like Mitch was stumbling through these caves, and paid the ultimate price for it in the end?

The figures were moving now, holding hands and shifting side-ways, round and round – allowing Mitch a glimpse of what was in the centre, what had been causing all that flickering, illuminating the scene much better than even his torch had done. Causing the heat. Another fire, built from kindling and moss or whatever else they could find here in these tunnels. The figures were going faster and faster, round and round like they were participating in some kind of schoolyard game. The chanting was growing louder, words rebounding off the rock, almost deafening him.

He could feel a tugging at his sleeve, his wrist, but when he looked there was no one there. Just a tugging *feeling* then, a need to be closer, to observe more, but at the same time not wanting to be within a million miles of all this. Mitch inched nearer, as the figures speeded up. Round and round, the flames they surrounded flickering furiously, casting shadow upon shadow on—

The figures suddenly stopped. So suddenly Mitch almost let out a cry of surprise.

One of them threw something into the fire and it exploded, the flames rising and licking the roof of the space. Mitch could see shapes in those flames, images. Wasn't this how they used to tell the future in the olden days? Looking into the fire, seeing what was to be? Or was something coming through from somewhere?

No, ridiculous.

Mitch shook his head, squeezed his eyes shut. Waited,

waited . . . When he opened them again, all the hooded figures were staring in his direction.

He caught a word, or thought he did then. A command, if anything: *'Brothers!'*

Then they started to move, letting go of each other and racing towards him. Mitch rose, turned, finally obeying that urge to flee – and scrambled back up the way he'd come. If nothing else, he didn't fancy a full-on fight in such a confined space with all of those people.

He ran back up, into another tunnel, *desperate* for the darkness now. To be away from the light, from the fire, from the people who'd been dancing and chanting around it. Mitch was aware of footsteps behind him, chasing him. Scratching and shuffling, shuffling and scratching. If he reached the blackness then he stood a chance of hiding from them, especially as the tunnels were turning and twisting once more. Surely they couldn't know them *that* well?

He rounded corner after corner, the sounds behind him at last receding. But he turned one too many, unable to see where he was going.

An outcropping hit him squarely on the forehead and he reeled backwards. Reeled and toppled against a wall, collapsing down it. Sliding and slumping to the ground.

Then, as much as he tried to stay conscious, as much as he fought it . . .

The darkness engulfed him totally once more.

Chapter 17

Blackness.

He stared into it, and it stared back. Then became brighter and brighter, swirled around . . . as the milk was added.

'Are you all right?'

The question roused him, broke the mesmerizing spell. Mitch looked up and across, seeing his Aunty Helen sitting there on the chair opposite at the kitchen table. Leaning forward, having just added the white liquid to his tea. 'Hmm?' he said.

'I asked if you were all right?'

Was he all right? It was a simple enough question, but frighteningly complicated. The blackness of the tea had reminded him of when he had been in the cave, when he woke in the darkness of the tunnel. The adding of the milk like the light that was coming in from somewhere. Not flickering this time, not the flame, but a chink of fading sunlight. A way out of the caves, not that far away: a hole he'd subsequently crawled towards, then squeezed through, out into what was left of the daylight . . .

It felt like he was being born again.

He'd held a hand up to block out that light, even though the sun was on the wane. Just too bright for him after all that dimness, and it was only then that the torch still in his other hand came back on. He sighed, switched it off again and put it back in his pocket. The sunlight explained how long he'd been in the caves, though. Hours: until evening actually. Unless he'd lost days? His watch told him it was quarter to nine, but not what day. Not important; all that mattered was getting home – his dad's home. Although hadn't he begun to think about it as his by now? Probably not a good thing, seeing as his real home was in Downstone with—

Shit! Lucy . . .

No, think about figuring out where you are. Where your bike is. And, as he'd stood up on shaky legs, touching his forehead and feeling a lump just under the hairline – but no blood, which was always a good thing – he'd spotted the edge of the woods. Had somewhere to aim for at least, and he should really get moving before night dropped completely.

As luck would have it, locating the bike hadn't been that hard – tracing the edge of the woods until he got to the other side of it where he'd originally entered. There it was, behind the tree exactly as he'd left it. Mitch wasn't sure he should be riding it, there was a risk that he'd lose his balance, wobble and come off it again, injure himself further, but night had definitely fallen by this time and he really didn't want to be out here till morning.

So, he'd taken it slowly. Managed to get back around midnight, pulling up outside the house and wheeling the bike round to the rear. By the time he'd made it to the front door again, and was letting himself in, Cat was there to greet him. Probably wanted more food. *Give me a break*, he thought, *I haven't had time to get to the shops. I've been too busy being trapped in a cave.*

Then he felt bad when the animal dropped something on the floor beside him: a dead mouse it had caught and had been holding in its mouth. It nosed the corpse towards him, returning the favour for all the fish and meat he'd fed it in the time Mitch had been at the house. He laughed. 'Look that hungry, do I?' The moggy nuzzled against his leg. 'As much as I appreciate the gesture, I think I'll pass.' He nodded towards the mouse. 'But please, knock yourself out.'

Cat had meowed, then picked up the mouse and carried it away into the building. If Mitch wasn't bothered, then waste not want not. He'd locked the door behind him, then managed to stagger as far as the living room, where he collapsed onto the sofa and fell into another sleep. Probably shouldn't have done, weren't you supposed to stay awake after a bang on the head? But he figured he'd made it back, and he was so, so exhausted. If he didn't wake up again this time, he really wouldn't have minded.

Wake he did though, with yet another headache. It was gone 8 a.m., so at least he'd had a decent sleep. And no nightmares, which was good. No shadowy figures, no scraping and shuffling. That had been in the real world, though. Hadn't it?

The more Mitch thought about it, the more he wasn't sure *what* he'd seen in those caves. Had he dreamed the whole thing? Knocked his head earlier and thought he'd seen what he'd seen? No, that had come afterwards when he'd been trying to escape from the figures chasing him. A reversal of what had happened in the woods, following those people into the caves in the first place.

More painkillers had helped with the head, then a shower had woken him up a bit. Drying himself, he happened to catch his reflection in the bathroom mirror. The bruises on his shoulder, his side, another one just below his hairline – not far from where his stitches remained hidden – which he attempted to cover up by brushing what hair he had there over it. He felt worse than he ever had pulling riot duty, like he'd been in a war – or caught in the middle of one? A battle between the people of Green Acres and those up at the Commune. A battle his dad had been caught in the crossfire of as well?

After more toast for breakfast, and digging out what was possibly the last tin of anything the cat might be interested in from a cupboard, placing that on the saucer he'd been using to feed it, he'd returned to the living room and slumped back down

157

on the sofa. It was then that the books he'd brought in here from the study caught his eye, piled next to the fireplace where his aunty and uncle had left them when they'd been tidying.

Mitch reached over, grabbed the first – entitled *Inside the Greatest Cults of Our Time* – and started flicking through it. Made sense to do some more research, he told himself. Know thine enemy and all that, because Mitch realized he knew very little about them in general; the extent of his knowledge was some vague memory of an episode of *Boy Meets World* where Shawn was suckered into almost joining a thing called 'The Centre' by a guy called Mr Mack. After yesterday, Mitch was more certain than ever that the Commune was one of those. That it was, to all intents and purposes, a cult itself.

Kicking off with 'The Children of God', which was established in the 1960s by travelling preacher David Berg, Mitch read all about how they used 'free love' as an incentive to draw members into their orbit. Former members reported the frequent abuse of children – a woman called Verity Carter claimed she was abused from the age of four onwards – and though Berg died in 1994, the group renamed itself the 'Family of Love' and then 'The Family International' after being labelled a cult and investigated by the FBI and Interpol.

'Heaven's Gate' was another cult he hadn't heard of, which preached that the end of the world was coming, and that God was an alien. Mitch had paused when he read this, wondering whether his father's research into UFOs might have a connection. Did the Commune believe something similar? Were those losses they'd talked about just collateral damage, or were abductions considered to be something akin to a holy experience? The founders of Heaven's Gate – Marshall Applewhite and Bonnie Nettles – encouraged members to give away their money and cut contact with families, which also smacked of the Commune. However, Mitch had no real proof any people involved with this one had been forced to break contact with relations.

The end of the world also loomed large in another cult leader's philosophy, and this time it was a name Mitch *was* familiar with. Though, again, he wasn't conversant with all the history of it. Charles Manson talked about something called 'Helter Skelter' – inspired by the Beatles' song – after he'd recruited his own Family of disparate youngsters. An apocalyptic event he used as the catalyst to get them to go out and murder innocents, most notably pregnant actress Sharon Tate, yet he always claimed he gave no such orders. Controlling and manipulating them through that cult of personality once more . . .

Something that was totally embodied in Jim Jones, founder of the 'People's Temple'. Jones would use tricks and misdirection to convince members of his own order that he was some sort of superman. Mitch read one account where the guy had sent his own people out to fire guns at him filled with blanks, so he could say the bullets had had no effect on him. A media personality of sorts in the '60s, his reign ended in the 1970s when he retreated to create his own 'paradise' called Jonestown. Mitch knew without even reading it what had happened there, the phrase 'drinking the Kool-Aid' referring to mass suicides Jones initiated when the authorities were going in. To have that much power over people, you could get them to end their own lives . . . It was just incredible.

There were more, of course, which he read about in some of the other tomes: like 'Aum Shinrikyo', founded in the '80s by Shoko Asahara, which started out as spiritual and became increasingly violent as time went on – members of that one even drank Asahara's blood, Mitch was shocked to learn; 'Buddahfield', begun by failed actor Jaime Gomez, a leader – or mentor – who again, it was said, exploited his position for profit and sex; right up to examples such as David Koresh and his offshoot of the Seventh-day Adventists, who all met their end at Waco after a standoff with authorities; and Warren Jeffs, who became the leader of the FLD church, someone who – despite being arrested – was still in charge of thousands of followers. It was all scary stuff and had aspects in common. Mitch had to wonder just how many of the smaller cults everywhere escaped attention, until it was too late.

Had Daniel struck him as someone charismatic who could inspire such loyalty? He must have had something going for him, to get people to give up on their lives, their savings, to come here to Green Acres and live that 'unique' life they'd talked about. Or was Leah the real brains behind everything, the true personality they'd rallied behind? Two – a couple – being stronger than one and all that, though who knows if their relationship was monogamous, or if relationships at the Commune were fluid. Everyone could be at it with everyone else, for all Mitch knew.

He'd been working his way through these books when a sudden knock at the door made him start. Mitch had got up, going over to the window and peeking out to see who it was – catching sight of his aunty stepping back, carrying something under a tea towel. It was exactly what they'd done when Mitch called at their house for the first time and there'd been no response to his rap at the door. Being careful, making sure it was friend rather than foe. An atmosphere of unease had descended on peaceful Green Acres since he'd been away, and a lot of that was probably to do with the presence of the Commune. Now Mitch understood perfectly how threatened people felt.

Making his way to the door, he'd opened it and the short woman had smiled. 'Hello love, how are you today?'

'I'm—' he started to say, then was interrupted by Cat speeding out through the gap, as if he'd been waiting for just such an opportunity to escape. Probably wanting to go off and hunt more prey.

Helen watched as it shot past her, pulling a face. He thought for a moment she was going to attempt a kick, but she didn't. For one thing it was moving too swiftly. 'Is that horrendous thing still hanging around?' she asked.

Mitch said nothing. He liked it hanging around. Instead, he invited the woman in, who explained she'd brought round a stew for lunch. 'I doubt you're looking after yourself properly,' she said, and was it his imagination or was she trying to sniff his breath again? Checking to see if he'd been drinking? 'I'll stick it in a pan to warm up, shall I?'

'Thanks,' he'd said, closing the door and trailing behind her – as she was already making her way through to the kitchen, rattling around in a cupboard next to the cooker for a pan to put on the stove.

It was as she turned to face him again that she pointed to his forehead. 'That from the other night, is it? I heard about your run-in with Cam Granger.'

Of course you did, he thought. 'No, no. Just an accident. A bump on the head.'

Her eyes narrowed as if she didn't believe him, and even if she did she probably thought he'd been soused again when he whacked it. 'Making friends and influencing people, eh?' said Helen after he rejected her offer to take a look at it, returning instead to the incident in the pub.

Mitch gave a small laugh. 'Something like that, yeah. Actually, I might have landed a job out of it. Or potentially a job.'

'Oh?' she asked.

'Security for Neil Sheldon,' he informed her, thinking she'd at least be glad he was working towards getting another gig. But she pulled a face worse than the one when she'd spotted the cat.

'Oh, *him*. The property fellow.'

'The developer, yeah.'

Her frown deepened. 'Hmm,' was all she said.

'I didn't say I was going to take it. Just that it was offered.' He held his hands out in a gesture of placation. 'I know how you guys feel about him. How most of the people here feel. I certainly know how that nutter of a farmer feels.'

'Well, it's only because Sheldon wants to exploit the area. Granger might not express his feelings in the correct way, but he speaks for a lot of us who have homes here.'

They left it at that, Helen busying herself with the stew – but making him his first tea of many before he could even sit down. Seriously, what was it with the tea? The British liked a cuppa, were known for it, but if she could, Mitch had a feeling his Aunty Helen would have it on a drip attached to her arm. Personally, it just made his bladder feel like bursting.

She served him up the stew on a plate, and he had to admit it was delicious. 'It'll save you having to go back into The Plough today,' she told him. Part of her plot to keep him away from the booze, regardless of the fact he'd been on the brandy two nights on the trot in this very house.

'You not joining me?' he asked her.

She patted her stomach. 'I already ate, Mitchel. Just wanted to make sure *you* did. Keep your strength up.' When he was finished, she'd taken the plate and popped it in the sink. Returning with yet another tea. That's when he'd stared into the blackness, when he'd been reminded of yesterday, at the point the milk was added. 'I asked if you were all right?' Helen repeated, once she realized he'd zoned out.

'Oh, right. Yeah, I'm fine.' He rubbed his eyes. 'Just tired, I guess,' Mitchel said, but she caught the lie.

'Events like those of late take it out of a person, whether they're sleeping well or not,' she informed him. 'I actually called around yesterday, brought lunch then – but you were out.'

'Yeah, I decided to go for a ride.' Technically not a false-hood, and as plugged into the Green Acres Matrix as she was, he very much doubted she would have heard about his visit to the Commune, or his exploits in the cave. Which may or may not have been real.

'Just you be careful, young Mitchel,' she replied, wagging her finger. He thought she might be talking about the drink again, but Aunty Helen had something else on her mind. 'There are some things that are better off left alone.'

It was his turn to pull a face. 'What do you mean?'

162

'Too much like your father, you are.'

'In what way?' he asked, but she wouldn't answer him. 'I want to know what happened to him, what's wrong with that? I seem to be the only one who gives a s—' She looked at him sideways, as if daring him to say it: 'Stuff.'

'That's not true at all,' Helen said. 'We all care.'

'Then why is nobody doing anything? Not even the local cops are looking into this, and by the time Wilkinson gets round to it I'll probably be dead too.'

'What a thing to say! And with your birthday just round the corner!'

'I . . .' Mitch realized how that sounded, how it had come out all wrong. 'I just mean I'll have died of old age, Aunty Helen. We all probably will! It'll be my hundredth birthday before we get any answers.' It was one of the reasons he hadn't bothered reporting what had happened in the woods, in the cave system.

She let out a long sigh. 'I know you're used to a different pace of life, you've lived so long in the city. But things work differently here.'

'They either work really slowly or not at all. There's stuff going on here that needs investigating or—'

'And it will be, Mitchel. In the correct manner.'

He didn't even know what that meant. The correct manner to him would be to get a DI or a DS here and on the case, someone who spoke the same language he did and at something approaching the same speed. 'Like what happened to mum?' he said then. 'How all that got cleared up?'

Helen winced, her eye twitching. The death of her sister, so long ago, was obviously still a sore point for her. 'There was nothing to *clear* up. Your mother died in a road accident.'

Mitch shook his head. He knew that, had no idea where the last thing he'd said had come from. His mum had been out walking, was hit by a car that was out of control; ploughed her right into a tree. Both her and the guy driving the vehicle – who'd been found to be drinking, which explained some of his aunty's hatred for it – had died. An accident, pure and simple. 'I know. I'm sorry.'

'That's why you're like him, Mitchel. Looking for conspiracies everywhere. Looking at the world a certain way.'

He hung his head. 'I dunno, I just feel . . . I can't help feeling cheated, y'know? She was my *mum*.'

Helen reached out and placed a hand on his arm, on his wrist. For a second he almost pulled away, recalling the way he'd been tugged down into that space where the hooded figures were. Then he relaxed. 'And she was my sister. She might have been a little . . .'

'What?' he asked, looking up. Helen wouldn't respond. 'Please. I never really knew her properly, Aunty. I only have vague memories. Like how she smelled, of lavender. Her smile. It was a bit like yours, actually. I think.'

Helen gave him one of those smiles now. Opened her mouth to speak, then closed it again.

'Please,' he begged her.

'She could be a little . . . odd,' Helen confessed.

'How do you mean?'

'Quirky, you know. Said she had . . . feelings about things sometimes before they happened, or what have you.' *Was his aunty telling him that his mother had her own version of his spider-sense?* thought Mitch. Had her own version of a copper's intuition? 'Of course it was all nonsense, like what your sister claims she can do. But we loved her all the same.'

No, he couldn't see that going down well with Helen at all. Scientific Helen, who also trusted in religion and all that – the dichotomy – who you couldn't swear in front of.

'So, you didn't believe her?'

'How could I? It didn't stop her death, did it? If she could . . . feel things about what was going to happen, wouldn't she have got out of the way of that car? Seen it coming before it hit her? Before it killed her? Maybe if she'd actually had that kind of foresight, she'd still be with us, Mitchel.' Helen began sobbing, the passing of her sister still quite raw for her, he guessed, regardless of how long ago it was. Yet Mitch still couldn't help feeling jealous, because this woman had known his mother, had spent time with her. *Grown up* with her, here in Green Acres. She'd known her in a way he couldn't possibly hope to.

'Yeah, I suppose,' said Mitch. He patted the hand that was still on his arm. 'It's okay. It'll be all right.'

Helen nodded, looked up at him with wet eyes. 'So much pain, so much tragedy. Not just back then, but in the world today. I don't have to tell you though, you've seen it for yourself.'

He had, and there was. Mitch decided to change tack again, or rather bring it back to what he'd been talking about before. 'My dad,' he started.

'Yes?'

'He was looking into a few things before he died.'

'Oh Mitch, he wasn't in his right mind. We've told you that.'

'Yeah, I know what you said – but actually some of it's quite interesting. They connect a few dots. Those Commune people, for example. Cults.'

Helen pulled her hand out from under his and jabbed a finger at him. 'Now, you stay away from those people. They're dangerous.' It was more or less what Wilkinson had said.

'In what way?' Mitch asked, though he had a pretty good idea himself.

'Just stay away from them, that's all. If you know what's good for you!'

'Was that what you said to my father? And he ignored you?'

'There are things that you don't . . .' Helen shook her head.

'So tell me! You and Uncle Vince, even that farmer Granger. You're all so worried about strangers coming in that—'

'The strangers are already *here*,' she butted in. 'That's half the problem. It's what's causing all this trouble.' She waved a hand around as if to say that everything that was wrong in the region was down to the new arrivals, and the potential ones to come.

'Everyone used to know everybody else here. It's how it's worked for centuries. The last time this happened, let's just say it didn't end very well.'

'The last time . . . Are you talking about all that black magic stuff in the past? Witches? That was something else dad seemed to be doing research on.' Was his aunty trying to draw a comparison between those people up at the Commune and the dark arts? Why not? Mitch thought to himself. How many cults were also linked to the occult? Hadn't he just seen people in robes performing some kind of Satanic ritual in those caves? And although he had no actual proof it was the Commune, it was a pretty safe bet.

'*Hello, brother . . .*'

'*Brothers!*'

Helen's face crinkled up, the tears from before all but dried. 'They were a plague on the area, Mitchel. If history teaches us nothing else, it's that.'

'So they deserved to be rounded up and killed, back then? Drowned in the lake or burned at the stake?'

'No,' she replied. 'No, of course not! They certainly didn't deserve that.'

'But the people of Green Acres were glad when they were wiped out, right? That the witchfinders came in and got rid of them all?'

'They were different times, Mitchel. That's all.'

Helen said nothing after that. What was there to say? She hadn't been around back then, didn't know *how* her ancestors had felt about the whole thing. Probably didn't even care, it was so long ago as she said. Just equated more strangers coming into the region with that terrible period in history. But maybe his father, with all his conspiracies and sticking his nose into places he really shouldn't have, had been on to something. His aunty looked at her watch. 'My, is that the time? I really should be making tracks. Vince will be wondering where I've got to.' She rose and he stood up as well. 'It's all right, lad. I can see myself out.'

She opened her arms wide, giving him another one of those

166

crippling bear hugs, before heading out into the hallway, calling back over her shoulder: 'You just take care, young Mitch. All right?'

Are you all right?

Mitch had been starting to wonder, but the chat had actually done him quite a bit of good, in more ways than one. He was beginning to get some kind of handle on things, was starting to see the shape of this particular mystery; the edges of it at least. All that remained was to solve it.

To finally see the light, where before there had only been blackness.

Chapter 18

Laying there, in the darkness, she wished she'd taken him up on his offer.

Should have gone straight away after he'd made it, when they'd been walking along the beach. The day after she'd seen them. More monsters in Bella's 'living room'. Not just the one that night, but three or more. It wasn't as if the space was that big anyway, not enough to accommodate too many of them. But the point was they shouldn't have been there in the first place, in her home!

Her sanctuary.

Yet there they'd been, large as life. Standing there having ransacked the place apparently, her belongings everywhere. Standing and – as she'd come out of her bedroom again, after hearing the noises: the bangings, shuffling, the creaking – looking over at her as if there *was* just one of them. Thinking with one brain, acting as if with one body. But more this time: the first shadow monster had brought friends.

And it had been the same story again, rushing at her, pushing her back, exiting the caravan and leaving it in that state. Leaving her in such a state that she hadn't been able to get back to sleep, hadn't even tried. Who the hell were these people plaguing her? What did they want? To drive her crazy?

The headaches were already doing that on their own, so painful at times they almost felled her more effectively than someone coming at her, attacking her.

Bella should have reported it this time, should have let Ashley Watts report the first incident – when there had just been the one intruder – but instead she'd left it. Then, when he'd come to check up on her, she'd hid what had happened. Not let him come into the caravan and see the mess, though it was obvious what a mess *she* was personally. Whatever he must have thought of her, probably that all this *had* succeeded in driving her crackers. But still he'd offered, towards the end of that walk, could see the fix she was in.

Had offered her a bed if she wanted one, at his place. Held up his hands quickly before she got the wrong idea. 'I'll take the couch. No funny business, honest.'

That had made Bella laugh, at a time when she couldn't imagine ever laughing again. She knew his intentions were honourable, Ashley was a good man. She'd known that for a long time now. It was the reason she'd asked for him in the first place at Golden Sands police station. However, as much as she'd appreciated the offer of a place to stay, she couldn't accept it. Felt that she needed to stay in her caravan, to, what, protect it? Guard it against the monsters in case they returned – and for some reason she felt that this was almost inevitable – not that she'd been any good at that so far.

If only she knew what all this was about, because it felt pretty personal. Like they were taking revenge for something, like it was connected to something in the past. Had she pissed someone off? *Let's face it*, Bella had said to herself when she got back to the caravan site after saying goodbye to Watts and gearing herself up to tidy the place, *you've pissed a lot of folk off in your time*. Most unintentionally, like Robyn Adams – the woman Ashley was so hung up on – but some definitely on purpose. Bella liked to think she was a good person, she did her best to help people after all, but she was still only human. Yet, as hard as she searched her memories, she couldn't think of anyone she'd hurt so much that they'd want to toy with her like this. So maybe it was somebody she'd accidentally hurt?

Or perhaps it was just someone who didn't like what she did, who she was? Some people didn't need much more reason than that for violence today, sadly.

Did it really matter? The consequences were the same. The lack of sleep, sitting and waiting to see if they'd come back – which they didn't that night, thankfully – the loss of days as she wandered around the place like some kind of zombie. The nightmares when exhaustion finally claimed her, the messages her mind was trying to relay about the monsters. There'd been more than one from the start in the dream, hadn't there, so had it really been so surprising when she'd seen them in reality? Prophetic somehow.

And when she closed her eyes, they were there again. Standing round in a circle, mumbling, chanting something in a language she couldn't understand – blocking out the departed who were attempting to get through to her.

Hooded figures in the dream, standing around that flickering flame. Then the movement, the shuffling – the creaking – louder and louder, as they danced (was it dancing? It looked like dancing) around that fire. Waking up at the last minute, drenched in sweat – staring into the darkness and wishing that she wasn't here dealing with all this on her own, that she'd gone to stay with Ashley when he'd made his kind offer.

Especially tonight, when Bella had heard the noises again out in her caravan. Except when she'd scrambled out of bed this time, snatching up the cricket bat she'd bought for protection – she'd bloody well defend this place if it killed her! – and raced out into the main section of the van, there had been nobody there.

Blinking, Bella had looked left and right, even behind her, in case someone had hidden in the loo; ready with that bat to

170

clobber them this time. There was nobody there, nothing. Just her imagination, definitely a carry-over from the nightmare tonight.

It was only as she'd looked up and faced forward again that she'd spotted it. The curtains she'd closed as night had fallen, the ones that ringed the bay window at the other end of the caravan, they were . . . glowing.

No, not glowing. Flickering.

Bella rubbed her eyes with her free hand, the one not currently holding her makeshift weapon, but the flickering didn't go away. Not even a little bit. If anything, it was brighter. Couldn't be the candles she'd lit in there when it got dark, she'd definitely blown all those out.

She'd made her way through the kitchen, past the breakfast table, towards the sofa that hugged the semi-circle just below the bay windows. Bella skirted around the small coffee table in front, kneeling on the padded cushions, free hand out to pull the curtains. Opening a tear in them at any rate, so she could see what was causing the—

But then she saw exactly what it was, and her mouth dropped open. Simultaneously, she dropped the bat, which bounced off the sofa and crashed into the coffee table.

She saw the light in the darkness. Then wished more than anything in the world that Ashley Watts was present, or that she was with the policeman in his place, away from here.

That she'd taken him up on his offer.

Chapter 19

It had come through the window only minutes after he'd returned.

Mitch had barely had time to place the leftovers he'd brought back with him on the floor for Cat when it happened. More trouble!

The crashing, banging, the smashing.

It had been a decent evening up to that point, mostly. Mitch had done a bit more reading, then – remembering about Lucy again, and how he still hadn't spoken to her since getting cut off – he'd wandered back over to The Plough. The one place he knew for sure had a phone he could use. He didn't want to pester the neighbour anymore, and figured his aunty had probably had enough of him that day, so really it was the only option, seeing as he still hadn't spotted a phone box in the village itself.

So off he'd gone to the pub. It was still only afternoon, but Denise was already behind the bar – a shift change, which meant she wouldn't be on that evening probably – and she greeted him with one of her warm smiles. 'Hello stranger,' she'd said and he couldn't help flinching at that title, given the conversation with his aunty. But, he supposed, he was a stranger here regardless of whether he'd been born in Green Acres. That wasn't what Denise was talking about, though. 'Thought we might have seen you yesterday?' Was that how it worked, you spent a night in here and it suddenly became your local? Somewhere you had to frequent every day? Having said that, Mitch had definitely developed a bit of a liking for the old Traditional real ale.

As if reading his mind, Denise was already pouring a pint even as he stepped up to the counter. 'Oh, hey. Yeah. I went out yesterday.'

'Don't blame you. Lovely weather, and they reckon it's only going to get hotter.'

He didn't know why he felt he had to explain he'd been anywhere, but for some reason he did – and he thought for a moment she might have asked what he was doing last night. Like his aunty, her eyes kept flitting from his face to the bruise under his hairline.

As it was, she asked, 'You all right?'

Mitch gave an uncertain nod. It wasn't the first time he'd been asked that day, and he still wasn't really sure he was. Felt better because he had a few more leads to go on in the case – was it really wrong he was beginning to think of what happened as *his* case? Wasn't it dangerous to be that closely involved having known the victim? Having been related to him? They warned you about that in training; how it can cloud your judgement. How he was suddenly starting to think about 'outsiders' and 'strangers' himself, judging them. Who else was going to dig into this, though, if he didn't?

But how did he actually feel? He turned the question back on Denise: 'You?'

'Bored. At a loose end,' she told him as she lifted the pint and put it on the bar, dark liquid slopping over the sides. 'Nothing new there, mind you.' She looked him in the eyes, but he glanced away. Mitch knew what she was driving at, that she could use some company: the company of an old friend, perhaps. But he had a girlfriend at home – hoped he still had a girlfriend – and that was the real reason he'd come here in the first place.

'Would you excuse me for a sec?' he said. 'I just need to . . .' Mitch pointed at the payphone. Again, he had absolutely no idea why he was explaining himself to the barmaid. There was no real reason to, except to be polite.

''Course, sweetheart. I'll still be here when you get back.' Denise winked at him this time, another practised move, which did nothing to make him feel any more comfortable. Wouldn't exactly put him at his ease when he was talking to Lucy.

In the end he hadn't been able to get hold of her anyway, couldn't get an answer at the flat or on her mobile, so he'd just left an apologetic and somewhat garbled message, fuelled by guilt. There was nothing else he could do really, couldn't give her a number to reach him. Definitely not this one, the last thing he needed was Denise taking messages for him here. He'd be lucky if Lucy ever spoke to him again.

It was as he replaced the receiver that his sister had flashed through his mind, and he decided to try her at the hotel. Was this the right day for her 'act'? He had no idea, but maybe he'd catch her – or at the very least could leave her a message. He was informed that she'd cried off her stage show this week, though. Wasn't feeling very well, apparently. Mitch had told the lady at reception to pass on his best (it was all he could think of at the time; love didn't sound right) and to say the next time she saw or spoke to her that he hoped she was feeling better.

His big sister, and they felt about as close as those strangers his aunty and Denise had mentioned. He couldn't help thinking now that Bella should have come. Then he wouldn't be tackling all this on his own, would have backup of sorts. Then again, did he really want her anywhere near this? Mitch forgot sometimes that there was a world outside of the police and cases and tracking down bad guys. Bella hadn't been exposed to any of that, as far as he knew. Probably for the best she was all the way over in Golden Sands right now.

'You get through?' asked Denise as he'd sloped back to the

bar with his drink. Mitch shook his head, then nodded. Denise laughed; it was a pretty laugh, he had to admit. A laugh he was remembering more fondly with each passing moment. 'Which is it?'

Mitch laughed himself. 'I got through but they weren't around.'

'Ah, right.'

'My sister,' he clarified. *Why the hell are you telling this woman?* he asked himself. But more importantly, why wasn't he telling her about Lucy? The first call he'd placed? 'You remember her? Bella?'

Denise stuck out her bottom lip, dredging her memory. 'She was older than us, wasn't she?'

'That's right. Not sure if she'd gone by the time we . . .'

She smiled again, at the thought of her and Mitch back in school. 'I can't remember meeting her, so probably.'

'Bella didn't really hang around long after she could get out of here.'

'In some ways I can't really blame her,' said Denise. 'What's she up to these days?'

Mitch opened his mouth to answer, but didn't really want to get into the whole psychic thing. It rubbed a lot of people up the wrong way, and around here was tantamount to being a leper if his aunty was anything to go by. 'She's in the entertainment business,' Mitch said finally, supping his beer.

Denise beamed, then leaned her elbows on the bar and put her head in her hands. 'Oh, really? That's something I always wanted to get into myself. I did a bit of singing and dancing when I was younger. Amateur stuff, but I did wonder if I could have taken it further. Acting maybe.' She stood up again, batting the notion away with a hand. 'What line is she in: TV, film?'

'S-Stage mainly,' replied Mitch. He had no idea why that made him so nervous, he wasn't exactly lying to Denise – just withholding some of the information. *And what about your girlfriend, Mitch? What does she do? Teaches lessons. Might teach you one if she finds out about these cosy chats with your ex!*

Hardly an ex, but he doubted Lucy would see it that way.

'Nice. Acting herself, or . . . ?'

'Magic tricks,' said Mitch. Again, not a fib as such. It was what some people called what she did.

'Rabbits out of hats and whatnot?' asked Denise.

'Something like that. She's in Golden Sands.'

'Ooh, lovely.' Denise looked about her, as if she was about to impart some government secret or something. 'I can't remember the last time I had a proper holiday, at the coast or wherever. And I've never been abroad.'

'What, never?' Mitch drank more of the Traditional. It was going down so nicely he'd almost finished his first. Should probably pace himself, needed to keep a clearer head.

'Naw. Well, you don't really, do you? Not when you live around here.'

He'd forgotten how the people at Green Acres felt about venturing outside of their little bubble, their comfort zone; how they passed that on to their kids. Fear of those strangers, outsiders. It extended to going out amongst them. Only his dad had never really been like that, encouraged his curiosity if anything. Wanted Mitch to learn about the world, travel. There had never been any attempt to stop him from doing that. But there was also the fact they lived in some of the most beautiful surroundings on the planet. What location could possibly measure up? It explained why they didn't want any of it to be sold off, to be ruined. Might be one of the few spots on Earth that hadn't been messed about with, beyond the settlement that had always been here – according to the keepers of those history books. The people who'd come down from those caves and built the very first dwellings.

Denise was already pulling him another pint of Traditional before he'd even asked for it, and before he had time to protest. She was talking about how she'd be finishing up before too long that evening. Mitch had nodded then asked if it was okay to use the pool table for a bit. 'Sure,' said Denise, looking crestfallen.

176

She'd clearly been waiting for him to ask her out or something. That way lay disaster, and Mitch knew it. He decided instead to spend a bit of the change he had left from the phone calls knocking the balls around that table. It was how he spent some of his free time with Vihaan and Tammy after work when—

Tammy.

He realized this was the first time he'd thought about her in days. Lucy and Bella weren't the only ones he'd been neglecting since he'd been here, and he thought then about how Green Acres had a tendency to do that. How time passed differently here and did a number on your priorities. She'd understand, he told himself. Tammy would be the first one to say he needed to get to the bottom of what was happening with his dad, the Commune, and whatever else was going on linked to this shitstorm.

'Seriously, what's got into you?'

It didn't stop him wondering how his friend was, though. Wondering if she was still hooked up to all those wires in that room? More than likely. He thought about going back over to the phone again to ring the hospital up, but spotted a couple of guys waiting for the pool table and wasn't ready to relinquish it quite yet. By the time he'd played a few more games and was fed up with it, Denise had wandered over to see if he wanted another drink – on her this time.

Mitch was just about to decline, when he was saved from that particular awkward conversation by another person joining them. Councillor Nuttall, who'd appeared behind them, leaning on his stick. Mitch had no idea whether he'd just come in, or had been in the pub a while and only just spotted him. Either way, the older man was offering to get the drinks in and before Mitch could say another word Denise had withdrawn to fetch them and put it on the older man's tab.

'How d'you like this heat?'

Mitch gave a half-shrug; it wasn't something he'd thought about all that much.

'Hottest day of the year coming up, so they say,' Nuttall informed him. 'Hottest for some time.' The Brits and their weather.

It never rains . . .

'Come on, come and sit with me, lad,' said the man. 'I never got a chance to thank you properly the other night for stepping in when, well, you know.'

'I do,' said Mitch, following the limping fellow to a booth. 'But it's fine. Happy to help.'

Nuttall was staring now and smiled when he was caught doing it. 'Ah, I'm sorry, but you really do look like him. Tommy, I mean. Especially now you've grown up a bit.' Mitch waited for the man to sit, which he did with a bit of trouble. That hip he'd been talking about the other night was obviously causing him a great deal of pain judging from the air he sucked in as he slid down onto the seat. 'Bloody thing,' said the man. 'Never get old, son. It's definitely no fun.'

'I'm not planning on it anytime soon, trust me.' Regardless of the fact he had another birthday coming up, which he kept getting reminded about.

'Not in any rush, I get you.'

'So, you knew my dad well then?' asked Mitch when they were both settled in the booth and Nuttall had leaned his stick up beside him. 'I don't really remember—'

'Oh aye.'

Of course he did, they both lived here in Green Acres for a start – but Mitch had to say he was struggling to recall Nuttall being around much. Wasn't just the politics; when you were the age him and Denise had been, anyone not related to you and over twenty-one was considered ancient, and therefore not really relevant. How stupid, how arrogant that sounded to him now. 'Then you know what happened to him.'

'Oh yes,' said Nuttall, but stopped before the requisite 'nasty business' comment that always seemed to follow. If it was such a nasty business, then why wasn't it being investigated properly?

Why weren't crime squads from the nearby town or city all over it like a rash? A man burned to death in the woods, not a stone's throw from a bunch of cultists who'd set up camp and might well be conducting secret rituals in the nearby caves! It was something he considered asking the councillor, but Mitch needed to be more subtle than that.

'I'm curious, what—' said Mitch, but didn't get to finish as Denise came over to plant two pints of Traditional in front of them.

'There you go, sir.'

'Thanks, love,' said Nuttall. 'Much appreciated.' She hung about for a minute – was she expecting an invitation to join them? Had she even finished her shift yet? – but when Nuttall gave her a 'that will be all' kind of look, she wandered off again. 'Cheers!' said Nuttall, holding his glass up for Mitch to chink. Which he did, thanking him for the drink at the same time. He would take this one slow, he'd decided.

'You were saying,' Nuttall prompted, which was probably a good thing as Mitch had forgotten he'd even started asking him anything. That Traditional crept up on you. *Definitely* take it more slowly.

'Right, yeah. That business the other night with Granger and Sheldon.'

Nuttall gave a bitter laugh. 'That's a whole pile of manure you might not want to get into.'

'Mr Sheldon wants to build some properties in the area, as I understand it?' said Mitch.

'You understand correctly. But it'll never happen.'

'Oh?'

Nuttall took a draught of his pint, sitting back in the booth. 'Just because he's got a foothold in the area, because he had relatives here way back in the day and scooped one of the nicer cottages on the fringes of the village itself, Neil thinks that gives him the right to come and shout the odds. In here and in the

179

council meetings.' The thin man shook his head curtly. In spite of the fact he'd tried to keep the peace the other night, that he'd even apologized to Sheldon for the ruckus, Nuttall came down on the same side of the fence as Granger, as Mitch's aunty and uncle. Progress, change and – when you got right down to it, money – could go and whistle. 'He'll get bored when things don't go the way he wants.'

'I'm not sure I understand, you're on the council and you *don't* want investment in the area?'

'Not his kind,' said Nuttall. 'Not if it means that things have to change beyond all recognition.'

Mitch took a sip of his pint, then wiped away the froth with the back of his hand. 'Things can't stay the same forever though, surely?'

'They have so far, more or less,' stated Nuttall, and actually Mitch found he couldn't really contradict that. Green Acres had stayed pretty much the same for as long as anyone could remember. 'Anyroad, what's so fantastic about change?' It wasn't something you'd expect a politician to say, but then again, the system here was more like a little kingdom in its own right, to be ruled as they saw fit with as little outside interference as possible. 'You've been out there in the world, my boy. Which would you say is better?'

Mitch thought then about the unrest in Downstone, the rioting in the streets he'd been in the middle of. The rioting that had resulted in Tammy – who he really did need to check up on – being in that coma in the first place. 'I'm not saying either way is better,' offered Mitch. 'Just that you can't hold back the tide.'

Nuttall nodded, then shrugged. 'Perhaps. Doesn't mean you can't try. Your dad, rest his soul, if he was sitting here, would have said the same thing.'

'My dad . . . ?' Was Nuttall saying that his father was as resistant to change and progress as the rest of them here? It was at odds with what Mitch knew about him, but apparently he was coming out with all sorts towards the end. Didn't know what planet he was on. Maybe even knew something that had got him killed? 'How about those people up at the Commune? You seem to share some of their views about a simpler life.'

Nuttall's lip curled. Mitch thought for a second the man was going to spit on the floor. 'Hardly. Those lunatics are nothing like the good people of Green Acres. They should never have come here.'

Now they were getting to it, the animosity Nuttall had for them was all too palpable, the same as his own family. Not for the first time, Mitch wondered whether his father had got caught in the crossfire of some conflict, between the villagers and the Commune. Whether Mitch should be asking if he could join whatever army was fighting them. 'They told me that things might be better if we just started again.'

'You went to *see* them?' Nuttall seemed both shocked and angry at the same time. 'What in the name of . . . What were you thinking, lad?'

Mitch held up a hand. 'Yeah, I know. They're dangerous, I've been told.'

'You don't know *how* dangerous. You need to steer clear of them.' The third time he'd been told that. Just what did this man know that he wasn't telling him?

Mitch went for broke, came right out and said it: 'I think they had something to do with what happened to my dad.'

That shut Nuttall up. Either this was news to him, or he suspected as much himself. But he didn't say anything in reply.

'And I think they're up to some stuff in those caves that they shouldn't be.'

'In the . . .' Once again, Mitch couldn't work out whether this was news to Nuttall or he was simply astonished that he knew about it. 'Look, young Mitch. You need to tread very carefully here. There are ways of tackling such things.'

'Correct ways, you mean?' he said, quoting his Aunty Helen.

Did she have the inside track on whatever was going on? The inside track on Nuttall? Had they known what his dad was investigating? Had they been helping him?

Nuttall finished his drink and started to get up, struggling to stand. 'I think I've said enough already.'

'I don't think you've said nearly enough, to be honest.'

Eventually, he got to his feet and leaned more heavily than ever on that stick of his. 'Have a nice rest of the evening, lad,' he told him. Then, as he passed, Nuttall patted Mitch on the shoulder. 'Don't go looking for trouble.'

He almost said back, 'I don't have to, it seems to come looking for me.' *Particularly these days, and since I got back here.* But then the man was gone, and Denise had returned – as if she'd been waiting for her chance to pop over. Before she could even say anything, he'd ordered a couple of bags of crisps to soak up what he'd already drunk; it had been a while since the stew. And was already deciding he'd get back to more research, which meant Denise was flat out of luck. Sad really, if she'd hung on to see if he was free. God, the ego on him!

Mitch remembered about phoning the hospital then, only to be told that they couldn't release any information about Tammy unless he was family. Even when he told them who he was, that not only was he a colleague (he left out the 'former' bit) who'd been there when she was brought in, but that he was practically family, he'd got precisely nowhere. Wouldn't have put it past Staton to have left orders for him not to be told, just out of spite.

But it was only when he was done that Mitch remembered he'd meant to go and get some more tinned food in for the cat. Consequently, he'd found himself asking Denise, 'I don't suppose you have any leftovers from the kitchen I could take back with me?'

'If you're hungry, we could—'

Mitch cut in and explained to her about Cat. 'I seem to have inherited it, but I'm running out of things to feed the animal.'

'Ah, right. Okay.' She appeared quite put out, but then smiled again. 'I'll go and see what we have in the back.' Denise returned a few minutes later with a plate of scraps covered in clingfilm. 'This should see you right. My shift's pretty much over, if you need some company . . . ?'

Mitch didn't have to fake the yawn, he was actually quite tired – and the alcohol hadn't done anything to help with that; though he hadn't had that much, had he? 'Do you mind if we take a raincheck? I'm pretty wiped actually.'

Another crestfallen look followed a smile. 'Sure. Absolutely. I'll hold you to that,' she said.

Mitch gave her an uncertain smile back, holding up the plate and thanking her one last time. 'See you soon.'

'Hope so. Don't be a stranger!'

With that, he'd left The Plough, making his way back home. Night had just started to fall, and the shadows in the village were lengthening. Mitch had that feeling again of being watched, which in a place this small was probably inevitable – though he did have enemies here, he reminded himself. By the time he arrived home, the feeling had died down a bit and Cat had returned to curl round his legs, sniffing the air for the plate of scraps. This distracted him enough that by the time he'd got through the door, put the food down, it was already happening.

The crashing, banging, the smashing.

What now? Mitch rushed into the living room and threw on the lights, wondering why he hadn't sensed what was about to happen – an after-effect of the Traditional perhaps? Though it had been ages since he finished that last pint . . . Didn't matter, he saw what the problem was immediately: it was hard to miss. His eyes darted from the hole in the window, which looked like someone had punched through it, to the glass sprinkled liberally over the couch, to the rock in the middle of the room. Going over, he noticed something had been painted on it in red.

It was a simple enough message: *Stop!*

Mitch ground his teeth, reached for the poker that had been

replaced and was back out through the door in seconds – the cat had apparently disappeared, frightened by the commotion and leaving the plate untouched. Glancing left and right, looking for the culprits, he waved the poker around, shouting: 'Who did that?' He must have looked like an American chasing racoons off his porch. Glancing back over his shoulder, he saw curtains twitching, including his neighbour with the phone.

Mitch hung his head, the culprit was long gone. Culprits? The same people who'd staged the robbery? Because it was starting to look more and more like it was a put-up job. 'I won't stop!' Mitch shouted a final time. 'I won't!'

Then he retreated back into the house, muttering to himself like that same American bemoaning his problem with pests.

Thinking that although he hadn't gone looking for it . . .

Trouble had certainly found him again.

Chapter 20

'Stop? Stop what?'

Wilkinson had turned the rock over and over, examining it through the plastic bag Mitch had placed it in. He thought for a moment the old policeman was going to take it out, and after he'd gone to so much trouble to make sure he didn't handle it personally. Picked it up with the bag and then turned it inside out, ensuring there was no contamination of the evidence. Not that it seemed to matter in this place, they didn't even bother when there was a burglary.

Or someone was on fire.

I wish this whole thing *would stop*, thought Mitch, and not for the first time that day. Wished it was over, wished he wasn't going through all this. Witnessing it. But he was. And apparently he was the only person taking it seriously, the only person getting close to the truth who could do anything about it. Which was why he'd been warned off. Again.

'Stop looking into all this,' he'd snapped. 'What do you think?'

Wilkinson, standing behind his desk in the station house, had shrugged. He even did that at a snail's pace, thought Mitch. 'Could mean anything.'

'But it doesn't, does it? It means stop poking around.'

'Hmm, is that what you've been doing then?'

He'd got him there. 'Well, nobody seems to be doing anything here.'

'It might look that way,' Wilkinson said in that drawn-out way he'd become used to over the last few days. 'But I assure you everything is in hand.'

'Maybe I should have a word with some of my friends back home. Perhaps they could—'

Wilkinson held up his hand. 'Already have. Seems that you're no longer a member of Her Majesty's finest. That right?'

Mitch looked down, couldn't even deny it. 'There was a bit of a . . . misunderstanding.'

'That what you'd call it, eh?'

He met Wilkinson's gaze again. 'Look, what's that got to do with someone lobbing that through my win— Through my *dad's* window?'

'Looks like vandalism to me,' Wilkinson told him, turning the rock over for the millionth time.

'Vandalism?' Mitch couldn't believe what he was hearing. 'You're serious?'

'Been a spate of it, same as the break-ins.'

A spate? It wasn't that big a bloody place! thought Mitch. 'Then why the message?'

'I'm not even sure that's what it says,' the sergeant admitted. 'It's a bit smudged.'

'*You're* doing that, rubbing it through the plastic!' he said, reaching for the rock – until Wilkinson pulled it away. He was quick enough when he wanted to be. 'Just what *is* your problem?'

'At the moment, lad, you are.'

'Not the vandals? Not the burglars? Not the . . . the Commune?'

The policeman froze himself then. 'The Commune? What have they got to do with this?'

'You tell me,' said Mitch.

Wilkinson just shrugged again.

Mitch let out a frustrated groan. He'd had enough of this. It hadn't been a great day so far, in fact he'd slept most of it away – not having got much the previous night. Had kept a vigil in case the people who'd thrown the rock came back, at least till it was light and he could fix the window.

At some point he'd dropped off in the wingback chair, and woke late. He was surprised Cat hadn't returned and nudged him, but when he had a look around and called out its 'name' there was no reply. Must have slipped out when he was doing his crazy person impression outside with the poker. He'd ended up tossing the scraps from last night, didn't want to poison the thing if it did come back.

Fix the window, that was the first priority. No, actually, it was to find a clear plastic bag and put the rock inside it – like he'd seen detectives do at so many crime scenes in the past. Once he'd found one, and sorted that out, he was left with the problem of securing his temporary home. Wasn't as simple as just closing and locking a back door this time, there was a ruddy great hole in the living-room window. Anybody could just reach inside and open it up.

He knew from the tidying that there was a hammer and some nails in one of the drawers, but what he really needed was some wood or something to patch it up. Of course, Mitch knew exactly where he'd be able to find some of that (his dad was a terror for saving bits and bobs in case they came in handy; amassed 'stuff' like he did information), he just wasn't relishing actually going in there.

The cellar.

The dark cellar, the place that was so like the caves. That he'd been doing his best to ignore, or pretend it wasn't even part of this place since his scare on the first night. But there was no other way, nothing else for it. He opened the door up and tried the light switch, but nothing happened – had he even been expecting it to? – so he went and fetched his torch, now it was working again. It hadn't got any lighter in there; if anything, even though it was daytime it was so much darker inside.

Mitch turned on the torch and the blackness immediately ate it up, the beam only stretching a couple of feet ahead of him. He started to descend, just like he'd done before. Tiptoeing down those steps, sweeping the light back and forth. The only blessing was that there weren't any noises on this occasion, no scratching or rustling or—

Something sprang at him from behind, and his first thought was that the intruders had returned. He noticed it again too late, his spider-sense still asleep it seemed, spinning and only catching the tail end – literally.

The damned cat again! Like it had been waiting to get back inside here, after making such a song and dance about getting out in the first place. 'Heaven's sake!' he said, letting it scamper down the steps to the bottom. Disappearing like a chameleon, black against the black. 'You nearly had me over!'

It was only afterwards that he considered maybe it was scoping out the way in front of him, ensuring it was safe for Mitch to descend. But what could be down there that might hurt him anyway? Nothing, that's what. Nothing to be afraid of.

Wood, he needed a bit of wood. Mitch continued down into that freezing cellar, colder even than the morgue, a contrast to the weather outside. The nape of his neck was prickling, hairs on his arms standing upright. Mitch swished the torch around, catching the edges of shelves with scabby pots of paint on them. In one corner there was an old washing machine, Christ alone knew how his dad had got the thing down here! It looked like it had been cannibalized, stripped for parts and left with its insides hanging out. There were boxes with old broken picture frames in them, and reared up against one wall a mattress with springs sticking out of it; again, that would have taken three men to get it down those steps. An old bicycle, looked like a girl's, so probably Bella's.

Mitch was on the ground level, searching around when he

heard a noise, which had to be Cat – and he swung the torch around, like a spotlight trying to trap an escaping prisoner. 'You'll have to come back up with me, you know. I'm not leaving you down—'

His torch beam revealed a face in the darkness and he let out the most unmanly yelp of his life. Mitch tumbled backwards, almost fell over a crate or box that had been left on the floor, but somehow managed to stay upright. His light showed that there was more than one face, a trio of people or more. How had they got down here: when he'd dropped off in the living room?

Mitch managed to keep his beam steady, then noticed the faces – the people – weren't moving. Just standing there, staring at him: eyes fixed on him, fascinated. Unblinking.

Mainly because they were painted on.

'Mannequins,' he whispered. 'Bloody mannequins.' He let out a long, relieved breath. It hadn't connected with him because he wasn't expecting to see such things down here – but then he remembered his mother used to design and make clothes. Did alterations for people, turned up dresses and trousers. Even had her own little market stall when they used to have a market in the village, selling her wares. Made a bit of extra money that way. Mitch guessed she must have used these – male and female – to see what the clothes looked like on 'people'. And, yes, there was even a dressmaker's dummy that could be adjusted for when she was working. Why had his dad kept all of this stuff, all this time? Just hadn't been able to part with it? Mitch guessed he could understand that.

Everything down here would need clearing out before they sold it, though he still suspected there were some people in the village who were expecting him to remain here. The baton passed on to the next generation, as was their custom. If he did put it up for sale, he'd be crucified if he sold it on to a stranger – not that Mitch was exactly part of the fixtures and fittings in Green Acres. Maybe one of the local's kids would be interested, someone who was getting married or something, looking to start their own family here? Thoughts for another time, the most important thing was—

There, he spotted a stack of timber. Offcuts and such. There was bound to be something in that lot he could use to cover that gaping hole in the window. Sure enough, a square bit of wood that looked like it had been part of a bookcase at some point caught his eye; a piece which had broken off or whatever. Discarded, but more detritus his father couldn't bear to permanently get rid of. Perfect for him though, at this precise moment.

Mitch grabbed it and made to get the hell out of that creepy place, only turning when he reached the bottom of the steps, remembering Cat was still down here. He didn't fancy leaving the door open at the top so it could come out when it was good and ready. 'Cat! Hey, Cat! I'm going now. Where the devil are you?'

Nothing. No response at all. If only he had another plate of leftovers to coax it with. He wasn't waiting around forever, so he decided to get on with the window and see if the animal emerged at some point during that. Needless to say it didn't, and he had to wait till he'd finished nailing the bit of bookcase to the wooden window frame, changed the litter and started rattling around in the kitchen to fix himself something to eat before the feline appeared.

'I'm not sure what I'm going to feed myself, let alone you,' he said to it, but went over and closed the cellar door while he had the chance. 'Do cats eat baked beans?' he asked, rooting around in the cupboards. Probably shouldn't have been feeding the animal fish from cans let alone anything else, so he decided against that course of action. 'I'll head out and get some meat. But in the meantime you'll have to make do with the dry stuff, okay?' The cat cocked its head, and wandered off when he put a plate of that down. 'Suit yourself.'

It was then that Mitch figured he could kill two birds with one stone – or rock. Would try to get Wilkinson to take notice

190

of the attack while he was out, then swing back into the shop on his way home. But the first part of that mission wasn't exactly going to plan. He might as well have been talking to a brick wall.

'So you're going to do what you did about the break-in, exactly nothing?' he asked the ageing sergeant.

'I'm not sure what you *want* me to do, lad,' the bobby told him.

Your job might be nice, thought Mitch. But he was getting precisely nowhere. Perhaps he should just take the rock to Larson, see what he made of it? 'Okay, fine. Then if you just give me—' Mitch reached for it a second time and it was pulled back again.

'Afraid I can't do that.'

'What do you mean? I brought it in!'

'Yes, but you handed it to an officer of the law. Like you said, it's evidence.'

'Of what? You've just stood there telling me there was no crime committed.'

'Never said that. The vandalism,' Wilkinson reminded him.

'Right, yeah. So you're going to be looking into this, then?' The sergeant stared at him, gave a half-nod, half-shrug. Mitch realized it wouldn't be a great idea to hold his breath while he was waiting. He slammed his hand down on the desk, drawing a look of disdain from the bearded man.

'Easy now.'

Mitch glared at him, then turned around and exited the station – back out into the baking hot sunshine. He'd walked this time instead of taking the bike, thought it would just be lazy to keep riding around everywhere. But now, with the trek back ahead of him, he was regretting that massively. Still, the sooner he set off, the sooner he could get something to eat from the shop for him and his – no, it *wasn't* his, wasn't anybody's – for him and *the* cat. He checked his pockets, checked the cash he had left on him (he'd need to get another sub soon from his aunty, if he couldn't sort anything with the post office; either that or ride out to find that local branch of the bank). He was wondering about more brandy, because there really wasn't enough left at home to take that edge off tonight. Realised it would be a choice between that or the food, and set off to see what else the spotty youth might have which would satisfy a hungry feline.

That had turned out to be some tinned ham, which he figured would last the cat a while, and he'd bought some oven chips for himself which he'd wash down with a four-pack of cider they had on offer (unsurprisingly, the post office was closed up again). Combined with the brandy he had left, it might just be enough. He didn't want to get paralytic anyway, because you never knew when those arseholes might be back and ready for a rumble. He'd see their rocks and give them a good pasting with the poker if they dared.

Hadn't worked out that way, though. He'd dropped to sleep early – the cider hitting him much harder than it should have done; he hadn't even touched the brandy – but he hadn't stayed under. Not after he'd dreamed about going down into that cellar, into those caves, the two interchangeable. Starting off in the darkness, making for the flickering light. Knowing what he'd find, but not really knowing.

Mannequins this time, ringing the flames. Hoods up, mumbling and chanting without moving their mouths. No dancing, because how could they? They were just lumps of plastic. Yet that still didn't stop their heads turning when they saw him, didn't stop them looking at Mitch with their dead, painted eyes. Nor one of them raising its arm, extending a finger to point at the flame. Didn't stop another pulling back its arm and casting a rock at Mitch, hitting him in the same place he'd banged his head on the cave wall.

When he touched the spot, expecting there to be blood pouring from the wound, Mitch found a ragged hole there with sharp edges. The more he prodded it, the more bits of flesh splintered and dropped into the wound or fell to the floor, tinkling like bits of glass.

Then suddenly the flame in the centre of this space was growing bigger again, the glowing, the flickering becoming brighter and brighter. And Mitch knew that however much he was scared of the dark, the blackness he'd encountered in the cellar – the cave – there was so much more to fear from the light. From that flame, the fire.

As it engulfed the area, the mannequins, him. Filling everything and burning it up. Burning it—

That's when he'd snapped awake in the living room, in the dark, in the chair. When he'd heard the cat's meowing, sounding like screams.

No. Those were from outside, where the light was coming from – flickering on the glass, on the walls, those bookcases looking for a moment like they were made out of rock. 'What the . . .' said Mitch, rising, still feeling a little out of it from the cans and tiredness, and drifting over to the window to get a better look. To see what it was that—

Then he smelled it, before he even saw the sight. The smell was like cooking flesh. And when Mitch peered outside, when he saw the most horrible thing he'd ever witnessed in his life, he wished it would stop.

Wished for this waking nightmare to be over.

Chapter 21

A waking nightmare, that's the only way Bella could think of describing it.

What she'd seen that night. The scene through the window. The figure, out there, alight. *On fire!* She'd been able to smell the meat cooking, hear the crackling of the flames. See the outline of the person standing there in the middle of the caravan park.

'M-My God!' was all she could manage, hands going to her face. Rising from the couch and almost falling backwards over the coffee table behind her. 'My *God!*'

Then she thought, I need to get out there and help them. Why isn't anyone else in the park doing that? Why aren't there loads of people rushing out to help? Yet no one was. They were leaving this person to just stand there and burn, to be burned up. On fire. Like her dad had died, in a fire. That much she knew.

The caravan was filled with light suddenly, flickering on the glass of the window, the walls – such as they were – and spreading out towards the back, illuminating the kitchen area with the breakfast table opposite.

She had to help, just like she always did. Just like she'd—

Failed to do with Mitch. Hadn't gone back with him, left him to it. Left him alone to—

No. Mitch was an adult now, a policeman. He could handle himself. He'd be okay. The real nightmare was happening here, outside. In her caravan park. Someone had been set alight, someone else was dying. And she had to save them. Get outside, get to the communal fire extinguisher there and . . .

Even as she was thinking it, Bella was moving, heading back towards the door. In some ways finding those people in her van would have been preferable to this horror. She could have done something about that, was readying herself to use the cricket bat – but they never showed up.

Instead, there was this! Even if she did what she was intending, got to the person and attempted to put them out, she knew their chances of survival were slim to negligible. What percentage of burns on your body could you withstand and come through something like this? She had absolutely no idea, wasn't medically trained. But then she didn't really need to be, because whatever the answer was, it wasn't *this* extent.

This person was dead, even if they didn't know it yet. They. Were. Dead. Simple as that. *God. My God!*

She'd fumbled with the door, with the locks, hands slick with sweat. Desperate to get out there quickly and not succeeding. Then suddenly opening it, nearly falling out, falling down those metal steps on the outside of the caravan.

Tripping instead and falling forward, almost hitting her Beetle that was parked there. Almost knocking herself out, but managing not to. What if the fire reached the car? she thought to herself. It would go up like a rocket, shrapnel everywhere. Would tear through the sides of these caravans flanking hers.

She had to—

Wait, no. Bella had used the side of the car to get herself upright, dragging herself along it towards the human fireball. Only—

Only it wasn't there anymore.

That couldn't . . . She could still smell the charred flesh, could still hear the crackling. Had the figure staggered off somewhere, maybe fallen through the barriers there and dropped down onto the beach, into the water now the tide would be in?

Bella made her way to the spot where she'd seen it, tried to examine the ground. But, of course, the flaming figure had taken all the light with it. 'W-What?'

She was aware of more illumination now, from different sources. Her neighbours flicking on lights inside their own abodes, wondering what all the racket was outside. Too late, they were all too late. There was only her out here now, the figure was gone – and still she was wondering where to? They were too late to rescue that person. The one who hadn't been a part of her nightmare, that had been real but she'd wished was a dream and seemingly had her wish granted.

Real, not real. A dream? No, it couldn't have been! But there was no sign now of—

How could she possibly tell anyone about this, they'd think she'd gone gaga for sure. Had she? Was that what was happening? How would she know? An early form of dementia, a result of what she'd been doing all these years? In touch with the departed, had that done it? Had that been a part of it all along? No . . .

Scared, more of what would happen if anyone found her outside like this, she'd raced back to her own caravan, locking herself inside. She wouldn't tell anyone about this, Bella decided; would keep it from people, especially Ashley. Couldn't tell him, couldn't take him up on his offer of somewhere to stay now regardless. How could she?

Keep the real, the *waking* nightmare a secret.

And with it, what she'd seen that night.

Chapter 22

He'd kept a certain part of it to himself. Kept it secret.

The waking nightmare, the thing he'd thought – hoped, wished – had been only a nightmare, but turned out to be real. What Mitch had been through was real: holy crap! Though it hadn't been a patch on what the victim had experienced.

Not imaginary, not a cider-fuelled hallucination.

Real.

A real-life death. No, that made no sense. And Mitch had needed to make sense for the statement, the witness statement. Telling Wilkinson what he'd seen the previous night, who he'd seen out there on the village square: tied, chained to the monument. Mitch had unlocked the door, flung it open just in time to see the man's face. He'd thought it was the cat meowing, but it was actually screaming. The man had been screaming because he was burning to death.

Sheldon. Neil Sheldon, out there roasting alive. In spite of everything, he'd looked over at Mitch and caught his eyes, begging to be saved. To be *in time* to save him. Mitch began to rush towards the figure, but had absolutely no idea how he was going to do that. His dad hadn't kept a fire extinguisher in the house, as far as he knew, and filling a bucket of water – assuming he could find one – would take too long. That man was dying out there!

But what could he do? Smother him with his own body?

No, but he could smother him with blankets or something. Mitch went back into the house, racing upstairs and stumbling, because he still wasn't that coordinated, and headed to his mum and dad's room, dragging off the blankets that resided on top. That weren't really needed because it was summer, because it was so hot (it was hot all right!). Weren't needed unless you had to put someone out who was on fire.

He'd dragged them from the bed, down the stairs, where they'd snagged briefly on a tack or something, and he'd had to tug at them and rip them before he could be on his way. When Mitch got back outside – how long had that taken? Even longer than the water would have done probably – he was amazed to see that there were still no other people coming out of their homes. Why weren't they helping? Were they even awake? How could you sleep through that screaming?

It was only now that he realized the screaming had stopped. Ceased because Sheldon's head was completely on fire, and his vocal chords had probably burned away. He was in no fit state to scream anymore, and Mitch had to hope that he wasn't feeling anything either. He got as close as he could with the blankets, but it soon became clear that he wasn't going to be able to put this guy out. Wasn't smothering anything anytime soon. Sheldon was past all that.

Lights were coming on in the surrounding houses, Mitch saw. People were emerging out into the night at last. Some had had the same idea as him, grabbed sheets or whatever and brought those with them. Others had gone to the effort of filling buckets, which they were passing along to throw onto the figure to try to put him out. Mitch recalled something then, that the shock of doing such a thing could kill a person as quickly as the flames themselves, but in the end it made no difference. Sheldon wasn't moving. He was slumping, held in place by those chains which had kept him rooted to the spot while the fire did its worst.

Dead, and perhaps mercifully so.

It was murder, there was no getting around the fact this time. Sheldon hadn't done this to himself, hadn't bound himself to that monument and then set himself on fire! *How?* He wasn't bloody Dynamo or David Blaine.

Mitch had been about to ask if anyone had rung for an ambulance, as he couldn't, but again there wouldn't be any point. There'd be no medical drama, last minute resurrections here, no pumping of Sheldon's chest and him taking a deep, coughing breath. They'd be carting him off to the morgue, where Mitch's dad was currently residing. A friend, a twin for him there.

Then he'd heard the sirens and realized that someone must have called for the emergency services, though bizarrely it wasn't an ambulance that showed up first. It was Wilkinson. The fastest Mitch had ever seen him get anywhere, though he guessed if the old sergeant had been told there was a man on fire in the village square that should warrant some degree of haste. But just Wilkinson, on his own again with no backup. He'd clambered out of the police car, which was just as archaic as its driver, and made his way over to Mitch to ask what the situation was.

Mitch hadn't even been able to find the words to answer him, had simply held out a hand as the flames were being dampened down. It was only at this point that Mitch thought to himself all the water they were chucking on Sheldon would also wipe out any forensic evidence at the scene of crime. But it was too late anyway, far too late for a lot of things. For Sheldon himself definitely.

By the time an ambulance did arrive, which didn't look in much better nick than Wilkinson's car, with Larson in tow, it was all over bar the shouting – which Mitch didn't have the energy to do on this occasion. He'd tried that all along the line, and where had it got him? There'd be no attempt to set up a cordon, or get any CSIs in to do a proper study. It would be yet another crime the people here would want to handle 'in-house', and he'd be stonewalled from the get-go.

Larson had made a stab at being professional, the same as last time he'd seen him, when Mitch had asked if he thought an accelerant had been used.

'I would have thought so,' the doctor replied, eying up the corpse – which was black, wet and, frankly, disgusting.

'Same as my father.'

The doctor had nodded. 'I'll need some time with the body to ascertain what exactly was used though.'

And that had been it: said body had been let down and placed on a stretcher by the ambulance man – Mitch was loath to call him a paramedic, because for starters he wasn't dressed like one, more like something from the '60s or '70s so no chance of any kind of *Casualty* heroics anyway – then loaded up into the ambulance itself, presumably to be taken to Green Acres Hospital. 'I'll be in touch,' Larson had told Mitch, who'd been joined by his uncle and aunty. She was busy making tea for him and the other people gathered, because it was good for the shock apparently. Mitch couldn't help noticing her look of disappointment when she sniffed his breath again, and realized he'd been drinking. Except he hadn't been, not much. Sheldon's partner – wife? – would probably need something a lot stronger when she eventually found out about all this. He'd heard someone say, Nuttall he thought, who'd been talking to Wilkinson, that she was away at the moment.

'Nasty business,' were his Uncle Vince's only words on the subject.

Yeah, waking to see a guy tied up and burning to death? Probably qualifies as nasty, among other things.

Denise had been present too, but hadn't come over when she saw he was with his relations. Just held up a hand, a concerned expression on her face. And Mitch couldn't help thinking then that actually she was quite a sweet person, always had been. That she really did care about him. Thought also that he should probably put her in the picture about Lucy, and not give her any false hope. Any *more* false hope.

Then Mitch had spent the best part of the morning making his statement at the police station, Wilkinson periodically asking him to repeat sentences so he could write them down at the same pace he did everything: glacial. But Mitch didn't see any point in getting mad, not anymore. Didn't see any point in questioning their methods here, the way they'd handle something more horrific than most of the stuff he'd seen out in the city put together. Didn't see how it would help to state again the parallels to his dad's death – that was obvious wasn't it, to anyone other than Wilkinson apparently – or to rant and rave about it. He'd only be told that what he thought was unreliable because he'd been drinking (which begged the question as to why he'd been asked to give a statement anyway). Mitch was beyond all that now, knew what he had to do. And that was not take a blind bit of notice of the authorities in this place.

What he had done was use the phone at the station to try to get through to his station house back home, to get hold of Vihaan at least to see if he might be able to help from that end. Somewhat predictably, he hadn't even been able to connect – his call dropping as it was ringing out.

Don't slam it down, he thought to himself. *What would be the use of that, either?* He should just thank Wilkinson and go about his business. The business of getting to the bottom of not just what happened to his dad, but now poor Neil Sheldon.

It was the reason he'd kept part of all this to himself. Kept it secret – in the aftermath and during his long-winded statement to Wilkinson – kept it to himself, so he could follow it up. Something that in the heat of the moment (very poor choice of words) he'd almost forgotten. About what he'd seen.

About who he'd seen that night.

Chapter 23

He knew where the man lived.

Mitch had seen him there, had encountered him there. So after he'd grabbed a quick lunch – Helen had left him a salad in the fridge, and he'd fed some more of that tinned meat to Cat, who'd returned once all the fuss had died down in the square and didn't fancy anything else on offer – he'd got on his bike and headed off again.

He'd been warned, been told to be careful, told not to go looking for trouble – by so many people. But Mitch thought to himself: sod it! This needed doing, needed looking into. Maybe he'd gather some evidence? He might not have been thinking straight, probably still wasn't, but he knew what he'd seen. Who he'd seen.

That face, casting a glance over his shoulder as he made himself scarce. As he made his exit, having done this in the first place. Who else could it have been? There'd been no one else around! Everyone had been in bed, hadn't even turned on their lights or come out of their houses until it was way too late to save Sheldon.

Must have gagged him or knocked him out or something while he was chaining him up and dousing him with whatever accelerant had been used (petrol?), but then the flames had kicked in and

Sheldon had begun screaming for all he was worth. Again, too late. He'd been a dead man even before Mitch had clapped eyes on him. An intentional act. A cowardly act. A terrible act Mitch didn't think anyone had in them. He was wrong.

As for motive, there was plenty of that too. Loads of it, in fact. Revenge for one, retaliation for what had happened in the run-up to last night. But, of course, it was bigger than that. So, what about all this was a good idea? Coming out here to snoop when he suspected that man was a cold-blooded killer? What did he hope to achieve?

Mitch had no idea, just knew he had to do something. That whatever he did, it would be a million times more than Wilkinson would be able to muster. By the time that man realized who was responsible and came to ask questions, if the sergeant could even be bothered, their suspect might be halfway around the world. Not that anyone ever seemed to leave this place. Apart from Mitch himself, he'd left, hadn't he? Had cause to. Then again, being wanted for murder – a double murder? – was probably more of an incentive to bolt.

Something told Mitch that the guy whose property he was on, covering the distance along the track, wasn't the running kind. Wouldn't bolt even if there was a lion after him: would instead just stand and fight the beast. So he needed to be careful.

He left the bike about halfway up, walking the rest of the way. Mitch would sneak in and have a look around the place, if he wasn't spotted beforehand, that was. And it seemed he was going to be lucky in that respect, to begin with at any rate, because there wasn't a soul around. Not anyone he could see, at any rate.

What he was expecting to find was anyone's guess. Cans of accelerant? There were definitely cans of petrol lying around, but then was that so unusual here? Probably not. He crept over to the nearest building, still unseen – no one had come out to stop him yet, call over to ask what he was doing, so that was something. It was big – huge, in fact – and made from wood, but had a chain just like the one that had held Sheldon looped through the handles of the door with a padlock attached. Mitch tried the door, found that it would open a crack – enough for him to get his fingers into, lever it open a bit more and peer inside.

From what he could discern it was just as big inside, but it was too dark to see right to the back. Storage for something? Wouldn't be unheard of out here, but what? As his eyes narrowed, he thought he saw a light back there. A glowing of some sort, but he couldn't be sure what—

There was a sudden pain in his fingers. Mitch tried to pull back but found that he couldn't. It was like his hand was stuck to the slatted wood, and it took him a moment to realize what had happened. Not stuck to the wood, but jammed in the gap. A gap that had been forced shut, kicked by a booted foot which was still pressed up against the door. Jesus, that *hurt* – felt like his fingers were going to be cut off completely. Too late now. It was too late to go back, too late to reconsider his rash actions.

Then just as suddenly as it had been there, the boot was gone again and the pressure was lifted. Mitch yanked his fingers out while he could, and jammed them under his arm to try to ease the pain. He looked up and over, tears in his eyes. Saw the watery outline of a man, someone who was no less huge than the barn he owned. The barn Mitch had been investigating without authority. He blinked away the saltwater, and it was only then that he saw what the farmer, Granger, was holding – training on him, on his head – the butt wedged in his shoulder. A double-barrelled shotgun.

'What d'yer think yer doin'?' asked the man with the humongous sideburns in a gruff voice, forcing Mitch to look at his face instead of the weapon he was holding. He took in the rest of the giant next, who had the same clothes on as the other night, except the tatty jumper which he'd taken off to reveal a chequered shirt that was full of holes too. 'I asked yer a question!' The man's cheeks were ruddy, not because of the hours that he worked out here in the fields, but because he was angry once again. Mitch noticed the purple veins in those cheeks now, running from the fellow's nose. A drinker then, not that he could talk lately.

'I . . .' said Mitch, his mind racing, not expecting to have this conversation just yet and certainly not after having had his fingers trapped in a barn door. He figured it was best to just tell the truth. 'I saw you, Granger.'

The farmer's right eye turned into a slit. Mitch hoped he wasn't aiming that shotgun, preparing to fire. Especially as it moved down slightly, the barrels pointed at his chest rather than his head. Actually, he wasn't sure which would be worse: a shotgun blast to the skull or the heart. Which would kill him the quickest? It depended on how good Granger was with it, he supposed. 'Saw me?' he asked, voice still sounding rough as sandpaper.

'Come on, let's stop playing games here, shall we?' Mitch took out his hand, flapped his fingers up and down, then experimentally made a fist and opened it up again to check none were broken. The injury was still killing him; he just hoped Granger's next move didn't finish the job. 'Sheldon. Last night.'

Granger let the gun fall again, and this time the barrels were pointing at Mitch's crotch. The worst of the lot, definitely. The farmer said nothing in reply.

'I saw you heading off, after he was attacked.'

'Don't know what yer talkin' about,' the larger man finally answered. 'Hey, yer that bloke from t'other night in the pub.' He said this last bit like he'd only just recognized Mitch as the person who'd restrained him.

'Yeah, when you were about to beat seven bells out of Neil Sheldon. Guess you found another way to shut him up. Once he'd finished screaming, that is.'

'An' I've always been a man of action anyway!'

The gun was lowering again, and Mitch was calculating his chances of reaching the bigger man, disarming him, then taking him down. They weren't good.

'I never did nothin',' snapped Granger, sounding like a street punk he'd just nabbed for graffitiing public property. Mitch thought about saying that was a double negative, which only compounded his guilt, but figured he might be pushing his luck.

'I *saw* you,' Mitch repeated.

'How could you when I weren't there when he was burned?'

'Who said he was burned?' asked Mitch. 'If you weren't there, how did you know that?'

'Was in the shop this mornin',' Granger retorted, but only after thinking about it for a moment. 'Talk of the village, it is.'

'Okay.' That was fair enough, it almost certainly would be. Look at all the people who'd gathered after it had happened. Most of Green Acres, Mitch guessed. Even if Granger hadn't been there earlier, he probably would have heard about it. That proved nothing, and when it came to Mitch's claim that he'd seen him, it was just his word against the farmer's. A stranger's word against a local's. 'So, what're you doing with those?'

Granger's eyes flitted over to where Mitch was nodding, at the petrol cans he'd spotted before. 'They're for Bessie,' the farmer explained, chuckling. When Mitch frowned, he went on. 'How d'you think I top 'er up?' Now he thumbed back towards the tractor he'd been driving when Mitch first encountered him on the road, when he'd almost run into him. It was only what he'd expected the man to say, and it was a decent explanation. Mitch had nothing on him really, apart from the evidence of his own eyes. If he could get hold of the man's clothes, then perhaps there'd be something on it that— 'I asked yer a question: what d'yer think yer doin' here?'

He'd made his allegations and this man had swatted them with the ease of someone killing a fly with a newspaper. So Mitch tried something else instead: 'What's your connection to the Commune, Granger?'

'The Commune?'

Mitch nodded. 'I think you know what I'm talking about. What they're up to.' It was just vague enough to perhaps get an answer. And that had been his first thought, hadn't it? The Commune, the cult. Using fire? Until he saw Granger fleeing the scene. Which meant one of two things, either he was mixed up with them somehow, in spite of his comments about trespassers. Maybe that's how he came into contact with them in the first place? Had he been brainwashed, all farmers in it together, back to nature? Either that, or he was just trying to make it *look* like them – put the blame on them for Sheldon. A convenient scapegoat for getting rid of a nuisance? Whatever way you cut it, Granger was in this up to his neck; Mitch just knew he was! What he didn't know was what it had to do with his dad. 'Something's going on here. Has been for a while, I reckon. Something involving my father.'

'Father?'

'Thomas Prescott.'

'Yer don't know what yer talkin' about, boy,' the farmer threw back, but Mitch noted the way a muscle in that ruddy cheek twitched at the mention of his dad's name.

'Did you kill him too? Set fire to him like you did Sheldon? Or was that *them*? Your friends? Why? What possible reason could . . . A defenceless man who didn't know what he was doing?'

Another chuckle from Granger at this.

'You think that's funny? My dad's dead and you think it's funny?'

'I'm glad yer dad's dead,' spat Granger.

'*What?*' Mitch couldn't believe his ears. 'What did you just say?'

'You 'eard me. I'm glad he's dead.'

'Why you—' Mitch lunged at Granger, not even thinking about the gun now, which had practically been lowered completely. But it was raised again in moments and he had to stop in his tracks.

'Yer trespassing, boy! I'd be well within me rights to blow yer brains all over that barn door,' growled Granger. That calm and collected killer speaking once more. Mitch was still tempted to rush him, gamble that he could reach the weapon before Granger could fire it – grab the barrel and shove it backwards. Shove it into that ruddy, sideburned face. Make it even more red than it was by smashing his nose to pieces. Yeah, sure, he was trespassing, but this guy murdered Sheldon – Mitch had never been so sure about anything in his life – and he'd all but confessed to the killing of his father, hadn't he? Wasn't it time for a bit of payback, some retribution of his own?

Before either of them could do anything, there came a voice. 'Cam! Cameron Granger, put that blessed thing down!' Mitch glanced sideways and saw a woman rushing towards them. She was the opposite of Granger, tiny in fact, wearing a plain dress with an apron tied around it – and she'd come from the direction of the farmhouse just a little further up that dirt track. Mitch had no idea why he'd thought Granger was on his own up here out of the way, a widower even – hadn't someone said that: Nuttall, his aunty? – but she was definitely acting like she was married to the guy.

'Caught 'im skulking around, Ellie. Figured I'd give him a little reminder of his visit.'

'You'll do nothing of the kind, Cam. And you know why.' She looked over at Mitch and apologized. 'My brother gets like this sometimes, het up about things.' It was what the landlord of The Plough had said too, excusing this man's behaviour on that night as well. Another relation?

'Brother . . .?' said Mitch.

'Good day, brother!'

'Brothers!'

'Aye, my thick-headed brother!' She reached up as high as she could, which really wasn't that high, and slapped him on the side. Mitch winced, expecting the shotgun to go off by accident. But instead, Granger shifted it across, pointing it away from Mitch, who let out a sigh of relief. He thought then about resuming what he'd been in the middle of, going for this giant because of what he'd said about his dad. Somehow that didn't seem appropriate now his sister had arrived, and since she'd probably saved him from that 'reminder' Cam Granger had been talking about.

There were other figures heading their way too, from the fields. Granger's workers perhaps, the people Mitch had thought might lie in wait for him after what he'd done to break up the fight with Neil Sheldon in the pub? His backup? More people who had connections to the Commune perhaps (a couple of them were even wearing those bloody cream clothes; had they just conveniently wandered on to his land?). They might even be the people who'd broken into the house that night, or thrown the rock? But Mitch didn't really want to hang around now to find out.

'He is right, mind. You *are* trespassing,' said the woman, which only convinced him more that it was time to make himself scarce. Though some trespassers were apparently more welcome than others: the 'hippy' kind.

Mitch held up his hands in a gesture of placation, backing off and turning to leave. 'I'm going, don't worry,' he said. As with the Commune itself, however, he didn't promise he wouldn't be back. That he wouldn't be keeping an eye on Granger. After all, he wouldn't be hard to find.

Mitch knew where this man – this killer – lived.

PART THREE

Farming in Green Acres has changed dramatically over the years, from the original tilling of fields by hand to the use of horse-drawn ploughs and then machinery, which made life easier for the average farmer in general. Naturally, not all change has been positive and depending on the farmer in question this has led to diversification in the form of renting out land, sometimes for the storage of caravans or other holidaying experiences, or even – in extreme cases – selling it off for the development of housing.

Perhaps understandably, this tends to be a last resort for many, who are reluctant to part with their property and cherished inheritances.

Chapter 24

She had nowhere to live.

Not now. And no choice but to rely on the one man Bella hadn't wanted to bother. The man, actually, who'd saved her when things had escalated. Who'd been so concerned, having not heard a thing from her since the beach, that he'd called one night after work and had been knocking on her door. It had sounded so far away, and she'd had no energy to answer. Couldn't even make it from the bed to the door to open it, or even shout, call to let him know she was okay. *Had* she been okay, though? Not even close.

The knocking had stopped and she'd assumed he'd gone away again, that he'd figured she was out somewhere. But she hadn't banked on how tenacious Ashley Watts was when he'd got the bit between his teeth. Like a dog with a bone, and a good job too because if it wasn't for him . . .

Bella had become lost, the pains in her head so far beyond agony that it felt like numbness really, like being drugged or something, slipping into unconsciousness. Every movement was too much effort, even when she woke up and heard the noises out there again in the caravan. The scratching and creaking, footsteps, people in there violating her home. Real, or not real? She couldn't tell the difference anymore, not since she'd seen the person out there through the window. The person who'd been standing around on fire, lit up like a Christmas tree, only to vanish when she went out to help.

The noises though: so loud! Banging around, voices not even trying to whisper this time, so thunderous they were stopping her from sleeping. Or was she still asleep? Bella had no idea. Nightmares, waking nightmares. Reality. Shifting planes, intersecting.

Had she even made it out into the main body of the caravan, seen the shadowy figures there? One minute she'd been in bed, then—

Had she seen the fire they were dancing round, celebrating, those hooded figures? They certainly looked like they were here, with her, in her home. She could feel the vibrations when they moved, the rocking of the van. Could smell the smoke, hear the crackling of those flames. And the heat, there was definitely heat. Bella could feel that on her arms, her legs. Burning. It was burning up her home, burning her up too – even as she fell and crawled around on her hands and knees.

Then the door was being bashed in, someone off to the side of her. Coughing, she could hear coughing – was it her? – and feel hands grabbing at her. Those men trying to pull her towards the fire they were dancing round, performing their rituals. Chanting so loudly. So loudly.

No, the hands were pulling her in the opposite direction. Away from the men, away from the flames. Pulling her out through the door, down those metal steps. Hands under her armpits, dragging her past her car – that car she'd saved up to buy, which she loved so much – out into the middle of the caravan park itself. Out into the night air, where it was easier to breathe. Slightly.

'Bella?' she heard, a soft, kindly voice. Then more urgently: 'Bella! Bella, are you okay?'

Her eyes had been pouring with water from the smoke, and when the face hoved into view above her she couldn't make out who it was – or if it was even real. Bella had opened her mouth to answer, then just coughed, rasped. Almost choked. She felt those

214

same hands that had pulled her from the caravan, from the fire, roll her over onto her side: the recovery position.

'It's okay, you'll be all right. The fire brigade's on its way.' She recognized that voice, as well. The same one that had been shouting through her door earlier, knocking on it. Ashley Watts. She'd had no idea what he was doing there, not back then. Had no clue that he'd waited in his car, thinking he might catch her when she returned from wherever he thought she was. Then saw the flames, caught sight of movement inside and realized she was still in there. In there with the fire. That's when he'd called it in, asking not only for the fire department but an ambulance, because there would be casualties. A casualty.

From her place on the ground, on her side, Bella could hear other voices outside; drawn by all the commotion. Her neighbours at the park, folk she didn't really know that well but made judgements about her on a daily basis. 'Holy . . . Is that the witch's van?' she heard one female voice say.

'Shouldn't even be here, living with us,' said another, a man this time. 'A nutcase, she is!' They all blurred into one, including holidaymakers who were just staying there for a little while during the summer. She heard parents keeping their children safe: 'The fire, mummy! Look at the fire!' 'Come here, Freddie, stay away from that – it's dangerous!' Mums and dads keeping their kids safe, and she felt a pang of jealousy. Her mum, long gone. And her dad—

Fire. On fire. Died in a fire, just like she almost had.

If it hadn't been for Ashley Watts. Dear old Ashley, who'd made the offer on the beach. An offer she'd had to take up finally, because she now had no home. After they'd done with her at Golden Sands' General – she was fine, just a mild case of smoke inhalation, could have been a lot worse – he'd been there, waiting again.

'A-Ashley?'

'Yeah. How're you feeling?'

Bella hadn't been able to help it, she'd thrown herself at him, knowing he'd catch her in those hands. The ones that had pulled her, literally, out of the fire. Watts had stood there in the waiting room, holding her as she sobbed; not an unusual sight for a hospital. A place of sorrow and death, as much as it was relief and luck. She'd been lucky, she knew that. If it hadn't been for Ashley, then—

'It's all right,' he told her, stroking the back of her head. 'It's going to be all right.' Then she'd stood back, tears flooding her eyes for a different reason. But his arms, his hands, were still holding her. Had moved to her shoulders so he could look into those eyes. 'I promise. Now, let's get you home, shall we?'

Bella had opened her mouth to say something, to ask if the caravan was all right now then? Had someone used the communal extinguisher, had the fire brigade got to it in time? Managed to save her belongings, such as they were? Didn't seem likely, but she could hope.

That hope was dashed when Watts had driven her to the opposite end of town, away from the beach. He'd come around and opened the car door for her, helping her out – her legs were still a bit shaky – and led her towards a small block of flats. 'We're just in here,' he said.

Are we? she thought. But where was 'in here', exactly? Turned out he'd taken her back to *his* home, the flat he'd offered to share when they'd walked together what seemed like a million years ago. They'd gone up in the small lift to the second floor, and walked down a corridor to his front door. Ashley had opened it, then waved a hand for her to enter. 'Excuse the mess,' he'd told her, but it really wasn't that bad. A few magazines scattered about, some clothes on the small circular table, dishes in the sink of the adjoining kitchen area. It looked okay to her, probably better than her place did right now. And he'd seen the questioning look on her face at that point. 'Oh, yeah. Your caravan's in a bit of a . . . It'll need some work, I think. But you're welcome to stay here as long as you need to, Bella. I've got most of the streaming services if you want to watch some movies? TV boxsets? Or if you like playing video games, I—' The look of bafflement she gave him prompted a, 'Maybe not. Like I said before, though, you can take the bed. I'll kip on the couch.'

'I-I can't take your bed, Ashley,' she told him, then started coughing again.

'You can and you will,' he insisted. 'Won't be the first time I've had mates staying. One time my friend from school, Bazza, he . . .' But she tuned out the rest of the story, the muzziness in her head making it hard to concentrate. Or was it the fact that he'd just called her a 'mate'? What else did she think they were, *of course* they were just friends. Ashley Watts was just a kind, very loyal, friend. Not to mention a police officer. A detective sergeant, she reminded herself. Was reminded anyway when he asked, 'This might not be the right time to broach this – to be honest, I'm not even sure when would be the right time – but can you tell me what happened, Bella?'

She'd shaken her head, then stopped because it hurt to do that. 'It's hard to remember. But there were men, Ashley. I think the men, the figures I saw, came back.'

'Figures? Bella, I thought there was only one person who'd been in your place? You're telling me there were more?' She'd had to confess then, about the people she'd seen – the ones who'd ransacked the caravan the night before she'd last seen him. The ones she thought she'd seen last night, back to start the fire in her home. 'I can't believe you didn't say anything.' He sounded hurt about that, like he thought she didn't trust him when that was so far from the truth . . .

'I was scared, Ashley. I didn't know what to think.' They were both on that couch now, Watts having fetched her a glass of water to ease her sore throat. 'I'm not even sure they're . . . I saw something else, not long ago.'

'Something else?' he asked, looking at her sideways.

'I saw, well, I thought I saw someone outside, through the window. They . . .' Tears were coming again, as she recalled the figure burning to death in the middle of the park. 'They looked like *they* were on fire,' she said at last.

'What?' The disbelief in his voice was palpable. 'And you didn't

217

report that? Christ, why didn't anyone else report it from your site?'

'That's just the thing, by the time I got outside they were gone.'

'Gone? What do you mean, gone? Gone where?' His eyebrows were stooping, he was rubbing his chin. Disbelief turning into concern.

'I-I don't know, I don't really understand it. I think I told myself they fell off into—' Bella was crying freely now, knew how all this sounded even as she was telling him.

The furrows were deepening in his forehead. 'You don't think this might be to do with, you know.' He raised his finger, thought about it, then decided not to tap the side of his head again. 'The . . . your . . . that thing you do?'

That thing, the psychic thing. 'I told you before, it doesn't work like that, Ashley.' She couldn't help the edge that had crept into her voice, but it was only frustration. 'The departed talk to me, but I don't see pictures, images. Anyway, I can't concentrate enough to hear them at all right now.'

'It sounds like a touch of exhaustion to me,' he said diplomatically. 'You look like you need a good night's rest.' As patronizing as that had come across, and Bella knew he hadn't meant it that way, she couldn't deny that it also sounded like the most perfect thing in the world to her. A good night's rest. 'We can pick all this up when you're ready, it's not going anywhere. But I promise you, if . . . The people who did this, Bella. We'll get them, don't worry.'

Get them, *if* they exist, is what he'd meant. If they weren't just in her imagination. She wasn't stupid. But she was tired, and she was grateful. To him for saving her, for providing a roof over her head – however temporary – and looking after her, which he was very good at, she had to admit.

Giving her a home for the time being, because she didn't have one anymore. Didn't have anywhere to live.

Had been left with no choice but to rely on this man Bella hadn't wanted to bother.

Chapter 25

'I didn't mean to bother you.'

She'd said that, looking down sadly, and of course he'd caved. Mitch had been intending to just ride through the village without being seen, head home and crash for the rest of the day. For the rest of the night. Barring any excitement later, like people in his dad's home, rocks being thrown in his general direction, people on fire. That kind of thing.

It just so happened, though, that she'd been outside when he rode up on the bike – on his way back from Granger's. Denise had been serving someone sitting outside The Plough on one of the tables there, a guy who looked even older than Wilkinson – skin like a prune – sitting enjoying the sun, the heat, with his collie dog who was panting. She'd placed a pint of what looked like Traditional in front of the guy, a bowl of water down for the dog, then looked up and spotted Mitch. Held up a hand, more urgently than last night, practically flagging him down. Standing nearly in the road, so that he'd had no choice but the pull up alongside her.

Mitch had flipped the visor up on his helmet and she'd said, 'Hey.' Today she was wearing a low-cut yellow satin top, with another short, black skirt.

'Hey,' he replied, though his voice was muffled by both the foam inside the helmet and the engine that was still running.

'You coming inside for bit?' Might have been his imagination, but had she made that sound like a proposition? A bit of what? He tried to keep his eyes level with hers, and failed, dipping them briefly.

'I . . .' He shook his head. 'I probably shouldn't, I'm still pretty wiped and—'

'I'm more or less done for the day, have a drink with me?' Now there was more than a hint of desperation in her voice. 'You look like you could use it. After last night, I think maybe I could as well.'

Mitch nodded slowly; he needed to remember that something like that had affected more than just him. Others had seen it, even if it was just the aftermath. It was probably the most excitement – and he hated thinking about it in those terms – this place had seen since, well, his dad. But while that had taken place out in the woods, away from the people who lived here, this had been slap bang in the middle of the village. In the village square. You could still see the tape from here, the scorch marks if you chose to look.

'I-I shouldn't, y'know.'

That's when she'd said it, looked down sadly as if he'd been rejecting her. Rejecting her company. 'I didn't mean to bother you. Another time.' Denise had made to walk away, and he should have just let her. Left it well enough alone. But for some reason Mitch didn't want her thinking he was some kind of dick. If there was one thing he'd been taught growing up, it was that politeness cost nothing. He could spare half an hour for a drink. With an old friend.

An old *girl*-friend.

Denise was a friend and she was a girl, he told himself. He was allowed to have those, wasn't he? Tammy, for example. But Tammy had a fella; Christ, he'd been out drinking with Zach himself and . . . The thought of those two, what they were both going through, made him actually want a drink. Not to mention this heat! His eyes flicked from the Traditional the old bloke was supping to Denise heading away from him.

'Wait. Wait! Denise, hold up.' Mitch climbed off the bike, wheeling it to the side of the pub, before kicking down the stand and securing it with the lock. The barmaid was beaming again, was doing as he'd asked and waiting for him. Mitch trotted up to her, helmet in one hand. Before either of them could say anything else, she'd slipped her arm behind his free one, linking them together to walk into The Plough. It should have felt weird, wrong, but it was strangely comforting.

'First one's on me,' she told him, smiling sweetly, complete with dimples. It was only then that he remembered about his financial situation. They might both be on her, he thought – but he'd pay her back. Because they were only having the two, and would be even when they'd bought a round each. He didn't want to risk any more than that.

Again, though, it hadn't worked out that way. Denise had got the first order in, a G&T for herself and Traditional – naturally – for Mitch. Then she'd asked if he wanted to sit outside, but he'd said no. The heat for one thing – he'd been glad to get his jacket off again – not to mention that line of sight to the monument.

'Right, yeah. I get it,' said Denise. So they'd occupied a booth instead where it was cooler, diagonally opposite to the one he'd shared with Nuttall not so long ago. Over in the other corner, and cosier somehow, or perhaps that was just the company? 'Do we know any more about what happened?' she'd asked him, sipping her drink.

'Apart from the fact it was Neil Sheldon, you mean?' Denise seemed shocked by the information, and he wondered then if he'd said something he shouldn't. If she didn't know who the victim was by now, then she was the only person in Green Acres. The moment was fleeting, the surprise passing over her face like a cloud across the sun – and then it was gone.

'Such a—'

'Nasty business?' he ventured.

Denise looked at him. 'Horrible way to die, I was going to say.'

'Aye,' said Mitch, only realizing afterwards he'd slipped back into Green Acre talk. 'Yeah, I mean. Yeah, it was. I saw him. His face, just before . . .'

'Oh my . . . Mitch, you poor thing. I didn't know.' She reached out for his hand now, but he moved it away. That was the one that had been trapped in the barn door, and was still aching. When he saw she looked sad, he offered his other hand and let her take it. Let her squeeze it. Mitch left it there for a few moments, then removed it and scratched a cheek that wasn't even itchy. If Denise was put out this time, she didn't show it. 'So, what do you think happened? You being with the police and all?'

With the police? He was hardly that. Especially around here. 'What do I think happened? The guy was trussed up like some kind of victim of the Spanish Inquisition, then set on fire. Strangely enough, I think he was murdered.' He hadn't meant the sarcasm to slip out, but he was getting a bit fed up with people around here just not 'getting it'.

'Well, aye. I mean, who do you think would—' Denise stopped and looked around her, lowering her voice. 'Who do you think did it?'

'Who do *I* . . .' Mitch touched his chest. He wasn't sure whether to say anything about Granger, like, 'As it happens, I've just come back from a run-in with my prime suspect!' (There he went again, thinking about it like his case, muddying the waters.) Then decided against it. Instead, Mitch said, 'I'm not sure, Denise. Do you have any thoughts?'

The woman pondered this for a few moments, then replied, 'Have to say, he wasn't best liked that bloke. You saw for yourself the other night. *Oh*, you don't think Granger might have something to do with it, do you?'

Bright girl. 'Possibly.'

'Honestly, though, it could have been anyone. Nobody's happy about him coming here with his schemes. Applications for planning permission or whatever. I heard someone say he wanted to build fifty houses on one field. Fifty houses!'

Mitch nodded. 'Doesn't surprise me. There's a reason that saying's a cliché, "When I were a lad, all this used to be fields."'

'Hmm, not heard of that one,' Denise admitted, drinking more of the gin.

'On the other hand, and playing devil's advocate here, where else are people like him meant to build houses? The towns and cities are overcrowded as they are. Homelessness is on the increase.'

'Crime as well in those places, I wouldn't be surprised. You don't see the link, Mitch? First Green Acres becomes a town, then more people move in. Then the trouble starts.'

Don't go looking for—

'From where I'm sitting, the trouble's already here!' Mitch said, raising his glass and taking a long draught of his beer. He went on to tell her about what had happened since he'd moved back into his dad's place.

'There you go!' Denise said. 'All down to more strangers appearing, those people up in that what's-it-called?'

'Commune.' Mitch practically spat the word out.

'Aye, that. What are they bloody well doing up there, that's what I want to know. What are they really up to?'

Now here was someone *finally* who was speaking his language, thinking along the same lines as him in every respect. Should he mention that there could be a possible connection to Granger, to his dad's death . . . murder? As it was, Denise brought the latter up herself.

'The way I heard it, those campers who found . . . Well, you know, who tried to help Tommy, they spotted some of those buggers hanging around the day afore.'

'*What?*' spluttered Mitch, almost spilling his drink.

'Oh, hey – you didn't hear it from me, though. I don't want to get anyone into hot water. But you do stumble across things, in this job and all. Overheard conversations and such.'

'Jesus,' whispered Mitch, running a hand down his face. Why the hell hadn't Wilkinson told him that? Probably thought it was a coincidence (was it?). More likely worried about him doing exactly what he'd done anyway, going up there and seeing what was what. Shouting the odds. He began to think about Granger again now too, about the possible link. His mind throwing up all kinds of theories.

Like father, like . . .

A relative perhaps? Hadn't the land come into Daniel's possession because of some kind of old family loophole? Had Granger spoken up for him, as his kin? Surely not publicly, after making such a song and dance about 'hippy trespassers'. Unless that had all been a distraction? Had Granger helped the leader of the Commune secretly? Maybe Mitch's dad had found that out? Had Sheldon? Or something else? God, it might be the breakthrough he was looking for. The thing that had been escaping him all this time, that caused everything to slot into place.

'Listen, don't go saying anything, will you. Only I'm not sure—'

'Denise, I could kiss you!' he said, forgetting himself in his excitement.

Denise blushed, flapped her hand. Then replied, 'Who's stopping you?'

Who? That would be Lucy, Mitch reminded himself. *Lucy, you know, your* actual *girlfriend. Move this along, quickly! Get back to talking about your 'case'. Denise could wind up being a goldmine of information.*

Mitch drained the final dregs of his Traditional, holding it up. 'Fancy another?'

Denise smiled, nodded.

Aren't you forgetting something, Mitchel? 'Oh, shit.' He put his hand to his mouth then, his aunty's influence.

Denise chortled. 'You can say shit, I'm a big girl. Have been for a while.'

'Oh, yeah. Blame my Aunty Helen, she doesn't like me swearing. Doesn't care for my drinking either, come to that.'

'You're probably talking to the wrong person, working here and everything.' Denise chuckled again. 'Although some people you see should probably cut down.'

Did she mean him? Mitch was being paranoid, after all she'd asked him for the drink. Denise was talking about the real hard drinkers. Those people you see in pubs when you're having breakfast, ordering their first pint of the day at something like 8 a.m. 'But yeah, no. The burglary, I still haven't sorted out my money situation. My aunty and uncle loaned me some, but a lot of that's gone on stuff like the cat.'

'Oh, the cat!' Denise said excitedly again. 'How is your cat? You're going to have to introduce us someday. After all, I did feed him that time.'

'Sure, aye. Yeah, I mean.' She'd *tried* to feed him . . . her . . . it anyway.

Denise laughed once more. It was a laugh he could get used to. Had been a long time since he'd heard Lucy laugh like that, always stressed about his job, or her work – budgets and lesson plans – or . . . other stuff. Like getting married, like having a family of their own. When had they gone from being that carefree (come off it, you were never such a thing) pair to Mr and Mrs Dull-as-ditchwater? When they moved in together? Before that? Denise gave another laugh, and he looked at her – *really* looked at her for the first time since he'd met the woman again.

No. Don't.

'It's okay, just get them to set up a tab. Tell 'em I'll vouch for you.' More vouching, that's how it worked here. Denise stared at him. 'You're not going to go running off on me now, are you?'

'I, er, not today,' Mitch promised. For one thing he had a mystery to solve, which Denise might inadvertently be the key to.

Now all he needed was something concrete to go to Wilkinson and Larson with. Something they could use to bring the big guns in: CID, the works. Maybe even higher up the chain if this was to do with a cult. As much as he'd hate to see another WACO here, Mitch was determined to bring that Commune down. And maybe Granger with it. 'I'll be right back.'

'I'll be here,' said Denise, placing her elbows on the table, folding her hands in front of her and resting her chin on them.

He looked over his shoulder once as he reached the bar. She was still watching him, staring. Smiling.

Mitch smiled back.

Two pints had turned into three, then four, five . . .

It was over the course of some time, however. Now he'd got a tab, and could 'buy' drinks in return (that's it, he told himself, you're here permanently – they own you!), the rounds had just continued, and so had the conversation. It actually turned into one of the nicest nights he'd had since he returned. Far from being a fact-finding mission, it had proved a welcome diversion from everything else that was going on.

They talked about his dad, not just about the fire, his death, but other things. Denise had filled Mitch in about the time that he'd missed out on. A regular at The Plough, she'd told him about the time Tommy had entertained them all with an impromptu rendition of 'I Am the Very Model of a Modern Major General' from *Pirates of Penzance* one evening, half out of his skull on Traditional and Brandy.

'Blimey, I don't think I *ever* heard my dad sing anything! Let alone Gilbert and Sullivan.'

'There's probably a very good reason for that,' Denise informed him.

'Where did he learn it, I wonder?'

Denise had shrugged. 'But he knew those words off by heart, let me tell you.'

Mitch laughed, at ease for a change, and asked her for more stories – which she was happy to provide. By the time she was finished, he felt he knew his father a little bit better. Not just through the eyes of a boy, but the man Mitch might have got to know when he'd grown up – if he'd bothered to return at all. It had brought on a bout of melancholy, not solely about Tommy Prescott, but also Mitch's sister. 'I-I really need to make more of an effort, you know?'

'How do you mean?'

'With Bella. Go and see her more often. She's my only sister. I mean, I know she left when I was . . . And she should be here now, with me. I mean, don't get me wrong, I understand why she can't, sort of. But I do love her, Denise.'

The barmaid nodded. 'I know you do, sweetheart. Of course you do. Family's everything, brothers, sisters and all that.'

Mitch thought then that Denise hadn't really spoken about her own folks or other relatives all evening, or indeed since he'd been back, so he asked how they were doing. Not that he could remember much about them. The alcohol wasn't helping with his memory, he supposed. Then again, it had taken him a while to even place Denise when he first saw her again.

'Oh, you don't know? But then, how *would* you know? Dad passed away a few years ago now.' Denise's eyes dipped, studied a spot on the table in front of her. 'Mum's doing all right, has good days and bad days.'

It was Mitch's situation in reverse – apart from the fact he'd lost both his parents now. Denise had been practically a grown-up when she lost her dad, though, while he'd been small when his mum went. He wasn't sure which was worse, Denise getting to know her dad only to have that torn away – girls and their fathers, the special bond – or him being barely able to recall his mother. The sense of having been cheated, as he'd said to Helen, but not really knowing what he was missing out on. 'I'm so sorry, Denise.' Before he knew it, he was reaching out his good hand this time, clutching hers to comfort the woman.

She looked up, as surprised as he was, gave him a weak smile – her eyes moist. 'Wasn't long after you left, as it goes. I really could have done with you being around, Mitch, if I'm honest.'

'I'm sorry,' he said again. An apology this time, rather than condolences, but not really understanding what he was apologizing for. Bailing and heading off to see the world? Had he owed this girl – this woman – more than that?

She gave him another squeeze of the hand. 'It's not your fault,' Denise said, so why did it feel like she was blaming him for something? 'I got it. Going off was something you had to do, find yourself or whatever. I got it.' The repetition told him that she really hadn't. Mitch wasn't even sure that he himself had. He was struggling now to remember how they'd parted, hadn't thought about it in years. Hadn't given Denise a second thought when he'd been off on his adventures, when he'd come back and got the job in Downstone. When he'd met and subsequently moved in with . . .

Lucy.

'I'm sorry,' Mitch said for a third time, and he wasn't sure whether he was saying it to Denise or the woman waiting back in the city for him.

'It's just that, I thought we were . . .' Denise shook her head. 'I guess I figured something more might happen. I was a little bit heartbroken. When you took off.'

'I . . .' He didn't know how to reply to that. Had Denise sat here and waited, pining, wondering if he'd return?

There was someone, for quite a while actually. But it didn't work out.'

Waited for him to walk through the doors of this pub and declare his undying love for her, say that he'd made a mistake and after seeing a bit of the world had returned to sweep her off her feet like in some romantic novel or movie? If so, why did that make him feel more guilty than ever – like he should have come back and been with her all along? Like Lucy was the mistake?

228

Except she wasn't. He loved her. The routine they'd got into was just a sign they were compatible, at ease with each other. Wasn't it? Yes, yes of course it was! Yet he couldn't help wondering what might have been.

'It's okay. I understood,' Denise said. 'Just wasn't meant to be, I guess.' She searched his face. 'Was it?'

'I . . .' Mitch began again, but at that precise moment he felt really uncomfortable – and not all of it was to do with the topic of conversation. There was a rumbling in his stomach, which let out a strange gurgle.

Denise couldn't help the laugh that popped out. 'You hungry?'

'No, I . . . Would you—' He wanted to say 'excuse me', but A) Mitch couldn't get the words out, and B) didn't feel like he had the time – just nodded over to the loos and hoped Denise got the message.

She did, letting go of his hand. 'Sure. No worries.'

Mitch tried to get up, but had to grab the edge of the table to make it. This was the first time he'd tried in fairness since he entered the pub, and once again the booze was suddenly hitting him hard. Four or five pints? Over several hours? What was happening to him? He didn't used to be this much of a lightweight. If anything, he should be developing a tolerance.

Or perhaps it was having the opposite effect, a cumulative effect. And his sleep patterns – his sleep in general – had been awful of late, understandably. He'd spent most of one day unconscious in a bloody cave!

He took a step, feeling like he was walking on the moon or something. Then decided the best bet was to just point himself at the gents and let the momentum carry him. It almost ended in disaster when he got to the door and banged into the frame, but he finally made it inside and promptly aimed for the nearest cubicle, locking himself in.

Mitch bent, hand out to steady himself using the cubicle wall. The toilet bowl veered left and right below him, a moving target, but no matter how much his guts churned, somehow he wasn't able to be sick. He got close a couple of times, but then started to feel a little better. Enough to come out again, before heading back in sharpish and at last throwing up. That seemed to take forever, until he was just dry-heaving, clutching the porcelain for support. When he felt like he was done, he straightened up and emptied his bladder, before flushing everything away like it never happened.

God, he hadn't been in this kind of state since studying for the police force – tying more than a few on during benders, some which lasted the whole weekend. Coming out of the other side of it, he'd always felt like he wanted to die, but a full English would usually sort him out. The thought of something like that right now just brought on the nausea once more.

Mitch opened the cubicle door, staggered to the sink and ran the water. He splashed his face, then washed his hands, drying both on the paper towels he got from the dispenser on the wall. He had no idea how long he'd been in there, but when he made it back to the booth at last, Denise had a worried expression on her face. 'I thought you'd got lost,' she said as he stood there, debating whether or not to sit down again.

Got lost . . . Had he been lost? Was he still lost?

'No. Just not sure that last one sat very—' He clutched his stomach again to mime it instead.

'Bad pint?' asked Denise, who looked like she'd seen her fair share of people suffering from those. How often did they clean the pipes in this place?

Mitch nodded, having no idea whether that was the cause. 'I just don't feel . . . I'm not—'

'Okay mister, I think we'd better get you back home, don't you?'

'I'll be—' Then he suddenly had to grab the back of the bench to stop himself from keeling over. Denise was up and there in seconds, the G&Ts she'd consumed having bounced right off her. Her tolerance, as a barmaid, was probably through the roof.

'Come on, sweetheart,' she whispered to him, helping him into his jacket and grabbing his helmet that was on the seat. Then she nodded over to the barman: 'Thanks Ted,' she called to him. Mitch had to wonder what for? Poisoning him? Yeah, thanks for bloody nothing, Ted! Arm in arm again, the same way they'd entered, she led him to the door, then pushed on it to let them both out.

He looked over, the road stretching out ahead of him for miles. 'I . . .' he started again; it was rapidly becoming one of his stock phrases.

'Yeah, I know,' said Denise, making sure he didn't trip as they wandered down that road. 'I know. Won't be long, almost there.'

'I . . .' he managed a final time, trying to say he didn't want to put her out. Hadn't meant to bother her, not like this.

But somehow he felt that it wasn't a bother, not a burden at all. On the contrary, Denise seemed to be quite enjoying it, being able to look after him. For some reason he trusted her to do it, though he had no clue why.

That thing again of thinking maybe he should have been with her all this time, all these years. All that time wasted, lost. Then he could have seen his dad singing in the pub, might have been able to help him when he started to go funny. Could have been helped back home so many times by Denise when he'd had a few.

Home. His real home sweet home. A place he was starting to wonder why he ever left.

And how different things might have been if he hadn't.

Chapter 26

Thought you were lost.

He'd lost so much time, recently too, judging from the light outside. It had been dark when Denise had helped him get back home, when he'd gone to sleep (when had that happened exactly?) and now he could see through the window that it was daytime. A little overcast, but no less warm. And not night anymore. The next morning then? Mitch had no idea, couldn't remember much after the bad pint. Or could he?

Snatches were coming back to him: the incident in the toilet; making it back to the booth; making it back here, Denise having to search his pockets for the key to the front door. Him laughing involuntarily because it tickled. 'Hold still, hold still – almost got it!'

She'd almost got it all right, but that wasn't the key, and he couldn't help chuckling himself at that joke.

'You like that, eh?' Denise had grinned, tickled him some more – which probably wasn't such a great idea, given how queasy he felt, though actually that was wearing off a little. 'Ah, here we go!' she'd produced the key, held it up in front of him. Opened the door, and—

Then suddenly, in the blink of an eye she'd helped him out of his jacket and they were on the stairs, the landing, Denise trying to get him to move towards his mum and dad's old room and Mitch shaking his head. 'Not in there.' Pointing to his old room instead.

'All right, soldier. Here we go.'

And they had gone, Denise taking him to his old room. What he wouldn't have given to have smuggled her inside when he was a teenager, instead of them having to sneak about all over the place, in the meadows, the woods. Near those caves.

Another laugh and he'd looked at his watch, though the hands were swimming. 'D-Do you want to know something?'

'All right,' the woman had replied.

'What time is it?'

'Knocking on for eleven.'

'Ha, yeah. Okay. It's almost my birthday,' he remembered saying. 'Yeah, tomorrow's my birthday.'

Denise had grinned. 'Is that so? Happy Birthday!' The memory came to him then: the kiss. Not the ones from way back when, but fresh. Abrupt, impulsive. She'd taken him off guard; he hadn't been expecting that, given the state he was in. Was she taking advantage of him? Come on, Mitch. Hardly that! If he hadn't wanted it, then—

He'd broken it off, though. Moving his head to the side so she couldn't do it again. Not that it hadn't been fantastic. 'Denise, please. I can't. I have . . . There's a——

Lucy. He had a Lucy, and even as Denise was kissing him, he was seeing her face. Longing for it, because he'd been away from her for far too long. Been away longer than they'd ever really spent apart. Was meant to be with her on his—

'What?' Denise had asked, because he hadn't finished his sentence, had he? Hadn't told her that back in Downstone he had a—

'Girlfriend,' he managed, unable to even look at her. 'I have a girlfriend.'

Silence then. 'Oh,' Denise had whispered. 'Have I just made an idiot of myself?'

'No.' Then more emphatically. '*No.*'

'Because, well, I thought . . . I've been getting mixed signals from you, but I just assumed that was because of—' My dad being murdered? Me being beaten up, seeing a guy roasted alive right in front of me, who was screaming for help (no, don't think about that). Telling you it's my birthday, and expecting . . . what? She shook her head. 'Doesn't matter.'

'No,' he'd repeated a third time.

'Then what? I don't understand. Is it because I'm here and she's not? Where is she anyway? Why isn't she—'

'Lucy,' he broke in.

Denise looked sick herself. 'Why isn't this Lucy woman here with you anyway?'

It was something he was beginning to wonder himself, right when he needed her the most. Where exactly was she? Doing prep for her students, who he sometimes thought were more important than him. He wasn't with it enough to offer Denise an explanation, however.

'If I was your girl then I wouldn't . . .' She sighed. 'No way you'd be here on your own, let's put it that way! You still don't have to be.' Denise placed a hand on the side of his face, turned his head back so he was facing her – but he still wasn't able to look at the woman. Not even as she was placing her lips on his again.

Mitch felt helpless. He liked Denise, and he'd enjoyed spending time with her again, but he didn't want this. Did he? No, Lucy – he *had* to think of Lucy! Again, he pulled away. 'This . . . It's not a good—' At the same time Mitch really didn't want to hurt Denise's feelings; she was a nice person, a kind person, and he should have filled her in about his situation long before now. 'I just don't feel that great.' It was true, he didn't. Wouldn't have been up to anything with the girl he was actually going out with, let alone Denise. 'I just want to . . .' He pointed at the bed, hoping she understood. That she wouldn't misinterpret it as some kind of invitation.

'Right, I get it. You want to go to sleep. Maybe, you know . . . Do you think we could pick this up tomorrow?'

A raincheck? A birthday drink?

Mitch gave her something that was partway between a half-nod and a shake of the head. Then he let her help him over to the bed. 'I'm going to hang around anyway, for a bit. Just to keep an eye on you. That okay?'

Another nod-shake, just like Lucy used to give. And that was all she wrote, all he could recall now he'd woken up, but he guessed there wasn't much else that had happened. Did he remember staggering to the loo at some point, or had he dreamed that? If so, it was all he'd dreamed, thankfully. The toilet had probably happened, because he didn't feel that overwhelming urge to go that he usually did when he'd drunk too much and woke up. Might just be dehydrated?

Whatever was the case, Denise had more than likely bailed at some point. Mitch couldn't say he blamed her, she'd watched over him till she was sure he wasn't going to choke on his own vomit or something; wouldn't exactly have been a great start to his birthday. It was more than he deserved for leading her on. Was that what he'd done? He hadn't thought so, had tried to keep her at arm's length if anything until yesterday – and then he just hadn't wanted to be alone, he supposed. Today of all days. Had wanted to reconnect with – Denise, Lucy – his dad. After what had happened, he just wanted to talk to someone who wasn't a . . .

Stranger.

So Denise hadn't woken him up, and he hadn't made a fool of himself last night which was something. Hadn't slept with her, though if he hadn't felt so sleepy and under other circumstances might he have? He hadn't though, that was the main thing. They'd just kissed. Get it right, *she'd* kissed *him*. He'd have to tell Lucy about it at some point, but at least he wouldn't have to explain anything more than that. Kiss, a birthday kiss when he wasn't really thinking straight.

Awake, right . . . Think about that. He was awake now, because something had woken him up. Noises, downstairs. *Was* Denise still here? Was she cooking breakfast or whatever? Mitch checked his watch. No, because it was late afternoon again already. The day had gotten away from him, his birthday – not that he had much to celebrate. He'd lost so much time, and God it was so, so hot today! Stick with it, Mitch. What had woken him? Not just the noises, but—

He heard a meowing in his ear, jumped at the movement. Cat, who'd been completely absent the night before, was now on his bed again crying. Probably wanted food. 'Okay, okay,' he croaked, his voice cracking. But that wasn't just because of the state he'd been in, his voice was hoarse because of the—

Smoke.

There was smoke, he could taste it. Faint, but there. And now the cat wasn't just crying, wasn't wanting to be fed. It was trying to get him up and out of bed. Trying to warn him. Screaming at him that there was danger, clawing at the mattress. Not only could he taste the smoke, but now he could see it, coming in through the open door. He could smell it too: acrid, unrelenting.

'Christ!' he hissed. Cat hopped down off the mattress and went over to that door, standing there and urging him to join it. Definitely had the right idea. At the very least he needed to see where that smoke was coming from, because there was never smoke without—

Mitch could see it, even as he got to the door of his old bedroom. The flickering on the walls of the landing, red and yellow fingers stretching upstairs, reaching for the upper levels. Just the reflection of it at the moment, but it wouldn't be long before the real thing reached them up here. He bent and scooped up Cat. It made no attempt to scramble free, to get out of his clutches (which was good because his hand was still throbbing a little from the barn door). Cat was apparently happy to let someone else do the legwork, now that its job was over and it had alerted him to the danger.

He got to the top of the stairs, looked downwards and saw those flames – angry, fierce. Coming from the kitchen, from where the cellar was. Had it started in there? Wherever it had begun, it was going to tear through the entire house – and them too if he didn't get them both out. Mitch took the stairs two at a time, ambitious given he still felt like seven kinds of dog crap. But the adrenalin was kicking in, getting him moving. The race was on, to get out through the front door before the fire prevented him. There were already smaller fires simmering in the living room, which meant that this wasn't a natural thing. Someone had started them, maybe the same person who'd set fire to Neil Sheldon. Farmer Granger, or his workers, or his co-conspirators in the Commune? Mitch had obviously become too much of a threat to leave alive.

Almost tripping on the bottom step, he stumbled forward, free hand already out to unlock and open the front door up. He tugged on the handle, but the wood was sticking: probably warped. The fire was on the left of him, behind him, coming at him in a pincer movement. Cat was going mental in his other hand, preparing to abandon him perhaps if he couldn't save them.

Mitch could feel the heat now, *real* heat, the sweat running down his back, dripping from his forehead. Running into his eyes and making them sting. Hoping that Denise really had left the house, she was probably well into another shift at The Plough by now, he gave one last almighty tug on the door and it opened, allowed him to tumble outside with the animal held close. Mitch ran forward a few metres, then stopped and did an about-turn. That seemed to be the only thing the fire was waiting for, and it burst out through the gap like a tongue attempting to lap at him and the feline.

Moments later it was on the upper levels. Mitch looked up and saw the flames at the windows there, the fire taking the whole of his – of his father's – house. It was mesmerizing, a few seconds more in bed and he would have been ravaged by the thing; would have been trapped. Cat let out another cry, legs kicking to be let down.

'Right, yeah.' Mitch set the creature down, and the action seemed to snap him awake again. He rushed to the neighbour's house, banging on the door to warn them – and get them to call the fire brigade if no one had already. If he was lucky and they called right now, the fire engine might be here in a couple of weeks.

Nobody answered, but it was as he was doing this that he spotted them. Men, dressed in black hoodies – no caps this time, because the hoods were pulled up – and jeans, getting into a dirty grey van that looked like it had seen better days. The kind of vehicle he'd spotted up at the Commune, or at the farm. At *both* places.

As they did a couple of nights ago, people started to emerge from their homes to see what was happening, and it was only this that made Mitch feel like it was okay to leave. To chase after those bastards even as the van set off trundling away from the square. Mitch ran after it, luckily still mostly dressed, with his shoes on from the night before, past the tape around the war memorial and thought to himself that his dad's old place would be cordoned off as well soon enough. Another crime scene in Green Acres. Another fire. Arson this time, to add to double murder. Oh, those guys were going to pay – whoever was responsible – he'd make sure of that!

The van sped away, leaving him behind – on foot as he was. But it was then that he remembered he hadn't brought his bike back to the house last night. He'd left it round the side of The Plough, which the van was now passing. Perfect!

As he made for the pub, Denise was outside, hands going to her mouth when she looked at the building he'd come from. Seeing the fire, probably thinking she'd been in there not so long ago. Almost certainly giving thanks for the fact Mitch was okay, knowing how she felt about him.

'Wha—?' he heard her say as he got nearer.

'Call the police!' Mitch shouted. He didn't have time for formalities. 'Tell them I'm in pursuit of the gits who did it!' He didn't say anything about where they might be heading, because he didn't know. At this stage it could have been anywhere: the Commune, the farm, the caves, the woods? Or none of them. That was why he had to follow them, trail them to their destination and make sure. Mitch unlocked his bike, got on the back of it. His helmet was back in the house, so he'd have to do without. Let them fine him, like he gave a toss! If they caught up with him – and he doubted very much it would be Wilkinson who did that – then they could give him a ticket, as they were arresting those hoodies in the van. Wouldn't matter then.

Mitch gunned the engine, ignoring Denise as she came over, leaving her behind. He glanced down in the rear mirrors, seeing her standing there and staring after him. Worrying about him, just like Lucy did when he was on duty.

Two of them now, he thought. *Well done, Mitchel!*

That was the least of his problems at the moment. Number-one priority was catching up with the van, now that he could match them in the speed department. It was only when he was on the bike that he started to feel it again, the queasiness from last night coming back in waves. Mitch tamped it down, there was no time for all that, no time for letting up. He had to push the machine harder, until he could see the—

There it was, the filthy grey van, just ahead of him. Mitch sped up, it wouldn't take him long to cover that distance, and before he knew it he was coughing from a different kind of smoke, the van's exhaust spewing out and hitting him in the face. He weaved, but managed to keep the Honda on track. Managed to keep behind the van, hopefully where they couldn't see him through their own side mirrors.

They must have spotted him approaching, though, because the van suddenly braked – and if he hadn't hit his own brakes and slowed down, he'd have slammed right into the back of the thing. '*Bastards!*' Mitch spat under his breath, leaning to try to get around the left-hand side of the vehicle.

The van steered the same way as him, and he had to pull back behind again. Mitch gritted his teeth, tried the other side. If he could get in front, he might be able to force *them* off the road and into a ditch or something. A long shot, as they were much bigger and in a virtual tank compared to him – at the moment he was like a fly buzzing around their heads – but he had to take the shot, hope that his luck (his birthday luck) held out. Already he'd escaped from a flaming house today, so he was pushing it.

As Mitch gunned the engine again and accelerated, he felt sure he was going to make it. Almost made it the length of the van, nearly to the front wheel – could see the driver through the open window, but not his face because of the hood, which was still up. *Almost there*, he thought to himself, *almost there*.

Then suddenly the driver jerked the steering wheel right. Like the fire, it was as if he'd been waiting for Mitch before making a move: in this instance it was to clip the bike, then accelerate. Mitch lost his balance, skidded and ended up being flung off his ride into the long grass. He hit the ground and rolled over and over several times, flattening the greenery. By the time he managed to get to his feet again, reeling sideways, the van had disappeared – but there were still plumes of blackness being pumped out behind it.

And he could see where it was heading.

Shaking his head to clear it, Mitch ignored the cuts and grazes on his arms, limped back over to his bike. Even before he reached it, though, he could see it was done. In a passing place, all right, as in passed away. The front wheel was bent, would have to be replaced altogether. There was no way he was getting back on that to trail the van. Left with no option, he set off on foot. It would take a while but he'd get there even if it killed him. At this rate, it just might.

Mitch set off, limping down the road. Making for the turning, which would take him to his destination.

* * *

It felt like he'd never get there.

He could have done with skipping over *this* part of the day, because the limp up there seemed like it took forever. Wasn't the first time he'd made this trip on foot, but he hadn't been in this kind of shape back then; had narrowly escaped serious injury, possibly death, twice. Now he just felt like death warmed up, that bad pint still affecting him.

But he had to come, there was no choice. There was nobody else who could do this. Every step of the journey, the walk up here, Mitch had an ear cocked for sirens. For the cavalry he'd asked Denise to phone. Who was he kidding? You had to be on fire yourself around here before anyone took notice of you, and even then they took their sweet time responding. Wilkinson did anyway. The guy was practically in a coma, even when he was awake. Tammy flashed through his mind again as he thought that; Mitch wondered whether he would ever see his friend again. If she'd ever recover.

He had to shove all that aside again, had other things to deal with that were more pressing. If he'd been thinking straight, Mitch wouldn't have come within a mile of this place – it hadn't exactly gone very well the last time, had it? And he'd felt like he stood half a chance then, unlike today. But he had right on his side and somehow that gave him the strength to carry on, like he was on some kind of one-man crusade. In a way he was.

They weren't even trying to hide what they'd done, which didn't exactly inspire confidence. There was the filthy grey van, parked outside the barn where he'd had the altercation with Granger. Where he'd been threatened with the shotgun, and who's to say that madman wouldn't be back again waving his cannon around like someone from a Guy Ritchie movie.

The place looked as deserted as before, so Mitch just lurched onwards. Moving towards the huge building again, which was open more than a crack this time. No sign of the chains or the lock at all, and a light was coming from inside.

Mitch looked about him, expecting to be ambushed at any moment – or maybe they assumed they'd dealt with him back there when they rammed his bike. They hadn't stopped to check, but had done enough damage that maybe they figured he wouldn't be getting up and coming here. Who'd be crazy enough to follow them after all that?

He had to wonder himself. Crazy. Is that what he was, is that what his dad had been? Forget about the dementia, this was just plain suicidal, right? The kind of action that gets you set alight in the woods. Gets you beaten up and the place where you're living set on fire?

When in Rome, however, and he needed to see what was inside that barn. What all this had been about. Felt sure the answers would be inside.

Mitch stepped through, following that light. And some of the answers he already knew; even before he'd discovered them himself by coming back, he'd known. Some of the things he saw in there shocked him. Shocked him to the very core. Made him feel like he was well and truly lost.

Then he was aware of someone just behind him, standing there by the door on the inside like he'd been waiting for Mitch to come through it and witness these sights. Not Granger, because as Mitch was turning he saw a fleeting glimpse of somebody else. As they whispered to him, a hand on his shoulder. One word, that made him lose time again. One word: more than simply a suggestion. Something embedded so deep he had no choice but to obey the command.

The voice whispered, 'Sleep.'

Chapter 27

As he yawned, he thought to himself: *Sleep*.

That's what he really needed, because Lord knows he hadn't had much of late. Not since Bella Prescott had waltzed into his nick, which seemed like such a long time ago now. No, Ashley Watts thought to himself, it felt simultaneously ages but only like yesterday. If you measure time by events then so much had happened since she'd come to see him, asked for him personally.

It had culminated with him taking her in, staying at his place – which was what he'd first suggested when she'd told him about the break-in. A break-in he could find absolutely no evidence of, and she didn't want to officially report. So off he'd gone again, looking into something that he really should have been keeping his nose out of. Speaking to a few of her friends after being so worried about her (like Vicky and Julie who went to her gatherings), following their chat on the beach. Finding out she'd been acting weirdly for a while, had cancelled things like the turn she did at The Majestic (was that the right name for it? Probably not – Bella saw it as more about helping people than a performance). Spending time investigating all that when he should have been working, had more than enough on. Going down that same rabbit hole he'd fallen into with Robyn when she'd been here.

Worried about Bella in the same way, actually. No, not exactly the same. Robyn was, well, Robyn. And he hoped, prayed, that one day something might actually . . . Then there was Bella. Who he'd only known fleetingly until the last week or more, but now considered a friend. A good friend. But that was beside the point, wasn't it? He'd have been concerned about anyone who'd come to him saying that someone had broken into their place, who'd looked the way Bella had when he called to see how she was. How distant she'd become, preoccupied, not the confident woman he'd met the previous summer.

He'd been worried enough to come back again, then stake the place out. Wait and see if she came back because she hadn't answered his knocks. A good job he had, because her caravan had caught light not long afterwards and he'd had to get her out of the place. Only to discover that the intruder – sorry, intruders plural, because if she was to be believed there were more than one now – caused the blaze.

If she was to be believed.

Because he'd seen no one else around, had he? It was entirely possible they'd come into the park the back way, but he still would have spotted them. Wouldn't he? Wasn't as if he'd been doing anything *but* waiting and watching. Watching as Bella's van caught fire, seeing her outline through the windows. Talk about a mystery.

If she'd had insurance, and she told him not long afterwards that she'd never really been able to afford any, then he would have said she'd done it for the payout. Looking for a way to get away from this place, this life. But that just wasn't her, was it? By all accounts Bella was – or had been – happy here. Had a life she was happy with in Golden Sands. Things had only really changed when she'd heard her father had died.

'If you ask me,' Vicky had told Watts when he'd spoken to her, 'I think it threw her. I think she cared more about him than she let on. A tragedy like that, it can do strange things to people.

Especially if you weren't around when it happened.' That woman definitely spoke from experience, she'd been through enough tragedy to last a lifetime: the whole family had. Yet Bella had been adamant about not going back home, it seemed. Had left her brother Mitch to deal with the arrangements, so maybe it was the guilt of that affecting her? But the death had nothing to do with whoever was staging these attacks. Or did it? Did Bella Prescott have enemies, *real* enemies? Organized enemies?

If you'd asked Watts a couple of years ago whether it was possible thugs could be breaking into places and starting fires here, he'd have thought you were mad. But things on the crime front had certainly ramped up recently. Not just the murder case he'd been involved in, but drugs, prostitution, even rumours of human trafficking. Someone having a grudge against Bella – maybe someone from her past who hadn't liked what she'd had to tell them from a deceased relative – and hassling her, driving her out of her home with arson. It wasn't all that hard to swallow really.

So he'd promised her he'd get to the bottom of it all, look into it. Watts had wanted to make it in an official capacity. Let's face it, she'd be dead if he hadn't been on hand to drag her out of the burning caravan. That was attempted murder, manslaughter at the very least – if the culprits had known she was at home. How could they *not* have known? It wasn't that big a place she lived in! But Bella had still insisted on keeping it between them, made him promise.

That hadn't prevented it from coming to the attention of his boss, O'Brien. Not a lot escaped her notice in that town, but burning caravans had a tendency to stick out. Especially when Watts was personally involved, when he said he needed to take some time away from their current cases to make sure Bella was okay. O'Brien had been uncharacteristically charitable about it all, had been in a house fire and only just escaped when she was younger, it turned out, so could sympathize. But she had asked, 'Is there anything we need to be worrying about with this one?'

'I'm not exactly sure yet. Waiting to hear what the official report from the fire investigator says.'

'And this is all about another woman, right?' O'Brien had looked at him sideways, as she often did. 'You're not going to start mooning about the office again, are you, Watts?'

Watts had shaken his head emphatically. 'It's not like that, guv. I'm just looking out for her.'

'Yeah, that's how it usually starts with you.'

O'Brien wasn't wrong, it was how he got into a lot of his messes. This time, however, he was genuinely just looking out for Bella. That's why he'd offered the use of his flat. Or was it because he wanted to keep an eye on her? A bit of both?

That, however, had resulted in his current exhausted state. The first night, when he'd taken the couch and she'd reluctantly taken his bed (also borrowing a pair of his pyjamas), he'd been woken by loud crying. Watts wasn't sure whether she was asleep and dreaming, or just upset about her home. No one would blame her. It had settled down sometime in the wee small hours, but that hadn't meant he'd been able to drift back off. Then, before he knew it, the alarm was going and it was time to make his visitor breakfast. He'd cooked scrambled eggs, his morning speciality – and it wasn't often he had guests, certainly not ones who stayed overnight (Robyn had never even seen the inside of his place), so he'd decided to push the boat out. He'd laughed at that thought as he put the eggs in the pan; where better to push boats out than at a place like Golden Sands?

Bella had emerged from the bathroom looking like a panda, the shadows around her eyes blacker than ever. If he'd thought she might feel more relaxed, more secure here – enough to be able to catch up on her rest – then he'd been sadly mistaken. All she'd done with her eggs was shove them around the plate with her fork, choosing instead to nibble on half a slice of toast, cut into triangles in honour of her staying.

It had crossed his mind to ask her about the crying, but Watts

246

had no idea how to raise the subject. Wasn't that great at chatting to the opposite sex anyway, didn't have that much experience of it (not that the lads down the station were aware of this). Wasn't your typical blokey bloke in the slightest. So all he'd said was, 'Bella, listen.'

She'd looked at him then with bleary, blood-shot eyes, and he'd never felt so sorry for anyone in his life. 'Yes?'

'You know you can talk to me, don't you? Tell me anything.'

Bella had nodded, but said nothing.

He'd needed to pop out, grab her more clothes apart from anything else (all of hers had gone up in flames), just casual stuff like jeans and T-shirts once he had her sizes, but wondered if he should really be leaving her on her own. Bella wasn't the type to do something stupid, though, was she? Hadn't been before – she'd been much more confident back when he first met her. Still wouldn't take too kindly to being babysat, he figured. So he'd headed out for a little while as she sat there and let old movies on the TV wash over her, knees pulled up and hugging herself on his couch. 'You going to be okay?' he'd enquired before he went out and she'd given a faint nod. 'You're sure?'

'Ashley, I'll be just fine,' she assured him, shades of her old self. 'Please stop worrying.'

She'd still been in the same position when he returned later on, hadn't moved an inch as far as he could tell. At least she hadn't tried to slit her wrists or anything. Then she'd headed off to bed quite early, he assumed to try to grab some of those z's that had escaped her the previous night.

The screaming had woken him at about 2 a.m. – he'd only just managed to get to sleep – but that was probably because Bella was standing in the middle of his living room bellowing her lungs out. 'Jesus!' Watts had cried, sitting bolt upright on the sofa and flicking on the side lamp that was next to him.

There she was, just gazing out into space, now that she'd roused him. Him and probably everyone else in the entire building, though there was no knocking on walls, the floor with the end of a broom or banging coming from the ceiling. 'Bella?' he'd called out to her, but she hadn't answered. It was like she was awake, but not awake. Seeing something that wasn't present, holding her hands out now as if he could help. *Sleepwalking?* he thought to himself. No, this was different; his dad had done a bit of that, so he had some prior experience. And this was infinitely more chilling.

He didn't know whether to call to her again or not. You shouldn't wake sleepwalkers, Watts knew that much. People in trances he wasn't sure about. And it occurred to him then that this might be connected to that thing Bella did, regardless of the fact she'd told him a couple of times now that it didn't work that way. That she heard voices, didn't *see* things like other mediums might.

Watts had been getting up though, which was just as well because as he did so Bella looked like she was going to keel over, drop forwards and land flat on her face. He'd just about got to her in time, catching the woman before that happened. She was mumbling something as she lay there in his arms, and he just made out the name, 'Mitch'.

Then she was out of it again, eyes closed and breathing heavily. She looked like Sigourney Weaver in *Ghostbusters* when Bill Murray catches her levitating. Watts had carried her back to the bedroom, returning her to his bed. He thought about calling for an ambulance, but she'd already settled down a bit. He'd hung around anyway, sitting in the wooden chair in the corner and watching her for a while in case she decided to start floating above the covers.

It had been Bella who'd woken him up that morning, after he must have dropped to sleep eventually. She'd shaken his shoulder, and he'd started. 'Wha—'

'Shh. Ashley, shh.' She was a fine one to be shushing him, the racket she'd been making the night before. 'It's okay.'

'Bella? What time is it?'

'Later than I'd like it to be, I overslept.'

248

He glanced at his watch, it was gone eleven. 'Probably needed it. Are *you* all right?'

She was simply staring at him, but in a different way than she'd been gaping at apparently nothing last night in the living room. 'No,' she admitted. 'No, I'm not. But I know what's happening now, I think. Sort of. Some of it anyway. The fog's beginning to lift.'

'You were screaming last night.' He thumbed back to the room beyond the door. 'Out there in the living room.'

Bella nodded; definitely seemed more lucid. 'Yeah, I'm sorry.'

'And you were saying your brother's name.'

Another nod. 'He's in really big trouble, Ashley. So much trouble.'

'How do you mean?'

'In Green Acres. I should have gone with him. I just hope it's not too late.'

'Too late for what?'

Then she held his gaze without blinking and said: 'He's in so much danger.'

Again, Watts was shaking his head, not understanding a word of this. Why was he in danger? Who from? But as chilling as Bella had been last night, the next thing she said chilled him so much more:

'I think . . . Ashley, I think they're going to kill him.'

Chapter 28

The only way he could think of describing this, was that it felt like his mind was rising up through layers of mist or fog.

This time Mitch did dream. He saw the figures, the fire. But that was hardly surprising given what he'd seen before he went under. *Interesting choice of words*, he thought. He hadn't just gone to sleep, he'd been *put* to sleep. One word doing it, like—

He'd seen this somewhere before, seen it done, but like everything else in this strange dreamscape, it was elusive. Hard enough to think, let alone anything else. So he just watched to begin with, watched as the hooded people in his dream did their thing. Muttering in their weird language, dancing round that fire. What he could see under those hoods looked like mannequin's faces.

Where was he? All right, so he was dreaming – but of what place? And he realized why it was so hard to pin down, because it was constantly shifting. First he was in his cellar, someone's cellar anyway – looked like his dad's – then he was in the caves again, where he'd seen that ritual recently, the first time.

Had it been the first time? He wasn't so sure anymore.

Wasn't sure about anything. Except that he'd seen it again just before being put to sleep. He'd been in the barn, Granger's barn.

Had chased the people in black there, the ones who'd set fire to his father's house.

The figures in the hoods . . . hoodies? No, definitely hoods now. Robes, too – dark robes. More maroon than black, now he thought about it. Preparing. Mitch had stared at the barn walls, painted red and yellow. Painted to resemble flames, to look like fire. The bunting and ribbons in those same colours decorating the tops, the corners of the barn: a celebration, like when he'd first arrived back. And in the centre of the room, a bonfire much bigger than the one he'd spied on in the caves, made out of kindling. On the floor encircling it were strange symbols and markings, again painted in reds and yellows. They were getting ready for something much bigger here, to *call up* something much bigger? Not a demon, but maybe the head guy himself? That's what they believed anyway. Wasn't real, couldn't be.

Nothing in his dreams was real, he reminded himself. But before, back out there in the waking world, he'd definitely seen those preparations in the barn. Hadn't he?

It was making him question everything, but yes. He remembered faces under those hoods, human faces. Some he didn't recognize, people who worked up here at the farm? But others he did. Granger was here, naturally. And his sister.

What he hadn't been expecting was Wilkinson. The old sergeant standing there in his robes, wearing one of those hoods. Just watching all the prep, because Lord knows if he was to help it would take them ages. Watching as . . . Larson put the finishing touches to one of the paintings. Hidden creative depths, the doctor had. Hidden lots of things.

It explained why Mitch had never been able to get any traction with the investigation, why things kept getting swept under the carpet. Or set fire to. The authorities here were in the Commune's back pocket, under their control. Mitch recalled some of the things he'd learned then about those cults, the methods they used. Cult of personality, Daniel and Leah. They'd wormed their way in . . .

But also how groups like that used persuasion, hypnosis. Were these people doing things against their will? Hadn't Mitch read that you couldn't do that, couldn't force someone to do something under hypnosis that they wouldn't otherwise do? Couldn't get somebody to kill, for example, if it wasn't already in their nature.

Still, the thought was there. That these people might just be the Commune's zombies, their workforce or foot soldiers, that they were being prevented from thinking for themselves. Innocents, being used to do the cult's dirty work. Key figures in the area, bent out of shape so they could get away with all this. Was that what his dad had seen, what he found out about? And he'd been too strong, or even too far gone with the dementia to turn? What about Sheldon?

Mitch had witnessed all this, was dreaming about it now too, but suddenly started to rise up through that mist. Rise to the surface again, back to the real world, the suggestion – hypnotic suggestion? – wearing off now. Or was he being brought out of this, what . . . trance?

I'm counting down from five. Four, three, two, one. You're back in the room!

I'm getting a Henry? Does anyone here know a Henry, he's trying to tell you—

No, nothing like what his sister did back in Golden Sands. Forget what he'd said to Denise, she wasn't really a performer.

She didn't hypnotize people like some corny stage magician, Mitch was bloody certain about that. Didn't fool them into thinking she was talking to their deceased loved ones. She actually believed it.

Why was he thinking about Bella again? Was it because he was worried about her?

Or because she should be here with him. Because he *needed* her, for Heaven's sake! Because he needed her help! Like he'd never needed anyone before.

Fight it. Bloody well fight it!

Mitch's mind was racing, pouring out gibberish as he rose through those layers of fog. As he returned to – what he hoped was – reality.

Back to the barn, goodness knows how much later. Minutes, hours? It was hard to tell. There were even more of the robed figures inside here now, he saw them milling around as he shook his head from side to side. And, yes, there was the ginger guy, the red-haired bloke he'd last seen at the Commune, and the acne-riddled – burned – woman. In their other, darker outfits.

'Well now, would you look who's back with us!' A female voice, followed by a clap of the hands as the small woman put them together in joy. Granger's sister again, what had her name been? Ella? Ellie, yes that was it! Her hood was down at the moment, and she was grinning from ear to ear, delighted Mitch was awake again. 'How wonderful!'

Mitch tried to move, struggled. Realized he was tethered to something. Chained to some kind of post, hands behind his back.

Just like Neil Sheldon had been.

Had they tried to do that to his dad? Maybe he'd got away from them, and they'd set fire to him as he ran? Or had they needed to restrain him anyway if he was having one of his bad days? So many questions. Some of which had already been answered, confirmed, some that were still hanging in the air.

'Cam! Cam!' Ellie called over her shoulder. 'He's woken up, tell the others! Tell all our brothers and sisters.'

'*Good day, brother!*'

'*Brothers!*'

She faced Mitch once more. 'Almost time, young man. Almost time. Oh, it's so exciting!' Ellie clapped again.

'Let me go!' he shouted at her. 'Unchain me!'

Ellie just laughed, had no intention of doing that. Was waiting for 'the others' to arrive, clearly. Daniel, Leah, all of their lot. Granger strode past his sister, nodded a grudging hello at Mitch. His opinion hadn't changed of the man from the night in the pub, from the encounter on the road: complete psycho! Unless he was also being controlled? Another innocent? Mitch doubted it somehow.

Over Ellie's shoulder he saw a familiar face. So Mitch hadn't imagined that bit, then? Hadn't dreamed it, assuming he was actually awake at the moment. 'Larson! Hey, Larson!' The man looked up and over, touched his chest like he was surprised Mitch was even calling to him. 'Yeah, you! Get me out of this!' Mitch strained against his bonds again, but it was useless.

Larson trotted over to stand not far away from Granger's sister. 'I'm afraid I can't do that. Sorry.' He said it like it was the most reasonable thing in the world, and he still had that bloody smug expression on his face – only now Mitch just wanted to wipe it off.

'Are you . . . Can you think for yourself? Are you being controlled?' It sounded barking mad even as he was saying it.

'Not that I know of,' came the reply from the medic.

'Then why are you—' Another thought occurred to him then. 'Are you being blackmailed? What do they have on you?'

Larson looked confused. 'Who?'

'The Commune!' snapped Mitch.

Wilkinson had joined them by this time, Ellie wandering off again to do something else. 'I'll handle this,' said the old man in his characteristic drawl.

'You'll handle . . . You mean like you've handled everything else, everything since my dad? What really happened to those campers, Wilkinson? The ones who gave the statements?'

Scared the life out of them.

'Sent them on their way? I bet you did! Couldn't risk anyone from the outside coming and poking around, could you? Anyone else that is!'

'People go missing here,' the sergeant told him.

'Yeah, I know. The lights, the UFO bull, right?'

He nodded. 'Something like that.'

254

'Oh no, the lights! Holy . . .You didn't? You did, you burned them to death, didn't you?'

The policeman said nothing. He didn't have to.

'And Sheldon's wife, partner. You did the same to her. She wasn't *away* anywhere at all, was she?'

'She was not,' came another voice off to the side of him. Mitch turned, saw another man in those robes, limping this time, leaning heavily on a stick.

'Nuttall? Not you as well?'

'*Never get old, son.*'

'*I'm not planning on it anytime soon.*' Might not get the chance.

Just how deep did all this go? The Commune was like a parasite, burrowing into the very heart of Green Acre's infrastructure, wasn't it? He shouldn't have been too surprised, they apparently had their hooks in the police, the medical examiner. Why not politics? All that talk about strangers and wanting them gone, it had all just been a—

A smokescreen.

And Mitch was the latest one to fall victim to it all. But why not just kill him when they broke into his house that night? Drag him away and set fire to him out in the square like they'd done with Sheldon? (He had to wonder now whether it had just been Granger on his own who'd done that, or if he'd had help . . . probably the latter.) Or drag Mitch off to the woods, the caves, to do the deed there instead?

'I can see you have a lot of things you want to ask, lad,' said Nuttall, then looked at his watch. 'I'm not sure we have time for all your questions, but we'll do our best to make you understand. It's the least we can do really, in exchange for everything you've . . . Everything you're about to do for us tonight.'

So it was night now? Early evening at the very least. 'You mean you'll get me to see, do that whole "look into my eyes, not around my eyes" bollocks.' Though he had to admit, nobody had looked at him when he fell into his trance. They hadn't needed

255

to, just touched his shoulder and whispered the word. That was how good they were.

'No. No more of that, we don't need to,' said Nuttall. 'No more drugs either.'

'Drugs?' Shitting hell! Seriously, drugs? 'When?'

'Ever since you arrived. Nothing much, just enough. Except for last night. The barman got a little carried away,' admitted Nuttall. 'Overzealous.'

'The bar—'

Thanks, Ted. What for? Poisoning him? Yeah, thanks for bloody nothing, Ted!

'But I was there to keep an eye on you,' said another voice, a female voice. Someone he'd asked to call the authorities before chasing the hooded figures up here in the first place, not that the call would have got through to the outside world anyway. 'Hi Mitch,' said Denise, holding up a hand in greeting. 'I told you, didn't I?

'Told you we'd pick this up again tomorrow.'

Chapter 29

He still looked so confused, and she could understand that.

Bella had tried her best to explain, as much as she could, even though it was still very much a muddle in her own mind. What she'd been seeing, a mixture of her memories and someone else's. Someone who'd been trying to warn her. Trying to get through a barrier – those headaches of hers, which had finally, *thankfully* faded away. The one thing she'd known for sure, that she'd been at pains to make Ashley Watts understand, was this:

Her brother Mitch was in grave danger. There were people at Green Acres who were going to kill him unless they stopped them. Unless they set off right that very moment, to prevent it from happening.

'Bella, if you think Mitch might be in trouble, why don't we just get in touch with the authorities there? I can—'

'It won't make any difference, don't you see? The authorities, they've been . . . They're not what you think, Ashley.'

'What?'

Bella had shaken her head, wasn't getting things across very well. Didn't really know how to. Not properly. 'They wouldn't listen, and by the time you get through it'll be too late. Ashley, please! You said you'd help me. You promised.'

'If you think there's an imminent threat to life, we should let O'Brien know. She'd be able to—'

'You think she'd believe you? Believe you based on my word. On my feelings?'

'Er, yeah.' A pause. 'Okay, maybe not.'

'So . . .'

'Look, I'm not sure what you want me to do here, Bella?'

She'd risen then, started to walk away from him, to get her clothes together. 'I'm heading off to Green Acres, I'll take the next train if I have to. But I have to go, have to save him Ashley. I've made a promise myself.'

'Train?' Watts got up out of the chair where he'd been watching over her, where he waited until she'd finally woken up, late: over-slept. Woken up as well to the fact that Mitch, her baby brother, was going to die if she didn't do something about it. How she could have left him back then she didn't know, but she really hadn't had a choice with that either, had she? Had left him all alone there.

She wouldn't leave him to suffer his fate alone now, that was for damned sure!

'There are no trains directly to Green Acres, none that I know of anyway.'

'I'll get as far as I can, then jump in a taxi,' she told him, at the same time realizing she didn't have any money.

'I can't let you do that,' Watts told her. 'Bella, this is insane!' He'd grabbed her wrist then and she'd looked down.

'You want to let go of me,' Bella said, in a voice she hoped would convey the urgency of what she was trying to do – but was aware was coming across as hostile. After everything he'd done for her, as well. He must think she was a complete bitch, but she just couldn't get him to understand. There wasn't the time! 'I'm sorry Ashley, I know you mean well. But this is important. It's *so* important, I can't begin to—'

Watts did as she asked and took his hand away, sighing. 'Can't we just talk about this?'

'Not unless we're talking on the way,' she said to him, hopefully.

She could see him thinking: it would probably take the best part of a day to get to Green Acres from there, even if he broke a few speed limits. But he was thinking about it. In the end, once he could see how determined she was to go anyway, he'd agreed to drive her.

They'd dressed, not even had time to eat, and headed off in his silver saloon. Hadn't spoken for the first few miles, as Watts drove them to the motorway, which was already rammed, but Bella caught him looking across at her every now and again, probably wondering when she was going to start talking.

But there was nothing really to talk about, they were doing the only thing they could do. They were the only people who were in a position to help Mitch, if he *could* be helped, and not even she was sure she'd succeed.

All they could do was try.

Once they were beyond the point of no return, she'd told him the one thing she did know. The thing that might have changed his mind about taking her to Green Acres at all. She'd debated whether or not to say anything, but if she wanted him to trust her she had to.

So the next time he'd looked over, expecting her to explain herself, she'd said, 'Okay, okay. I'm going to tell you something now, Ashley. Something you might have suspected, but hear me out before you stop the car or turn around or anything.'

'I'm listening,' he said.

'I think I saw my mother the other night,' she said. 'My dead mother.'

Bella thought he was going to run the car off the road. 'But I thought you said, I mean, you don't see things, right? You hear them? Get messages.' He sounded like he didn't even believe that, let alone anything else.

'I didn't say I understood it, just that I think that's what happened. She was the figure out there in the caravan park.'

'The one on fire?'

Bella nodded. 'She was in an accident, was hit by a car when Mitch was small. The car went up in flames, and both she and the driver died.'

'O-Okay.'

'Look, there's a lot more to this and it's all so complicated, but before I get into it, I just need to tell you this one other thing.'

Watts nodded now.

'Ashley, I think I was the one who ransacked my place, my caravan. I didn't know it was me but, well, I think I did that and—'

'Yes?' he asked, his voice cracking; he sounded terrified.

Bella looked across at him. She didn't think she'd ever seen anyone so confused in all her life as she went on:

'And I think I was the one who set it on fire.'

Chapter 30

'Don't look so confused,' Denise said to him.

Mitch didn't know how he was supposed to look. The woman he'd spent much of the previous day with, who he thought was quite possibly in love with him – had been since they'd been at school – she was *in* on this? Had been turned by the Commune like the rest of them? Sure, the barman had drugged him – why not? Wasn't the craziest thing that had happened since his return. But for some reason he'd never thought Denise might have known. She'd been so lovely, and he'd felt so guilty about letting her down. She'd turned out to be quite the actor after all.

'Hey, I know what you're thinking. But it was all genuine, what I said. How I feel,' she offered then as if reading his mind. 'How I've *always* felt about you, Mitch. It was so hard to let you go back then, you have absolutely no idea.' Her eyes were moistening again like last night. 'But, well, we all have to sacrifice things. We all have our parts to play in this.'

'Parts to . . . ?'

Denise stepped forwards, the maroon robe she had on, hood down, swishing around her. In another time or place he might have said that it suited her. She ran a finger down his front, down his chest. 'What a shame you had that reaction to the stuff they gave you last night, because I think it would have been pretty special, y'know? Best night of your life, I reckon. You'd have known it was your birthday, all right! I still tried, but you weren't really into it.'

'Into it? God, Denise, *of course* I wasn't into it. I'd been drugged.'

'They've been doing that since you got here though, just a little bit.'

'A *little* bit?'

'Just to dampen things down. You know, dull those heightened senses of yours. Sharpen other ones.'

He thought about the paranoia he'd been feeling since he got to Green Acres, seeing things in the cellar, possibly in the caves. Had that been down to the drugs? From where Mitch was standing, chained up, he'd been right to suspect people were out to get him. He suddenly realized: 'The fire! The house! You knew about it and didn't warn me?'

'I told you.' She sounded annoyed now. 'I was keeping an eye on you. I wouldn't have let you die there.' Denise, rushing towards him from The Plough. Had she been watching as the fire had been set, making sure he got out? Would she have come to get him if he hadn't?

'Why?' he asked. 'Why bother? Why not just let it happen?'

Denise shook her head. 'Because everything has its time. Has to be handled correctly.'

'But the house, why—?'

'Because it was its time. Everything burns eventually. To pave the way.' Denise smiled that sweet smile, dimples included, as if it explained everything. 'I get it, trust me. You're still having trouble, while the rest of us . . .' She waved a hand around to indicate the members of the cult still busying themselves with prep for whatever this was. 'Our family. We've known about it all for such a long time.'

Family's everything, brothers, sisters and all that.

'Known about what?' he gasped. 'What exactly are you hoping to achieve here?'

262

'Something wonderful!' exclaimed Denise. Her eyes were wide, she looked like she was the one on drugs.

'Right. Call up the Devil, ask him to grant you three wishes. That kind of thing?' He'd seen it a million times in films, on TV.

Denise's smiled faded. 'You really don't understand at all, do you?'

'No,' admitted Mitch. 'Enlighten me.' He winced then at his poor choice of words again.

'Why would we need demons, devils? When we have . . .' Denise turned and nodded back to the bonfire that had been erected. 'It cleanses, purifies. It teaches.'

Okay, officially time to call the looney bin, thought Mitch. 'You worship fire? Is that it?' He should have seen it before, worked it out from the way those hooded figures had danced around the blasted stuff. But he'd thought they were trying to make something appear *in it*.

'Haven't we done so since the first cavemen huddled in caves?' said Denise. Was this the sales pitch? he thought. If so, it was wasted on him. 'It kept us safe from the ills of the world. And the Great Flame spoke to us, showed us the way.'

'You've lost it, Denise.'

She scowled at him. 'You're the one who's lost, Mitch. Or you were. Now you've been found again.'

'This is it, isn't it? This is what my dad found out about,' spat Mitch. 'It's why he had to die, isn't it? You sat there telling me all those stories about him, reminiscing with me. And you let it happen? You did nothing when they took him out to the woods, poured petrol or whatever over him – a man with dementia! – and set him on fire. Did nothing while he screamed and burned alive!'

'Don't judge her too harshly,' came another voice he knew altogether too well, also female.

'There was no other choice,' said a second. Deeper: a man. 'And she wasn't alone.'

He hadn't realized there were even more people inside with

them until he turned, saw the couple standing there. His worst nightmare: *worse* than a nightmare actually. 'A-Aunty Helen? Uncle Vince?'

And Mitch suddenly realized he was more confused than ever.

Chapter 31

He'd almost stopped the car, backed it up, turned it around. Done what she'd predicted he might, before it was too late.

Almost.

What had stopped Ashley Watts from going through with that when Bella had confessed about the ransacking of her home, about setting it on fire – a fire he'd had to bloody well save her from, risking himself – had been yet another traffic jam they'd had no option but to brake for, a Mini parking right up behind them and sandwiching them in.

That and the look on her face. The pleading there, an expression of someone who desperately needed his help. The confident Bella had come back in leaps and bounds, yet she was still vulnerable – and Watts could resist anything but someone close asking for his help.

Even if she was off her head.

'It was me, but it wasn't me,' she'd told him. 'I didn't know what I was doing. I was seeing, remembering something. But my memories and my mother's were getting all mixed up. And I was recreating . . . Look, I know you don't have any reason to believe in me, especially now. But I really need you to, Ashley. I really need *someone* to. You promised you'd get to the bottom of all this, and the answer's waiting there. If you don't do it – get us to Green Acres as soon as possible – for me, do it for Mitch. A fellow police officer.'

That one was hitting below the belt; Bella knew his loyalty to the boys in blue. But he should be doing this officially. They should be doing this right, if Bella thought her brother was in as much danger as she claimed. He'd told her as much yet again.

Bella shook her head. 'They wouldn't listen. Nobody would. Look, we get there and something's happening, you can call in your buddies. Okay?'

'What exactly are we talking about here? Who do you think's after your brother, what kind of numbers are we talking?' Watts took a hand off the gear stick long enough to rub his head, then gripped the knob again. 'I'll be honest, heading into a potentially hostile situation without backup—'

'It'll be okay,' she assured him.

'How do you know?' Watts queried, pulling on his collar because of the heat, regardless of the air conditioning.

'I just do.' But her voice had wavered as she'd said that, like she didn't know for sure. Like she couldn't see it, hadn't been *told* everything would be all right. 'You have to trust me.'

Strangely, even after all this, he did. Didn't trust that she knew what she was doing, but trusted she thought her brother was in some deep shit. Watts had been there himself, been in countless situations and prayed that someone would dig him out. He thought back to one such predicament last summer in fact, with that killer. Had hoped that would work out, and it had.

When the traffic finally started to move again, albeit slowly, he'd had a difficult decision to make. Carry on or go back? Bella was looking at him, biting her lip. 'Please, Ashley.' Now her hand was on the arm closest to her, a reversal of his clumsy, panicked attempt to stop the psychic from leaving. Bella was forever helping others, so maybe it was her turn for a change and maybe it was down to him to do that. See this through.

Watts let out a weary breath. 'Okay, all right. But once we've scoped this out, I'm calling it in,' he told her.

'Yes, definitely. Agreed.' She'd removed the hand then, let him put the car into gear and head off again. Head to Green Acres, a journey that had – including several more jams, especially in rush hour – taken them till the evening. Bella hadn't even wanted to stop to get any food, they might already be too late.

It was as Watts navigated the winding roads of the place itself, passing some woods, that they saw it – the sun sinking into the horizon at the same time. It looked for all the world like the glowing orb had set the village itself on fire, smoke billowing up from it.

'Jesus, is that . . . That's Green Acres village, isn't it?' Watts exclaimed.

Bella could do nothing but nod. She seemed to be in shock, probably at the sight of her old home going up in flames. He wondered then how it had started, why there were no fire engines like the ones he'd called for when the caravan was going up.

It was as they got a little further down that narrow road Bella told him to take the turning, head up the road towards a group of buildings. 'Where are we going? What about the—'

But the words had died in his mouth, because Watts saw the people. The figures heading in their direction: lots of figures. It was then that he was forced to stop the car again, not because of a queue or anything else, but because the shapes had reached them, were surrounding them. Behind and to the sides. So many – too many. And he'd listened to Bella, come here without any tactical support!

He stopped, wanted to turn around again – but couldn't – and he began fumbling for his phone, dropping it on the middle console, hearing the crack of the screen.

Ashley wanted to back up, turn the car around, but couldn't. Because the figures were already tugging on the handles of their doors.

Already opening those doors up and pushing their way inside.

Chapter 32

'Wait a second, back up a minute. What did you just say?'

Mitch had heard what his aunty and uncle had told him, just didn't – couldn't – believe it. Couldn't believe his ears, or his eyes come to that – thanks to the combination of drugs he'd been given (not just in the Traditional, but the tea – all that bloody tea! – even probably in the food in the fridge and brandy that had been left for him, those biscuits when he first arrived . . . his aunty's stew) and a certain skill of his uncle's.

'Vincent was a therapist before he retired, *of course* he used hypnotism in his work,' Helen had told Mitch, like it was a no-brainer. Had been using it on Mitch too, since he got back – although apparently the trigger for susceptibility was in that original phone message, the groundwork laid long ago. Vince had also been the person, Mitch remembered now, who'd been behind the door when he first entered the barn. The one who'd put him under with a word when they needed to chain him up.

'Just for a little while,' Vince had said, as if that made it all okay.

None of this was all right, not a bit of it! He could promise them that. 'Just long enough to bloody well truss me up.'

His aunty winced at that. So she was still sticking with the whole not swearing thing? 'Restrain you, for the moment. For your own good.' Helen, and his uncle come to that, sounded so reasonable. Like they had when he'd called in to see them after he first arrived (had Vince been doing his 'thing' even then?). Sounded like family.

Family's everything. It's all we have at the end of the day.

There was so much about his family he didn't know . . . Maybe he'd discover more while he was here, get to know these folks a bit better. Reconnect.

'Till we were ready,' added his uncle. 'Till it was time.'

Time . . . lost time . . . Those people 'abducted' by little green men. The ones that hadn't gone missing, hadn't been set on fire, they'd lost time. Like he had. Maybe some had been released, but had their minds tinkered with? His uncle must have been a hell of a find for Daniel and Leah! Or had they hypnotized the hypnotist?

When Mitch asked them about the UFO stuff, Vince had just smiled in reply.

'Some simply weren't . . . suitable,' his aunty clarified. 'Had to be let go, but we couldn't have them remembering anything about their experiences so we had to plant false memories.'

'Not suitable? Suitable to *murder*?' Mitch shook his head, didn't understand.

'For sacrifice,' said Helen. 'Only the worthy are given to the Great Flame.'

'Jesus Christ!' Mitch couldn't help noticing then that his aunty didn't pull a face. The worst possible swear word and she . . . But hold on, she was still religious – just not in that way. Didn't give a monkey's about that kind of blasphemous swearing anymore. It explained why the church – or the building he'd thought of as a church – in the village was in such disrepair, why nobody went (had they ever?). Mitch couldn't remember attending a single service there, now he came to think of it, no Christmas or Easter celebrations, nothing. Just those harvest festivals, carols, strange songs. Pagan rituals? He couldn't rely on his dodgy memory. It explained why nobody was in a rush to do his father's funeral.

'And Sheldon, was he worthy? I thought you hated his guts! Didn't want him bringing in outsiders.' Though the irony of it was the outsiders had brought all this in to start with: the bloody Commune.

'Worthy, or powerful. Sometimes it is for the common good, and he did have a lineage as he said – even if his kin abandoned this place many years ago. I personally wouldn't give people like that the privilege, but . . .' And he thought then about what she'd said about the witches, how Helen wouldn't have burned them if she'd been around in those times. That they hadn't deserved it. A privilege, she was calling it now.

'*Stuff and nonsense, the lot of it!*'

Perhaps that's what they thought they were giving his father, doing him a massive favour? Yeah, right, some privilege! 'I doubt my dad would have seen it that way when you cooked him.'

Vince laughed. 'Your dad. Oh Mitch, you never really knew him at all, did you?'

He didn't, but what had that got to do with this?

'Thomas volunteered,' stated Helen. 'Insisted.'

'*No!*' screamed Mitch.

'I'm afraid it's true,' Vince informed him, like he could believe a word that came out of the faker's mouth.

'But he didn't know . . . There was something wrong with his mind, his brain. The dementia.'

'Think about it, young Mitch. Who told you that?' asked Helen, sticking her tongue in the side of her mouth, proud of the misdirection. What had they done, drugged him like they had Mitch?

'*Who knows what he might have been seeing, or hearing at the time . . .*'

Apparently not, as she continued: 'He was of perfectly sound mind when he agreed. Knew he needed to provide you with a mystery to bring you back, for you to investigate in the run up to . . .' She pointed behind her now. 'The clues he left, the break-in, us leaving those books in the living room when we were tidying up, the rock through the window – they were his idea, all parts of the puzzle for you to solve. To ultimately bring you here. Fanning the flames, if you like. He wanted to keep you here once you'd returned, keep you occupied. After—'

'Keep me isolated!' Mitch broke in, remembering how his phone had been stolen, the landline crippled. He wasn't going mad, *hadn't* left the back door open at all like Wilkinson said: they'd had the keys to the place! His aunty and uncle had given them access!

'After all,' Helen continued, ignoring the interruption, 'your father was the one who sent you away in the first place.'

'Nobody sent me away, I—' But hadn't Thomas Prescott encouraged him to get out there and see the world? Experience all it had to offer?

'You needed to see what a mess it is out there,' Vince said, folding his arms. 'So you'd understand why we have to start again.'

'Start again?' Mitch was still trying to get his head around the fact his father had sent him away with all this in mind, with a purpose. But that had been before the Commune ever came here – hadn't it? *Fucking hell!* he thought then, exactly how long had they had members planted in Green Acres? Ten years, twenty years? More? And he had a flash of the cave drawings now, the rituals they'd depicted. The Commune had only managed to settle there because of relatives, hadn't it? How far did that line stretch back? No wonder they'd been able to set up their base of operations so easily, the arguments about them just another rouse. 'Was that why Bella left? Was she forced to go as well?' he asked. If it had all been going on back then, it explained a lot of things.

Aunty Helen spat at the floor then. '*Bella!* That monstrosity!'

'My sister!' he cried out.

Helen's right eye twitched. 'Your . . . half-sister.'

'What?' spluttered Mitch. 'What do you mean?'

'Same mother, descended from Wiccan stock. That whoring

Apple Hill Coven from the darkest part of our history. That *whore* Elizabeth Croft! Different father, though.'

Different . . . What did that mean, his dad wasn't Bella's?

'It's like I said to you, your mother wasn't quite right. Never had been, never would be. It's why she had such a problem with all of this, young Mitchel. The ceremonies, the worship of the Flame. We tried with her. Mum and dad tried to put her on the right path, so did your father. But in the end, she just had to be helped on her way.'

Like those victims of the UFOs, like the backpackers who were witnesses to his father's death. 'No.' Tears were flooding Mitch's eyes. His mother! His actual mother! They killed her!

'Don't weep for her too much, she went with her lover,' his aunty continued. 'The man who'd fathered Bella. Of course, when we found out, we orchestrated the whole thing, made it look like an accident. And, though again it wouldn't have been my first choice, we gave them both to the Flame.'

No wonder she hadn't 'seen' her death coming, they either drugged her or implanted something; messed with her mind too. 'She . . . she was your sister!' Mitch yelled, struggling against his bonds once more but still getting nowhere.

'Adopted,' said Helen. 'Her parents had been put out of their misery as well, and our family took her in. Sometimes, though, things just don't work out, do they? But she had some good years with your dad, I do believe that. He loved her. It broke him, mind, when he found out she'd been unfaithful. All that time, and with a man from the next town along. Not even a local!' Helen spat again. 'But then you came along and we knew – knew you were his. The blood tests confirmed it: your mother's final gift to Thomas. Just like the Great Flame prophesized. A child born of "magick" and of fire, a worshipper of the fire.'

'Your mum would have wanted us to look after you.'

'We had to wait until you were settled first, naturally, but once you were, we knew we had to act before your mother fled with

272

you. Fled with Bella and her father. Thomas did so miss your mother afterwards; I think that's why he turned his attentions to Bella. She reminded him of her.'

It was too much, all too much to take in! Now what were they telling him, not only was his father not Bella's real father, but he was also a pervert? What exactly had he done to her back then? This man he'd wept over when he died, whose death Mitch had investigated when in truth he'd committed suicide for the cause? For the Commune?

A necessary evil.

'That's why she ran away, isn't it? The real reason?'

'Not that she'll ever remember it, but . . . yes,' his uncle said. 'I made sure she wouldn't. Just that she thought it was about some guy. Not a lie really.'

Girls and their fathers, that special bond.

Mitch felt like he was going to be sick again, but there was nothing left in him after the previous night – and he hadn't eaten all day. 'It's why she didn't want to come back,' he whispered after a moment.

'Why would she? That bit's real, though she won't have a clue why she doesn't wish to return to Green Acres.' Vince was smirking, having messed with her memories, a job well done.

'Probably a good thing. If she ever did come back we'd just kill her on sight,' Helen proclaimed, smiling; not his mother's smile at all, an imitation rather than genetics. 'Be done with it.'

'No.'

'At least this way, she'll die along with everyone else. In the Final Conflagration,' Vince chirped up.

'The Final . . .' More mumbo jumbo lunacy.

Staunch believers.

'Yes, and it's almost time. Hottest day of the year!' Helen exclaimed, with the same kind of excitement Denise had displayed earlier. Where had *she* gone? Mitch hadn't even noticed her leave. Too busy trying to work all this out, digest what he was being told. 'That's where you come into it, my lad!' she told Mitch, pointing at him.

'Me? What the fuck has—'

'Language!' Helen admonished.

'Go fuck yourself!' Mitch snapped back. She wasn't even a blood relative! 'Your Great Flame can go fuck itself as well! It's not *my* god.'

She sighed, but carried on regardless. 'You're more powerful than you can possibly imagine, sweetheart. You needed to go away, yes, but then return when you'd come of age.'

'Growing boy . . .'

'All grown up and everything!'

'And on your birthday, this particular year,' Helen continued, 'it will begin and it will end, only to begin anew. As the prophecy foretold. When your magick meets the fire, you'll be the spark that sets the whole world alight! Moving from place to place, not even the oceans will be able to stop it!'

Mitch wasn't important; he was nobody special.

Hottest day? It was about to become even hotter . . . for him!

Never rains . . .

'Alight, just like Green Acres is right now, spreading from your father's house.'

'The village.' Why did that suddenly matter to him? Because it was his home, where he'd been born? Far from being the middle of nowhere, did these nutcases believe it was the middle of *everywhere*. 'Why my . . . Why start it there?'

'Your father's house is built on one of many sacred spots,' Vince informed him. 'And especially his cellar.' Those dreams of the hooded figures, were they repressed memories of actually witnessing rituals in there? Had he actually seen people being killed in there, set alight? Mitch wondered in horror. 'The caves are another, the woods. All places where we worship.'

'Where you murder!'

'Sacrifice,' Helen corrected him again. 'Though not always.

274

Sometimes we just talk to the Great Flame, sometimes it talks to us.' This was beyond the Commune – or whatever they were really called – and their influence, this was deep-rooted. This was something those people had been doing for a long time, their faith like a cancer at the heart of a village that had once been good. Hadn't it? He didn't know what to think anymore, it depended on where the Commune originated from, he guessed. 'That's how the prophecy occurred, how we knew you would come to us eventually. Be born unto us.'

'You think *I'm* going to end the world? My death will?'

'Why not?' asked Vince.

As I live and breathe . . .

Not for long.

'We all have to sacrifice things . . .'

'The Great Flame is all-powerful, all seeing.' Mitch thought the man was going to get on his hands and knees right there and then and start praying. 'You've seen first-hand what it's like out there, the hatred, the violence. How sick society is.'

'Not half as sick as you monsters!' argued Mitch, though he couldn't help flashing back to certain things he'd seen on the force. Teenagers addicted to drugs, huddling in crack dens, choking on their own vomit. Domestic abuse, husbands hitting their wives, or vice versa – partners causing abuse in other ways, manipulating or eroding their confidence (not that the people here in Green Acres could bloody well say anything about that, they were masters of it). Serial killers like the ones that were in the news, how much heartache they'd caused. Governments lying to and cheating the very people who'd put them in those high-up positions, creaming off money and power, letting the poor go poorer while the rich got richer. Mitch thought about the riot he'd been involved in just before he came here, how his warnings had been ignored. How it had ended in so much destruction, ended in Tammy being battered into a coma. Though if he hadn't been so thrown by that call, the start of these people working on him, picking up where they'd left off . . .

'Yes, you know what we're talking about,' Helen said then. 'I can see it. Oh, there have been attempts to try to control it, in Redmarket for example. Those people had a very different kind of belief system, one that stretched back almost as far as ours. But in the end none of it ever works, because none of it can. It's even infected Green Acres, the modern world. Thomas was always quite comfortable with it, liked his mod cons.' Mitch doubted he would ever have called any of the stuff in that house a mod-con, but then maybe they were to Helen and Vince? 'But a line has to be drawn. When the weeds strangle the lush grassland, the green, what must we do to get rid of it? Burn it, Mitchel!'

'Maybe try weed killer?' Mitch said, but his black humour fell flat. Helen wasn't really listening anyway, she was in full flow.

'Burn it and start again! The light must drive out the darkness. Can't you see that?'

Mitch was reminded of the speech Denise had made about lighting fires back at the dawn of time, to keep people safe. To keep away animals – and the darkness. Without light, human beings felt like he did back in that cave when his torch went out. Panicked, scared. Made sense that they would worship whatever gave them that luminescence, kept them warm. But people had come a long way since those days – hadn't they? Not looking around at all this, hearing these people speak, they hadn't! Civilized, his arse! It was only now he noticed folk from the village were beginning to congregate, the barn getting quite full.

He spotted individuals from Green Acres itself now wearing those robes, they probably had nowhere else to go since the entire place was ablaze. His dad's neighbour who'd rung the authorities, the old man Denise had been serving outside The Plough, the youth who'd served him from the shop . . . And younger still, kids being dragged inside this barn to witness what was about to happen, the children who'd been with their parents that day. Just like they'd done with him as a boy, taking him by the arm into the cellar, Bella too more than likely. Down into those caves . . .

He couldn't help thinking about the lad who'd been lost in there, now; what had been his name? Who was he? Had it been *him*? Mitch was beginning to think it might have been; maybe that's how he found his way out again? Those hooded figures Mitch had seen before – after – he'd banged his head, had they simply been more repressed memories of another time, when he'd been trapped in there? It was looking more and more likely.

'The last of the drugs should be out of his system by now,' Vince said to his wife. 'It's almost time.'

This was it: they, the Commune, were going to kill him. It was their version of Helter Skelter, Armageddon, the Apocalypse. They were looking to Mitch to light the fuse. 'Wait, wait! If the world burns, like you believe it's going to do, you die too,' he said to them. A flaw in their plan, he was hoping. Not much of a hope because all this had been set in motion a long time ago.

'Our Lord will grant us a favour,' Vince replied. 'We'll be reborn, the world will start again. Like a phoenix from the ashes!'

'It will begin and it will end, only to begin anew.'

'New seeds can be planted, once the weeds are gone,' Helen added, returning to her previous analogy about nature.

A reboot, like rebooting his dad's old computer so it would work? These people – these crazy, deluded people – believed they were going to come back and repopulate a better world? Frolic in the fields and the woods that those new seeds would provide, with no threat from—

What was he thinking? None of that would happen. He wasn't going to start an apocalypse, all that would happen would be another killing. Another person dead, burned to death. Him, Mitchel Prescott.

Helen looked him in the eye now, and asked seriously: 'Mitchel, do you pledge to go to the Great Flame willingly?'

He couldn't help laughing out loud at that one. 'Throw myself in the fire, you mean? Are you fucking kidding me?' There were no qualms now about swearing in front of her.

'Even after everything you've seen of the world outside?' asked his uncle, amazed. 'Look inside yourself, search your feelings.' Really? Vader again trying to get him to join the dark side. Except they claimed they were on the side of the light, didn't they? There were plenty of flames in Hell, though, weren't there? Paths and good intentions. Not that these intentions were particularly good; not from where he was standing.

'I'll say this very slowly, very clearly: no. What're you going to do now? Have I ruined everything?' Mitch laughed bitterly once more.

Helen just shook her head. 'No. You came here, to this most sacred of places—'

'What, a sodding barn?'

'It is hallowed ground!' Vince snapped. 'Show some respect!'

Helen went on regardless. 'You came here willingly, we shall help you with the last few steps. Vincent, it is time we took our places.' She held out her hand and her husband took it, both pulling up their hoods at the same time. When he hadn't been looking, someone had lit the bonfire and already the fire was spreading through the wood. For the second time that day, Mitch smelled the smoke, heard the crackling. This time there would be no escape.

As his so-called relatives joined the others forming a circle and chanting, ('*Family's everything, brothers, sisters and all that*'), other figures in robes set about unchaining Mitch. As soon as he was released, he made a bid for freedom, lurching forwards, even trying to get a punch in. He wasn't under the influence of drugs or hypnotism, the sacrifice wouldn't work if he was, but Mitch *was* still weak – and there were just too many of them. Three on each side at least, holding him by the arms. Then Mitch looked up and saw Granger again, brandishing his shotgun.

'*I'm glad your dad's dead!*'

His words when they'd been in this position last time. Of course he was, because it meant Mitch would come. Meant he'd eventually be here, now, today.

'Stop,' said the man in his gruff voice; it was the message from the rock, and Mitch wondered if he'd done the deed himself. Relished it, in fact. 'Stop struggling.'

There was no choice but to do what the farmer ordered. As Mitch was being led across to the hooded, chanting figures, who were dancing in a circle around the fire as it rose higher and higher; Mitch had never seen a fire spread so quickly. Culminating in a huge flame at the top. Their Great Flame, as they'd have everyone believe. He could feel that same spider-sense coming back now, the one that had worked just that bit too slowly, poorly, to help him in Green Acres, or not at all, hampered by drugs or suggestion. He felt it now as strongly as he had in the riot, as wound up as he was: a gift from his mother?

Not that he needed it to let him know things were about to go to shit. Had the capacity to get even worse. That he was about to get tossed on a bonfire like a Guy Fawkes doll! Or maybe it was something else?

Because someone was missing, weren't they? All the gang were here – Granger, Nuttall, yes there was Denise, his aunty and uncle – everyone apart from the star turn. Their leader—

Leaders.

But, as Mitch now saw, they'd opened the door of the barn and appeared at the back. Daniel and Leah, here to oversee the final few moments of the great ritual, even as a gap opened in the circle of dancers, paving the way for the men to lead – half carry, because Mitch freely admitted he was dragging his feet now – their most important sacrifice ever to the fire.

'Brothers!' shouted Daniel loudly. Proudly, opening his arms. 'Put him the fuck down!'

That's when everything really did go to shit.

Chapter 33

He couldn't believe what was happening.

This was it, surely. The end. Daniel had arrived, Leah had arrived. But they weren't alone. They'd brought more of the Commune with them, flooding into the barn, including that bald man with the fleshy lips he'd seen there before. Only, as Mitch looked back over his shoulder, still being pulled towards that bonfire, the heat so intense it was causing him to sweat profusely again, none of them were dressed in those maroon robes. They were all still wearing cream tunics and trousers.

'I said: put him down!' Daniel repeated, his words aimed at the hooded men who had hold of Mitch. Were they doing it wrong? Had there been a change in plans? After all this work, all this preparation, surely not! And why was Granger turning, aiming – with that shotgun – at Daniel.

'Get out of here!' yelled the farmer.

Why? They didn't want their leader here? Unless . . . Yes, Mitch could see now that the members of the Commune were branching off, seeking out those in the maroon robes and hoods and tackling them. One man he spotted had a hooded figure in a choke hold to restrain him. Another – that same bald guy – had dropped a person to the ground, rolling them in a move he was all too familiar with from his own self-defence training. For each hooded figure there seemed to be an equivalent counterpart dressed in cream, attempting to subdue them. Like a wave moving over them, this was the real light driving out the darkness.

For his part, Daniel was moving forwards – heading towards Granger. 'Get out, I'll fire!' shouted the large man, but it didn't put the Commune leader off at all. Mitch jostled the men holding his arms, leaning sideways and pushing the ones on his left into the farmer. It affected his aim and the shot went high, into the ceiling of the barn.

By the time the men had a grip on Mitch once more and Granger was readying to shoot again, Daniel was already there, had hold of the weapon and was wrestling it sideways out of the farmer's grasp, flinging it to the ground. Granger immediately lashed out with a ham-fisted punch, which Daniel neatly avoided, bringing his own hand up, palm outwards to smack him under the chin. The large farmer toppled like a chimney being demolished.

Meanwhile, the men were still pulling Mitch towards the fire, had been tasked with throwing him on it and they were bloody well going to carry that out no matter what was happening around them.

He was vaguely aware of one of them letting go of him on his right – so Mitch turned, saw another bloke there. This one was in a suit, however: shirt, tie (loosened, granted), jacket, in spite of the heat; and a haircut which looked like a wave was crashing over his forehead. He'd obviously grabbed Granger's gun, because he'd just felled one of the men with the butt of it, was bringing it around to swipe another with the side of the weapon.

Mitch couldn't be sure of it, of course, but he was willing to bet that this guy was a copper. Plainclothes perhaps?

The policeman brought a knee up and the remaining hooded man on the right crumpled up like a used tissue. 'Wotcha!' said the man to Mitch, before two other hooded figures grabbed him and dragged him back into the crowds.

There were still the others on the left pulling Mitch, desperate to get him into that fire. But Daniel was helping now, dropping one by kicking him in the back of the knee. Chopping another on the back of the neck. The remaining hooded man Mitch elbowed in the face himself, causing the guy's nose to explode with redness.

He heard a scream at that point, spun around just in time to see his Aunty Helen coming at him like a missile. It was clearly her intention to hit him, pushing him those final few feet onto the pyre.

She was intercepted at the last moment by another woman: Leah sideswiping her, rugby-tackling her to the ground. They went down in a blur of maroon and creams, rolling over and over. But where was his uncle Vince?

Mitch spotted him, too late, advancing on the other side, trying to do what his wife had failed to. Except he was gazing at Mitch, trying to do something with his eyes. Mitch looked down immediately, looked away. Had fallen for that trick too many times lately. But that didn't stop the man reaching him, trying to shove him backwards.

Instead, Mitch angled his body to the side and Vince stumbled, tripped. Ended up ramming into the bonfire himself headlong. It was only now that Mitch looked, seeing the flame on top rising even higher, being fed with a sacrifice – albeit not the one it was expecting. As a consequence of Vince hitting those piles of wood, though, it destabilised the entire bonfire at the base.

Logs began to drop, flaming branches rolling off and along the floor. One, he saw, rolled to the side of the wooden wall of the barn and set that alight. In no time at all this entire place, mirroring Green Acres itself, would be an inferno.

Then he felt it, a hand snaking into his. Tugging.

Still a bit dazed and confused, Mitch looked down, then up into the face of the person who'd grabbed hold of his hand.

And, in all honesty, he couldn't believe what was happening.

Chapter 34

Ashley Watts couldn't believe what he was doing, how he'd got here.

When they'd been surrounded by the figures at his car, he thought they were done for. Here, without any kind of official blessing and definitely without the benefit of any sort of official backup. It wasn't only going to be Bella's brother that was killed at this rate.

Leaving them no way forwards, no way back, and opening up the doors. Then the pair of them were outside of the car, surrounded, with people asking what they were doing there. Why they were at some place called 'The Commune'. Jesus, Bella had never mentioned this might be about a cult! Watts suddenly felt in way over his head, and here with a person who'd been 'seeing things', who thought she might have set fire to her own home! He'd read about folk like this, what they did to interlopers.

Then Bella spoke up, 'I'm here to talk with Daniel. Daniel and Leah.'

It was even worse than he'd feared: she *knew* these people. Whether she was in this with them, or just knew the people by name who'd snatched her brother, he had no way of knowing. All he did know was, she hadn't let him call the police – even before he'd dropped and smashed his mobile – and it probably explained why. She definitely seemed quite chummy with those two when they arrived, wandered off while Watts continued to be watched by the members of this Commune, all dressed in cream pyjamas not dissimilar to the ones he'd lent Bella when she'd come to stay.

He watched as she chatted to them, saw her point back at him a couple of times. Imagined her saying something along the lines of, 'We must dispose of the unbeliever I've lured back here,' like some kind of old-school villain or femme fatale. The tall man she'd called Daniel nodded, then Leah did as well. Finally, they returned and Daniel shouted for someone called James, to explain and spread the word.

Bella came around to his side of the car, the people who'd been 'guarding' him dispersing. 'What's going on?' he asked her.

'You wanted backup, Ashley. Here's your backup.'

'I don't understand.'

She promised she'd tell him everything later. For the time being, though: 'We need to go and find my brother, before it's too late.'

Luckily, she'd known exactly where he would be, too – as if she was being directed somehow. Her mother perhaps, not that Watts believed she'd been in contact with the dead woman. Not really. Or did he? Because there was the bike, run off the side of the road like Bella said it would be. And there was the barn, where she said they would find Mitch. They'd headed up there like some kind of convoy, all the folk from the Commune in tow and in their vehicles. Watts had worried that maybe they'd make too much noise to sneak up on anyone, let alone the numbers Bella reckoned were involved in this at the farm, but they were otherwise engaged in the barn. 'They're going to kill him in there,' Bella said, pointing to the building.

'Why?' he said, shaking his head. 'I still don't—'

'You don't need to, Ashley. Not yet. There'll be time for all that later on. You just need to trust me. To help me.' She'd placed a hand on his arm again and he found himself nodding.

Then suddenly they were there. James and a couple of others had instructions to phone the authorities from the farmhouse (they were assured they'd get through), making sure they were put through to the regional division. While the rest of them stormed that barn, trying to save Mitch.

When Daniel opened the door, Watts' mouth had hung open in disbelief. This was the real cult, some real *Wicker Man* and *Midsommar* shit going on. And in the middle of it all, about to be chucked onto the bonfire, was Bella's little brother.

Next came the fight, the battle of the barn, and he'd run off to try to prevent Mitch's fate – scooping up a discarded shotgun in the process, which he had hoped he could fire and disperse the enemy. No such luck. In the end he'd whacked two or three of the nutjobs with the butt of it, then been dragged back into the fray again, the shotgun knocked out of his hands.

But he had seen Bella rushing past, heading for her brother. Taking him by the hand and leading him away from the bonfire, as bits of it fell off and started more fires on the floor, the walls. Trying to get him to safety. Watts lost sight of them momentarily, someone grabbing him by the throat. It was all too familiar, this: the way certain murders had been committed the year before.

Watts brought up his hands and grabbed the wrists of his attacker, trying to lever those fingers away from his neck. However, the grip was strong, so strong he couldn't believe it. Couldn't believe what he was doing: fighting for his life.

Fighting for his life in a burning barn, so far from home.

Chapter 35

It was good to see him again, even under these circumstances.

Good to see him *alive*, definitely. Bella had worked her way through the crowds, through the fighting, to get to her brother. Daniel and Ashley had been trying to help him, clearing away the robed figures holding him. And Mitch himself had just narrowly escaped being shoved into the fire by their Uncle Vince, who was now languishing in the flames himself; Bella wasn't about to shed any tears over that particular relative.

Leah was busy holding down Helen, which left the way clear for Bella to get Mitch away from the immediate threat. When she'd taken his hand, he'd gaped at her like he couldn't believe she was really there.

'Bella? Bella, is that you?' he'd asked.

'Yeah, it's me,' she told him.

'What are *you* doing here?'

'Later,' she said.

He let her pull him away, and Bella was pleased to see members of the Commune grabbing children and getting them to safety as well, carrying some outside. They shouldn't have been in here in the first place, but certainly not now the barn was burning up. They were almost at the door themselves when someone stepped in their way, pushing Mitch to the ground and taking a swipe at her.

It was a woman, about Mitch's age. She thought she heard her brother call out, 'Denise!' and that name rang a vague bell for her, from her time living in Green Acres.

'Can't let you take him, love,' said the woman.

'I'm not your love.'

The woman grinned, then pulled out a large knife from under her robes. She swiped it from left to right, and Bella arched herself to avoid the blade. The woman lunged and Bella grabbed the arm, but had trouble hanging on to it because it was moving around like a live snake. Denise brought up her free hand, which had curled into a fist, but Bella managed to dodge the blow to her temple. She'd fallen for that move before.

Then Mitch was back on his feet and helping her with the knife-hand, yanking it back and forcing Denise to let go of her weapon.

'Mitch, don't do this. I love you!' she screamed. Just who the hell was this crazy cow?

'You're trying to kill me!' he yelled back at her.

Denise shook her head, like he just didn't get it. Then she wrestled herself out of their grip, kicked Bella and launched herself at Mitch again. It was like a lover's embrace gone wrong, like she wanted them both to go into the fire – so they could stay together forever, presumably.

What stopped them was Ashley Watts, shotgun raised and pointed at Denise's head. 'I wouldn't if I were you,' he said, wrenching his neck where Bella could see finger marks; obviously one of the robed figures he'd had to deal with. 'I'm having a really bad day.'

'*You're* having a bad day,' Mitch answered.

Watts smiled, then prodded Denise so she'd let go. 'Okay, Bella, get your brother out of here,' he told her and she thanked him.

'Ashley, look out!' Bella shouted.

But it was too late, Denise was rushing him, grabbing for the shotgun. The pair struggled with it, and both Mitch and Bella stepped forwards but were afraid to get involved in case they made things worse. There was a sudden *bang*! It was impossible to see who'd been shot. Then they both started to slide to the floor, keeling over together, Denise on top of Watts.

Neither of the prone figures moved for a second or two, then Denise twitched. Bella's hands went to her mouth: 'Ashley! Oh God, no. *Ashley!*' Mitch was there in moments, arm around her shoulders.

Then Denise flopped off, Watts' hands shoving the woman – the dead woman – from him. He staggered to his feet, tossing the gun aside, and Bella rushed to him, hugging him. 'I thought—'

'You won't need to have a séance to talk to me just yet,' he told her. 'Come on, let's get out of here.'

They found Mitch again, said as much to him. He was staring at an old man on the floor, his stick abandoned. Mitch looked like he knew him, was going to go to him – but the guy was already on fire and screaming out. 'It's too late,' she whispered.

The members of the Commune, including Daniel, were helping as many robed figures out of the barn as they could. But some were simply walking into the fire, like they wanted to die. Bella knew their names, some remembered, some she was 'told': Wilkinson, Larson, Ellie, giving themselves to the Great Flame. Another was their Aunty Helen, having shrugged off Leah – who'd backed away from the lady. Figured it was her lookout. She probably just wanted to be with her husband, Vince.

Helen turned around once before walking into those flames, shot both Bella and Mitch a chilling look. Then she was gone.

Finally, the three of them made it outside, where members of the Commune and worshippers of the fire were congregating: some of the latter having to still be restrained because they were trying to get back inside. Bella was happy to see that most of the members of the Commune had made it out, though.

The three of them stood well back from the barn as the fire raged through it. Angry that it had been denied its prize, Bella thought to herself. She realized she was still holding on to Ashley Watts for dear life, her arm around his middle – while Mitch was on her other side and had his arm across her shoulders again. It was bizarre, but for the first time in so long she felt at peace. She felt safe. 'Happy birthday, little brother,' she whispered to Mitch, and he nodded. The best present anyone could have given him.

Even under these circumstances, it was good to be here. Good to be here with Ashley Watts. Good to see her brother again, to know she'd reached him in time.

Good to, quite frankly, still be alive.

Chapter 36

Mitch stood there, watching the barn go up in flames.

He had his arm around his sister – and he was still quite surprised she was there, had thought immediately about his plea for help. When he'd called out to her. But still, he hadn't expected her to come. Really thought it might have been better if she hadn't, given what his aunty had said would happen if she did. But she'd had help from the guy in the suit, from the . . . from the Commune, and he was still owed an explanation about that.

All in good time, he said to himself. For now, he'd got to the bottom of one mystery: the major one. Everything else could wait. Everything apart from getting home, getting back to Lucy. God, he hadn't realized until then quite how much he'd missed her!

Something touched his leg and he started, causing Bella to jump as well. Mitch looked down and was surprised again – or not – to see Cat there, meowing. All this way, and the animal had found him, sought him out. Okay, after all the fighting was over, but the thought was there. The animal that had never, ever belonged to his father. That had come to the house for him and him alone.

'I think you have a new friend,' Bella said when she saw the black cat.

'Yeah,' Mitch replied, then nodded at the suited man. 'You too.' He bent and picked up the feline, who began nuzzling his neck and chin.

'What a night,' he heard the man on the other side of his sister say.

'Yeah,' repeated Mitch, then whispered to himself, 'Nasty business.' A business he doubted he'd forget as long as he lived, that would definitely stay with him no matter how far away from here he went. And as he made out the sirens in the distance – police, ambulance, fire brigade . . . all three? – he wasn't surprised to also hear a clap of thunder; a storm coming to break up the heat. Finally raining, pouring, but that might be for the best; might help put out the fires. And Mitch thought to himself how quickly things had turned again. From nasty to—

That there was always scope for them to get worse, so much worse. But also better, the calm now before a very different kind of storm . . . For things to work out, as they had done here.

Scope for things to turn out okay in the end.

PART FOUR

Those who leave Green Acres always find themselves returning eventually . . .

Either that or they take away memories which will last forever,
a little bit of the place that they will always carry with them.

Chapter 37

It had been one of the best night's sleep she'd had in ages.

Bella woke in the bed, no headache, no worries. Woke from pleasant dreams for a change. Even the voices were giving her a breather, it seemed. They'd be back, she knew they would. Things would soon return to normal, or as normal as they could be around here.

Not even the fact she wasn't in her own home was bothering her today, because Ashley was letting her stay as long as it took to fix up the caravan; she'd been amazed that it *could* be fixed, frankly. Amazed at the generosity of her friends as well, the people she saw on a regular basis, the people who came to her stage show – not to mention the hotel itself – everyone had chipped in. Ashley had even had a whip round at the station, O'Brien herself kicking a note or two into the pot, surprisingly.

The investigators had put the fire down to a candle that had fallen over, and warned her about leaving those unattended and lit, especially at night-time. Bella had nodded and promised she wouldn't do it again, had said nothing about the fact that she could now recall lighting the candle, touching it to her sofa. It was still a bit of a haze as to why she'd done that, recalling some of the rituals she'd seen from her youth, or her mother's memories, or maybe the suggestion had been planted that if she ever started to remember some of that stuff she should just kill herself? Her Uncle bloody Vince!

It had definitely been her mother who'd helped her break down some of those barriers: the ones he'd put in place, that had caused the headaches, stopped the voices from coming through. That woman, who'd been murdered so brutally along with Bella's real father, had been trying to help her right from the start. It was against the rules, apparently, for people from her own family to get in touch, but they'd been 'relaxed' or 'bent' – something to do with the balance of things. Then when she'd seen her mum outside in the caravan park, that human candle – not a usual occurrence, something to do with the bond they shared – the race had been on as to whether Bella would recover or just go mad. Or simply end it all.

The turning point had been at Watts' that night, when he told her she'd been sleepwalking, screaming. That's when her mother had finally got through, was able to clear her mind, that fog – though God, had it hurt! She could tell Ashley was still having trouble with bits of this, as would anyone else – which was why she'd only talked to him about it – but that was okay. He wasn't a true believer . . . yet. But he'd believed in *her*, enough to take her to Green Acres—

Bella Prescott, racing off to save the world!

—and for that she could never thank him enough. He had done what she didn't think anyone else in the entire world would have, flying in the face of logic and just going with it, regardless of the fact he might be putting himself in harm's way. Might even die. He'd been expecting a bollocking from O'Brien, but it hadn't been as bad as he'd feared. The official line, of course, had been that they'd stumbled upon what was happening accidentally – when Watts took Bella back home, as part of her convalescence, but also to see her brother on his birthday. They'd stumbled on the plot: an entire village that had turned out to be insane, all members of a cult that wanted to bring about the end of the world and for some reason believed sacrificing Mitchel Prescott would initiate it.

How come the Prescott siblings hadn't known about it beforehand, growing up there? Conditioning and hypnotic suggestion, wiping their memories – more and more of which were surfacing all the time. Bella had probably blocked a lot of those out herself, it had to be said. The ones involving her 'dad'. The man she'd thought was her father, who had been the first person she'd seen in her caravan that night, she later realized. The creaking outside her bedroom door the same as the ones she used to listen out for on the landing when she was a girl. She would almost certainly need some therapy at some point to deal with that, but for now she'd deal with it herself like she did everything else. Maybe she'd talk to Ashley about it too, because they were becoming quite close, weren't they? It was nice. It felt nice. And for once in her life, Bella was starting to hope.

They'd defeated the cult with the help of a . . . cult. Another cult, except it had never really been one regardless of what people thought. What Mitch had thought. Daniel, Leah, and the others really were just trying to make a new life for themselves in Green Acres away from everything. Had been allowed to settle there because one of the members had old family ties to the area, a family that had died out of natural causes. Allowed to settle, but with a few members of the real Green Acres cult infiltrating it to keep an eye out, joining them and wearing those cream clothes; one a red-headed guy, and another a woman with burns, both of whom Mitch had pointed out as 'double agents'. They hadn't wanted to miss the great ceremony at the end, though.

Ironically, they had similar goals to the villagers at the Commune, apart from the rituals and killings and the worship of the Great Flame, of course. And Daniel's use of the word 'brother' that had puzzled Mitch? Just something he'd always said, apparently. A term of endearment and a consequence of his religious upbringing. Not used in the same context as the brothers – and sisters – from the real cult.

'But I still don't get how you could talk them into helping,' Ashley had admitted, and she'd said she would explain that to him when it was all over, hadn't she?

'Because of Oscar,' Bella told him, as if it explained it all.

'Who?'

'Their kid. I heard him, he spoke to me.'

'You mean he—'

Bella had hung her head. 'They lost him, yeah. He was being bullied at school, they didn't know about it – too wrapped up in their own lives to spot the signs – and in the end he hanged himself.'

'Christ almighty,' Ashley had exclaimed.

'I know.' There were tears in Bella's eyes as she told him the story, thinking back to Oscar first coming through to her, once that fog had begun to lift: the barrier gone that allowed her to talk to the dead. 'That's why they upped sticks and left it all behind in the first place, wanted to strip everything away and get back to basics. They weren't the only ones who felt the same. Wasn't any coercing, no cult of personality. Just people trying to make a new life for themselves. A better life.'

'I still don't understand how you convinced them.'

Bella smiled. 'I gave them a message from Oscar. And told them something only the three of them would know. Told them he wanted his parents to help.'

'Right,' said Ashley, still struggling with the concept. 'But how come they were all so . . . I mean, some of those guys could give my constables a run for their money in the fighting stakes!'

'One of their members teaches it. It's a class offered at the Commune, quite popular by all accounts. Self-defence comes in quite handy when you get hassled like they do, Ashley. They were not exactly welcomed with open arms when they moved there.'

'I can imagine. And they're talking about moving on again, is that right?'

'Yeah, I think what happened has kinda soured things for them there. But they'll be okay. I know they will.'

'So, all's well that ends well, eh?' He'd beamed at her then, and why wouldn't he be happy? This on top of the high-profile case last year, there was even talk of a promotion for him over it. Praise from high up, uncovering corruption the likes of which hadn't been seen since Redmarket all those years ago. Corruption that even stretched to Mitch's boss, Staton. Turned out he was originally from Green Acres, as well; that he even arranged for some of the more violent protesters to turn up at the riot in Downstone, initiating everything there, giving it a nudge, all to mess with her little brother. To 'convince' him the world needed to change. But Staton's once powerful friends (who conducted ceremonies behind closed doors), and the 'higher authority' that they all worshipped, couldn't help him this time.

Bella couldn't be happier for Ashley, though, because it really couldn't have happened to a nicer person. A nice person who she was starting to think of as more than just a friend. Ever since she'd thought he was dead, when she'd thought that woman Denise had killed him, she hadn't been able to stop thinking about how much she'd miss Ashley if he wasn't around. How much she'd relied on him lately, and how he'd been there for her.

'*Let someone look after you for a change.*' Vicky's words not that long ago.

She'd even thought about telling him a few times how she felt, taking that chance she'd never had the courage to before. Asking him if maybe they could have dinner sometime, which she knew was ridiculous because they had dinner together every night! Dinner out somewhere special, though, somewhere nice. Nice, like Ashley Watts was.

So, she'd got up that morning full of the joys of, if not spring, then late summer, almost autumn. Opened the bedroom door, ready to make him a strong cup of black coffee, just the way he liked it. Calling out: 'Ashley? Ashley, where are you?' Then she saw him walk across the living room, not in the kitchen like he usually was making breakfast (another bonus in a guy, one who cooked). 'Morning, I was just—' Bella saw that he was on the phone, mouthed an apology and put a finger to her lips.

He finished talking to whoever it was a few moments later anyway, saying goodbye. 'Hey, Bella, how're you? How'd you sleep?'

'Like a log, thanks!' She thought about asking who was on the phone, but it wasn't really her business. He told her anyway seconds later, like he was trying to apologize for something.

'Oh, that was just Robyn.' Bella's heart sank immediately, at the very mention of that name.

'E-Everything okay?'

'Yeah, everything's *great* in fact. Actually, not altogether great. You know those two campers that were murdered? The ones that discovered your . . . well, the ones that were there when your dad died?' Theirs were amongst the remains that had been found, buried in the graveyard behind the church: bones, burned and charred. People the villagers had killed to keep them quiet, along with Neil Sheldon's partner.

Bella nodded.

'Turns out they were students of hers. A couple, just finished their course. Had their whole lives ahead of them.'

'Oh no. That's so sad,' said Bella and meant it, even though she hadn't known them.

'Yeah, she's a bit cut up about it. I mean, obviously she's heard all about what happened.'

'Obviously,' said Bella. Heard all about his adventures, heard about who he was with as well. Why it happened. That had probably gone down like a lead balloon.

'But, well, there is some good news. She wants to see me.'

'Oh.' Bella's heart was in her feet now and getting lower by the second. 'That's—'

'Turns out there might even be a position for me on their investigative team.'

'In Hannerton?' That was miles away! She'd barely ever see him if he took that.

'Yeah. Can you imagine, hunting serial killers and the like!' He was grinning all over his face. It would have filled most people with dread, but it was Ashley's dream job.

'I . . . congratulations,' Bella said, mustering as much enthusiasm as she could – which was the same as a condemned prisoner on their way to the gallows.

'Thanks!' Ashley said, barely noticing. 'I haven't got it yet. But, hey, I can dream, right?'

Which broke her own dream, reminded her what it had been about. Her and Ashley somewhere in a meadow, having a picnic, laughing and joking. Kissing. 'Y-You'll be able to see a lot more of Robyn, I guess.'

'I know, right? That's the plan.' He noticed she was frowning then, came over to her, putting down the phone. 'Oh Bella. I know she's not exactly your favourite person in the world.' It was mutual, thought Bella. 'But look on the bright side, while I'm away you'll have this place to yourself! You can still stay till the caravan's fixed up, of course. And without me getting in your hair.'

Bella nodded (*but I like you being in my hair*) and he made things worse then by giving her a hug. She'd hugged him back, so hard, trying not to cry. Had bitten it back through breakfast, when he was bouncing around all over the place – didn't even notice she'd barely touched her eggs this time. Just called out a goodbye – soon it would be a permanent one – as he went off to work and wished her a lovely day.

Once the door had slammed, she let it all out. Sank down on the couch and cried her eyes out. Cried and cried and cried. Heart having travelled through the floorboards and on its way to the Earth's core.

It was probably why she hadn't noticed it at first, the voice that came to her. The voice coming through, one she knew by now. Another person wanting to say goodbye, it seemed.

'Mum?' said Bella, her own voice weak. She'd wiped the tears away with the backs of her hands.

Then her mother spoke to her one final time, had something important to tell her before she went.

And Bella began to cry once more.

Chapter 38

There had been tears, naturally.

But tears of joy in the end, that he was all right after his ordeal. That he was back with her, the taxi having dropped him off (his bike in the shop, being fixed up). Mitch worried that things would be a little weird, and felt uneasy on his return. But Lucy had just wrapped her arms around him as he came back through the door, hugging him so, so tightly. Kissing every inch of his face.

'Oh Mitch, I'm so glad to . . .' More tears, but of guilt this time, about the way they'd left things. Lucy knew by now all about everything (mostly), how he'd been cut off and his calls 'monitored' at the pub. How they'd made it hard for him to talk to anyone, because of what they had planned. How they'd drugged him, used hypnosis, the works. 'I'm so sorry,' she told him then.

'You don't have anything to be sorry about,' he said.

'But I should have been . . . And I was such a bitch, before you left. The last time we spoke!'

'Forget about it,' Mitch told her. 'All that's important is I'm back, I'm safe. And I have you.' He'd had time to think, time to realize what was truly important in his life.

'You've got me, all right,' she'd said and kissed him again. Then she looked down at the box he'd left on the floor, not the bags

302

he'd taken with him – they'd gone in the fire that had claimed his dad's place, claimed the rest of Green Acres too – but a pet box. A cat box. 'What's that?' she'd asked, hearing the mewling that was coming from inside.

'I-I seem to have adopted a cat.'

'A . . . Mitch, you know they don't allow animals here.'

'I do, but it'll only be for a while.' He was telling her that, all the time knowing that he was going to talk to the landlord; was planning on keeping Cat, even if it meant moving. It wasn't as if she had been much trouble (the vet had told him the sex, as he'd checked her over and given her some shots), they'd hardly seen much of her since Mitch got back. Apart from when she wanted letting out; he'd sort out a cat flap in due course. Or at mealtimes, obviously. Food from cans, as she'd grown used to that routine. The very fact she hadn't eaten anything fresh in Green Acres, not even those leftovers from the pub, should have told Mitch something. (Had those been laced with something more deadly, he had to wonder now, in an effort to get rid of the animal? *'How is your cat?'*) The fact she'd brought him that mouse . . .

Lucy had taken some time off work to spend with Mitch. And they'd barely made it out of bed, it was just like when they first met. Hadn't been this happy in ages. They'd talked, a lot. Him about his ordeal, her about how much she'd missed him and how she was going to pamper him for a good while yet. She'd looked a bit wary when he said he was going to see more of his sister, that they'd reconnected and had promised to keep in touch – but Lucy would get used to it. She just didn't know Bella very well, was all. Had apparently had quite a terse exchange with her while he'd been away, which hadn't helped.

'She was going through some stuff, as well,' Mitch told Lucy. 'But she's okay now.' At least he thought she was, had Ashley Watts helping her through it. Mitch really liked him, they'd got on like a . . . Don't even go there. Got on *well*, then. Ash had even straightened things out at work for Mitch, sorted out that bastard Staton and co. Ash had friends in high places apparently – or friends of friends was how he put it. If Mitch's old job didn't work out, there was always a place for him at Golden Sands nick, he'd said, though he hadn't passed that on to Lucy yet either. Mitch was actually secretly hoping his sister ended up with Ash, he was a good guy and she deserved a bit of that. He could tell she really liked him. A sibling thing, or maybe something else?

There was also good news in the form of Zach calling up to let him know Tammy was out of the coma. Best news he'd had in a long while! He'd promised to swing round the hospital with Vihaan when he got a sec. When Lucy had finished with her pampering.

That, last night, had involved cooking him the most delicious meal, accompanied by champagne no less. 'A late birthday treat,' she'd called it, finally getting to spend that special time together she'd wanted. He'd drunk a bit more champers than he should have done, had got used to drinking more while he'd been away (would cut down now he was back, once things had returned to normal, he'd promised). But hadn't drunk so much he'd been unable to negotiate the stairs. Not too much he didn't enjoy the night that followed, Lucy appearing at the bedroom door in that short pink and black nightie he liked so much.

'Wow!' was about all he could manage to say, then she'd climbed in with him and they'd spent one of the most wonderful nights he could remember. Passionate, but tender. Urgent, but loving.

He'd woken early, with a bit of a headache and Denise on his mind; perhaps the two were connected, but the former was probably the booze he'd put away. There was definitely guilt about what had happened with that woman, what had *almost* happened – he wouldn't have let it – fuelled by whatever they'd slipped him at The Plough. Mitch knew he had to tell Lucy sometime, he was just waiting for the right moment and last night definitely hadn't been it.

Neither had that morning, as it transpired, because she'd brought him coffee and waffles in bed. 'You've really got to stop spoiling me like this,' he'd protested. 'It's not my birthday now!'

'Close enough,' she'd said with a grin. And when he'd finished, they'd ended up making love again, before she'd gone off to the bathroom.

It was only after eating that he'd begun to feel more of the effects of that alcohol from the previous evening, headache getting a bit worse, his stomach rolling. His new mobile ringing had taken his mind off things momentarily, and he checked the number. Watts . . . Or more likely Bella ringing from Watts' place where she was currently staying – and once again he hoped those two made it the distance. He had a funny feeling they might.

Mitch pressed the green button to answer. 'Hey sis, what's occurring?' If anyone had told him a month or more ago that he'd be on such good terms with Bella, he'd have laughed them out of the place.

'Mitch! Oh, thank God!'

He sat up. Something was wrong. 'Bella? What is it?' No longer light, not a joke, no longer funny.

'Mitch, you have to listen to me. I need you to—'

He was aware of Lucy coming back into the room, still wearing that nightie. God, she was gorgeous! 'Who is it?' she asked.

Mitch put his hand over the speaker. 'It's Bella, love. I think something's—'

Then it happened: he was suddenly wet. Soaking. Mitch frowned, sucked in a breath of shock. What the fuck? What the actual fuck? For a second he couldn't work out why, or what was happening – then he looked up to see Lucy holding some kind of container she'd had behind her back. He'd never been one for practical jokes, and neither had she. So why would she chuck water on him from the bathroom, and why in the middle of—

'Mitch! Mitch, can you hear me? Are you still there?'

Bella's voice seemed so far away, because he was trying to process what was happening in the bedroom. He could smell something, a strange smell. Smelled a bit like petrol, but it couldn't—

Lucy had such a weird expression on her face. One he'd seen before somewhere.

Don't look so confused.

What a shame you had that reaction last night, because I think it would have been pretty special, y'know?

Best night of your life.

You'd have known it was your birthday, all right!

Mitch dropped the phone, just as he heard the words: 'It's Mum. She's been trying to warn me again. You need to get out of there, Mitch. Lucy . . . You need to get away from Lucy!'

He moved forward, but suddenly felt so much worse. Felt sick but also weak again.

'The witch, eh?' said his girlfriend. 'Well, she's too late. I never knew why I hated her quite so much until now, or why she didn't want to go back. Not until the fog lifted this morning. Until I woke up. *Really* woke up.'

'Lucy, wha—'

'You see, I couldn't really remember anything . . .'

That was dangerous: Lucy remembered everything.

'. . . about where I came from, why they sent me away. Why I was rejected – except I wasn't. Never really knew what my mission was. I just knew when I met you, I had to look after you.'

'I don't—'

'Understand? You should do, they did it to you too. When you were younger. Planted the seeds . . . It was so that damned sixth sense of yours didn't pick up on it, so you wouldn't suspect. And I do love you, Mitch. *Truly* I do! That was the real reason why . . . Oh, it was so hard to let you go, let you go back. But I get it now. I think. Unless . . .' She paused. 'It might have been that final push to *make* you go, because I wanted you to stay. Or to be there, with you, with them, when it happened. Only I couldn't. I had to stay here, in case . . . In a way I'm glad they

306

failed, because I wanted to be the one to do it anyway. Had this need inside me, though I didn't really know what it was. Thought it might be marriage, a family. But it was our real future, Mitch. I wasn't rejected, I'm important. And so are you! This is our destiny. It always was.'

'Mitch? Mitch, talk to me!' The phone sounding like it was a million miles away, a million years . . .

Mitch clutched his stomach, groaned loudly.

'Not feeling so great? That'll be what I put in your breakfast, in your coffee. I distracted you – in the best possible way – until it had a chance to work.'

'Work . . . Lucy, what have you . . .?'

'You make me sound like some kind of heartless monster.'

'I was always the fail-safe, you see. In case things went wrong. You didn't think we met by accident, did you?' She laughed. 'Nothing *ever* happens by accident. I was drawn to you and—'

Mitch was crawling along the bed, it felt like so much of an effort. 'Luc . . . Lucy, please.'

'Forgive me, I'm savouring the moment too long, aren't I? Need to get on with it. Might not be your birthday, might not be the hottest day, but it's close enough. This needs to be done, you do understand, don't you?'

'Mitch! Mitch! Answer me!' Bella! Oh God, Bella . . . 'Just wait there, hang on! I've rung for the—'

'It needs to start anew, we need to be reborn. All of his . . . the true believers.' Lucy looked insane now, eyes wide, smirking. He'd just about made it to the end of the bed when she brought out the matches, freed one. 'Then it'll all be all right. You'll see. It'll—'

Mitch used the last of his strength to throw himself off the bed, grabbing Lucy, trying to grab her hands before she could strike that match. But she was so much stronger than him, might even have been without the drugs: fanaticism fuelling her actions now. He was hanging on to her as much as anything, even as she backed off. Backed towards the doorway, out onto the stretch of landing there. It looked for all the world like they were dancing, but not in circles, not round and round mumbling, chanting.

That bit didn't seem to matter, Lucy just needed to set him alight. Kill him. Then that spark would light the—

Lucy was still stepping back, carrying his weight. He was losing his grasp on her wrists, only holding on now because he knew if he let go, she'd—

Then suddenly Lucy had wrenched free and he was dropping to his knees, totally naked in front of her. Too weak to even get up. Mitch tilted his head, saw her raise the match to strike it. 'I love you so, so much,' she told him, taking one last step back.

One too many – because she was tripping on something, falling. Trying to get her footing again, but failing miserably because she was at the top of the stairs. The matches from the box flew into the air, as Lucy fell backwards. Fell back and back. There was a massive thump as she landed.

Then a meow, and Mitch saw why she'd lost her footing. Saw what had tripped her, as Cat strolled over and was about to rub itself against him, then sniffed Mitch and turned her nose up at the smell.

Was extremely good at hunting and . . .

He just about had enough energy to crawl to the edge of the top step and look over. There she was: Lucy. Although there weren't a huge number of steps, she'd fallen awkwardly, landed at the base of them, her head twisted in a way it really shouldn't be, her tongue sticking out of her mouth. Mitch didn't need to check her pulse to know she was dead. Felt a mixture of emotions: loss, grief, relief.

It was then and only then he heard the sirens, just like the night outside the barn. Heard the sirens as he started to pass out, everything going black. Knew they'd break in, find her, find him. That it was finally, truly over this time. Knew also that when he woke up again, it would definitely be in a new world.

Born again, rising up. From the darkness . . .

And into the light.

Epilogue

A light.

In the night-time, the darkness. A light in the woods, but not actually in the woods. Somewhere close by, not far away from the clump of trees. The village that had taken this area's name was ashes now, same as the barn. Not even the rain had stopped it. Nothing left. Ripe for development, which meant that at some point all this might start again. That more might see the wisdom of worshipping the Great Flame.

Denied on this occasion, there would be other opportunities. In time, always in time.

But if anyone had been around that night, they might have been able to trace the light back to its source. Back through the woods, to the cave system. A fire burning deep inside it that some said had been burning since time began and would never burn out. A legend. A myth.

A promise yet to be fulfilled.

Acknowledgements

As always, I won't start naming names here because I'll inevitably leave someone out. There are just *so* many people who've helped and supported me during my years as a professional writer. But I do owe a huge debt of gratitude to my tireless and excellent editor Belinda Toor; her comments, notes and edits have made all three P L Kanes much better than they were originally. I also want to thank everyone from the HQ/HarperCollins family, from Abigail Fenton and Lisa Milton, to Suher Sofi and Audrey Linton. Thanks, as well, to anyone and everyone who took the time to read, review or offer a quote for the first two thrillers. Finally, thank you to my actual family for their support, help and encouragement while writing this novel; it wasn't easy for any of us, I know, especially as it was during the first lockdown. And a massive 'words are not enough' thank you to my better half Marie for, oh, just everything really! Love you more than I can possibly express in words, sweetheart.

Keep reading for an excerpt from
Her Husband's Grave . . .

HER
HUSBAND'S
GRAVE

Some secrets are worth
killing for...

P L KANE

Prologue

He'd been looking for something else when he made the shocking discovery. The grisly, stomach-churning discovery that would change everything . . .

He had been walking along, here on the beach, looking for treasure no less – buried or otherwise – if you can believe such a thing. And he did, had done all his life. Believed the tales his father had told him about this place when he was young, about the smugglers and the pirates. Loved it when his old man had read *Treasure Island* to him at bedtime when he was little.

Jeremy Platt had only recently moved back to the area, partly to keep an eye on his ageing dad now that the man's wife, Jeremy's mum, had passed away; partly because his own marriage to Alice – who he'd met at college in the nearby town of Mantlethorpe – had fallen apart. Now, here they both were . . . alone, together.

They'd joke about it sometimes, over a pint in their local, or a game of dominoes, though their laughter would fade quite quickly. But at least they had each other, the roles reversed from when Jeremy had been little; now he had to read to his father because of his failing eyesight. Something that had put paid to the old bloke's hobby of amateur writing, and one of the reasons why he liked to stand at the window with those binoculars, looking out over the sea. Or had done, until a couple of days ago.

Until the heart attack.

Jeremy had been the one to make the discovery then too, calling round early because he couldn't reach him on the phone; all the while telling himself it was just lines down because of the storm. Instead, finding him collapsed on the floor, phone off the hook after clearly trying to reach it and ring for help. Jeremy had rung for an ambulance instead, straight away. They'd whisked him off to hospital, and there had followed an anxious few hours, waiting to hear the worst.

When the doctor came out and told Jeremy his dad had stabilised, he'd almost hugged the fellow. 'What he needs now, more than anything, is rest,' the physician had said to Jeremy, 'and time to recover.' He'd been allowed to sit by the bedside, even though Mr Platt Snr was still pretty out of it – wires running in and out of him, like some kind of robot. And Jeremy had cried, watching him, realising just how frail he was for the first time. How he might lose another parent before long.

To be honest, he'd come here today to give himself a break more than anything. The hospital had promised to call if there was any change and he could be back in no time.

So here he was, on said beach, looking for excitement, looking for treasure. Just like his old man had promised. All part of a hobby he'd taken up, something to occupy his time while he looked for – and had failed so far to find – work in the area. So, with what was left over from the redundancy package and his share of the marital savings, he'd treated himself to a metal detector.

Jeremy had often spotted people wandering up and down the sands, sweeping those things from left to right, and thought it looked like fun. Well, you never knew what you might find out there. The guy in the shop, that fellow with the beard and cargo trousers – front pockets bulging, so full Jeremy wondered how he walked without falling over – had done nothing to dissuade him. Had been a self-confessed expert on the subject, happy to give him lots of tips . . . Not to mention sell him the best detector

314

on the market, or so he claimed: the Equinox 800 with the large coil, perfect for places like beaches.

It had continued to rain off and on since the storm, and that made for perfect conditions as far as detecting was concerned. 'When everything's wet,' the bloke from the shop had told him, 'it soaks into the ground and helps you spot anything that's deeper down. Ground's had a drink, see?'

He'd also advised Jeremy not to be in a rush, to expect lots of trash. 'Ninety-five per cent of what you'll find,' cargo guy had said, simultaneously showing him how to swing the machine – not too fast and not in great arcs, 'it'll be junk.'

He hadn't been wrong. In the months he'd been doing this, Jeremy had found enough bottle-tops to pebbledash a house, old-fashioned keys, the backs of watches, tin cans, safety pins, bits of shiny metal that looked like mirrors . . .

However, he'd also found enough to encourage him to carry on: toy cars (a couple of which had actually ended up being collectors' items); an old whistle once (which he hadn't dared blow, recalling an old ghost story he'd read in his teens); a few lighters; a couple of rings; and, though they weren't doubloons as such, quite a few pound coins that must have fallen out of wallets, purses or pockets. The point was, he had fun while he was doing it – and at the moment he needed that, needed to take his mind off things. Off his dad lying there in bed looking like C-3PO.

He stopped when the beeping in his earphones intensified. Jeremy stared at the screen in front of him: 12 . . . 13 . . . no, 14! A pretty good reading, he thought, pulling the 'phones from his ears to wear them around his neck. Bending and taking out his trowel from his pack, he placed the detector down and began digging in the spot it had indicated. What would it be this time – a gold chain perhaps? Down, down, and further down . . .

Jeremy stopped when he saw the metal, couldn't help grinning to himself. The last few bits of sand he dug out with his gloved hands, fingers clawing, eager to see what it was he'd uncovered.

He stopped when he reached it, plucked the item out and held it up in front of him – where it glinted in the early morning sun. His smile faded. 'Just an old ring-pull,' he said to himself, the kind you wouldn't get these days because they were fixed to the lid. Sighing, he bagged it anyway, to stop another hunter from making the same mistake – and to keep those beaches clean, of course. They were a far cry from what they'd been when he was a kid, or indeed when his father had been a boy, and Jeremy wasn't even sure they deserved the name Golden Sands that had been given them now, their colour dull even when it hadn't been raining.

But it was as he'd contemplated this that he spotted it. Something in that dull sand, along the beach. Something not that well buried at all, sticking out in fact – just ripe for the taking. He looked around him, the beach deserted – though to be fair you wouldn't really get many tourists on this stretch of it anyway. They'd stick to the main beach for swimming and so they were closer to the pier and shops. Grabbing his stuff, he clambered to his feet and started over. He couldn't be sure what it was really, but it was glinting.

It was metal. It was gold . . . *Golden* at any rate.

Didn't even need his detector this time, which was real irony for you. All that sweeping, all that beeping. The closer he got the more he saw of it, some kind of strap . . . a watchstrap! Looked like it belonged to an expensive one, too. Just a bit of it sticking out, but there it was.

Jeremy got down again, started to uncover the find as he had done with the ring-pull. He hadn't been digging for long, perhaps only a few seconds, when he pulled back sharply. It was a watchstrap all right, with a watch attached. But there was skin there too.

And a wrist.

Swallowing dryly, he moved forward again. His imagination surely, eyes playing tricks on him. He dug a little more, pulled back again.

There was a hand attached to that wrist. A human hand.

Jeremy hadn't uncovered much of it, but he could tell now – and though it was at an angle, it looked for all the world like a much dryer version of The Lady in the Lake's hand reaching up for Excalibur. Except there was no sword to catch. And this was no *lady's* hand.

He scrabbled backwards again, felt the bile rising in his mouth. That was a body, no doubt about it – and his mind flashed back to when he and his mum used to bury his dad when they went on the sands (*might be burying him for real soon*, a little voice whispered and he promptly ignored it). But surely nobody would have done that by accident? Left a relative here, especially in this isolated spot.

Jeremy frowned, then reached into his pocket for his mobile. Began to dial a number.

There you go, that same voice had told him, *you wanted excitement. An adventure*. He shook his head again, shook those thoughts away too.

'Yes, hello,' he said when the ringing at the other end stopped and a voice came on the line. Not asking for an ambulance this time, because it was far too late for that. Instead: 'Yes, could you give me the police please.'

Part One

Golden Sands acquired its name because the first people to settle there were struck by the colour of the beaches. The sands, a vibrant golden shade, remain some of the most impressive and cleanest in Britain. Located on the east coast, not too far from Dracula country and only a hop, skip and a jump from places like Redmarket and Granfield – which is why it remains a popular holiday destination with people who live in those localities – it is a family-orientated town (population of around 12,000, who live there the whole year round . . . lucky souls!).

For those history buffs among you, Golden Sands was once known as a smugglers' cove and notorious pirate haunt – you can still ride in the galleon that departs from the harbour at twelve o'clock, midday, and which will take you all around the bay area. Some also say that Golden Sands got its name because those same smugglers and pirates used to hide their treasure in caves or indeed on the beach itself, which is why it attracts its fair share of divers and treasure hunters, keen to uncover a welcome surprise.

Chapter 1

Why did she put herself through this, time and again?

She had no idea. No, that wasn't true. She knew exactly why she came here: to learn; to document; to look for hidden clues that might help with future cases. With hunting people like this – those who did so much harm. But that wasn't the main reason, was it? As Robyn Adams made her way down this corridor, having already gone through the various security checks so far, she thought once more about the why of it. The real reason.

And that reason was to see if she'd been right.

Robyn caught a glimpse of herself in some security glass as the guards escorted her, noting how tired she looked. Her blonde hair, which was streaked through with more and more silver these days, was yanked back into a bun, but that was still doing nothing to stretch and conceal the wrinkles that had appeared over the course of the last couple of years or so. Wrinkles that coincided with taking this job on, not that it was – had ever really been – her real job. More of an extra-curricular activity that the university allowed her to partake in, the kudos they got for having someone like her on their payroll more than compensation enough; all those mentions in the academic papers she had published, those stories in the newspapers. As long as she kept up with her lectures and marking, they were happy enough. And as long as she was helping the police to put away the bad guys, their government funding was also more or less assured.

It had been a total accident, how she'd ended up working for the cops. She'd been at a charity event to raise awareness for cancer research, representing their faculty, and due to her lack of a plus-one had been placed at the table for dinner next to a man who introduced himself only as Gordon, which for most of the evening she'd assumed was his first name rather than his last. He was about ten years older than her, but wore it well, even with the dyed hair – had aged better than she was doing recently, that was for sure – and at first she thought he was trying to chat her up. He'd asked about her work, taking more of an interest than she usually expected people to, especially at an event with free wine.

For a couple of hours or more, he'd quizzed her about various disorders and treatments, ranging from OCD to schizophrenia, and when it came time for them to say goodnight she realised she knew barely anything about the guy, aside from the fact he was a widower and a huge Bruce Springsteen fan.

'Well, it's been nice talking to you, Gordon,' Robyn had said, holding out her hand when their respective taxis arrived.

'You too, Doctor. I'm sorry I monopolised your time, but it was all genuinely fascinating . . . Oh, and please call me Peter. Or Pete if you prefer.'

Robyn had assumed that was that, because he didn't ask for her number or anything and didn't proffer his own. She didn't find out until a day or so later that she'd spent the entire evening talking to one Superintendent Peter Gordon (whose nickname in some quarters was 'The Commissioner' after that famous character in a certain comics series). He got in touch with Robyn through the uni and asked for her to come in to their local station at Hannerton. It had been weird seeing him out of context – the switch between dinner jacket and bow tie to full dress uniform jarring – but he'd given her that same warm smile from the other night, then offered her a seat across from him as he settled down behind a huge, oak desk.

'Am . . . am I in trouble?' had been her first question to him, and he'd laughed.

'Far from it, Robyn. Far from it. Indeed, I think *we* might be ones in trouble and could really use your help.'

Over tea and biscuits, he'd told her about a case his people were working on that had stumped them all. A series of killings that had been in the news – young girls who'd been found dumped in various locations. Who'd been killed, bitten and partially eaten, then wrapped up in rope. 'Some kind of bondage thing, was our initial assessment,' Gordon informed her and Robyn had frowned. 'What?'

'I don't think the tying up is a sex thing, Superintendent.'

He shook his head and for a moment she thought he was disagreeing with her, but then he said, 'Peter, or Pete. Or plain old Gordon. Look, maybe it's best if I take you over and introduce you to some of the team working on this. Get you to have a look at what they've come up with so far . . .' He paused suddenly. 'If that's okay with you, of course?'

She'd nodded and that's exactly what Gordon had done: he introduced Robyn to people like DI Rick Cavendish and his loyal band of DSs and DCs, many of whom had worked together for ages. She hadn't exactly been welcomed with open arms by everyone, some saying that Gordon was too trusting and they didn't need a person like her – a psychologist – sticking her nose in. But once she was given access to the findings so far, the evidence they'd been sorting through, she'd come up with some theories, and even the naysayers had started to take notice.

Then, after she'd drafted a profile that helped them catch the person they were looking for, Robyn was definitely flavour of the month – especially when she insisted it be classed as a team effort. 'You guys had already done the legwork on this; it just needed a fresh set of eyes was all.'

Fresh eyes to see that the cannibalism was the key, that the person they were looking for – Adrian Nance – thought he could outdo Iranian serial killer 'The Spider', Saeed Hanaei. But Nance not only lured women back to his place like flies into a web, he also tied them up and ate bits of them, 'becoming' the arachnid he wanted to emulate. That extended to actually keeping spiders, the more exotic the better, and that was how they found him in the end: tracking anyone who'd bought such animals in the area.

So now, whenever Cavendish and his team needed those eyes of hers, she was called upon. In the time she'd spent with them, she'd helped with cases such as the so-called Postcode Killer, who was chopping up people who lived in a certain location; and Dennis Wilde, who some called The Baby, because he was leaving bodies in the foetal position . . . Right up to this last case she'd worked on, paying a personal price for his incarceration.

Kevin Sykes. The one who'd taken her prisoner, who'd almost killed her. The man she was on her way to see right now, today. Who was the reason she was hesitating, questioning why she was coming here in the first place and putting herself through all this.

Breathing in deeply, she just placed one foot in front of the other. The material of her trouser suit was swishing with each step, causing her to wince, every sound magnified in this place of echoes. Even her shoes – flats rather than heels (for one thing, the latter could be used as a weapon if any of the inmates got hold of them) – were still making clacking sounds, beating out the rhythm of her journey, matching her heartbeat that was quickening with each metre she covered in this place. The place they called Gateside. Located out in the middle of nowhere, this maximum-security facility for the criminally insane was definitely a misnomer, because it only had one gate – at the front, rather than on the sides – which was so heavily guarded that even if an inmate somehow reached it they would get no further.

Those who called Gordon 'The Commissioner' also referred to Gateside as Arkham, though once again they were totally wrong.

Far from the gothic monstrosity that asylum was, this was new and clean – all white walls and metal and toughened glass. None of which made her feel any better about being inside its walls. Because as much as she knew the science of how the people kept here ticked, as much as she'd studied things like nature versus nurture, behavioural patterns and brain scans showing whether people had shrunken amygdalae (the seat of emotion, of empathy, conscience and remorse) or not, when you got right down to it, the prisoners shut away in this place were just plain scary.

Robyn usually did her best to hide her fear, putting on a front as always, because showing it only made things worse. You'd get nothing out of subjects if they thought you were terrified; it would just make them want to 'play' with you more. Serial killers liked to be in control, liked that feeling. If Robyn was to find out anything during her visits to Gateside, she had to at least appear as if she was the one in the driving seat. Easier said than done, when the man you were facing had once towered above you and been ready to take your life.

All too soon she was there, at the final door. Robyn peered in through the square of glass in an otherwise solid metal barrier, seeing him handcuffed at the table there, attached to chains that ran through metal hooks welded to the table – which itself was bolted to the floor for added security. She would be safe enough, especially with the guards just outside the doors here. Sykes wasn't deemed as dangerous as some in Gateside, who you could only communicate with through bars or toughened glass, guards on either side ready to Taser the person. She was at least allowed to sit in a room, sit down at a table with her . . . patient. A patient Robyn knew would never, ever be cured.

She swallowed again, sucked in another breath, and nodded at one of the guards who'd been with her since the inner door. He was dressed like something out of Judge Dredd, everything padded for his own protection, baton hanging from a belt at his waist – Taser on the other side, looking for all the world like some kind of futuristic handgun. When he nodded back, helmet wobbling slightly, he reached out with gloved hands and undid the lock with a key card, then held his hand out for Robyn to enter, like he was a butler at some kind of swish stately home.

Sykes barely looked up when she stepped inside the room, which was probably a good thing because the door slamming shut again made her start a little. Instead, he kept his head down, as if he was studying something in front of him on the table – though there was nothing there – bald patch on top clearly visible; premature for someone of his age. He wore the pale-yellow, boiler-suit-style uniform of all the prisoners here, the theory being you wouldn't then confuse them with the guards who were in muted blues and greys. Here, yellow rather than orange was the new black, but then Robyn doubted any of them were concerned about fashion.

Only when she reached the table itself did Sykes acknowledge her presence, looking up slowly and regarding her with those penetrating eyes. The ones she'd gazed into when she thought she was about to die.

'Hello, Dr Adams,' he said with a smile that sent shivers down her spine. 'I wondered when I'd see you again.'

Dear Reader,

Thank you so much for choosing to read *The Family Lie*.

The first two P L Kane novels dealt with family ties. The first, *Her Last Secret*, was primarily concerned with an estranged father and daughter, while in *Her Husband's Grave* it was cousins who were more like sisters. Both were also about coming home or back to a hometown, such as Redmarket or Golden Sands. In *The Family Lie*, I wanted to take things a step further.

So, not only do we tackle head on the relationship between a son and his father this time, but also Mitch Prescott's relationship with the rest of his family – including his sister, Bella, who is a bit of a black sheep because of her 'line of work'. And Mitch is returning to his childhood home, in the form of Green Acres, which allowed me to talk about how much things change – or maybe shouldn't – as you get older. I've wanted to write something about cults and the phenomenon of the cult of personality for a while now too; I just find the whole subject fascinating, including people's beliefs when they're in a cult. This book allowed me to dovetail all these subjects and more.

Although totally standalone, if you've read the other two P L Kanes you will definitely spot links. Bella, Ashley and O'Brien, for example, first cropped up in *Her Husband's Grave*, so if you want to know the full story of what happened with Robyn Adams, it's there waiting for you. But anyway, I hope you enjoyed reading *The Family Lie* and, if you did, perhaps you might consider leaving a review . . . even just a line or two would be very welcome.

Warmest wishes once again,
P L Kane

Dear Reader,

We hope you enjoyed reading this book. If you did, we'd be so appreciative if you left a review. It really helps us and the author to bring more books like this to you.

Here at HQ Digital we are dedicated to publishing fiction that will keep you turning the pages into the early hours. Don't want to miss a thing? To find out more about our books, promotions, discover exclusive content and enter competitions, you can keep in touch in the following ways:

JOIN OUR COMMUNITY:

Sign up to our new email newsletter:
http://smarturl.it/SignUpHQ

Read our new blog: www.hqstories.co.uk

 : https://twitter.com/HQStories

 : www.facebook.com/HQStories

BUDDING WRITER?

We're also looking for authors to join the HQ Digital family!
Find out more here:

https://www.hqstories.co.uk/want-to-write-for-us/

Thanks for reading, from the HQ Digital team

If you enjoyed *The Family Lie*, then why not try another gripping thriller from HQ Digital?